From Notting Hill
with Four Weddings ...
Actually

Ali McNamara

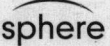
sphere

SPHERE

First published in Great Britain in 2014 by Sphere

A CIP catalogue record for this book
is available from the British Library.

ISBN 978-0-7515-5024-5

Typeset in Caslon by M Rules
Printed and bound in Great Britain by
Clays Ltd, St Ives plc

Papers used by Sphere are from well-managed forests
and other responsible sources.

MIX
Paper from
responsible sources
FSC® C104740

Sphere
An imprint of
Little, Brown Book Group
100 Victoria Embankment
London EC4Y 0DY

An Hachette UK Company
www.hachette.co.uk

www.littlebrown.co.uk

For Jim, we made it to twenty . . .

Acknowledgements

My acknowledgements seem to get longer with every book! So this time I'm going to keep it as short as possible.

A million thanks go to –

Rebecca, and everyone at my publishers Sphere and Little, Brown who help me turn my babbling stories into these wonderful books for you to read.

Hannah, my brilliant and always Zen-like agent, who always manages to remain calm whatever madness is going on around her!

All my brilliant readers! I say this every time, but your lovely messages about my books really mean so much.

My wonderful, patient and amazing family, who often get to enjoy the spoils of my writing, but also have to endure the tantrums, mood-swings, and often late mealtimes that come with living with a writer ... I love you all more than you know!

Special thanks also go to my very clever son, Tom, who wrote Scarlett's brilliant rap for me.

And Christmas competition winner Pamela Dean – whose prize was a cameo in this book! See if you can spot her.

Until the next time ...

Keep Smiling ☺
Ali x

One

'Scarlett!' I hear a voice that sounds very much like Oscar's calling my name. But he sounds far away and muffled, like I'm underwater and he's on dry land.

'Scarlett,' he calls again. 'Wake up this instant! This is highly embarrassing.'

I open my eyes to find my good friend Oscar glaring down at me. I turn my head to the other side to find my other good friend, Maddie, looking at me with concern.

'Oh ...' I say, pushing myself back up in my chair. 'I must have dropped off.'

'Dropped off!' Oscar yelps. 'You were snoring so loudly at one point the bride and groom stopped at the end of the runway and pointed at you. You were the highlight of the two p.m. showcase!'

I look around me at the empty auditorium where just

minutes earlier I'd been watching models parade down the long runway in wedding gowns and designer morning suits. Had I really managed to fall asleep with all that going on?

'Sorry – it's the jet lag,' I explain, by way of excuse. 'It was really late by the time I got home last night.'

My regular journeys back and forth across the Atlantic between London and New York were usually problem-free, but last night we'd been delayed by some heavy January snowfall arriving into Heathrow Airport. We'd landed on time, but there was such a backlog of planes that we'd had to wait on the tarmac for over two hours for a gate.

'I guess we can let you off this once, then, darling,' Oscar says with a wink. 'Heaven knows I wouldn't want to be stuck on a plane for two extra excruciating hours after a seven-hour flight. I'd be bouncing off the ceiling so hard people would think I'd been fired from an emergency ejector seat!'

I smile at Oscar; he definitely isn't at his best when he has to sit still for a long period of time. Oscar is much better 'uncaged', I guess you'd call it, so his natural enthusiasm for life can be allowed to burst free.

'The actual delay wasn't that bad,' I tell them. 'I got into conversation with a young man sitting next to me and the time passed quite quickly after that.'

As so often happens when you're flying alone, I'd spent the majority of the flight exchanging the odd pleasantry with the passenger in the seat next to me – we briefly spoke when our food was served or I needed to allow him to pass when he wished to visit the lavatory, as he was in the window seat. But all that changed when we became united in our despair at being stranded on the airport tarmac for so long, when all we wanted to do was disembark the plane, go in search of our bags and be on our way home ...

'I guess we should consider ourselves lucky we were actually allowed to fly,' my neighbour remarks after we've been sitting waiting for about twenty minutes. 'Lots of flights into Heathrow were cancelled last night due to the weather.'

'Yes,' I agree, relieved I don't have to sit in silence any longer. The entertainment system had been switched off when we were preparing to land, and assuming it wouldn't be long before we left the plane, I'd stowed all my paperwork and my half-read novel in the overhead locker. 'I wondered if I'd even be getting home today when I saw the forecast on the internet this morning.'

'Where's home?' he politely enquires.

'London, Notting Hill.'

'Nice. I have some mates in Notting Hill. How long have you lived there?'

'About two and a half years. I live there with my fiancé, Sean,' I proudly tell him.

He nods. 'Yes, I noticed your ring. Are you getting

married soon?' Then he flushes a little. 'Sorry, is that too personal?'

'No, it's fine. We may as well chat – we could be here a while. This year, we hope. I'm supposed to be planning it right now.'

'Supposed to be?' He raises his dark eyebrows.

'I mean, I *am* planning it. I've just been a bit busy lately – with work.'

It was the truth. I really couldn't wait to get married to Sean, and planning our dream wedding was always at the top of my to-do list. But just lately work seemed to be taking over everything and I longed for a thirty-six-hour day to try and fit everything in.

'Yes, I know that feeling well,' my new companion says. 'My life is often like that too. What job keeps you so busy?'

I'm quite surprised at all his questions – we've hardly spoken during the flight, he's kept himself very much to himself reading his fitness and men's fashion magazines, and when he wasn't doing that or watching a movie, he's listened to music through a pair of bright red Beats headphones.

'I own a couple of businesses,' I reply, trying not to sound too boastful, even though I am immensely proud of both of them. 'The one based in London I run with my father. We sell popcorn machines.'

'Popcorn machines!' he exclaims in delight. 'Cool. What, to individuals or cinemas?'

'Cinemas, mainly. We used to be solely based in the UK, but we've recently expanded overseas too.'

'Awesome. And what's your other business – hot dogs?' he grins.

I smile politely at his joke. 'No, completely different. I run a charitable trust over in New York.'

'Really?' he says, turning towards me a little. 'I do a lot of work for charity. Will I have heard of yours?'

I look at him more closely as I answer. He's quite a good-looking young chap. His thick black hair is cut into a sharp, angular design, and I suspect his casual but trendy clothes all have designer labels.

'Probably not. It's called The Dragonfly Trust. We search for missing people: children, parents, whoever needs our help. Our aim is to reunite families. We're part charity, part private business. The paying clients help fund the charity side.'

'Awesome. Why Dragonfly, if you don't mind me asking?' He glances around the cabin. 'I see our air stewards are up and moving about now, so it doesn't look like we'll be going anywhere just yet.'

'Gosh, it's a very long story,' I tell him. 'The short version is, I was over in New York tracing the history of an antique dragonfly brooch when I managed to stumble on my half-brother whom I'd never met before. The trust sprang up as a result of me wanting to help others be reunited with their long-lost relatives like I was with mine.'

I decide not to mention doing something very similar

with my then estranged mother some years ago too. The fact I'd searched for and eventually been reunited with her in a cinema in Notting Hill was another long story I hoped there wouldn't be time to tell him during our enforced delay.

'Wow, that's wicked!' he exclaims. 'Not just the trust, but finding your half-brother too. And he didn't know he had a sister?'

I shake my head. 'No, Jamie was as much in the dark as me.'

As I'd just told my new friend, I'd met my half-brother, Jamie, when I visited New York with Oscar. We'd bumped into each other outside Tiffany's, not knowing who the other was. Although I'd felt a connection to him right away, it took a series of random events for us to find out exactly what we meant to each other.

'And do you get on OK?' he asks, seeming genuinely interested.

'Oh yes. It was a little awkward at first, but Jamie and I are really close now.'

'Excellent. So this Dragonfly Trust, is it just in the US?'

'Yes, it is right now. Peter – he helps me run the trust – and I have talked about bringing it over to the UK, though.'

Peter does more than simply help me run the trust. Without him, it would probably never have got off the ground in the first place. Peter is a very well-respected businessman over in the States. We too met on my first trip to New York, and he's not only become my business partner but my very good friend. Peter introduced me to a children's home called Sunnyside over in Brooklyn, and it was in part due to this association that The Dragonfly Trust was born.

I'm about to ask what my travelling companion does for a living when an air stewardess offers us some drinks.

'I'm very sorry but it seems we may be delayed a little longer,' she explains. 'Please help yourself to some refreshments.'

I take a glass of orange juice and stretch out my legs, glad I'm lucky enough to be able to fly premium economy on long-haul flights.

'So what brings you back to London tonight?' my companion asks, sipping on his own glass of juice. 'Just catching up with your fiancé?'

'Yes, and my friends. We're going to a wedding fair tomorrow at Earls Court to get some ideas for the big day. My friend Oscar has had it all planned for ages. He and Maddie, my other friend, are going to be attendants at my wedding.'

Maddie has been my friend since we were at school together, and I met Oscar when I first came to Notting Hill to house-sit for a month. I'd been so excited that I was going to be staying in the place where one of my all-time favourite movies was filmed, I'd never expected the trip would completely change my life and I'd meet the man I would fall head over heels in love with, Sean.

'I've just realised I know all about your friends and

family and your work, but I don't actually know *your* name!' my travelling companion says now. 'How rude of me.'

I laugh. 'Don't worry about it. I do have a tendency to waffle on if given the chance. My name is Scarlett. And you are?'

'Louis,' he says, holding out his hand for me to shake. 'We should have started this conversation earlier, Scarlett. I would have enjoyed hearing all about your exciting life during the flight.'

'Oh, it's not really that exciting,' I tell him. 'It has its moments, but I bet yours is much more thrilling. Come on, your turn now – tell me something wonderful that's happened in your life.'

Louis smiles. 'Yes, mine has its moments too. Like the time I won a silver medal at the 2012 London Olympics. That was pretty cool.'

I feel my mouth drop open . . .

'Scarlett!' Oscar blinks in astonishment as he and Maddie stare at me open-mouthed. 'Are you telling me you flew from New York to Heathrow sitting next to the divine Louis Smith and you didn't realise!'

'You know who he is?' I ask in just as much amazement. 'Louis told me all about his gymnastics career, but I didn't realise he was famous too.'

Oscar simply shakes his head in disbelief.

'Of course we know him,' Maddie says gently. 'But we can't believe you don't. Didn't you watch the Olympics?'

'Yes, of course, as much as I could. I didn't watch much gymnastics, though. Perhaps I *have* seen him before.'

'*Perhaps!*' Oscar exclaims. 'What about when he was on *Strictly*? Oh my, I nearly fainted when he did his show dance with no top on. I think half the nation did, actually!'

I look at them still none the wiser.

Oscar pulls out his phone. 'Look,' he says, turning it to face me. 'I had this as my wallpaper for weeks afterwards.'

I peer at the photo Oscar is showing me. It's of a very fit man holding a female dancer over his head in a *Dirty Dancing*-style pose. He has his shirt off, showcasing a very well-defined chest and upper body.

'Yes, that's him!' I say, looking at the photo. 'That's Louis.'

'We know!' they both call in unison. 'We just can't believe *you* didn't!'

'What can I say?' I hold my hands aloft. 'I didn't watch that series of *Strictly*. I think I was mostly in New York then.'

'My God,' Oscar says, putting away his phone. 'If I'd been sitting next to Louis Smith, I'd have had him tangoing me down the aisle by the end of the flight. Actually, no, make that the rhumba!' He gyrates his hips suggestively.

'That, my dear friend,' I say, standing up, 'is why I now fly alone!' Then I wink at him. 'Come on, you two, I thought we had a wedding fair to visit today! What are we waiting for?'

'You, Sleeping Beauty!' Oscar calls as we begin to make

our way down some steps and back towards the entrance to the main fair. 'I seem to remember the gentle snores coming from your delicate lips were our main delay!'

'To be fair to Scarlett, the show *was* a little dull,' Maddie suggests. 'They weren't the most exciting wedding gowns I've ever seen.'

'Exactly!' I agree. 'See – I wasn't the only one snoozing.'

'Well, I thought it was simply marvellous!' Oscar says, clapping his hands together in joy at the thought of all those outfits. Oscar runs his own vintage boutique on the King's Road; he adores clothes, and definitely has a unique style when it comes to his own choice of outfits. 'I wish I was getting married. I'd have a simply splendid time choosing the cake, the venue, the gown . . .'

Maddie and I glance at each other.

'And just who will be wearing the gown at *your* wedding?' I ask, smiling.

Oscar flicks his head away. 'You know what I mean. Just because it's a gay wedding doesn't mean it can't have the full works.'

'If you ever get married, it will certainly have the full works,' I wink at Maddie, 'and probably a side order of works thrown in for good measure.'

'It certainly would that,' Oscar agrees wistfully. 'I'd make sure of it. Now then, Rip Van Winkle, we'd better get a move on. We've got so much more to see at this bridal show, and as your chief bridesmaid, I'm going to make damn sure we make the most of it.'

'Oscar,' I call, as he skips merrily off in the direction of the door, 'I haven't chosen a *chief* bridesmaid. You and Maddie are just going to be my attendants.'

Oscar swivels round on the heels of his snakeskin boots and poses with his hands on the hips of his emerald-green trousers. 'Darling, you've known me long enough by now to know if there's a shimmer of silk or the glimmer of sequins to be had, I'm the perfect man for the job!'

Two

⌘

'Can't we go home yet?' I plead, as we trail past yet another stall showing what looks like the same display of long ivory dresses as the last dozen we've passed. 'My legs are really starting to ache.'

'Soon, darling, soon,' Oscar soothes, taking my hand and pulling me even further into the realms of icing, sequins and confetti.

The stands at this vast wedding fair in Earls Court are showcasing absolutely everything you could possibly need to create your perfect day – from the usual wedding necessities like invitations, flowers and cakes to more unique wedding trappings like magic shows, instant photo booths and companies that will not only shoot a basic wedding montage for you to remember your special day but also make a full-length music video that features you and your guests singing along to your favourite pop song.

'Oh, darling, you have to get one of those,' Oscar enthuses when a stallholder thrusts a brochure under our noses as we try to pass. 'Imagine us all singing along to yours and Seany's favourite tune.'

'That would be virtually impossible, since most of my favourites are by Robbie Williams and Take That, while Sean's are Bon Jovi and Coldplay,' I reply, watching the happy couple miming to 'Fairytale of New York' by the Pogues and Kirsty MacColl on the promotional video that's playing at the back of the stand.

'No, Oscar, it's not for us.' I thank the man, hand him back his glossy brochure and walk quickly away to where Maddie is gazing wistfully at a stall showcasing a quite incredible range of wedding cakes covered with intricate ice sculptures.

'Do you remember our wedding cake?' Maddie asks me quietly as I stand next to her.

'Of course I do! Yours and Felix's cake was awesome.'

Maddie and her husband, Felix, had got married at Disneyland Paris almost four years ago now, and I'd been her bridesmaid. The wedding, even though it had had a Disney theme throughout, hadn't been cheesy at all, and had been a very special day for all of us. Their wedding cake had been decorated to look just like Cinderella's castle and had been quite spectacular.

'What a shame fairy tales never last,' Maddie mutters as

she wanders off towards a cafeteria selling coffee and sand-wiches.

'What's up with Mads?' Oscar asks as he catches up with me. He thrusts yet more brochures into one of the free goody bags already hanging over his arm. 'She's been quiet all day. Not at all like her usual self.'

'So you've noticed it too?' I ask, looking over to where Maddie is now browsing the cafeteria menu. 'I wasn't sure. I thought it might be because I was feeling a bit off with the jet lag that she seemed a bit odd.'

'Right,' Oscar announces, slipping his arm through mine. 'I think it's time we put the world to rights over a coffee! I'm sure we can rustle up some medicinal chocolate cake from somewhere to accompany it.' He glances at Maddie. 'I've a feeling it's going to be needed.'

We buy three large cups of coffee from the vendor, while Oscar persuades us into three huge slabs of some very yummy-looking chocolate fudge cake to go with them. Then we find a quiet table at which to sit down and enjoy our treats.

'So . . .' Oscar enquires when we've just started to get that warm comfortable feeling that only good chocolate cake can bring, 'what's going on with the two of you right now?'

I look at Maddie. She shrugs and spoons more cake into her mouth.

'Scarlett, we'll start with you, then,' Oscar declares like a lawyer about to cross-examine a witness. 'Why aren't you leaping around this wedding fair like Darcey Bussell?' He gestures out into the hall. 'And don't give me the jet-lag excuse again. You're getting married – you should be like the proverbial pig rolling around in all this bridal mud.'

'If I eat much more of this chocolate cake, I'll look like a pig by the time my wedding comes around,' I try and joke.

But Oscar simply lifts his fork and prongs a tiny sliver of chocolate cake from his plate. He slips it calmly into his mouth and chews thoughtfully while he awaits my truthful answer.

Oscar, for all his flamboyant ways, is incredibly sensitive towards others' feelings, and he knows me too well for me to pretend there is nothing wrong.

'All right, you win,' I sigh. 'I'm just finding it a bit difficult to cope with everything right now, that's all.'

Oscar nods silently, waiting for me to continue.

'I'm trying to run the popcorn business here in London, and then I'm always jetting over to New York to deal with The Dragonfly Trust. Don't get me wrong,' I say when I see them both frown, 'I'm not complaining. The trust is growing so fast right now it's wonderful watching it flourish, and a life that I lead half in London and half in New York is something I could only dream about when I lived with Dad in Stratford.'

Maddie smiles now. She's the only one who knew me when I lived a quiet, sheltered life in Stratford-upon-Avon with my father and could only dream of living the exciting jet-set lifestyle I do now. Oscar didn't know me back then, but even he knows how much I've changed for the better over the last few years.

'And I really enjoy running both businesses,' I continue, 'but having the wedding to organise now as well, I'm finding it so difficult to cope with everything.'

'Is that why you fell asleep earlier?' Maddie asks gently. 'Are you exhausted?'

'Yes, that's exactly it. I'm incredibly happy and excited by the prospect of all this.' I gesture back out into the wedding fair. 'And I can't wait to marry Sean, you know that, but I'm just too damn tired to enjoy it right now.'

Maddie puts her hand on mine. 'Oh, Scarlett.'

I attempt to raise a smile. I don't want to let either of them down. I know they're both as excited as me at the prospect of my big day with Sean. Especially Oscar. Even though he and Sean don't always see eye to eye, he's more enthusiastic than any of us when it comes to talking about our wedding plans.

'Don't look so down, you two,' I say in a brighter voice than matches my spirit. 'I'll get there! You've just caught me on a bad day, that's all. A bit more sleep and I'll be as right as rain! What you said earlier was true, though, Maddie – that catwalk show *was* very dull. I'm surprised I was the only one snoozing through it.'

Maddie smiles. 'None of those dresses would have suited you anyway, Scarlett. You need something much

16

more special and wonderful to wear when you marry Sean. Don't you agree, Oscar?'

'Without question, darling.' Oscar sits to attention. 'I can't have my Scarlett wearing any old off-the-peg gown!'

'But it's just so difficult to find anything I like,' I say, screwing up my face. 'They all look the same to me. Everything here is made of ivory satin or cream silk, with a few sequins, beads or a lace frill to try and make them look different. I just want something a little more unusual. At least when you got married, Maddie, you had a theme to work with.'

'Themed weddings aren't always the best way to ensure a long and happy marriage,' Maddie says, a pensive expression appearing on her face. 'I wouldn't recommend it.'

Oscar and I exchange concerned looks.

'What's wrong, Maddie?' I ask. 'Are you and Felix having some problems?'

Maddie's face tells us everything her reply does not. She pushes the remnants of her cake around her plate with her fork. 'I'd rather not talk about it right now, if you don't mind. This is your day, Scarlett, and you don't want me bemoaning my marriage when you're just at the joyful beginning of yours.'

'But if you need to talk—' I begin.

Maddie cuts me off. 'Not now,' she insists. 'We'll talk later, Scarlett. Promise.'

I nod. But I'm worried about my oldest friend.

'Right, then!' Oscar enthuses, trying to lift our mood.

'This wedding party needs cheering up. There's a guy over there doing teeth whitening. What say we all go home with gleaming smiles tonight?'

'Oscar, if your teeth get any whiter, when you go out at night you'll have aircraft trying to land on them!' Maddie grins.

'As long as a uniformed pilot is flying the plane,' Oscar winks, 'I don't mind where he parks his aircraft!'

Three

'So what do you think to your first taste of haggis, Scarlett?' Sean asks as he tucks into his own plate of haggis, neeps and tatties at the Burns' Night dinner we're attending in a pretty London restaurant in Belgravia.

'It's actually really nice,' I say, surprising myself by enjoying this traditional Scottish meal.

We agreed to come to this dinner at the request of Oscar's boyfriend, Luke. Yes, for all his joking about pilots (and any other uniformed men for that matter) Oscar now has a regular boyfriend.

Luke is an actor – Scottish by birth, but you'd never know it to listen to him. He has a highly cultured, theatrically trained voice that will completely entrance the audience of a theatre when he's on stage, or draw them right into the heart of their television screens when he's appearing in their living room. They met when I put Oscar in touch with a costume designer who had just moved in across the road from Sean and me in Notting Hill. She was working on the period drama that Luke was appearing in, and Oscar had agreed to provide a few items from his vintage clothing shop for her. But when the pair of scarlet knickerbockers Oscar originally provided weren't big enough for Luke, he'd had to go to the studio to measure him again, and that's how they met. Oscar still insists the colour of the knickerbockers was a sign of good things to come, and now, over a year into their relationship, I have to agree.

'You're enjoying your haggis, then, Scarlett?' Luke calls across the huge table we're all seated round this evening. There's a great gang of us here. Sean, Oscar, Luke and I sit at one end with Maddie. (Felix is working late.) Then there's Ursula, Sean's sister and Oscar's close friend, and a few more of Luke and Oscar's friends, some of whom I've met and some I haven't. They're a lovely, friendly, at times quite rowdy bunch, and it's turning into a fun-filled evening.

When Luke first invited us to this Burns' Night supper, I was quite sceptical, imagining reams of tartan, sporrans and bagpipes everywhere, with lots of beardy Scotsmen drunk on whisky. But apart from the haggis being piped in earlier by a quite handsome young piper in full Scottish regalia, sporting a very nice pair of legs under his kilt, the night was progressing much like any other meal in a top London restaurant.

'Yes, Luke,' I call back over the chatter round the table. 'It's really tasty. I never thought I'd enjoy turnips and potatoes mashed together as much either!'

Luke smiles. 'Ah, neeps and tatties have filled many a Scotsman's stomach when he's an important job to do!' He takes a swig from his glass of whisky. 'You're not drinking your whisky, though?'

The neat malt whisky had for a few seconds taken my breath and my voice away, when, like Sean, I'd tried to down it in one go. Much flapping with my hands had made the others round the table understand that I needed water, and fast. So now I'm sipping slowly, but much more pleasurably, on a nice glass of chardonnay, which is far more to my liking.

'No.' I lift my glass. 'This is more up my street.'

'I don't blame you,' he smiles. 'At least you're not drinking the hideous monstrosities my magnificent partner here is currently downing.'

We both look at Oscar, who is deep in conversation with Ursula about something; he reaches for his bright blue cocktail. 'What?' he asks, seeing us staring at him.

We smile.

'Nothing,' Luke says, touching the back of Oscar's hand gently. 'You just keep being you, Oscar – never change.'

They exchange a look that makes my heart ping with joy. It's been so wonderful to see Oscar so happy over the last year, and Luke is definitely the reason why. Although they are complete opposites, in looks as well as personality – petite Oscar with his flamboyant, outrageous ways, and tall, dark Luke with his calm, considered, almost methodical approach to life – they seem to make a great couple: two sides of the perfect coin.

Sean squeezes my hand. 'What are you thinking about?' he asks.

'Oscar and Luke,' I reply. 'They really make a great couple, don't they?'

Sean nods. 'Yes. Don't quite see what Luke sees in him myself . . .' he winks, 'but I'm glad Oscar's happy at last.' He glances at Maddie. 'Is everything all right? Maddie seems very quiet tonight.'

I look over at my friend; she's barely touched her food, but is seemingly doing very well with the alcohol side of things this evening.

'I don't think so,' I whisper in Sean's ear. 'I think she and Felix are having some problems.'

'Oh no, really?' Sean looks with concern at Maddie.

'I'm afraid so. I keep trying to get her to talk about it, but she's being very evasive. I don't think she wants to bother me with hers and Felix's troubles because of all our plans.'

Sean frowns. 'That's very generous of Maddie. But everyone goes through sticky patches with their marriage – it's how you work through your troubles that matters. We're her friends. She should know we're there for her if she needs our help.'

22

Sean can be so lovely sometimes; I just want to kiss him. So I do.

'What's that for?' he asks.

'Just because I love you,' I say, smiling at him. 'And because you're you.'

Sean looks puzzled yet pleased.

'You're right, though,' I continue, 'about Maddie. I should try a bit harder to get her to talk.'

'The pair of you don't usually have any difficulty talking.' Sean grins. 'It's all I can do to stop you sometimes!'

'Funny!' I reply, pretending to give him a scathing look.

Sean winks. 'Anyway, talking of our wedding, how're the plans coming along?'

'Ah ... about that,' I say coyly, picking up my wine glass, sad to see it's already empty. 'That's something I need to talk to you—'

'Ladies and gents!' Luke suddenly announces, standing up and clinking his glass with a spoon. 'If I could just have your attention for a few moments ...'

We stop talking and turn to look at Luke; he seems edgy and a bit nervous, which is not like him at all.

'I'm so glad you could come along tonight to help celebrate Burns' Night with me. I know I don't sound much like a true Scot, but I can guarantee you I'm one through to my core. In fact, if you'd asked me a number of months ago where my heart would always lie, I'd have answered you Scotland every time.' There's banging on the table, and a couple of 'Hear! Hear!'s from the Scots in our party. 'But then this beautiful, wonderful man came skipping and twirling into my life –' Luke turns his gaze towards Oscar, who gazes up at him with just as much, if not more love in his eyes '– and I knew that my heart had found a new home.'

I can feel tears beginning to well up in the corner of my eyes, so I reach down into my lap for my napkin.

'Oscar,' he says, taking hold of Oscar's hand, who is for once speechless, 'I know there are so many ways in which someone can propose. Some set the bar so high –' he flits a glance towards Sean '– that it makes anything us mere mortals do seem dull and without thought. But that doesn't make our declarations of love any less meaningful. And that's what this is, my dazzling, wonderful Oscar – it's *my* way of declaring my everlasting love for you.'

Oscar, still bizarrely silent, claps his hand over his mouth in shock.

'Oscar St James,' Luke says, dropping to one knee, 'will you do me the greatest of honours by becoming my husband?'

There's a collective sharp intake of expectant breath from round the table as we all await Oscar's answer. I feel Sean's hand grip mine even tighter.

Eventually, after what seems like forever, Oscar speaks.

'Of course I'll marry you, my big Scottish Braveheart.

Nothing would make me happier in this world! But I do have one condition.'

'Yes?' Luke asks, his expression of joy rapidly turning to concern.

'I'm the one who gets to wear the big white dress!'

Four

'I can't believe Oscar is getting married,' I say to Sean, as we're getting ready for bed that night. 'We were only joking about it at the wedding fair the other day.'

Sean climbs into bed, props some pillows up against the headboard, then leans back against them. 'I know. Can you imagine what an Oscar-inspired wedding is going to be like? There will be more sequins and feathers than a Kylie Minogue concert.'

I laugh as I rub some cream into my hands. 'But Luke isn't like Oscar, is he? Maybe that will tame things a bit.'

'A whole circus of lion tamers wielding whips couldn't tame Oscar when he's in full flow.'

'You're probably right. Blimey, don't mention whips to him – he might like that!'

Sean pulls a face. 'At least you quashed the "let's have

a joint wedding" idea immediately. As much as I can just about *tolerate* Oscar these days, there is no way I'm sharing our special day with him and Luke.'

Sean and Oscar's relationship is a funny one: although they both claim to dislike each other intensely, and often behave accordingly, underneath all the pretence they actually get on very well. There's a certain mutual respect between the two of them, which is lovely to witness on the odd occasion it's allowed to find its way to the surface.

'Oh no, as much as I love Oscar, I would never agree to that. I want our wedding to be *the* most perfect day ever.'

'Me too,' Sean says, as I climb into our super-king-size bed and snuggle up next to him. 'How *are* the plans coming along?'

'Ah, that's what I've been trying to talk to you about . . . They're not, exactly.'

Sean looks down at me. 'What do you mean?'

I lift my head off his chest and sit up to face him. 'I've been so busy lately I just haven't had much time.'

'For what?' Sean asks, his forehead wrinkling. 'Sorting out a venue, a dress, flowers, what exactly?'

I swallow hard. 'Anything.'

Sean pulls himself up in the bed so he can turn to face me properly. 'Anything? But we're supposed to be getting married at the end of the year. I don't know much about these things, Scarlett, but I know you have to book certain aspects of a wedding a long way in advance.'

'Well, you haven't been much help, have you?' I reply defensively. 'What have you done towards it?'

'I came with you to look at venues – I thought you were going to choose one of the ones we shortlisted.'

I shake my head. 'No, none of them seemed right, and anyway, it's something we should do together.'

Sean considers this. 'True, but it's a bit difficult to do when you're hardly ever here.' He looks at me with a sad face and I know in a moment his pale blue eyes will go all puppy-like. 'You spend most of your time over in New York these days.'

'No, I don't,' I respond firmly. 'It's been working out about half and half lately, and you agreed it would be OK for me to work like this. It was your idea to get the apartment in Manhattan instead of me staying in hotels all the time.'

'I know –' Sean takes hold of my hand '– but I didn't realise quite how often you'd be gone. I miss you so much when you're away, Red.'

Uh-oh, he's using my nickname now. Sean is the only person who calls me Red. It started as a joke when we first met and Sean was teasing me about losing my temper. But now he uses it as a term of endearment.

'And I miss you too – you know that. I'd love it if we could be together all the time. But the trust is going so well now, Sean – I can't take a step back.'

'And I wouldn't want you to. You've done such great work over there, and I know how much it means to you.'

Sean is right: The Dragonfly Trust has really spread its wings and soared in the last couple of years. Through fundraising and private income we've been able to reunite children with estranged parents, and clients with family members whom they'd given up all hope of ever seeing again. We are like a last resort for people who need our help, and we – my growing team of employees and I – are good at what we do. Our high success rate has been the subject of many media reports over in the States, in news-papers and magazines as well as on TV.

'Yes, it does. And just between you and me, there's talk of some possible new backers who could make a huge dif-ference to our fundraising in the future. We've a big board meeting coming up when I return to the States.'

Sean leans back against his pillows again and sighs. 'This is what comes of having two high-flyers in the family, eh?' he smiles. 'Who would have thought when I bumped into you in the Travel Bookshop all those years ago that you'd be running two successful businesses now? And on both sides of the Atlantic, too. You make my little empire look insignificant in comparison.'

'Hardly,' I reassure him. Sean runs a huge and very successful property company. I likened him to Richard Gere in *Pretty Woman* when we first met. 'Back then all I was interested in was movies,' I say, remembering how my passion for the cinema had led me away from Stratford-upon-Avon to London. 'House-sitting in Notting Hill was the height of excitement for me. Remember how I used to pretend I was in a movie?' I still do this occasionally, but Sean doesn't know. 'If I'd bumped into Hugh Grant or Julia Roberts, I would have thought my life complete!'

'How could I forget?' Sean winks. 'But we've come a long way since then.' He links his fingers through mine. 'Together.'

'We have,' I agree, smiling up at him, 'and now we're finally getting married.'

Sean nods. 'Although it doesn't seem like two minutes since I was proposing.'

My mind wanders happily back to Sean's wonderful romantic proposal on top of the Brooklyn Bridge in New York, our friends and family around us.

'I think that's part of the problem. We thought back then we'd got ages to organise our dream day, but suddenly it's January in the year we're supposed to be getting married and we've made no plans. We're both so busy. If we just had a few more hours in every day . . . !'

I say this lightly, but Sean releases my hand, folds his arms across his bare chest and proceeds to stare at the wall opposite the bed.

This means he is thinking. I know him well enough by now to know that when he gets that little crinkle in his forehead between his sandy eyebrows, he usually comes up with a good idea, often one involving me. So I relax back on my pillows and let him think.

After a few minutes he turns confidently towards me.

'I'll do it,' he says, smiling at me, his eyes shining with enthusiasm.

'Do what?'

'I'll organise the wedding.'

It's just as well I'm in bed or I might have found myself lying horizontal on the floor right now, after fainting in shock.

'*You'll* organise the wedding?' I ask him, aghast. 'We are still talking about *our* wedding?'

'Yes, of course.'

'The wedding where when we added up the guest list, it came to nearly two hundred people, with all our family, friends and your business contacts?'

Sean flinches slightly. 'Yes, well, maybe we could cut that list down just a tad … But at least think about it, Scarlett. It would free you up and take some of the pressure off your shoulders. You have seemed a little strained just lately, and you do look exhausted much of the time.'

'Thanks very much! I love you too!'

'You know I didn't mean it like that,' Sean says, putting his arm around me. 'I'm just trying to help.'

But my brain is already racing. 'Just say for one moment I did agree to this – tell me what you know about organising a wedding.'

'Right now about as much as you, it would seem.' Sean raises his eyebrows.

'Funny,' I reply. 'No, it's lovely of you to offer, Sean, and

I really appreciate you trying to help, but it's a silly idea. It just wouldn't work.'

'Why wouldn't it?' Sean asks. 'Let's have some reasons.'

I think quickly – I hate it when Sean does this. This is his practical business head kicking in. Whereas I always jump straight in with my heart on my sleeve and worry about the consequences later, Sean wants to work through any idea, ironing out the pros and cons until we reach an informed and sensible decision.

'Hmm, I know one straight away. If I let *you* organise the wedding, it will be based on practicalities. You'll choose flowers that last the longest rather than look the prettiest, a car that does the most miles to the gallon rather than one that looks the most fantastic driving me and Dad to the church, and probably a venue that's closest to an airport or a major motorway, so it's more accessible for our guests.'

'Good idea,' Sean says, considering my last suggestion. Then he shrugs. 'I *may* consider things at a more practical level than you would, but that wouldn't be my only criteria for organising our day. I'd choose what I think we would both enjoy, in all aspects.'

Hmm ... I think again.

'Ooh, I know – what if some big business comes up for sale while you're in the last stages of planning everything and you have to jet off abroad like you sometimes do to negotiate a deal? Who will take over then – Marjorie?'

Marjorie is Sean's PA. She is excellent at her job, and

would actually make quite a good addition to a wedding-planning team. But that isn't the point.

'You're right,' Sean says, calmly considering this. 'Marjorie would simply inform me of anything I needed to know while I was away and would keep me up to speed on any necessary developments.'

Damn . . . he's got an answer to everything.

'It's just not the done thing for the groom to organise the wedding,' I throw in as a last shot.

'But isn't there a whole television show dedicated to just this same process?' Sean asks. 'I'm sure I caught you watching it one day.'

'Oh my God – if my wedding turns out like any of the disasters on that show, I would be the first bride to become a spinster in the same day!'

When Sean and I first got engaged, I watched every bridal show I could Sky+. I read all the bridal magazines from cover to cover every week, and I even had a go at making a wedding mood board, before the irritation of cutting scraps of fabric and tearing pictures from magazines put me in such a *bad mood* I gave up and threw them and the board across the room.

'No,' I insist, 'you just can't do it. You've already been given one job and you haven't even done that as far as I'm aware.'

'What's that?' Sean asks, puzzling.

'To find a best man.'

'Oh, I have one of those.'

33

'You have? When did this happen? Who is it?'

Sean smiles knowingly. 'You see – I can do things when asked to. I'm not a complete wedding loser.'

'You still haven't told me who this mystery man is.'

'His name is Alex, and he's an old friend of mine.'

'You've never mentioned an Alex before. How come I haven't met him?'

'He's been abroad for the last few years travelling. I've known him since university days. Then we shared a flat together in London for a while. We made a sort of pact that we'd be best men at each other's weddings, should we ever be lucky enough to get married.'

'When was this?' I'm a bit put out. I thought I knew all about Sean's past.

'Er . . . ' Sean thinks. 'Bit before I met Jen, I think.'

My stomach twists into a knot at the sound of her name. I have a *history* with Jen, Sean's ex-girlfriend. But she is also Oscar's sister, so occasionally I'm forced to tolerate her.

'So Alex knows Jen?'

'He did, yes. Why? Is that a problem?'

'No, of course not. Does he know Oscar?'

Sean thinks again. 'Do you know, I can't remember if they ever met or not. Oscar and I didn't really know each other all that well back then. He was more Ursula's friend. It was when I started dating Jen that I got to know him a little more.'

It is in part thanks to Ursula, Sean's lovely sister, that Sean and I are together now.

'Anyway, why is any of this relevant?'

'It's not, I suppose. I'm just trying to build up a picture of this man who's going to be an integral part of our wedding yet I've never even heard of.'

'Oh, you might have heard of him,' Sean says mysteriously. 'And you might have seen him, too.'

'What on earth do you mean? How can I have seen him if I've never met him?'

Sean grins at me.

'Sean!' I say, rolling on top of him now, so my legs are straddling his bare body. 'Stop teasing me. Tell!'

'I'm not too sure I want to,' Sean says, grinning up at me. 'I quite like teasing you in this position.'

'Tell!' I say, pinning his hands above his head.

'Even better,' Sean laughs.

'If you don't tell me now, Sean, there'll be no teasing of *any* part of your anatomy for a very long time! If you get my meaning . . .'

'You're so nosy, Red,' he torments. 'Can't bear it when you don't know everything, can you? OK, OK,' he relents, when I press even harder on his wrists. 'Alex is like your brother.'

'Whatever do you mean?' I puzzle, releasing my grip on his arms slightly. 'How can he be like Jamie?'

'He's a news correspondent – well, he was. Foreign affairs. He got sent all over the world for years and he was very good at it – won awards for journalism, that kind of thing.'

'Would I have seen him on anything?'

'You might,' Sean says, easing his arms entirely from my grip now and placing them on my hips, 'when you were over in New York. He used to work for American TV – they loved his accent, apparently, that's what got him the job to begin with. He started with basic reporting, then he was gradually promoted to the more serious stuff. Alex has been to all sorts of war-torn areas. Pretty brave guy. I wouldn't want to do it.'

'Oh ...' I think about the kind of news programmes I watch when I'm over in New York. They mainly consist of *The Today Show* on NBC first thing in the morning, an incredibly popular US breakfast-TV programme. But to be honest, I take more interest in Kathie Lee and Hoda, who come on directly afterwards – they are like a sort of US cross between the Loose Women and Holly and Phil from *This Morning*, full of showbiz gossip and useful tips like summer barbecue recipes or Christmas gifts to buy your nearest and dearest, depending on the season. 'Maybe I have seen him at some point,' I say lightly, trying to conceal my lack of knowledge of American news channels. 'But since I don't even know what he looks like, I'm hardly likely to know, am I?'

'Oh, you'd know all right if you'd seen him,' Sean says as he begins to trace his hands gently up and down my back, making my spine tingle with anticipation.

'I would? How?'

'You'll see when you meet him at the wedding.'

'Our wedding?'

'No, the wedding we're going to up in Edinburgh in a few weeks. Like me, Alex knows the bridegroom, Callum. Alex is back in Scotland for a while catching up with his family while he's between jobs.'

'Alex is Scottish?'

'Yup, just like Luke, only his accent is broad – well, as broad as it's going to be now it's been ironed out in the States.'

'Well, I look forward to meeting this mystery Scottish friend of yours – he sounds intriguing.'

'Alex, yeah, he's a good guy.'

'He would have to be if he's *your* best man ... Although –' I lean down and kiss Sean, powerless as always to resist the effect his touch is having on my body '– I don't think there's any better than the one who's below me right now.'

'Red, you never said a truer word,' Sean agrees, 'and I think I should prove that to you again right this very minute ...'

Five

'And the award goes to ...'

This is so exciting, being here tonight among all the celebrities in their finery. We – me, Sean, Oscar and Luke – are at the Stardust TV Awards at the O2 Arena in London, and we're surrounded by the glitterati of television past and present, who are here to see if they've received an award, to present one of the sought-after silver stars or just to lap up the free champagne that's being handed out on silver trays during the advert breaks by scantily clad waitresses.

The costume drama on whose set Luke and Oscar met has been nominated for several awards, so when Luke was offered several free tickets to tonight's event, he invited Sean and me, along with Oscar, to come and enjoy the show.

Never one to miss an opportunity to celeb-spot, Oscar and I of course jumped at his invitation. Sean was a little harder to persuade, but eventually he agreed, and tonight he looks absolutely gorgeous in his black tuxedo and white shirt. Oscar is wearing one of his usual colourful creations – a purple velvet suit with a red silk shirt, and I'm in my new sky-blue Ted Baker evening dress, which I bought specially for the occasion. I casually name-dropped to the sales assistant exactly which occasion it was going to be worn at, and was pleased when he seemed as enthusiastic as me to talk about the awards.

The assistant was also quite excited when I mentioned which TV show we were going there to support, and who had got us the tickets. Apparently Luke, in his footman's uniform, has caused something of a stir in certain communities and has built up a bit of a following.

'Oh, oh, isn't that Ian Beale?' I whisper to Oscar, as we peer down from our seats in the front row of the side tiers. Luke is sitting down on the ground floor in front of the stage with his cast members.

'Yes, it is!' Oscar exclaims. 'And there's Max Branning with the rest of the *EastEnders* cast.' Oscar and I have nearly fallen over the safety barrier in front of us a couple of times when we've been desperately peering down into the audience to try and spot our favourite TV stars.

'Will you two stop it,' Sean says, calmly flicking through a programme next to us. 'They're just people like you and me.'

'I know that,' I say, sitting back in my chair for a moment, trying to appear cool and composed. 'We're just playing a little star-spotting game – a bit like TV bingo.'

Sean's lips twitch in amusement. 'Bingo? What happens when you get a full house? Do you leap in the air and Dermot awards you a cash prize from the stage?'

Sean was referring to Dermot O'Leary, the presenter of tonight's awards. Oscar and I both squeaked like demented hamsters when he appeared on stage. I've loved Dermot since his *Big Brother's Little Brother* days, and Oscar – well, Oscar just fancies the pants off him.

'No,' I say calmly. 'It's simply a bit of fun to pass the time while we wait. We're only here to support Luke and his show – you know that.'

Sean lets out a deep belly laugh. 'Yeah, right. That's about as likely as me ending up on that stage tonight with one of those silver stars in my hand.'

I laugh too. 'Sean, you hate the spotlight – that will never, ever happen.'

'Too right,' Sean agrees. 'But I bet you'd love to be down there, wouldn't you? I bet you've even thought about your acceptance speech since we've been sitting here.'

Sean has this amazing ability to know me better than I even know myself. He is right, of course: I'd love to be down there on the stage with the audience and the spotlight focused on me. Winning an award is something I dream about. Years ago I used to have a fantasy about winning an Academy Award in Hollywood. It was usually presented by Johnny Depp or Colin Firth. I don't have that fantasy any more. Obviously I've matured and grown up a bit these days . . .

Now my fantasy award is presented by Will Smith, Ryan Gosling or sometimes my old mate Bradley Cooper!

'I might have considered it,' I admit. 'But I'm never going to be accepting an award for anything, am I? So what harm is there in pretending?'

'Look,' Oscar calls, waving a purple velvet arm towards the celebrity audience. 'They're on the move again.'

We've witnessed this strange procedure taking place several times during the course of the evening already. When celebrities leave their seats for toilet/cigarette/goodness-knows-what breaks, a small swarm of prettily dressed women suddenly appear to fill the vacant spaces – presumably to keep the audience looking full for the TV viewers.

'How odd,' I commented when we first noticed this going on. 'Imagine being told to go and sit down next to Alan Carr to fill the gap Ant and Dec have left.'

'If you were told that, darling, you'd be putting yourself on a serious diet the next day,' Oscar mused, watching the bizarre routine with as much interest as me.

I looked across at him. 'What do you mean?'

'Ant and Dec may be tiny, but *two* spaces, darling!'

'Ah yes,' I agreed, getting his joke. 'But seriously, how sad would it be to do that job for an evening? Have you noticed no one talks to the space-fillers? It's as if they don't exist.'

We watch again now from our vantage point, the girls being blanked by the celebrity they're sitting next to, and it's quite depressing to witness.

'TV's a bit fake, isn't it?' I whisper to Oscar. 'I mean the stuff that goes on behind the scenes, not just the programmes.'

He nods. 'That's what Luke tells me all the time when I get excited about him doing telly stuff. He says the money is good, but it's too controlled. That's why he prefers the theatre. He says it's more real. More genuine.'

'Yes, I reckon he might be right.' I think about my half-brother, Jamie, who's a television correspondent, and our friend Max, who's a cameraman over in New York. Some of their tales were much the same; they never understood why I would get so excited about anything to do with the big or small screen. It was just commonplace to them, and they would often warn me it really wasn't as exciting or as glamorous as it was made out to be.

'You know something, Oscar, when you see peculiar things like this going on, you realise that people like Luke, Jamie and Max might be right after all.'

'Might be right about what?' Sean asks, sitting back down in his seat again. While we've been dissecting the seat-filling issue, Sean nipped out to the loo.

'Scarlett has decided television is a sham,' Oscar repeats for Sean's benefit in a loud enough voice that the people around us all glance in our direction.

'Hush, Oscar!' I hiss, my face flushing. 'I didn't quite

say that,' I whisper to Sean. 'I said it seems a little fake at times.'

'Well, of course it is,' Sean agrees. 'It's hardly going to be real, is it? Take reality shows for instance – they're either scripted, or edited the way they want us to view them.'

'No,' I disagree, thinking of my favourite, *Big Brother*. 'You simply couldn't invent some of the stuff that goes on in them – it's nuts.'

Sean nods down at the audience below. 'Red, that's what all these luvvies and darlings do for a living – pretend. Of course TV is fake.'

'Oi, my fiancé happens to be one of those luvvies!' Oscar grumbles at Sean. 'And I can guarantee you there's nothing *fake* about any part of him!'

Sean pulls a face.

'No, you're wrong. Jamie isn't fake,' I say. 'Or Max.'

'Scarlett ... Jamie can play up to the camera when he wants to,' Sean grins. 'I've seen him turn on the charm when he's interviewing a pretty girl. It's all for show, and completely false.'

I know Sean is only joking, but I feel myself bristle at this slur on Jamie. We've only known each other for about a year and a half, but I'm still very protective of my half-brother.

'I think I'll just take a visit to the ladies' room,' I announce, standing up, 'before it's time for Luke's award.'

'Now look what you've done,' I hear Oscar hiss at a surprised Sean as I begin to climb the stairs of the O2 Arena and head towards the toilets. 'Wait up, Scarlett – I'll come with you!' Oscar calls after me.

We meet up again in the corridor outside, after we've both used the appropriate facilities.

'Shall we head back, then?' I ask in a subdued voice, looking towards the exit we've just come from.

'He didn't mean anything, you know,' Oscar says. 'Sean, when he said that thing about Jamie. He was just using him as an example of how media types can play people sometimes to get what they want – even the good ones.'

'I know. I just miss Jamie now he's got his new job. When he was in New York, we'd see each other all the time when I was over there. But now he's travelling so much, I hardly hear from him, let alone see him.'

'I bet Max misses him too,' Oscar says. Jamie had been a UK reporter based in New York when I first met him, and Max had been his cameraman. But after Jamie had been headhunted as a foreign correspondent for NBC, Max had been assigned a new correspondent to work with. She seemed nice enough – I'd met her a couple of times – but both Max and I missed having Jamie around.

'Yes, he misses him a lot.' I sigh. 'Like me.'

'That's enough of that!' Oscar snaps. 'I've heard you sigh far too often recently, and there's been much too much of this.' He pulls a miserable clown-like expression and pretends to wipe away a tear. 'This is not the Scarlett I know and love. Where's all your fun gone, your excitement, your lust for life?'

'You were always the one with the lust for life, Oscar,' I smile, 'not me.'

Oscar grins. 'And I still am,' he says knowingly. 'I don't hear Luke complaining too often!'

I roll my eyes.

'But enough about fabulous me!' he says, pretending to smooth his dark hair. 'I think *you* need some fun tonight, Scarlett. Something that's going to brighten you up and put a smile back permanently on your pretty face, and luckily for you, I know just where we're going to find it!'

Six

'Where are we going?' I pant, as Oscar tugs me quickly by the hand up a long corridor. 'We can't go down here, can we?'

Oscar had told me to ask no questions when, from the small man bag he was carrying across his shoulder tonight, he'd produced a couple of laminated cards on red silk ropes for us to hang round our necks. Sean's eyes had nearly popped out of his head when he'd seen Oscar carrying the bag earlier. But he was fairly used to Oscar by now, with his outlandish ways and even more outlandish dress sense, and the small purple leather purse wasn't exactly an eyesore against his brightly coloured suit.

'Where did you get these?' I ask Oscar again, waving my pass at him.

'I told you – no questions, Scarlett,' Oscar insists. 'Let's just say I found them *lying around* in an office when Luke went to collect his own pass the other day. I simply picked up a couple of spares in case they came in handy!'

'Oscar!'

'Well, they are coming in handy now, aren't they?'

'Handy for what?'

'Some much-needed Scarlett and Oscar fun!' Oscar says, flashing his pass at a security guard as we go through a door marked RED PASSES ONLY.

On the other side of the door, I find myself in a large open area. There are lots of people milling about with clipboards, iPads and walkie-talkies, furrowed brows and worried looks on their faces. Occasionally, in among a small gaggle of the stressed-out brigade, there is someone in a suit or a long evening gown having their make-up touched up, or their hair fiddled with, and as I stand there watching them, I suddenly realise where we are.

'Oscar,' I exclaim, swivelling round to look at him, 'we're backstage!'

Oscar nods excitedly. 'Come on, darling,' he whispers, grabbing hold of my hand. 'Let's explore before we get rumbled!'

We walk around the area hand in hand as casually and nonchalantly as we can, trying to blend in with everything that's going on. But it's actually quite dull. Even when we do spot the odd celebrity, they're either being ushered in to present an award or ushered away because they've won one and they're off to do press interviews.

'You two, over here!' we hear someone shout behind us. We turn round to see a woman with an earpiece and a clipboard. 'Yes, you two. Quick – we need seat-fillers and fast.'

'No, Oscar,' I insist, as I see his eyes light up. I firmly shake my head. 'This is far enough. We've had our fun. We're not crossing *that* line.'

But Oscar, with a surprisingly tight grip, pulls me towards the entrance to the main arena, where the woman is madly gesturing now as she directs the fillers to their temporary seats.

'Perfect,' she says, looking us up and down. 'We have two gaps in "talent shows".' She gestures at me. 'You'll do for Nicole Scherzinger. Your long, dark hair will be spot on. Slip in over there next to Gary Barlow for me, sweetie. And you.' She pulls Oscar towards her. 'See that space in *Strictly Come Dancing*?'

'I'm there!' Oscar says, virtually pirouetting across the room towards the gap.

The woman stares after him. 'He could be Bruno Tonioli's twin with moves like that! He's a perfect match for him while Bruno's presenting the next award.' She looks at me. 'Are you OK, sweetie? You look a bit pale.'

'You want me to go and sit next to Gary Barlow?' I squeak. Gary Barlow the *X Factor* judge, but more importantly a member of one of my all-time favourite bands, Take That.

'Yes, now hurry up before we cut back from the

commercials.' She gives me a shove from behind in the general direction of Gary, so I stumble forward in my heels and begin to totter towards him.

What on earth am I going to say to Gary Barlow? I think as I get ever closer. *I can't possibly be one of these mute girls who just sits and says nothing – that's not my style at all.* I take a deep breath. *I have to calm down. There's nothing scary about Gary. After all, I've had conversations with many a Hollywood A-lister before – Johnny Depp, Kate Winslet and Bradley Cooper. How bad could Gary Barlow be?*

I notice as I pass that Oscar is already deep in conversation with Len Goodman, another of the *Strictly* judges. His hands gesticulate in the air as if he's showing Len some of his dance moves, and Len looks highly amused by his actions.

Right – if Oscar can do this, so can I.

I slip into the seat next to Gary. But he doesn't appear to notice me and continues to chat to the person on the other side of him, who I'm guessing must be a member of the *X Factor* production crew because I don't recognise him as anyone famous.

I clear my throat.

But that doesn't gain Gary's attention either, so I shuffle about in my seat a bit in the hope he might notice me.

Gary turns briefly, nods his acknowledgement of my presence, but immediately turns away again.

No! This isn't the way it's supposed to go at all.

So for some inexplicable reason I decide to start humming the first thing that comes into my head, and then when that still isn't working, I begin to sing the lyrics to the song quietly to myself: '... and through it all, she offers me affection ...'

Gary swivels round in his seat to face forward and I suddenly realise we've gone live again as Dermot O'Leary reappears on the stage.

'Were you singing just then?' Gary whispers, leaning towards me while continuing to face forward with a fixed smile on his face. He looks a bit like a ventriloquist trying to smile and talk without his lips moving.

'Yes, I was. It's one of my favourites,' I gush, glad I've got his attention at last. 'Take That are one of my all-time favourite bands.'

'Then you should have known you were humming a Robbie tune just now,' he says gravely, turning to glance at me quickly while trying not to take his eyes from the stage. He's obviously very aware there are men all over the auditorium floor running around with cameras that could poke a lens up his nose at any moment. 'And not only that, you got the lyrics wrong. It's "protection", not "affection". That's the next line.' He looks at me reprovingly.

I think about this. Oh shit! I was humming, then attempting to sing the lyrics from 'Angels'. How could I one, have got the lyrics wrong, and two, sung a solo Robbie Williams hit to Gary Barlow! My face flushes as bright as my name.

'Oh God, I'm so sorry! I'm just a bit star-struck to be sitting next to you,' I babble. 'Only, me and my friend, we were sitting up there a few minutes ago.' I point, and as I do, I see Sean looking quizzically down at me from his seat, so I hastily withdraw my hand. 'And then we sort of got lost, and then this woman suddenly thrust us out here, and, well, here I am ...'

Gary forgets about the stage now and turns to look at me properly. 'Well, that's a story,' he says in that monotone way of his. 'Does this sort of thing happen to you often?'

'Yes, it does actually,' I have to admit. 'My whole life is full of incidents just like this. I'm Scarlett, by the way.' I hold out my hand.

Gary grins while he shakes it. 'Great life you have, then, Scarlett. I'd stick with it if I were you.' Then he winks. 'You don't want to be known as *boring*, do you? Oh, look sharp – it's time for another award.'

I turn towards the stage and realise it's one of the awards Luke's TV show is nominated for, and they've only gone and won!

As the cast and crew from the show fill the stage, I can see Luke up there too, so I applaud extra hard, but out of the corner of my eye I notice a kerfuffle going on in the *Strictly Come Dancing* section of the audience. Oscar has stood up on his seat and is yelping and wolf-whistling his support of Luke's win. Len Goodman, next to him, is trying to coax him down, and the cameras are loving it! He's now being shown up on the big screens that surround

51

the stage, which I guess probably means he's also being beamed live into people's living rooms right at this very moment.

I look up at Sean. His face suggests he's not impressed by our escapades.

Gary shakes his head next to me. 'Never could control themselves, that *Strictly* lot. That's why I never did the show when they asked me to be a contestant.'

'Really?' I mumble, still looking across at Oscar, who, after being physically removed from his seat, is now being escorted rather swiftly through an emergency exit by a couple of burly bouncers. 'You sure it wasn't because you're a rubbish dancer?'

I slap my hand over my mouth the minute the words escape from my mouth, but Gary just smiles.

'You really *are* a Take That fan, aren't you?' he grins.

I see the same woman who placed Oscar and me in our seats fiercely beckoning me towards the wings.

'Looks like that's your cue to exit,' Gary whispers as we cut to another break. 'Nicole must be on her way back.'

I sigh. 'It was lovely to meet you, Gary. Really it was. I'm so sorry about the dancing thing. My mouth just gets a little carried away with me sometimes. You're a great songwriter, if it's any consolation?'

'And you,' Gary grins, looking up at me as I stand up and smooth down my dress, 'are ... ' He pauses and I stand awkwardly waiting for him to finish, aware of all the pairs of very green eyes that are suddenly trained in my direction.

I'm hoping to hear a phrase like 'stunningly beautiful in that dress' or even 'a breath of fresh air in among all this celebrity nonsense'. In fact, a simple 'completely mad' would have done after what I'd said to him in the last few minutes.

'... quite obviously a Robbie fan,' he finishes. Then he winks. 'Don't worry about it. I'll let you off. Give me a shout the next time we're on tour, Scarlett, and I'll get you a backstage pass to meet him.'

I'm about to jump up and down on the spot with excitement; then I remember I'm in heels and refrain from doing so.

'Thank you!' I whisper. 'Thank you so much!'

'Now go!' Gary waves me away with his hand. 'Before that woman over there explodes! You don't want that on your conscience, do you?'

I hurry over to the exit, where the woman with the clipboard glares at me ferociously before she hurriedly escorts me back into the 'holding area' behind the stage.

'Who the hell are you and your friend?' she hisses, gesturing over at Oscar, who is being frogmarched towards me by a security guard in a fluorescent jacket. 'You're not from the agency, are you?'

'Er ...' I hesitate, looking at Oscar as he wrestles himself from the man's hands.

'You didn't have to be quite so rough,' Oscar complains, brushing at the sleeves of his velvet suit. 'I don't normally complain about a bit of manhandling by someone with muscles the size of yours –' he eyes the man's biceps '– but when I'm wearing vintage Armani . . . '

'That's vintage Armani?' the guard says, looking with new interest at Oscar's jacket. 'I thought the fabric felt a bit special, and I feel a lot of suits in my game. I'd have placed it as Versace maybe, or a McQueen, but not an Armani.'

The three of us stare up at the huge security guard. He doesn't look much like a connoisseur of men's fashion, in his high-vis jacket.

'What?' he asks. 'Just 'cos I'm made to wear this right now don't mean I don't know good clobber when I feel it!'

'Anyway,' clipboard lady continues, shaking her head, 'about these passes . . .' She pulls on the two passes still hanging round our necks.

'Oscar! There you are!' It's Luke and he's heading our way. 'I saw you from the stage. What were you up to jumping on the seats like that? Honestly,' Luke gushes, laying it on thick for the woman, 'I can't take him anywhere these days.'

The woman appears to know who Luke is without even inspecting his pass, which I notice is on a blue rope.

'Are these two with you?' she asks, still holding on to our passes as though she's handing over two stray dogs to Luke.

'But of course they are!' he grins. 'They're my friends!' He takes hold of the passes and begins to lead us away before she can argue. 'I'll take care of them now, Mary. Thank you for looking after them for me!'

We leave Mary looking suspiciously after us, and allow Luke to lead us quickly out of her eyeshot.

Luke drops the passes as soon as we're safe. He turns to Oscar and raises an eyebrow. 'Well?'

'Never a dull moment with Oscar. You should know that by now, darling.' Oscar blinks innocently as he looks up at him.

'Scarlett?' he asks, turning to me. 'This has your name written all over it. I've heard about your antics from Oscar.'

'Not me this time, Luke,' I say, shaking my head. 'I can assure you I was just an unwilling accomplice. I do hope we didn't spoil your evening, though.'

Luke looks at the two of us and smiles. 'No, of course not. Nothing is going to spoil my night tonight. In addition to the show winning the award, I just had a phone call.'

'Ooh, from whom?' Oscar asks, pleased Luke is not angry.

'From the director of the play I auditioned for the other day.'

'The one you didn't think you'd get?' Oscar asks, and I notice he seems less enthused suddenly.

'Yes, that one! I've only gone and got it! I start rehearsals in a few weeks. It looks like you'll be seeing a lot more of me when you go back over to New York, Scarlett. Because I'm going to be on Broadway!'

'Wow, that's fantastic news, Luke!' I say, hugging him. 'Congratulations.'

'Yeah,' I hear Oscar mutter while I do. 'What is it about that city? First it stole my sister, then my best friend, now my fiancé too. I think I'll get a T-shirt printed, but instead of "I *heart* New York", mine will say, "I *bloody hate* New York".'

Seven

'What on earth are you two doing in the back there?' Sean takes his eyes off the road for a moment and tries to steal a quick glance in his rear-view mirror at Oscar and me.

'We're trying to watch an episode of *Dallas* that Oscar has downloaded onto his iPad,' I say, removing my headphones for a moment.

'Both of you at the same time?'

'Yeah, we can with these new headphones Oscar has. He plugs them into the machine and I plug my set into his headphones.'

Sean shakes his head. 'And what about you, Maddie?' he asks, looking across at Maddie, who's swapped seats with me and is sitting next to Sean in the front passenger seat. 'Is *Dallas* not your thing?'

'No, not really,' Maddie replies, still looking out of the

windscreen at the long stream of A1 traffic stretching out in front of her. 'I have enough drama in my own life right now without adding to it for entertainment.'

I exchange glances with Sean through his rear-view mirror. I couldn't get my head around this Maddie. She was usually so upbeat about life. Maddie worked for an aid charity back in London, so she dealt with horrendously sad stories of poverty and despair on a daily basis, and yet she was always so positive about life. Her problems with Felix must be serious if they were bringing her down this badly, but still she didn't seem to want to discuss them with me. She was vague and evasive when I tried to get her to talk, and usually we shared everything in our lives – good and bad.

Today we're all on our way up to Scotland for a wedding to be held at Edinburgh Castle tomorrow. Sean and Oscar both know Callum and his bride-to-be, Louisa; they met through Sean's sister, Ursula, about ten years ago, when as students they had all worked as ushers one summer in the open-air theatre in Regent's Park in London. We'd chosen to drive up instead of fly or take the train because Sean wanted to take a quick trip over to Glasgow after the wedding to do some business and to visit his father. So Oscar and I had decided to turn the wedding into a mini Scottish road trip and had persuaded Sean (well, we'd blackmailed him really) by saying that if he was going to conduct business while we were away, then we wanted him to do something for us in return –

that something being a trip to Gretna Green on the return journey home.

'Gretna Green!' Sean had protested. 'Why do you want to go there? It's just a tourist trap these days, isn't it?'

'Because Oscar is still looking for the perfect wedding venue for him and Luke,' I'd explained, 'and besides, it might be romantic to go to the place where so many people have eloped to over the years.'

'Sure, if that's what you want,' Sean had agreed with a shrug of his shoulders. 'I'll drive us back that way. But don't go getting any ideas, Scarlett, about us tying the knot in a blacksmith's forge . . .'

'Duh . . . as if,' I'd said at the time. But it *had* actually crossed my mind. As well as it being quite romantic, it would be so easy just to elope and exchange our vows at Gretna Green.

Maddie had been a late addition to our road trip. I'd decided it might help her to get away for a while, and although a wedding might not be the best of events for her to be attending right now, a long weekend away in Scotland with her friends could be just the boost she needed.

Maddie had been extremely reluctant to gatecrash Louisa and Callum's wedding, though, and had said she'd just amuse herself while we were there. But Louisa had been extremely understanding when Sean had spoken to her over the phone about Maddie. The wedding was going to be huge, apparently, and Louisa said she had spaces on a couple of the tables at the reception. So eventually, after a lot of coaxing, Maddie had agreed to come. Probably more to shut me up than anything else, but that approach quite often worked for me . . .

'I can't see the fascination of *Dallas* myself,' Sean says, still referring to Oscar's and my choice of viewing on the iPad. 'What's so wonderful about a bunch of Stetson-wearing cowboys? You can get that in a good western.'

'Oh, hark at you with all your movie knowledge now,' I respond, teasing him. 'Time was when you wouldn't have known Gary Cooper from Bradley Cooper.'

'I hardly think I was that bad!' Sean defends. He winks at me in the mirror. 'You've taught me well, Obi-Wan.'

'Do you ever hear from Bradley these days?' Maddie asks. 'I couldn't believe it when I turned up in New York that time and he was running around with the rest of us on your proposal treasure hunt.'

I smile as I remember. I'd met Bradley at a charity auction in New York on my first trip there with Oscar, and through a strange sequence of events we'd subsequently become good friends. 'Yes, we text sometimes – depends what he's doing movie-wise. He's pretty busy most of the time.'

'Just to be able to say that you can text Bradley Cooper is so cool,' Maddie coos, turning to smile at me in the back seat. 'You're so lucky, Scarlett.'

'I know. It always puts a smile on my face when his name flashes up on my phone.' I glance at Sean, but he doesn't seem too concerned. 'Anyway,' I say, changing the subject away from Bradley, 'technically in *Dallas* most of the characters aren't cowboys – they're oil barons. And what's wrong with a Stetson on a man? I think it looks sexy. Maybe that could be a theme for your wedding, Oscar?'

'Ooh, now there's a thought! Cowboys . . . ' Oscar's eyes glaze over.

'Scarlett, don't give him any ideas!' Sean grumbles good-naturedly. 'He'll have you dressed as an Indian squaw before you know it.'

Oscar huffs. 'Just because you're dull and boring, Seany, doesn't mean the rest of us have to be!'

'So *have* you got any ideas for your wedding yet, Oscar?' Maddie asks. 'Real ones, I mean, not daydreams.' She's smiling again, and I'm pleased to see it. Obviously this trip *was* a good idea. I knew it!

Oscar shakes his head. 'Nooo! It's a nightmare. There's so much to think about and do. I hope when I find the perfect venue, the rest will start to fall into place.'

'Didn't I say planning a wedding wasn't all fun and games?' I say, nodding knowingly. 'I definitely agree about the venue. I think that's a really important starting point.'

'Aren't you two any further forward yet either?' Maddie asks, looking between Sean and me. 'I'll have to step in soon and help all three of you out. Probably not a good idea, the mood I'm in right now. I'll have you all wearing black veils and dressed in mourning as you walk down the aisle.' She laughs, but I know her joke isn't too far away from the truth.

61

Oscar suddenly whoops with joy next to me. 'It's ready! Come on, Scarlett, it's time for a bit of Mr John Ross *sexy* Ewing. Mmm, that man can screw me over any day!'

'Oscar!' Sean raises his eyebrows in the rear-view mirror.

'What?' Oscar asks, slipping his headphones off again. 'That's what he does, doesn't he, Scarlett?'

'He's right. John Ross is the main villain of the show now J.R. Ewing has passed away. Although actually the whole show is filled with them. It's quite mad really – no one would be plotting and scheming to be that mean to someone else in real life, I'm sure.'

'My wonderful, innocent Scarlett,' Sean says. His pale blue eyes, filled with affection, are reflected back at me in the mirror. 'You'd be surprised what real people are capable of if pushed. You, my lovely, have lived a very sheltered but lucky life if you've never met anyone like this John Ross before.'

'But really, Sean, the characters in it are quite vile sometimes. If there're people like that out there in real life, then I'm glad I've lived the sort of life where I've never met any of them, and I hope I never do!'

We arrive in Edinburgh after the long journey and check in to the hotel we're all staying in tonight. The Balmoral is just along from the castle where Callum and Louisa's wedding will be held tomorrow. Their actual ceremony is taking place in a tiny private chapel within the castle walls, with just enough room inside for close family and friends, but the reception is to be a huge affair held back at the hotel.

After a brief rest in our rooms, we're now heading off for dinner at a strange-sounding restaurant called The Witchery by the Castle, which Sean's friend Alex has recommended and booked for us all.

'Wow,' I exclaim as we walk in through a tiny, almost hidden entrance leading off the Royal Mile and stand for a moment wondering at the intricate and exquisitely designed candlelit interior. 'It's so pretty. Your friend has great taste, Sean.'

'Why thank you,' I hear a smooth Scots voice say behind me. I swivel round to find a tall, dark and rather handsome stranger grinning down at me. 'I always like to hear that from a beautiful lady.'

'Cut the charm, Alex – this one's mine,' Sean says jovially, putting his arm protectively around my shoulders. 'Scarlett, meet my good friend and soon-to-be best man, Alex. Alex, meet Scarlett, my, as you so accurately pointed out, beautiful bride-to-be.'

Alex, still smiling, holds his hand out for me to shake. But as I take hold of it, he swiftly turns my hand over and gently kisses the back. 'Delighted to meet you at last, Scarlett,' he says. 'I've heard so much about you from Sean. And these are your friends who are also coming to the wedding tomorrow?' He looks towards Oscar and Maddie.

'Er ... yes, they are.' I've been quite thrown by Alex. He is not what I was expecting at all from the way Sean described him. With his chiselled good looks and piercing blue eyes, he looks more like a Hollywood movie star than a boring news reporter. But then my own brother, Jamie, also went against the 'dull male' stereotype I appeared to have when it came to TV news correspondents. 'This is my good friend Oscar,' I say, gesturing to Oscar. Oscar presents his hand palm down in the hope that Alex will give it the same treatment he gave mine, but Alex merely shakes it and smiles.

'I think we've met before, Oscar, haven't we, many years ago?'

'Yes, quite possibly, according to Sean,' Oscar says, nodding. 'Although I'm sure I would never forget a face and –' he looks Alex up and down '– a physique like yours in a hurry.'

Alex takes Oscar's flirting with good humour and winks at him.

'And this,' I say, lightly touching my hand on Maddie's back, 'is my other good friend, Maddie.'

'Now I know *we've* never met,' Alex says, showing much more interest in Maddie than Oscar. 'I never forget a beautiful face. Delighted to make your acquaintance, Maddie.' He kisses the back of her hand. 'And how are you enjoying this magnificent country of my birth?'

'What I've seen of it so far I like very much.' Maddie blushes a little as she retrieves her hand from Alex's.

'I'm glad to hear it,' Alex says, offering Maddie a dazzling smile. 'Now, I've reserved one of *the* best tables in the restaurant for us all. Please allow me to escort you to it.' He immediately links his arm companionably through Maddie's, then leads her and the rest of us to our table.

Alex, for all his cheesy charm and old-school charisma, is actually a pretty funny guy and I can see why Sean would have been friends with him at university. He's a wonderful, and entertaining, dinner guest and keeps us all amused with tales of his exploits from around the world.

'So, Oscar, Sean tells me he's not the only one to be getting married this year,' Alex says in between our delicious main course and our dessert, which we've just ordered.

'That's right. I'm getting married too.' Oscar simply radiates joy at the mere thought of his impending nuptials. Unlike Sean and I, who have had a fairly long engagement, Oscar and Luke are diving straight in and getting married as soon as possible. 'Luke and I plan on an autumn wedding later this year.'

'So where is this mystery Luke hiding tonight, then?' Alex asks. 'I do hope he's not wedding-shy – it doesn't bode too well, does it?' He laughs and takes a large gulp of his red wine.

'No, not at all,' Oscar says, and I see a flicker of annoyance cross his face. 'He's over in New York rehearsing for a Broadway show that he opens in very soon.'

'New York, eh? That's cool. Maybe I'll have to go and see this show when I'm over there next.'

'Oh, are you heading to New York soon, Alex?' I enquire, always keen to talk about my favourite city. 'For a holiday?'

'Nope, I'm going over for business. Just got the call today, actually.'

'New York, bud?' Sean asks. 'So soon. I thought you were slowing down for a while in your "semi-retirement" and you were going to spend a bit more time in this country from now on.'

'The only sort of retirement I'm taking is from news. You have to go where the money is – you know that, Sean – and this is too good an opportunity to turn down.'

'So will I be seeing you on my TV again when I'm in New York?' I ask.

'No, not this time. This is a different sort of business.'

Alex doesn't enlighten us any further, so we don't ask.

'Well, I think it's all very exciting,' Maddie says, picking up her wine glass. 'All these people living in New York ... I think I'll have to come over for another visit sometime.'

'Oh yes, Maddie!' I'm about to sing excitedly, but Alex cuts in first.

'Yes, you must,' he says, his gaze lingering on Maddie. 'I'm sure you'll have plenty of volunteers to show you round the city ...'

Maddie toys playfully with the stem of her glass. 'In that case, I think I'll *definitely* be taking a trip over this summer, or maybe even sooner.' Maddie draws her blue eyes slowly away from Alex. 'What do you think, Scarlett?'

'Of course you must! You were there such a short time on your last visit when we got engaged. It would be brilliant to have you come and stay for longer!'

'That sounds like a date, then,' Maddie says, still smiling at me, but I see her eyes flicker towards Alex again.

'It will be good to know another person in Manhattan, Alex,' I say, my smile slightly warier now. 'I'll look forward to seeing you around.'

'Yes, indeed, Scarlett. It will be fun getting to know Sean's fiancée better.' Alex clinks his glass against mine. 'I'm sure you and I will become great pals.'

Eight

The wedding up at the castle the next day is truly spectacular. Sadly we can't all squeeze into the tiny twelfth-century St Margaret's Chapel, where the ceremony is taking place, so while the main wedding party watch the bride and groom exchange their vows, the majority of us guests wait outside on the cobbled courtyard in the very welcome February sunshine. On her arrival at the castle, Louisa had looked like a model from a bridal magazine as she alighted from an ornate closed carriage pulled by two immaculate grey horses. And her groom, Callum, had looked every bit her match as he'd climbed from a shiny burgundy Bentley in his dapper slate-grey morning suit and tartan waistcoat. Now, while a few *unofficial* tots of whisky are added to the *official* coffees provided to keep us warm, we wait while the newly-weds have some photos taken in front of the ancient walls of the castle.

'Do you think Luke would like to get married here?' I ask Oscar, looking up at the castle's huge stone walls, which dominate the skyline in front of us as we stand within its protective shadow. 'It seems pretty perfect, doesn't it?'

'I did wonder before we arrived if it might be an option,' Oscar replies. 'And as you can quite clearly see, I do suit the thread of a fine Scots tartan very well.' Oscar spins round so his kilt, which he insisted on wearing today, billows out around his small but surprisingly muscular calves.

'I do hope you're not wearing your kilt in the traditional way if you're doing that!' I say in alarm, watching him.

'As if I'd go without my Calvin Kleins, darling!' Oscar looks at me with mock horror. 'And in February too! I'll have no wedding tackle left for my groom come autumn if it got frostbite and fell off!'

He takes another sip of his coffee, while I shake my head at him.

'Now, as I was saying,' he continues, 'yes, I had considered the castle as somewhere quite suitable for my handsome Scots groom, but now, standing here in this freezing cold, I'm thinking it's not such a fabulous idea after all.'

'But it won't be quite as cold in the autumn, will it?'

Oscar wrinkles up his nose. 'No ... that's true. But it's just a bit ... Hmm, how can I put it delicately? *Dull*.'

'The castle is dull?'

'Not the castle per se, but getting married in an old building like this. I want my wedding to be exciting and flamboyant and full of life. Not solid, static and heavy.'

'Heavy? Whatever do you mean?'

Oscar grimaces. He pulls his tam-o'-shanter (yes, he's even wearing traditional Scottish headgear!) from his head, deep in thought. 'Don't you feel a tad claustrophobic in here, Scarlett?' he asks. 'Among all these thick walls and cannons and armour every which way you turn?'

I look around me. 'No, not really. Why? Do you?'

Oscar nods quickly. 'Actually, darling, I hate it. Can't wait to get out of here. Keep thinking someone is going to come along and lock me up in a dungeon forever!'

I stare at Oscar. 'Really?'

'Yes, really. I never lie. You should know that about me by now.'

Now I look at him properly, he does look genuinely spooked. 'Here,' I say, handing him my coffee, 'take this. I think Sean put a bit more than a wee dram of whisky in mine.'

Oscar gulps down my coffee and some of his usual colour returns to his cheeks.

'Thanks, sweetie. I'm fine really. Just don't do well in old buildings, I guess!'

Sean returns to us. He's been having a scout round the castle while the photos are taking place. 'Isn't this great!' he exclaims happily, purposefully taking in a deep, cleansing breath of cool Scottish air. 'This could be somewhere for us to consider, Scarlett,' he says, much to my and Oscar's immediate horror. 'You don't have to get married in the chapel – they have bigger venues that can hold many more people – but apparently Louisa has wanted to get married in St Margaret's Chapel since she was a little girl.'

I look at Oscar; he's already turning pale again.

'No,' I say, hurriedly trying to think of a way of stopping Sean before he can go any further. 'It wouldn't be right for us.'

Sean looks a little put out. 'But why?'

'Erm ... neither of us has any Scottish ancestry, that's why.' I hold my hand up before he can interrupt, knowing exactly what he's going to say next. 'I know your father lives in Glasgow, but he's not Scottish, is he?'

Sean concedes that point.

'And ... it's too far away. It would be too complicated and difficult for everyone to get here.'

'I hardly think Edinburgh is complicated to get to, now, is it?' Sean asks, his eyebrows raised. 'It's straight up the A1. Our guests wouldn't exactly have to row themselves across a loch to get here.'

'You know what I mean.'

'So you're saying we can only get married in London, then?' he asks, beginning to sound irritated.

'No, but I thought that's what we'd agreed to do.'

Oscar clears his throat. 'Much as I hate to interrupt an imminent argument about wedding arrangements when it isn't for once about my own forthcoming nuptials, I think the newest happy couple are about to leave for the reception.'

We turn to see Louisa and Callum climbing into an open horse-drawn carriage this time, ready to take them back down the hill to the hotel.

'I'm sorry, Red,' Sean says, kissing me on the cheek. 'Let's not bicker about this today, eh?'

'Let's not bicker about it ever,' I whisper in his ear. 'I want to remember our wedding day as being absolutely perfect, just like today is going to be for Louisa and Callum.'

The reception back at The Balmoral is a very glamorous affair. There's a red carpet upon our arrival, a master of ceremonies and a luxurious gold and cream colour scheme throughout. From the banqueting suite, where the reception is taking place, we can still see the castle dominating the Edinburgh landscape, so in a way it's like we've never left the place where the newly-weds exchanged their precious vows.

'Impressive, isn't it?' Sean says, as I gaze around me in wonder at the spectacle of romance and beauty that has been laid on. Long-stemmed white lilies stand elegantly in the centre of each table in tall, slim glass vases, becoming the focal point for all that is so perfect about today.

I nod silently.

'Are you OK, Red?' he asks. 'You're a bit quiet.'

'It must have taken them ages to plan and organise all this, Sean,' I say, still looking around me. 'Every detail has been covered. Every possible problem teased with a fine-tooth comb until it can no longer contain any tangles to spoil the day. Look at this seating plan, for instance.' I gesture at a sheet of paper we've been given on entering the room. 'Instead of simply telling people where to sit, they've spent time working out who might get on with who, and suggested possibilities of who we might like to sit with during the evening. We even have a shortlist to mingle with first!'

Sean pulls a face. 'That's just a bit *too* organised, don't you think?' he asks. 'They obviously have a lot of spare time on their hands.'

'It doesn't matter. The point is, they've done it.' I run my hands through my hair. I can feel myself starting to stress again. 'I want our wedding to have delicate little details like that. I want it to be just as lovely as today. But if I can't find the time to organise the basics, how can I do things like this?'

'Then let me do it,' Sean suggests, 'like I offered to before.'

'No.'

'Why?'

'Just because,' I insist, not being able to think of anything better right now.

'"Because" isn't a valid reason, Red.'

'A valid reason for what?' Oscar asks, skipping over with

73

a glass of champagne in his hand. 'Isn't this simply divine?' He waves his glass at our surroundings. 'So much better than that draughty old castle.'

'That's what we were just discussing,' I say, replacing my empty glass with a fresh one from a passing waiter. 'Sean wants me to let him organise *our* wedding.'

Oscar chokes on his champagne, so I slap him hard on the back.

'Oh, I'm so sorry,' he says, pulling a handkerchief from the top pocket of his jacket. He dabs delicately at his mouth. 'I don't know what came over me there. I thought for one moment you said Sean wanted you to let *him* organise your wedding.'

'She did,' Sean says flatly, eyeing Oscar.

Oscar's eyes open wide, and his mouth does the same. '*You!* Let loose on a wedding? But it would be all … all functional and utilitarian.'

'*That* is exactly what I told him when he first suggested it.' I knew I could rely on Oscar to see my point of view. I link my arm through his and he gives my hand a reassuring pat.

Sean folds his arms and observes the pair of us. 'I shall say only two things. The London Eye and the Brooklyn Bridge.'

'Ah … ' Oscar tilts his head to one side. 'See, he has got a point there, darling. That *was* quite romantic.'

'Er … *quite*?' Sean protests. 'It was bloody brilliant. If we'd filmed either of those two declarations of love, they'd have had as many hits on YouTube as that Tom chap from McFly had of his wedding speech!'

'Oh my gosh, did you see that?' Oscar swoons. 'That was so fabulous. I just sobbed and sobbed when I first saw it. Luke came in and thought someone had died I was in such a state. Tissues everywhere and—'

'Anyway, back to the point,' Sean insists. 'I *could* organise our wedding. And I'd make just as good a job of it as the one we're at today, if not better!'

'Yes, of course you would, Sean.' I slip my arm from Oscar's to take hold of Sean's hand. 'But *I* want to be a part of our big day. It should be something we both have a say in, not just one of us doing everything and making all the decisions. Our day can be just as perfect as this one if we work on it together.'

Sean shakes his head. 'No, it won't be *just* as perfect,' he smiles. 'It will be better than perfect! OK, you're right – I understand completely. But the offer is always there ... You only have to say.'

I kiss his cheek. 'I know. I love you,' I whisper in his ear.

'Aw ... you two,' Oscar says, pretending to dab at his eyes with his hanky. 'Please stop with all the love!' He holds up his hand. 'Or it'll be a McFly moment all over again!'

Nine

'Where did Maddie end up sitting?' I ask Sean a bit later, when we're sitting down to eat the delicious five-course meal that has been laid on. 'I haven't seen her in a while.'

The room the reception is being held in is so big, and there are so many guests that it's easy to lose people very quickly. We lost Oscar quite early when he met two of Louisa's actor friends who are currently appearing in the West End in a production of *Chicago*. Oscar engaged them in conversation about Luke to begin with, and is now having a whale of a time at the table next to us with his own stories – sometimes true, but mostly embellished with a little Oscar-like flourish – about costuming the rich and famous from his King's Road shop.

'She's over there.' Sean points to a table at the far end of the room and I can just make out Maddie as two waiters who are serving her table their desserts move aside. Her long, blonde hair cascades down over the shoulders of her midnight-blue dress, and I'm pleased to see she's smiling and laughing.

'Why is she all the way over there?' I ask. 'I'd have thought she'd rather have sat with us. She doesn't know anyone else here other than Oscar.'

But Maddie looks like she's enjoying the company of whoever she's sitting next to, and it's good to see her that way.

'I think she's sitting with Alex,' Sean replies, as another waitress comes to our table with some delicious-looking desserts for us to choose from. 'Gosh, I don't know . . .' he says, trying to decide. 'They all look so good.'

'Alex? Why would she be sitting with him?' I demand.

'Madam?' the waitress asks. 'Dessert for you?'

'Yes . . . er, the sorbet is just fine, thank you,' I reply, not taking a lot of notice of my options.

'Why did you choose the sorbet?' Sean asks, while I crane my neck to try and see exactly where Alex is sitting. Is he next to Maddie? 'You hate sorbet.'

'I don't know. Does it really matter?'

A woman with a big pink hat gets up from the table and I can now see clearly that Alex is indeed sitting next to Maddie. She's smiling at him and he's . . . he's spooning dessert into her mouth!

'Yes, it matters if you're not going to eat it,' Sean grumbles. 'The food might be delicious, but the portions are bloody small. I could have had two decent desserts instead of one.'

'Oh, stop your moaning for a minute,' I shush him. 'Look over there!' I gesture towards Maddie and Alex, but they're both chatting with the guests either side of them now and, instead of eating dessert, are sipping at their wine.

'What?' Sean asks.

'Just now – they were flirting with each other.'

'Who was?' Sean asks with a mouth full of raspberry roulade.

'Alex and Maddie.'

Sean finishes chewing and swallows. 'Don't be daft, Scarlett. Why on earth would they be flirting with each other?'

'I don't know, but they were. She was smiling at him, and he was letting her try his dessert.' As I hear the words coming out of my mouth, I know they sound lame. But I know what I saw.

'And ... ?' Sean asks. 'Is trying someone else's dessert a crime? Ordering a sorbet when you're not going to eat it, perhaps ... '

'Stop with the dessert thing now – this is serious.'

Sean puts down his spoon. 'What's wrong, Scarlett?'

I shake my head. 'I don't know. I've just got a bad feeling.'

'About?'

I look back towards the table, but both Maddie and Alex still appear to be quite happy in conversation with other guests.

'About them?' Sean asks. He shakes his head. 'No. For one, they're both married, and—'

'Wait. Alex is married? He never said last night.'

'Didn't he?' Sean thinks about this. 'No, come to think of it – I don't think it was mentioned. Yes. I was his best man, as he's going to be mine.'

'Don't you think that's odd? He goes out to dinner and doesn't talk about his wife once during the whole evening?'

Sean shrugs. 'Not really. They've always had a different sort of relationship, with him travelling so much for his job. Charlotte is quite successful in her field too, from what little I know of her. I only really met her at the wedding.'

I give Sean a meaningful look. 'You travel overseas with your job a lot too. Does that mean you don't ever talk about me to people?'

'No, of course it doesn't, but we're different.'

'Why?'

'Because we *are*. Look, Scarlett, there's really nothing to worry about with Alex. He's a good guy. You can trust him with Maddie. And don't you think you're being a little unfair to your friend?'

I look at Maddie again. It was good to see her looking so happy for once. 'It's not that I don't trust her, but you know she's not been herself lately. I'm worried she might be vulnerable.'

'Maddie vulnerable? Now there a word I wouldn't have associated with her!'

'I know she comes over as quite confident, but she's not

really. And we know she's having problems with Felix right now.'

'Has she actually *told* you that yet? Herself?'

'No, but—'

'Scarlett,' Sean says, gently putting his hand over mine, 'you seem to be doing an awful lot of assuming. Don't let that very active imagination of yours start working overtime again, now, will you?'

Sean is right. I do have a tendency to let my mind become a little 'inventive', shall we say, on occasion. Maybe this is one of those times.

I nod at him. 'OK, maybe you're right.' I take one last look at Maddie and Alex. They're talking to each other again. Nothing wrong in that, I tell myself, about to look away. But before I do, I see Alex reach over and gently brush a stray lock of Maddie's hair away from her face, tucking it carefully behind her ear.

Maddie blushes and looks coyly back at him.

I turn back to Sean to see if he's witnessed any of this. But he's already returned to his dessert.

I close my eyes. *Scarlett, you really must give them the benefit of the doub*t, I tell myself sternly. *For now, anyway . . .*

Louisa and Callum's wedding doesn't turn out to be quite as perfect as its matching gold seat covers led us to believe it was going to be.

During the speeches Josh, Callum's best man – who I would say had downed way too many free glasses of champagne – let it slip that Louisa and he had a 'history' that Callum apparently knew nothing about. Well, we could only assume this was fresh news to Callum, given the fact he immediately sent Josh flying across the table with a punch Mike Tyson would have been proud of. I wonder, as I watch Josh being escorted away by two of the waiters, if removal of bloodstains is factored in to the price for weddings at establishments such as this. I bet they weren't called to remove them from their pristine white tablecloths too often.

I catch Oscar's eye across the room. I know just what he's thinking: *My Big Fat Gypsy Wedding.* But surely this elegant and expensive Edinburgh wedding won't disintegrate any further into the realms of the show Oscar and I watch as one of our guilty pleasures.

But sadly it does.

Shortly after the glitch in the speeches has been smoothed over by Louisa's father, we are just toasting the happy couple (who actually don't look all that happy any more) when a bright pink cloud of chiffon, sequins, beads and lace bursts into the room.

'I hope you're all enjoying yourselves!' a girl calls from inside the pink cloud. Her dress reminds me of the Christmas tree Oscar had last year: far too bright and gaudy but perfectly suited to its owner. As she begins to strut around the tables, the guests don't know whether to laugh or be horrified, unsure whether she's real or wedding entertainment laid on by the hotel.

'Isn't this just *beautiful*,' she says, pretending to admire the lilies, and the gold candelabras on each table. 'Very elegant. Not the sort of place someone like *me* would fit in at all ... I mean, why would you want to invite someone like *me* to your wedding? I'd only ruin the look of the occasion – especially wearing something like this.' She twirls round in her dress. 'I might even embarrass you in front of all your posh friends. Isn't that right, Callum?' She swivels round on her crystal-encrusted pink stilettos and points accusingly at him. 'I mean, I'm only your baby *sister*, aren't I? Why would you even think of inviting *me* to your own wedding?'

There's a collective intake of astonished breath around the room at this revelation.

'Sophie,' a red-faced Callum says, standing up, 'I ... I thought you couldn't make it.' He turns to Louisa, who avoids meeting his glare. 'You said Sophie wouldn't come back from Ibiza for the wedding. You said you'd sent her an invite but she'd said no.'

'I should have known it would be *her* doing!' Sophie turns to Louisa. 'Miss Fancy-pants, Nose-in-the-air, Too-good-for-the-likes-of-us. She never liked me!'

'Madam, I think perhaps you'd better leave now.' The maître d' tries to lead Sophie away.

'Don't touch me!' she yells, snatching her arm away from his hand. 'I'll go quietly, if that's what you all want. But I'll say this before I do. I saw your poor best man outside a few minutes ago, Callum, and I heard all about what

82

happened.' She shakes her head. 'Oh, my poor innocent brother, you don't know the half of it.'

Louisa stands up now too and glowers threateningly at Sophie. I don't know about *My Big Fat Gypsy Wedding* – this floor show is better than an episode of *EastEnders* and *Dallas* rolled into one! I look over at Oscar again; his eyes are wide with a mixture of delight and horror as he watches the scene unfold with the rest of us.

'Cal,' she says gently, walking over towards her brother at the table, 'I hate to be the one to tell you this, but the truth is, Josh and her weren't just an item before the two of you got together – they've been at it ever since! I caught them in bed together before I left for Spain, when I had that temp job cleaning up at that motel on the Glasgow road.'

It feels like we're at a pantomime, as the guests 'ooh' and 'ah' appropriately at each new revelation.

'And *that* is why *she* –' Sophie points at Louisa '– really didn't want me here. She was worried her dirty little secret might seep out. Well, guess what, Louisa? Secrets have a habit of outing themselves when you least expect it!'

As Callum sinks down into his chair, his head in his hands, the bride has to be physically restrained by her father from clambering over the top table.

Sophie decides enough is enough. 'I'm sorry, Cal,' she says, patting her brother on the shoulder, 'but you had to know the truth. Mum, Dad,' she says calmly, acknowledging her horrified parents sitting on the top table, 'pretty cool wedding you and Lou's parents have laid on – congrats. Gramps, looking good,' she says, high-fiving her granddad as she walks past him. 'Catch you later, dude.'

He grins back at Sophie and winks.

And then as quickly as she's burst into our lives she's gone, leaving a pink tornado-like carnage in her wake.

In the silence that now encircles the whole room, I can hear several people sobbing at the top table, and not just the females.

'Not such a perfect wedding after all, is it?' Sean whispers to me, his eyes wide. 'Did that actually just happen?'

I nod, as amazed as he is. 'I think it did. It just goes to show, though, that *nothing* is ever perfect. Even a wedding.'

Ten

The day after the wedding we head over to Glasgow.

While Sean is meeting with a client, and Maddie has decided to do a bit of shopping in the city centre, Oscar and I take a trip out to the House for an Art Lover at Bellahouston Park. As Oscar explains while I drive Sean's car over there, it's a house built exactly to the 1901 design of Charles Rennie Mackintosh, an architect and designer of the Arts and Crafts movement at the beginning of the twentieth century. It all sounds a bit dull, if I'm honest, but Oscar seems keen, so I go along with it. Plus, he's promised me a fabulous afternoon tea later in some famous tearooms designed by this guy back in the city centre. That's if we can manage afternoon tea; we're meeting Sean, his father and stepmother for lunch when we're finished here. I'm glad I only had toast for breakfast!

We pull up in the car park outside a fairly plain white building. Nothing special, I think, as we begin to approach by foot. But as we get closer, I'm intrigued by some carved wood panelling on the outside of the building. I can't think why the design seems familiar to me. It's as we pay our entrance fee and go inside that I immediately realise why.

Every room is decorated in simple, neutral colours like black, white and cream. But intertwined through this starkness are sinuous, elongated, curvy hints of colour, in the form of flowers, leaves and women. The reason I recognised the wood panelling outside, and so much of the interior now we're inside, is because I've seen these same designs produced on jewellery and interiors in shops and catalogues many times before.

'I know this stuff!' I exclaim, looking around at the dining room we're in now. 'I've seen these designs loads of times before.'

'Isn't it superb?' Oscar says, examining some coloured glass. 'I adore Mackintosh. I wonder if Luke would like to get married here.'

'They do weddings?'

'Oh yes. When we've had a good look around, I'm going to see if there's anyone I can speak to about it.'

We continue to explore the house. Every room is exquisite to view. From the high-backed chairs to the stained-glass windows, to the gorgeous light fittings that hang above us, it's just faultless. There're no frills, no fuss, no confusion, just simple, clean lines.

While Oscar goes off to find someone to talk to about holding a wedding here, I take another look around myself and find I'm particularly drawn to some ceramic tiles, recessed in dark wooden panelling. On each tile is a graceful-looking abstract woman. They all have long, flowing, flower-adorned hair and wear simple cloaks and dresses to match.

'Gorgeous, aren't they?' Oscar says, returning to find me staring up at the panels, transfixed. 'So simple yet so chic at the same time.'

'Now, if I could look as elegant and graceful as they do in my wedding dress, I'd be very happy.'

Oscar smiles. 'You should have been born in the art nouveau era, darling. You'd have suited the Pre-Raphaelite look, with your willowy figure and sumptuous long locks.'

'Ah yes.' I run my finger over the panelling. 'But sadly my life isn't much like it would have been for these ladies. It's a little bit more hectic these days.'

'When do you head back over to New York?' Oscar asks, as we begin to make our way towards the exit.

'Next week, as soon as we return from Scotland. I've got some important funding meetings coming up for the trust.'

'Excellent. I miss those little devils at Sunnyside, you know,' Oscar says fondly, as we climb into the car. 'I definitely want to visit them again when I come over for Luke's opening night.'

'Oh yes, you must. The kids adore seeing Uncle Oscar!'

Sunnyside, the children's home in Brooklyn, is one of

the main charities The Dragonfly Trust helps to fund. Both Oscar and Sean have visited it with me several times since my first trip to New York.

'So,' I ask him as I switch on the sat nav, put the car into gear and begin to drive over to a pub on the outskirts of town where we're meeting Sean for lunch, 'what did they say about holding a wedding there?'

Oscar pulls a face. 'The lady I spoke to was very helpful.'

'But?' I ask, sensing all is not well.

'It's a lovely venue, and I'm sure they would throw you an excellent wedding. It would be elegant and classy and sophisticated, but . . . '

'But it's just not *you*, right?'

'Exactly! How did you know?'

'Because that's how I feel about it too. When I go and view possible venues, or I look at wedding dresses or flowers, they all seem perfectly fine, but they're just not *me*.'

'Oh, darling, do you think we're awkward, horrible brides-to-be!' Oscar asks, assuming a dramatic diva-like pose in the passenger seat next to me.

'Probably,' I agree. 'But I do know one thing.'

'What's that?' Oscar asks, slipping a pair of designer shades on now as we begin to zip along the motorway.

'When we do finally manage to organise our weddings, I can't wait to see our bridal gowns!'

Eleven

'*This* is Gretna Green?' Sean asks as we pull up in the visitor centre car park at the famous site so many people have eloped to over the years.

'Apparently,' I reply, looking dubiously at the buildings, which have 'tourist trap' written all over them.

'But I thought it would be so quaint and romantic,' Oscar says from the back seat, sounding disappointed.

'You're almost as bad as Scarlett,' Maddie says, gesturing to me in the front. 'Life isn't always perfect and like a fairy tale, you know.'

I sigh. I'd been hopeful when I'd seen Maddie smiling and laughing again during our trip that she had returned to her usual bubbly self, but it seemed that as we began to edge closer to the English border, she was leaving her newly found happiness back in Scotland.

'What's got into you this morning, Grumpy?' I try and joke. 'You were all sweetness and light yesterday when you got back from shopping. Now we're on our way home, you're like a bear with a sore head again.'

After the Rennie Mackintosh house, we'd gone out for lunch as planned at a strangely named pub called The Swan with the Two Necks with Sean's father, Alfie, and his wife, Diana.

The landlady, Pamela, was an old friend of Alfie's, and we had a fabulous time and a wonderful lunch that went on late into the afternoon. Sadly there was no time for the planned afternoon tea, but to be honest I don't think my stomach would have coped with any more food, I was absolutely stuffed!

When we got back to our hotel, I had been surprised to find Maddie had only just returned from her shopping trip – bag-less, which never, ever happened when she or I went shopping, and yet she was surprisingly chipper.

'Girls, girls,' Sean interrupts now, 'I am not putting up with bickering all the way back to London today. Now, first things first, who's going into this Gretna place?'

'Me,' Oscar and I both say at once.

'Maddie?' Sean asks.

She shakes her head and turns away.

'Right, I think I'll give it a miss too.'

I'm about to protest, but Sean continues, 'Maddie and I will go for a nice quiet coffee somewhere.' He gives me a meaningful look.

'Sure.' I nod, understanding. 'That sounds like a great idea.'

The Gretna Green visitor centre is a small tourist complex of gift shops and restaurants, but in the midst of all this is an exhibition about the history of Gretna Green and the original blacksmith's shop where weddings have taken place for hundreds of years and still do to this day.

I find the exhibition fascinating and am captivated by reading the many stories of young couples who have eloped here over the years, some alone, some chased by their families in the vain hope of stopping the couple from making what they considered a dreadful mistake.

'Have you seen this?' I ask Oscar, pointing to some letters on the wall. 'Some people even tried to use the Gretna Green blacksmith as an early type of dating agency in the hope of finding a mate.'

'That's priceless,' Oscar says, inspecting the letters. 'It's quite an interesting place, isn't it? Can't imagine myself getting married here, though, can you?'

'No.' I shake my head. 'Not my sort of venue at all. It's been cool to see the genuine wedding anvil, though, in the blacksmith's forge.'

Oscar nods. 'I wonder what sort of couples do get married here these days.'

'People like us, perhaps?' An elderly couple stands behind Oscar and me. The lady is wearing a purple floral

91

dress, with matching jacket and shoes, and is clutching a small posy of violets in her hand. The man wears a grey suit with a tie that coordinates perfectly with his partner's outfit.

'Gosh, are you getting married here today?' I ask them in surprise.

'You haven't eloped, have you?' Oscar jokes.

Luckily they have a sense of humour. 'Cheeky!' the woman says to Oscar, winking at him. 'No, young man. We're actually here renewing our vows. We got married here fifty years ago today.'

'Oh, how wonderful.'

'It's a miracle,' the man says, 'that it's lasted that long!'

'Hector!' the woman scolds. She rolls her eyes. 'I don't know – I can't take him anywhere.' She looks with interest at Oscar and me. 'Are you two thinking of getting married here?'

I turn to Oscar and we burst out laughing.

'Ah, I thought not,' she says before we can even reply. 'No offence, dear –' she pats Oscar on the arm '– but you don't look the type.'

'I am getting married this year,' Oscar announces proudly. 'To my boyfriend. We both are, actually.' He smiles at me.

'Not the same boyfriend, you understand,' I hurriedly explain when the couple look confused. 'Different men at different weddings.'

Hector nods. 'Ah, I see. Well, that's wonderful, for both

of you.' He looks at Oscar. 'In our day that sort of thing was all hush-hush, you know. It still went on, of course, but it was kept under wraps – like it was a bad thing. But you can't help who you fall in love with, can you, Evie?'

'No, Hector.' They look adoringly into each other's eyes for a moment. 'The truth is, dears, we did elope here fifty years ago. My father didn't want me to marry Hector at all. He forbade it. He thought Hector was after my money – well, my family's money.'

'You weren't, were you, Hector?' Oscar winks. 'You old cad!'

Hector smiles. 'Wouldn't have mattered if I was. Evie was cut off the moment we got married. Never saw her family again from that moment on.'

Evie looks sad suddenly. Then she brightens. 'It didn't matter, though. It was worth it. I spent the rest of my life with the man of my dreams.'

'And on Mondays, Wednesdays and Fridays she saw me!' Hector jokes. But I notice he squeezes Evie's hand extra tight.

'It's wonderful you two met each other, and so fantastic you've been together this long,' I say, turning to Evie, 'but that's very sad about your family.'

'No, lovey, don't you fret yourself. We have a lovely family of our own now – children and grandchildren. We're having a big party next week for them all. Well, some . . . ' she says, trailing off.

Hector nods reassuringly at her.

'But we wanted today to be just for us,' Evie continues. 'Like it was the first time.'

'That's lovely.'

'Would you like to be our witnesses?' she asks, looking at Oscar and me. 'We don't strictly need them for renewing our vows, but I always say everything happens for a reason. And I've a feeling we've bumped into you two today for one.'

I suck in my breath. 'That's one of my favourite sayings too!' I exclaim excitedly.

'Then I'm right,' Evie says, taking my hand. 'Please, come and be a part of our ceremony. I'd like you to. *We'd* like you to, wouldn't we, Hector?'

'Better do as the lady says,' Hector replies. 'I've found that's the best way to a long and happy marriage. Not quite sure where that leaves you, young sir!' He winks at Oscar.

'Hector,' Oscar confides, '*I* always get my own way, lady or not! Now, lead on, my fine fellow!'

Evie and Hector's renewal ceremony is charming, and quite touching at times. Imagining them here in this tiny blacksmith's forge on the run from Evie's parents all those years ago is a very powerful thought as they declare their continuing love for each other on this same spot fifty years later.

As we exit the blacksmith's shop, and thank them for allowing us to be a part of their special day, they have some words of advice for our own impending nuptials.

'Don't worry too much about the day itself,' Hector says. 'It's what comes after that's important.'

Evie nods. 'Yes, by all means have a wonderful wedding day, one you'll remember for the rest of your lives, but after that remember to love one another, be patient and above all keep trying when things get tough. If we'd given up the first time we had a big argument, we'd have barely celebrated our first wedding anniversary, let alone our fiftieth!'

'Thank you so much,' I say, giving Evie a hug. 'I'll remember that, I promise you. Would you mind if I gave *you* something now?'

'Why, of course, dear.'

I'd been thinking throughout the whole ceremony about whether this was the right thing to do, and I'd decided to go for it.

'I run a charity over in America that specialises in looking for lost relatives. If you should ever want to look for yours – for whatever reason – you just let me know.'

Evie looks down at the card I've pressed into her hand.

'Thank you, dear. That's very kind,' she says, trying to pass it back to me. 'But that was a long time ago. Things have moved on and been forgotten. Some things are better left buried.'

'Yes, I completely understand, of course.' I don't take back the card. 'But keep it. Just in case?'

She nods and slips it into her bag. 'Take my number too, dear. It's not such a fancy business card like yours – my son did them on his computer for me because I was always forgetting my mobile number when I wanted to give it to anyone.'

I take Evie's plain white card.

'Now, we must be going,' she says. 'We've a second honeymoon planned too, haven't we, Hector?'

'We sure have,' he replies. 'However, although we may be able to replicate many things about our wedding day, I'm not sure *that* is one of them.'

Evie laughs and shakes her head. 'Thank you again, my dears. It's been lovely to meet you both. Good luck with your own wedding days.'

'Thank you,' we call as we walk them to their chauffeur-driven Daimler and wave them goodbye.

I turn to Oscar. 'If Sean and I are like those two in fifty years, I'll be well happy.'

Oscar grins. 'If Luke and I are still going on honeymoon in fifty years, I'll be more than happy – I'll be ecstatic, darling!'

Twelve

'Hot towel, madam?' the air steward asks as I gaze out of the window at the disappearing British countryside below.

'Thank you, yes.' I take the warm white towel and dab it over my neck and hands.

My flights over to New York these days are so different to the first time Oscar and I flew over, nearly two years ago. Two years. I can hardly believe it. We were so excited back then. So eager to seek out the tourist hot spots and discover for ourselves this wonderful city in which I was now lucky enough to spend so much of my life.

Sadly these days my flights to the Big Apple don't end in a fabulous holiday like Oscar and I enjoyed. They're a business necessity. I haven't quite managed to manoeuvre myself into first class yet in the hope of bumping into the odd A-lister jetting back and forth across the Atlantic, but the extra space and legroom of premium economy, or the equivalent, is most welcome, and gives me room to work and sleep on my long journeys.

As I gaze out of my window at the clouds below, I'm thinking about Maddie. After we drove back from Glasgow, Sean sat me down and explained he'd had a long chat with Maddie while Oscar and I had been in the Gretna Green visitor centre. Not that Sean was a stranger to Maddie in any way, but it seemed she'd found it easier to pour out her troubles to him than to me, her best friend.

'But they've barely been married four years,' I'd said sadly, when Sean told me that, as we'd suspected, Maddie and Felix were indeed having marital difficulties, quite serious ones from the way Maddie was talking.

'You don't need to have been married for decades to have marriage problems,' Sean had told me. 'They can strike at any time.'

'What's wrong *exactly*? Did she say? Is there someone else?'

Maddie was my oldest friend, and even though I'd suspected it, for her and Felix to be going through this so soon into their marriage was just horrible.

'She didn't say. I don't think there's anyone else on either side. It sounds as if they're just drifting apart with Felix being away so much for work.'

Felix worked for the same big aid charity as Maddie, but unlike Maddie, who was usually office-based in the UK, he quite often had to travel out to Africa and countries where the charity's much-needed funds were being put to good use.

'That won't happen to us, will it?' I'd asked Sean with genuine panic. 'That's what I do, isn't it – charity work abroad?'

'My darling Red,' Sean had said, putting his arms around me, 'it's not the type of work – it's the fact they hardly see one another. And when they do, it doesn't sound like it's very pleasant for either of them any more.' He'd stroked my hair. 'We have a wonderful time when we're together, don't we? Of course, I'd much rather you were by my side all the time. I miss you so much when we're apart.' Sean kissed the top of my head. 'But I actually think our short separations make our relationship stronger, and the time we do spend together that little bit more special. Don't you agree?'

'Yes, of course I do,' I'd said, burying my head into his chest. 'We're not like Maddie and Felix at all, I know that. We are *very* different. I miss you so very much too, Sean, you know that.' And I'd pulled him that little bit closer to me.

But as I fly over the Atlantic again, back to the apartment in Manhattan that I love so very much, it's with an unusually heavy heart. Even after Sean's reassurances, I'm still worried about Maddie, and now about us. I didn't have much time before I left the UK, but I tried to call Maddie to get her to open up to me, like she had with Sean, but when I did eventually get through to her, as always she was evasive in her responses, and I wondered why.

But Maddie would be over to visit me very soon, wouldn't she? Maybe we'd be able to talk then and I could try to be of some assistance to her and Felix. I didn't know how right now, but she was my friend and I was determined to try and help her.

My yellow cab from JFK Airport pulls up outside my apartment block on the Upper West Side of Manhattan.

When I first started travelling back and forth between London and New York, I stayed in hotels, but as time went on and my trips became more frequent, it made sense to rent a small apartment to stay in.

Sean made some enquiries, and luckily for me, through a friend of a work colleague we stumbled upon someone who was looking to sublet their apartment. When he said it was on the Upper West Side of Manhattan, I nearly exploded with joy. The Upper West Side was Nora Ephron territory, the lady behind some of my all-time favourite rom-coms: *When Harry Met Sally*, *You've Got Mail* and *Sleepless in Seattle*. It was going to be like living in a movie all over again.

But of course I didn't mention this to Sean.

And unlike when I first went to Notting Hill a few years ago on the hunt for movies in which to live my life, living on the Upper West Side really was like being in some of those movies. I bought coffee from the Starbucks Meg

Ryan used in *You've Got Mail*, shopped for my groceries in Zabar's, the same delicatessen both she and Tom Hanks frequent in the movie, and I often visited Riverside Park and the exact same spot where they meet up at the very end of the film.

So although I missed Sean terribly when I was here and he wasn't, I loved my New York life, and my lovely little apartment.

It's in one of those beautiful brownstone houses that you see in movies and on TV programmes set in New York, with huge stone steps leading from the sidewalk up to the communal front door, and a little intercom on the top step listing all the residents' names.

My apartment is on the third floor. It isn't huge; I have an open-plan living area with a small kitchen at one end, and a little balcony leading off that where I can sit outside in the warmer months. There is one large bedroom, a small box room I use mainly for storage and a bathroom. It isn't anything super special, but in my eyes it is perfect.

I actually don't like to admit how much I adore being here in New York. Of course, I love my life back in Notting Hill with Sean, Oscar, my mother and our friends there, but I have another life over here now too, with a second set of family and friends. My father lives here with his girlfriend, Eleanor, and I also have my good friends Max and Peter, to name but a few.

It's like I lead a double life. And except for the fab times when Sean or Oscar come over to visit, the two halves stay completely separate. But I have a feeling that this will be the year they're going to mingle more than ever before, and I want more than anything for that blend to be smooth.

The next morning I take the subway to my office, which is in the TVS building, which my friend Peter owns, on Sixth Avenue.

When I first came to New York, I met Peter quite accidently when he saved me from choking in an Italian restaurant, and then I bumped into him again in St Patrick's Cathedral. We may have met accidentally, but we came into each other's lives for a reason; the two of us recognised that fact the moment we met. Peter was the person who first introduced me to Sunnyside, and the children there, and subsequently was a great help to me in setting up The Dragonfly Trust. Together we've turned it from a twinkling of an idea of how I might be able to help reunite children with their families into the thriving and successful charitable foundation it is today.

But more than that, Peter has now become my very good friend. He is like a business partner, mentor and surrogate dad all rolled into one.

This morning Peter and I have a meeting with the full board of The Dragonfly Trust – yes, we even have a board of directors now! This to begin with had made me feel incredibly glam and uber-important, like I was some hotshot New York businesswoman. But I soon found out that in reality it just means all major decisions about the trust have to be passed by the board. This works both ways; it means we get more money poured into the trust to help those who need our help, but it also makes doing everything that little bit more complicated than it was in the early days, when I was the only one saying yes or no to everything.

But both Peter and Sean had assured me this was the best way forward, so of course I had bowed to their greater business knowledge.

However, every time we sit round Peter's huge oval boardroom table, which he kindly lends us for the trust's meetings, I always feel like I'm in a scene from *Hitch*, one of my favourite movies, in which Albert, egged on by Will Smith's character, Hitch, first stands up to his own board members to gain the attention of a pretty girl.

Adding movie scenes to dull episodes of real life is something I haven't quite grown out of ... yet.

After I've caught up with what's been going on in the office while I've been in London, both work-wise and gossip-wise from Jessica, my PA – even that sounds odd. Me having a PA! – I head up to Peter's office on the top floor to catch up with him before today's meeting.

'Morning, Scarlett.' Bella, his secretary, smiles up at me from her desk. 'Back again! How are your wedding plans coming along?'

'Good, thanks, Bella,' I sing happily, thinking this will be the simplest approach.

'Wonderful! Are you getting married in London or here in New York?'

I open my mouth to say London and then pause. I hadn't considered that option. We *could* get married in New York. A lot of our friends and family are here – well, mine are. Sean's seem to be scattered all over the world by the look of our current guest list.

Could New York be a possibility for us?

'New York would be fantastic,' I say confidently. 'Just a few tiny things to iron out first.'

'How fabulous – a Manhattan wedding! Good luck with that. They can be a devil to coordinate, I've heard, but simply wonderful if you pull it off.'

Oh Lord, that I didn't need to hear . . .

'Is Peter in?' I ask hopefully, deciding now would be a good time to change the subject.

'Yes, he's expecting you, Scarlett – just head on through!'

I knock gently on Peter's door to be polite, and as I enter his office, I can just see his silver-grey head poking over the top of his huge leather chair. He has his back to me as he gazes through a vast plate-glass window out onto the Manhattan skyline.

'Scarlett,' he calls, spinning round in the chair, 'good to see you again.' He leaps up and strides round his desk to hug me. 'How's things?' he asks, holding me at arm's length while he inspects me. 'You look tired.'

'Cheers, Peter,' I say, trying to laugh it off.

But he still looks at me with concern.

'Truth is,' I admit, 'I have been a little stressed recently.'

'I'm sorry to hear that. Any particular reason why? Take a seat. We have a few minutes before the meeting.'

There is something very special about Peter that means I can talk to him about anything. He always has a calming effect on me, and ninety per cent of the time he'll have an answer to my problems, both business and personal. And the rare ten per cent of time he doesn't, he'll help me find an answer.

I tell him about my issues organising the wedding – how wonderful yet at the same time stressful it all is, and how even though I keep trying, nothing seems to feel right. Then how a few minutes ago Bella gave me the idea of getting married here in New York.

'I think that's a fantastic idea,' Peter says approvingly. 'You love New York. It's your second home now.'

'You're right – it really is. I love being here. But the question is, will Sean be keen?'

'Sean will want to get married wherever makes you happy, Scarlett. He loves you.'

I feel a tug in my heart at Peter's words. 'Yes, I know. But I'm pretty sure he wants us to get married in London.'

Peter simply looks at me across his desk. 'Then why don't you talk to him? I've met Sean enough times now to know if *you* really want to get married here, then he will too.'

'Can we, though?' I ask now, my brain starting to race, as it always does when it begins to formulate a plan. 'Get married here?'

'Yes, I believe so. You just need to get the appropriate licences.'

I can't contain my delight at the thought of a New York wedding. 'I *really* like this idea, Peter.'

'I can tell.' Peter nods knowingly. 'That's a genuine Scarlett smile I'm seeing on your face now, not the pretend one you had when you walked in earlier. So where would you like to hold your wedding if you got married here?'

'Gosh, I don't know.' I shrug. 'This is all happening so fast. There must be loads of places.'

'There's really only one.' Peter leans back in his chair and smiles. '*The* one.'

I look at him with a puzzled expression.

'The Plaza Hotel,' he replies. 'That's *the* dream wedding venue, I'm led to believe.'

'We can't get married in The Plaza!' I exclaim.

'Why?'

'For one, it'll be way too expensive. We're lucky enough to have a fairly good budget, but a wedding at the Plaza must be extortionate. And two, we're getting married *this* year. I bet it gets booked up way in advance.'

Peter shrugs now, mimicking me. 'There's always a way if you want it badly enough. You should know that by now, Scarlett.'

'Peter … what are you suggesting? That you know someone?'

'I'm not suggesting anything. I'm asking how badly you want it.'

I think about this. A New York wedding would be so special ... I'd be getting married in my favourite city in the world. As I think more, I can physically feel my stress start to float away across the Atlantic.

'Oh, I want it, Peter. I want it very badly indeed.'

Thirteen

The board meeting, as I expected, is quite dull.

We go through the usual business: minutes from the last meeting, things on the agenda, a financial report, requests for money, then on to 'any other business'.

'Right,' Peter begins. 'This wouldn't usually be classed as any other business, but this client has expressly asked for her business to be included at the end of our meeting.'

I look at Peter. This is a bit odd. He didn't mention anything before. But then with all my wedding chat, I guess I didn't really give him the chance.

He presses a buzzer on the boardroom table. 'Bella, would you show Miss Romero in, please?'

The board members all murmur to each other in low voices, then turn towards the door. Bella comes through first, followed by a sight that immediately silences any murmuring.

Miss Romero is only Gabriella Romero, pop star, recently turned movie actress, daughter of Vincenzo Romero – multi-millionaire business tycoon and entrepreneur – and darling of all the celebrity gossip magazines on both sides of the Atlantic.

As she stands in the TVS boardroom this morning, flanked by a man in a smart suit, who I assume is her security guard, she looks every inch the global superstar. She's wearing a skintight black leather minidress that shows every curve of her figure, black patent stiletto court shoes that must have heels five inches high, and her beautiful long chestnut-brown hair has been coiffed into glossy waves that bob about seductively on her shoulders when she moves. Every man in the room, straight or gay, is transfixed by her.

'Miss Romero, please come and sit here,' Peter says, standing up and pulling out a chair for her.

'Thank you, Peter.' She smiles graciously at him and a set of gleaming white teeth are revealed to complement her flawless appearance.

'I will just give a brief explanation as to why Miss Romero is here,' Peter explains to us, 'and then I'll hand the meeting over to you, if that's OK?' he asks, looking for her approval.

'Of course.' She nods graciously.

I'm as mesmerised by Gabriella as my male colleagues appear to be.

She's absolutely perfect. I've never seen anyone look so immaculate and unblemished in the flesh. When I look at celebrities in magazines, like everyone else I dismiss much of their faultless appearance as airbrushing, and of course most of the time their flawless looks *are* down to a quick touch-up here and there with a fancy computer program. But not so in Gabriella's case, it seems. She's simply stunning.

'Miss Romero has kindly offered to donate to the trust in a rather big way,' Peter begins, smiling at Gabriella. 'If you'll take a look at these sheets I'm passing round the table now, you'll see just what she's proposing.'

We all look at the sheets of paper that Peter has passed to us and there are small gasps at the figures written there.

'However,' Peter says, 'Miss Romero does have some conditions to her donation. Isn't that right, Gabriella?'

Gabriella smiles at Peter now. 'Hello, everyone,' she begins. 'Forgive me for not standing up to address you all, but my stylist has put me in these very silly shoes today, and I'm sure you don't want me toppling over on your lovely table, now, do you?'

Everyone laughs, even though I'm sure a few of the men would have quite enjoyed seeing Gabriella do just that.

'Thank you so much for allowing me to come along to your meeting today. As you can see from the document you've just been given, I do indeed wish to donate to the wonderful trust you have created here.' She turns to me. 'Miss O'Brien, I remember watching you on TV when you were first setting up The Dragonfly Trust. Coming from a large, close family myself, your story about how you were reunited with your brother genuinely touched me.'

'Thank you.' I smile at her. I know almost as much about Gabriella's large family as I do about her. The Romero family are well known across America for their enormous wealth. Vincenzo Romero built up his huge fortune over many years, from humble beginnings as a delivery boy for a small hardware store in Little Italy to owning one of the biggest and most well-known delivery firms across the globe. Gabriella is a celebrity in her own right now due to her singing and, more recently, acting career, but the Romero family have long been minor celebrities, having taken part in a fly-on-the-wall documentary many years ago, before anyone had even heard of the Kardashians.

'I've followed The Dragonfly Trust's progress ever since,' Gabriella continues, 'and the wonderful work you do helping reunite families. So now, as you can see, I wish to do my part to help.'

'That's very kind of you.' I'm still wondering what her conditions are going to be. There has to be a catch. Some of the figures on the sheet of paper in front of me are quite astronomical.

'My first donation, as you can see listed on your sheet, is completely unconditional,' she says, looking around the table. 'That is my gift to the trust. But there will be other, more substantial donations – as you can also see listed – if my other conditions can be met.'

There's silence round the table while we await these conditions.

'Miss O'Brien, I wonder if we may talk privately?' she asks, to my surprise.

'Er, yes, of course.'

I look at Peter.

He nods. 'You can use my office, Scarlett. It's closer than yours.'

Gabriella and I get up from the table and I lead her through to Peter's office.

'Please, take a seat, Miss Romero,' I say, gesturing to a leather sofa.

'Thank you.' Gabriella sits elegantly down on the sofa with her legs pressed neatly together to the side of her.

'First, I'd like you to call me Gabi,' she says. 'All my friends do, and I'm hoping that's what we'll end up being if you can do for me what I'm going to ask of you.'

'Sure,' I reply, completely bewildered now. 'And I'm Scarlett.'

She smiles. 'Well, Scarlett, you'll have probably guessed I'd like you to find someone for me.'

Ah . . . it's beginning to make sense now.

'But because of who I am and my family's fame, I can't under any circumstances have this getting into the press. Do you understand?'

I nod. 'Yes, of course.'

She looks at me for a moment, as if she's sussing out whether I genuinely do understand the importance of her request.

'Really,' I insist. 'We at The Dragonfly Trust offer complete anonymity.'

'That is exactly why I wanted us to talk alone, Scarlett. I don't want just anyone at The Dragonfly Trust to search for my missing person; I want you to do it. If only you're involved, no one else, I can guarantee it's kept private.'

When we first started up the trust, I *was* the only person searching for lost relatives. I got a lot of joy and satisfaction from bringing estranged families back together. But since the trust has grown bigger and more successful, and our services are so much more in demand, I now have a fantastic team of people who do all the complex stuff for me, and they have a fantastic success rate too.

But I do miss being hands-on, at the centre of all the action. I also miss the thrill I used to get when I finally made a breakthrough with a search. Maybe it's time to get back down to grass roots again.

'Who do you want me to find, exactly?' I ask her, as I feel my heart start to beat a little bit faster.

Gabi hesitates again.

'Gabi, really, you *can* trust me. Honestly.'

She nods. 'Yes, I know. I knew that the first time I saw you on TV. There's just something about you, Scarlett. But when you're in the business I am, you become very wary of people.'

'I'm sure.'

'It's my grandmother's younger sister,' she says at last. 'Nonna hasn't seen her since she was a young girl, a teenager to be exact. She ran away, apparently, and was ostracised by the family. Eventually they lost touch altogether. That's all I know. Between you and me, I think there may have been a baby . . . You know how things were back then.'

'So why does she want you to find her now?' I ask.

'She doesn't. I do.'

'Why? Sorry to ask so many questions, but I have to have as much information as I possibly can if I'm to help.'

Gabi nods, but her expression immediately changes – she looks pale and drawn, even behind all her make-up, as she thinks about her grandmother. 'Nonna has cancer, Scarlett. She's dying.'

'Oh, I'm so sorry, really I am.'

Gabi takes a deep breath. 'We've known for a while she won't pull through this time. That's why I want to find her sister. Family is everything to people of my background, Scarlett. Nonna doesn't talk about her that often, but in the few times she has spoken to me about her sister, I know she would like to see her again to make amends for what happened all those years ago.'

I nod. Poor Gabi. She was one of those people who you

114

thought had everything. Money, looks, fame. Who knew under her glamorous facade she was going through all this heartache with her grandmother's illness?

'But no one else must know. I can't stress that enough. Everyone thinks my family's fortune came from my father originally – self-made man and all that – but it actually came from my mother's side. She was the one who set my father up in business all those years ago – her family were very wealthy. But all that's been hushed up over the years – stupid male pride. And the success story of delivery boy to global delivery magnate is one my family has happily fed to the press on many an occasion when it suited them. The press will have a field day with it if they find out the true story of our wealth. And if you do find my great-aunt, not only might stories from the past emerge, but *if* there is any scandal around her, they'll feast on that too.'

'I understand completely, Gabi. Really. Our little project is completely safe in my hands.'

'You'll do it, then?' she asks, looking astounded that I've actually agreed.

'Of course,' I smile. 'It will be my pleasure.'

'I warn you, Scarlett,' she says, 'this won't be as easy as you think. The press are on my tail twenty-four hours a day. If they even sniff there's something new going on they might be able to hook their shark-like teeth into, in either my or my family's lives, they'll be after you as well for a story.'

'I can handle it,' I assure her. 'We'll be just fine. This will be our little secret, Gabi. No one else need know anything.'

Gabi takes my hand and cradles it between her own delicately soft palms. 'That's just what I hoped you'd say, Scarlett.' She looks me affectionately in the eyes and smiles. 'My friend.'

Fourteen

After the board meeting I get off the subway a few stops early and decide to walk back to my apartment. Even though it's quite chilly, it's a bright, sunny March day, and a walk in the sun will give me some time to think.

Gabi and I spent a few more minutes discussing things in Peter's office before heading back into the boardroom with the good news that Gabi would be making the first of her generous donations to the charity with immediate effect.

I could tell the others, including Peter, were desperate to know what we'd been discussing, but of course I said nothing. Only that I'd agreed to Gabi's terms and I hoped I'd be able to ensure her future donations to the trust very soon.

And now, as I walk back up the elegant tree-lined avenue of Central Park heading towards the Bethesda

Fountain, I'm thinking about two things: what Gabi has asked me to do for her and what Peter suggested before the meeting.

A wedding at The Plaza ... Surely that isn't possible for Sean and me? But how wonderful would it be if it were? The Plaza is an iconic New York hotel, not only to get married in, but it's featured in so many movies too, like *The Great Gatsby*, *Crocodile Dundee* and of course *Home Alone 2: Lost in New York*. It's also the only hotel in New York to be bestowed the honour of being a National Historic Landmark. It's unique and special and glamorous; it would be magical to hold our wedding there. I decide to do some initial investigations, just as soon as I can get an appointment with someone at the hotel.

There's a skip in my step for a change as I look up and smile at the Angel of the Waters in her usual vantage point, calmly watching over Central Park. Maybe I'd finally found somewhere I'd like to get married – I just hoped Sean would feel the same.

'Scarlett!'

I look up at the angel again. No, it wasn't her. This voice was coming from the ground.

'Scarlett,' the voice calls again, 'I thought it was you!'

I turn to my right to see Alex heading round the outside of the fountain. He's wrapped up against the cold in a long black overcoat, green scarf and dark shades.

'Alex, hi,' I say as he catches up with me. 'I didn't realise you were in New York yet.'

'Yeah, I arrived a couple of days ago. Just finding my feet again. How about you?'

'Yesterday. Doesn't take me long now though. I'm kind of used to it.'

'Yes, Sean said you were quite the jet-setter these days.'

'You could say that.' I pull the collar of my coat up around my neck; it suddenly feels chillier than it did a few minutes ago when I was alone.

'Actually you've saved me a job, I was just on my way over to see you.'

'Were you – why?'

'I just thought it would be nice for us to get together sometime,' Alex says, removing his shades. 'It would be good to get to know Sean's bride a little better before I'm your best man.'

'Yes ... yes, we should do that.' I'm slightly thrown by his suggestion. I hadn't considered the possibility I might actually have to see Alex while I'm in New York. But I don't want to seem rude. 'When is good for you?'

'How about tomorrow night?' Alex suggests. 'I know a fantastic restaurant in the Village if you don't mind travelling down that far?'

'No, of course not, I don't mind at all – it's always good to try somewhere new.'

'Right, that's great. I'll text you the address and a time when I've booked us a table. See you tomorrow, then!'

'Sure, see you. Wait – you don't have my number!'

Alex pulls his phone from his pocket and waves it at me. 'Already sorted!' he smiles.

'Right . . . ' I guess Sean must have given it to him at the same time as my address. 'Well, I'll see you tomorrow night, then.'

'Looking forward to it already, Scarlett!' Alex calls, and I'm relieved to see him head off in the direction from which I've just come.

'I wish I was,' I mutter under my breath, as I turn and walk towards Strawberry Fields, the memorial to John Lennon, and my apartment. Usually I enjoy having dinner with new and interesting people. And in theory Alex should be one of those. He leads an interesting life; he's a friend of Sean's, so it should be a fun evening.

But there's just something about Alex I don't like.

Or trust.

I get back to my apartment, make myself a coffee and get straight onto my laptop and my phone.

Diligently I deal with as much of Gabi's request as I can first, sending a few emails and making notes of things I need to ask her at our next meeting. Then I make a couple of phone calls related to those notes.

Then it's Plaza time!

First I google 'weddings at the Plaza' and I'm immediately thrown into a luxurious, sparkling world of chandelier-filled ballrooms, with ornate cream and gold archways and candlelit splendour.

I'm hooked.

I jot down their telephone number and give them a call.

'Hi. Would it be possible to talk to someone about holding a wedding at The Plaza?' I ask, my heart beating quickly as I gaze at the pictures tempting me from my MacBook's screen. 'Yes, I can hold.'

I wait while I'm put through to the correct person.

'As soon as possible,' I say as the man at the other end enquires when is a suitable time for me to come in and discuss my requirements.

'A cancellation! That's excellent. I mean, not for them, or you, obviously. But yes, I can make tomorrow at three p.m. . . . Fantastic. I'll see you then. Thank you so much!'

I hang up the phone and look again at the beautiful Plaza ballroom. It looks like something a princess would get married in. Suddenly visions of myself spinning round the floor like a Disney princess fill my head, with Sean holding me in his arms as my handsome prince. I'm wearing a beautiful white and gold dress with a huge white tulle skirt that wafts up and down as I move, and Sean wears a long blue and gold tailcoat, matching knickerbockers, long white socks and shoes with gold buckles.

I quickly shake my head. Maybe that was taking the fantasy a bit too far!

But still, it didn't hurt to dream about The Plaza . . . I just needed to rein in the Disney part a little.

*

The next day is a busy one.

After an early morning Skype call with Sean (lunchtime for him), during which I decide not to mention The Plaza idea until it's more than just a fantasy, I have a breakfast meeting with my father to discuss how everything is going with our popcorn-machine business both back in the UK (my end) and over here in the States (his). It's always good to catch up with Dad when I'm over in New York and find out all his news. Also to check on whether things are still going well for him and Eleanor.

Eleanor is Jamie's mother. She and Dad reunited after Jamie and I found out we were siblings when I first came to New York. Dad had been as much in the dark about having a son as I was about having a brother, and after a shock first meeting in Central Park, much to my joy they had kept in touch and had renewed their old romance from many years before. Eleanor now rented an apartment in New York and used it as her semi-permanent base when she wasn't away touring as an actress, so she could be close to Dad.

To see my father happily in a relationship again after so many years alone gave me so much pleasure, and Eleanor definitely put a spring in his step and a twinkle in his eye.

The inevitable 'How are the wedding plans coming along?' question doesn't take long before it springs up, but I'm quick to deflect it with my own 'How are you and Eleanor getting along?' – a question always guaranteed to make Dad squirm. He hates discussing his private life with me. So we're then swiftly carried into our safe zone of business-related topics, where we both immediately feel more at ease.

'I have some exciting news, Scarlett,' Dad announces, when we've been chatting a while and have just finished eating our breakfast. 'I'm going out to Australia for a while.'

'Australia!' I exclaim, nearly spitting my coffee over the white tablecloth. 'Why?'

'Eleanor has got an acting job over there, on one of those big Aussie soaps.' He pulls a face. 'It's not usually her thing at all, but the money they were offering was too good to turn down.'

'But ... but why are *you* going?' I ask in dismay. These days Dad and I don't see each other anywhere near as much as we used to, with me living my transatlantic lifestyle, but he's never been that far away from me before.

'To be with her, of course,' and he adds, 'Plus, I'm thinking it might be an idea for us to branch out the business over there, so it seems like the ideal opportunity. What do you think, Scarlett? It could be a whole new venture for us.'

'Er ...' I don't know what to say. Of course I want the popcorn business to continue to flourish, but I don't want to lose my dad to Australia.

'You can keep an eye on things here for me, can't you?' he asks. 'The team will do most of it, of course, but if you could just oversee things, like you do in London.'

'Yes, of course I can,' I say eventually, trying to sound enthusiastic at not only the prospect of his trip but of looking after the US side of the business in addition to everything else I have going on.

'It will be my pleasure, Dad.'

After my meeting with Dad, my mood has dropped, but as I hail a yellow cab and head out to Brooklyn, it begins to brighten again because I'm now on the way to one of my favourite places in the world – Sunnyside.

The very first time I visited Sunnyside I immediately fell in love with the positive, optimistic spirit inside its four walls. I wanted to help the children there, and future children and adults like them who through no fault of their own were separated from their families, as I'd once been from my own mother, and it was from this need to help that The Dragonfly Trust had been formed.

'Scarlett!' A barrage of children scream my name as I walk through the door. 'You're back!'

'I am! And I bring gifts!' I shout above the noise, holding aloft a bag of goodies. 'Where's Kim? Is she about?'

'Right here, honey!' Kim, one of the wonderful team that helps run Sunnyside, calls, appearing amid the crowd of children. 'Good to see you back where you belong.'

I smile at Kim and give her a hug.

'Can I give the children some little treats I brought back with me?' I ask hopefully. 'It's mainly candy, I'm afraid.'

Kim looks at her watch. 'Hmm, I really shouldn't allow it. It's not long till lunch.'

'Aw, please, Kimberly!' a chorus of small voices call in unison.

'But since it's you, Scarlett, just a little bit!'

'Yay!' they all shout.

I sit down on the bottom step of the long wooden staircase in the hallway and hand out mini bars of Dairy Milk, tubes of Smarties, packets of Jelly Babies and anything else British that these children might not have seen in their local 'candy store'.

'What's in your other bag, Scarlett?' Bethany, a young girl I got to know quite well the last time I was over, asks me.

'These,' I say, holding up my second carrier bag, 'are some books I've brought over from the UK. Books I thought you might all like to read. They're to go in the fun room, so you can all share and borrow them from time to time.'

'Oooh,' they coo. 'Let's see!'

I pass the books round. 'Some of them you might have seen before,' I say as they look at paperbacks like Harry Potter, 'and some you might not.' Bethany picks up a Famous Five book. 'That was one of my favourites as a child,' I tell her. 'And these.' I pass some of the younger children Topsy and Tim books. 'I think you'll enjoy them.'

One of the boys, Jack, comes up to me and puts his arms around my neck. 'I love it when you come back to us,

Scarlett,' he whispers in my ear. 'Don't go away for too long again, will you?'

I hug him tightly. 'I love it when I come back again too, Jack. Just between you and me, I'm going to try and be in New York and here at Sunnyside a lot more often in the future. It really feels like my home now.'

I have a lovely morning at Sunnyside and stay much longer than I anticipated, which is often the way on my visits. Just as I'm about to leave, conscious I need to go back to my apartment to change before I head to my appointment at The Plaza, Peter arrives unexpectedly.

'Hey, Peter. I didn't know you were visiting today,' I say as I'm gathering my things. 'I'm just about to head off.'

'Ah, you know me, Scarlett – I often drop in unannounced.'

The children are now dancing around Peter in the same fashion they were on my arrival. Peter is always a popular visitor at Sunnyside. He has a way with the children that they just adore. It's strange, really, because even though Peter has two grown-up children of his own, he doesn't seem to have much family at all other than that. Friends, yes. Peter has more friends than I've had visits to the cinema. But no close family. None he ever speaks of, anyway. Sadly, he rarely sees his children because they and his ex-wife now live in Texas.

'You do indeed,' I agree. 'And you're always so popular!' I laugh at the children pulling on his jacket sleeves. 'You've made my exit much easier, anyway.' I wink at him, grab my bag and coat, and hurry to say a quick goodbye to Kim.

'See ya soon, you lot!' I call as I head out of the door. 'Enjoy yourself with Peter!'

'Bye, Scarlett,' some of them call back. But most are now busy with their newest visitor.

I don't mind, though. I'm always pleased to see them happy, and they deserve as much joy as possible in their young lives.

I smile contentedly as I close the door and head down the street to hail a cab. Who would have thought coming to Sunnyside with Peter all that time ago would have changed my life for the better in so many ways, and also that it would become one of my favourite places to spend time in New York City.

Fifteen

By the time the evening comes I really don't feel like going out with Alex. And my reasons are many.

Firstly my meeting at The Plaza was not a success.

It started extremely positively. A very nice man called Geraldo, wearing an immaculate black suit and white shirt, greeted me at three p.m., just as arranged, and took me on an extensive tour of everything The Plaza had to offer in terms of a wedding venue. I was hooked from the moment we walked inside the magnificent opulence of the Grand Ballroom. I could just imagine us there, me walking down a tree-lined aisle – Geraldo said we could have trees of our choosing to line the route, our guests sitting either side on gold chairs with flowers strewn across their backs – the chairs, that is, not the guests. Then us all sitting down to a sumptuous dinner served by impeccably dressed waiters.

Followed by dancing, and me and Sean swirling round the ballroom just like my Disney fantasy.

I started to get a bit panicky when we went back to Geraldo's office and he began to talk prices. Sean and I hadn't really ever talked about the cost of our wedding. We were very lucky, with Sean running his own business for so long and me now running two (make that three after Dad's shock announcement!), that we weren't going to have to scrimp and save to afford all the trimmings. But I'm pretty sure the prices Geraldo was quoting were a lot more than we'd had quoted at other venues we'd looked at.

But it was when Geraldo took out a large black book and asked what sort of date I was thinking of that my newly found enthusiasm dropped back to its usual level of stress-filled wedding gloom ...

'Do you have any dates in mind, Miss O'Brien?' Geraldo looked keenly at me, his silver fountain pen poised hopefully over the pages of his book.

'We were hoping for a winter wedding,' I said eagerly. 'We've even talked about Christmas as a possibility.'

Geraldo filed through a few pages. 'Ah yes, we could fit you in for a date very near Christmas if that's what you would prefer.'

'You could – really?' I couldn't believe this. It was amazing. I knew I'd find the perfect venue eventually. Now I just needed to persuade Sean ... But he'd be OK. I'd bring him here when he next came over. He'd see the ballroom and fall in love with it just like—

'Yes, Christmas 2016. We have many dates around the holidays available then. What would you prefer, Christmas Eve, or a weekend maybe? What would be better for your guests?'

'Wait – Christmas *2016*?'

'Yes, madam.'

'But I thought you meant this Christmas – Christmas 2014?'

Geraldo looked at me as if I was a little bit unhinged.

'Er, no, madam. The Plaza gets booked up months, sometimes years in advance for weddings.'

'Do you have *anything* this year?' I asked hopefully, looking at his book.

'Madam, we even have a waiting list.' Geraldo produced a sheet of paper from the back of the book and I saw a list of names on it. 'I do apologise if there's been any confusion.'

'No, it's fine, Geraldo. It's not your fault. I should have known it wouldn't be that simple. My life never is.'

'Should we put you down for Christmas 2016?' Geraldo asked expectantly.

I shook my head. 'Thank you, but no. Although, if I don't get something sorted soon, it might well be 2016 before we get married!'

Geraldo smiled sympathetically and walked me to the door.

'Goodbye, Miss O'Brien. I do hope you manage to get the wedding of your dreams. I'm just sorry the Plaza won't be the venue providing it for you.'

'Thank you, Geraldo. You don't know how sorry I am too. Really you don't.'

So all I want to do tonight after my long and now disappointing end to the day is order a pizza, lie on my sofa and watch one of my favourite movies on TV. The last thing I feel like doing is travelling all the way down to Greenwich Village to have dinner with Alex. Right now the thought of trying to make polite conversation with him all evening seems like a huge effort.

I sigh. Perhaps I'm being unfair. After all, if he was Sean's best friend in the past, he can't really be that bad, can he? Maybe we just got off on the wrong foot. Actually, maybe I did. Alex didn't seem to have any issues with me.

I drag myself into my shower and begin to get ready. I really must make an effort with this dinner tonight, if only for Sean's sake.

The restaurant that Alex has suggested is actually very lovely and I'm quite impressed with his choice. It serves a Mediterranean menu, and its décor matches accordingly. Bright, vibrant pieces of pottery adorn the walls and the scrubbed wooden tables, and the waitresses are similarly dressed in colourful mismatched outfits. The whole ambiance is cheerful and fun, and not at all what I was expecting from Alex.

'So how has your day been?' Alex enquires after we've ordered.

I'm also surprised at Alex's choice of outfit tonight. He's

wearing pale tan trousers, a white shirt and a navy sweater. When I met him before, he was wearing quite stark, formal colours – white, black or grey.

He seems more relaxed and at ease than he has been previously and I wonder why.

'It's been up and down, if I'm honest,' I say, taking a sip of my white wine.

'How so?'

'It started well. I had breakfast with my father – part business, part pleasure.' I omit to tell him about Australia: I really don't feel like discussing that tonight. 'Then I went over to Sunnyside, which is the children's home in Brooklyn I help fund with The Dragonfly Trust.'

'Ah yes, I've heard all about that. It must be very rewarding.'

Is there anything Sean hasn't told you? I wonder. But I smile politely and reply, 'Yes, it is. Very.'

'I've done quite a lot of work for charity myself. You know, fundraising, that kind of thing, but I've never had my own trust. It's something I'd quite like to look into for the future. I'll have to pick your brains sometime, Scarlett. See if you can give me a few pointers.'

'I'm sure I could help you out a bit. But I'm no expert by any means. Peter, my right-hand man, he's the expert on the business side of things.'

'Peter?'

'Peter Butler. You might have heard of him. He's quite a well-known businessman here in New York.'

132

'Yes, of course I've heard of Pete Butler. Who hasn't? I didn't know you knew him, though.'

Alex seems to be regarding me with a newfound respect.

'I've known Peter since I first came to New York. He's a good friend of mine.'

Alex takes a long sip of his red wine.

'Impressive, Scarlett. What other hidden talents do you have?'

'I don't know what you mean. Peter isn't a talent. Like I said, he's my friend.'

It's my turn to drink from my glass again now. But I don't place it back down on the table; I nurse it in my hands and look around the restaurant as an awkward silence falls over our table.

'I'm sorry,' Alex says eventually. 'I didn't mean anything by that last comment. I just didn't expect you to know Peter. He's a very well-connected, successful businessman in this city.'

I glance at him and raise my eyebrows.

Alex pulls a face. 'I'm digging my hole even deeper, aren't I?'

I nod. 'Yep.'

'Hmm, let's draw a line under that then and I'll try again.' He thinks. 'You said your day had been up and down. You've told me the ups. So what were the down parts?'

'Ah, it's nothing,' I reply, not wanting to reveal my mistake at The Plaza, and my subsequent let-down.

'Come on. Our dinner isn't here yet, and we can't just sit here in silence, can we?' He pulls a dejected face at me over the table.

I have to smile.

'OK, I went to The Plaza Hotel today to talk to them about possibly holding our wedding there.'

'The Plaza – very nice! I heard you were having a few problems finding somewhere, but I had no idea the two of you were thinking of getting married in New York.'

'Yes, well, we aren't now. We can't have it. It's booked up right through until 2016.'

'Really?' Alex asks. 'That's madness.'

'I know. But it was a nice dream while it lasted.'

'Is that where you and Sean really want to get married?'

I glance at him, not knowing whether to discuss this any further with Alex when I haven't even talked with Sean about it. But what does it matter? It isn't happening now, is it? 'I do. It's the most perfect venue. I haven't actually told Sean about it yet, though. I only got the idea the other day.'

'Spur-of-the-moment gal, eh?' he smiles. 'A bit like my good self.'

'You could say that.'

Our food is delivered to the table then.

'This looks good,' I say as I begin to tuck into my dish of spiced vegetables and wholegrain rice.

'What you were saying before,' Alex says, cutting into

his beef, 'about The Plaza . . . Do you think Sean would go for it, if you could get a date?'

'Probably. I think he'd just be relieved I'd actually booked something at last.'

'And the cost?'

'It's certainly not cheap, but it would be the wedding of a lifetime.'

'It surely would be.' Alex chews thoughtfully. 'You know, I could put in a few calls for you.'

'How do you mean?'

'I know someone who is very high up on The Plaza board. They might be able to pull a few strings . . .'

My fork clatters onto my plate, so I hurriedly pick it up again, while trying to look calm and collected in front of the other diners.

'But Geraldo said they were fully booked.'

'That's what they tell people like you and me,' Alex says, smiling. 'It's like if we'd turned up at one of the top restaurants in New York tonight demanding a table. We'd have been laughed at and told to come back in three weeks. But I bet you any money there would have been a table if J-Lo had done the same, or Brad Pitt.'

'Probably true.'

'You know it is. I bet it's the same at The Plaza. I bet they keep a few dates free – just in case. When is it you and Sean want to get married ideally?'

'December. As close to Christmas as possible.'

'Right then, I'll see what I can do. Leave it with me.'

I'm in shock. Maybe I did get Alex all wrong.

'Really? You'd do that for us?'

'Of course. Sean is one of my oldest friends, and I'm hoping you, Scarlett, are going to become one of my newest.'

Sixteen

This morning I'm heading across Central Park again.

It's another bright morning, albeit still a bit chilly, and I'm protected from the cold in my red wool coat and black leather boots.

I've made a special effort today with my outfit because I'm meeting with Gabi. I knew whatever I chose to wear I was going to feel plain and drab next to her perfection, but at least I've given it my best shot.

Last night's dinner with Alex didn't turn out too badly in the end. After his offer to help with The Plaza, we chatted about Sean, and my businesses, and what I got up to when I was over here in New York. Then we talked about his career, and all the interesting countries he'd visited as a foreign correspondent. I mentioned Jamie and Max, what they did and how we'd met. I was surprised to find Alex to be quite pleasant company, but even more surprising was the fact he didn't mention or ask after Maddie once during the whole evening.

I was actually quite pleased, and a little relieved.

Maybe I really had got the wrong idea about Alex after all.

I breathe in the cool morning air as I walk through the park. I always love walking through Central Park. Whatever the season there is always something new to see – whether the beautiful blossom on the trees in the spring, the gorgeous golden shades when autumn falls over the park, the skaters skimming the ice rinks at Christmas, or the New Yorkers who spill out of their apartments and onto the grass to picnic and play ball games in the hot sunshine of the summer.

It didn't take me long to stop feeling like a tourist when I was over here. As soon as I'd been asked for directions a few times, begun to get irritated by tourists milling about in front of me on the sidewalk when I was trying to get somewhere in a hurry, ridden with a couple of surly cab drivers, knew where to get the best coffee, pizza and Chinese near my apartment and had found myself walking almost everywhere with my earphones plugged in, I knew I was no longer an outsider to this great city, but that she had now welcomed me as one of her own.

I'm meeting Gabi in her apartment, which overlooks Central Park from the east side. I know how much apartments like these cost to rent – I'd googled them enough times in the past when living in New York was only a dream to me – but this particular block was supposed to be one of *the* most exclusive in Manhattan and I couldn't wait to see inside.

The doorman, who greets me with a genuine smile, is wearing a top hat and a smart green tailcoat and trousers. 'Good morning, miss,' he says, holding open the door for me. 'And how can I help you today?'

'I have an appointment with Miss Romero,' I tell him proudly.

'I'm sorry, miss,' he says in a tight voice. 'We have no one of that name staying in this building.'

I stare at him for a second with a puzzled expression. 'But I have an appoint— Oh, wait,' I say, suddenly remembering what Gabi told me to say. 'I'm sorry – I meant Miss *Sinatra*.'

'Ah … yes, miss. That would be the top floor, the penthouse. Cedric will see you safely up in the elevator.' He gestures across the foyer to some ornate-looking lifts, and a young man steps out of one to escort me up.

'Thank you. Sorry about my mistake – I'm a bit new to all this.'

'Understandable, miss,' he smiles. 'You'll soon get used to it, if you're spending any time with Miss *Sinatra*.'

I walk across the foyer and step inside the elevator. Cedric gives me a brief smile as the doors close, and we whizz up to Gabi's floor.

'Just along there, miss,' Cedric instructs as I exit the lift.

I can hardly miss it: Gabi's is the only door on the long, opulent corridor. I walk along the plush carpet, push the bell and stand back a little to wait. I'm not really sure what to expect next. A butler maybe, or a maid? But Gabi herself opens the door.

'Hi, Scarlett. You found me OK, then?' she asks, standing back to allow me in.

'Yes, eventually. Although I made a bit of a mistake downstairs when I asked for you by your real name. I forgot about the Sinatra thing.'

Gabi waves her hand at me. 'Oh, don't worry about it. They're used to it. It's not them I'm protecting myself from – the staff here are fine. It's the paparazzi trying to infiltrate where I am to get their sad little stories.'

'Like in *Notting Hill*?' I suggest.

Gabi looks blankly at me.

'When Julia Roberts checks into hotels in that movie, she gives herself silly cartoon names to protect her privacy – like Bambi and Pocahontas.'

'I don't think I've ever seen that movie.'

'You've never seen *Notting Hill*!' I ask, aghast. 'It's one of my favourites.'

Gabi smiles. 'Then I shall definitely have to check it out one day. Now, Scarlett, what can I get for you before we get down to business?'

I follow Gabi into the penthouse properly now, and my

jaw almost hits the ground as I stand and stare open-mouthed at the vast room bathed in bright natural light pouring in from the many enormous windows that run the length of it.

'Scarlett?' Gabi asks again. 'Are you OK?'

'This is beautiful,' I gasp, looking around me at the white and pale wood décor. 'And look at your view!' I dash across to the window. 'Oh my God, if I lived here, I'd never move away from this window!'

Gabi laughs. 'It is pretty special, isn't it?'

'It's spectacular.' From her window Gabi has a simply amazing view of Central Park. It's like looking at one of those panoramic photos that someone has taken with a wide-lens camera where you can see everything at once.

'You should see it at night,' Gabi says, 'when everything is lit up – it's magical then.'

'I'd love to! Oh, sorry,' I say, hurriedly turning away from the window. 'I didn't mean—'

'It's fine, Scarlett. You'll have to come back when I'm having one of my parties up here. We often go out on the terrace at night when it's warm. Come see.'

Gabi leads me further along the length of the penthouse and slides open a set of French windows so we can step outside onto a patio area with decking, a pool and a large Jacuzzi.

'Parties out here in the summer months are great fun. People love watching the sun go down and then later seeing stars up in a clear night sky.'

I look from the balcony we're standing on across at all the buildings and skyscrapers nearby and imagine them lit up at night. 'It must look amazing.'

'It does. I'm very lucky to get to stay here when I'm in New York.'

'You mean this isn't your permanent home?'

'Oh no. I have another house in LA, and we have a few little holiday homes scattered around the world. Although, the majority of my family don't live too far away, on Long Island.'

I wonder what she means by 'little' homes.

'Yes, you are very lucky, then.'

'Come back inside. Let me get you a drink,' Gabi offers. 'Tea? That's what you English drink, isn't it?'

'I'd prefer coffee if you have it, but tea is fine if not.'

'Oh, I gave my barista the morning off, as I did all my staff. I wanted to keep your visit a secret. That's why I'm here all alone.'

'You have your own barista!'

'Of course,' Gabi says as if it's quite normal. 'Guido makes the best cup of coffee this side of Naples.'

'That's so cool. Do you actually have a coffee machine, then?' I ask hopefully. 'One we can use?'

'Er . . . I think so,' Gabi says. 'The kitchen is this way.'

Gabi leads me through to a pristine-looking stainless-steel and walnut kitchen with every mod con you can think of, including a very complicated-looking coffee maker – the type you might see in a high-street coffee shop.

'Do you know how this works?' I ask her.

'No,' she says, looking at it as if she never even knew her kitchen had such a thing. 'Do you?'

'Er ... no. That's a little bigger than my Tassimo machine at home. Why don't we just go out for some coffee?'

Gabi looks at me as though I've just suggested we abseil down the side of the building. 'Go out? For coffee? What if someone sees me?'

'Can't you put some dark glasses on or something? Isn't that what celebrities usually do?' I ask, smiling.

'But I'm not dressed for going out.' Gabi gestures to her clothes, which look perfectly acceptable to me. She's wearing a very nice pair of blue designer jeans, a white shirt and high-top Ugg boots.

'You look great,' I tell her. 'Plus, if you don't dress up too much, no one will notice you, will they?'

'I'm not sure, Scarlett,' she hesitates. 'Usually I have security.'

'Are you telling me you never go anywhere without a pair of heels on and a big, burly security guard? It's no wonder you get pounced on by the press and the public! Come out with me in what you're wearing, a warm jacket and a pair of shades, and I promise no one will bat an eyelid, let alone turn a head.'

Gabi looks at me, and for a couple of seconds I think she's still going to refuse. Then she grins. 'Go on, then!' she calls, turning and running into her bedroom. 'Let's go for it. Scarlett, I'm trusting you – this had better not go wrong!'

I take a deep breath as I wait outside on the thick cream shagpile carpet for her to get ready.

When does anything I do ever go wrong?

Seventeen

We head out of the front of the apartment block together, me wearing my long red coat and boots, and Gabi still in her jeans and Ugg boots, but with the addition of a tan sheepskin jacket and huge dark designer shades, and with her dark brown hair scraped back into a ponytail. She'd toyed with the idea of a NY Yankees baseball cap for a few minutes in her apartment, but we'd both decided it was just a bit too OTT and might do the opposite of what we wanted, by drawing too much attention to what would then be a person with terrible dress sense.

'Come on,' I encourage her, as she hangs back behind me. 'You'll be fine.'

We head to the nearest Starbucks and join the queue.

'What's happening?' Gabi asks.

'We're waiting to be served,' I reply.

'Why?'

'Because that's what you have to do here unless you want caffeine-deprived New Yorkers to jump you because you've prevented them from getting their coffee fix as fast as possible.'

Gabi looks bewilderedly around the interior of the coffee shop and I wonder if she's ever had to queue for anything in her life.

'Yes, ma'am?' the jolly-looking counter assistant asks.

'I'd like a grande skinny vanilla latte, please,' I say. 'Gabi?' Gabi digs me hard in the ribs with her elbow. 'Oh ... I'm sorry, er ... Anna?' I improvise, thinking of Julia Roberts's character in *Notting Hill*.

Gabi looks at me with a puzzled expression, as does the Starbucks assistant. 'Could your *friend*,' she emphasises, 'just hurry up and choose? We have a line.'

I look behind us at the queue of people beginning to gather. 'Won't be a min!' I smile.

Gabi is staring hard through her dark shades at all the options listed on the menu behind the counter.

'There's so much to choose from,' she whispers to me. 'Guido just makes me my usual.'

Oh Lord. 'Do you know what that is?' I ask her.

She shakes her head.

'Is it sweet?'

'No, not really.'

'Milky?'

'No.'

'Frothy?'

She grimaces.

There're a few 'humph's and loud sighs behind us.

I think quickly.

'Is it a small or a large coffee?'

'Oh, tiny.'

'And black?'

'Always black – think of the calories.'

I shake my head. Gabi has a barista and he only makes her espressos! What a waste.

'Will you two get a move on!' someone shouts at the back of the queue. 'I have an appointment with my orthodontist in three weeks' time.'

A few people laugh.

Gabi spins round. 'There's a time and a place for manners, and this is it!' she says succinctly to the man. 'My friend here is politely trying to ascertain what coffee I usually drink. However,' she says, spinning back round towards the counter, 'that now sounds way too boring. So today I'll simply have what she's having,' she says, smiling at the assistant while inclining her head towards me.

'At last!' the rude man mumbles.

Gabi lowers her glasses and fires him a scathing glance.

He stares back at her and a fleeting look of recognition flickers over his face.

Gabi hurriedly replaces her glasses and drops her head.

'Two grande skinny vanilla lattes, then?' the woman repeats. 'Is that it?' She looks pleadingly at me in the hope we're not going to start the whole process again with muffins.

'Yes, that's it,' I say, thrusting a twenty-dollar note at her and taking my change. 'Thank you for your time.'

We move along the counter to wait for our coffees.

'That man is checking me out, Scarlett,' Gabi whispers, leaning in towards me. 'He knows.'

'Perhaps he might have recognised you when you lowered your glasses, but it was only for a split second. He'll probably be trying to work out why he thinks he knows you. Or perhaps –' I grin at her '– he simply fancies you!'

Gabi's head turns sharply away from her surveillance of the city type in his suit and tie to me. 'Fancies?'

'Thinks you're attractive,' I explain.

'Oh ...' She nods as if that's quite standard. 'It might just be that, I guess.'

I'm grinning as our coffees are produced by the barista and we head out of Starbucks's door.

'What's so amusing?' Gabi asks, taking a sip of her coffee. 'Mmm, this is good!'

'I'm glad you like.' I look at Gabi and wonder how she will take what I'm about to say. 'You are.'

Gabi turns swiftly towards me. 'Me? What have I done?'

I shake my head. 'It doesn't matter.'

'Yes,' Gabi says, stopping abruptly on the sidewalk now with her coffee-free hand on her hip. 'If you're finding me so hilarious, I want to know why.'

Oh dear, this wasn't the best way to start a relationship with a new client.

I swallow and try to choose my words carefully. 'It's not you as a person that's funny. I really like you.'

'Then what?' she demands, still holding her sassy pose.

'It's just your ways that make me smile.'

'Such as?'

'Such as the fact you have your own barista but he only makes you espresso – how dull must the poor man find his job, only being requested to make black coffee all day?'

Gabi thinks about this.

'And I'm pretty sure you had no concept of the principle of queuing until I made you stand in one just now.'

Gabi wrinkles her forehead as much as her Botox will allow.

'I mean waiting in line,' I explain. 'Do you ever do that?'

'I'm on a waiting list for the new Prada bag when it arrives in store. Fredo promised me I'd be the first in Upper Manhattan to get one.'

'It's hardly the same, is it? And what about that guy who was checking you out in Starbucks? You just took it as standard he was attracted to you when I mentioned it as an option. Most women would at least be a little coy if the possibility was suggested.'

Gabi drops her sassy pose and now stands coolly on the sidewalk as she takes a thoughtful sip of her coffee.

'So, don't you want to be friends and help me now, then?' she asks, lifting her shades for a moment and looking at me with doleful eyes that blink steadily. 'Am I that annoying?'

'No, of course you're not. You're just different to anyone I've ever met before. And that's why I was smiling. It doesn't mean I don't like you. I like you very much, actually.'

Gabi smiles. 'Good. Because I like you too, Scarlett O'Brien. No one ever speaks to me in the honest way you do. And I like that. I like it a lot!'

She slips her arm through mine, and we begin to walk contentedly down the street together like two old friends. I'm sure we don't look like an English movie addict and an international singing star as we sip happily on calorie-laden but very delicious shop-bought coffee.

Eighteen

I don't push Gabi's first time out in the city 'un-minded' for too long. We wander through Central Park to begin with, to get her used to the fact that every single person we pass isn't going to jump on her for an autograph or a photo, and as I originally suspected, in this city where everyone is always rushing here, there and everywhere with their own worries, no one bats an eyelid in her direction.

'See,' I tell her when we've been out and about in the park for about half an hour, 'no one notices you.'

'I have to say I'm surprised,' Gabi says, sounding a little miffed. 'It's not what I'm used to at all.'

I smile. 'That's because you're probably surrounding yourself with the wrong people.'

'How do you mean?' she asks. We've paused now at the Alice statue, a huge bronze sculpture built for children to climb and play on, filled with all the characters from her adventures in Wonderland.

I need to tread carefully here.

'Well, I bet you have staff, like a manager and a publicist, at your beck and call twenty-four hours a day, don't you?'

'Madrid and Marcus are with me most of the time, yes. But I don't see—'

'Wait.' I hold up my hand. 'Madrid?'

'Yes, she's my publicist, and Marcus is my manager.'

'Oh ... OK.' What sort of world have I unwittingly stepped into here, where people are called Madrid! 'Do those people say yes to everything you ask for?'

Gabi thinks about this. 'Pretty much. But that's what I pay them for.'

I nod knowingly and smile again.

'What!' Gabi demands. 'Stop doing that smug smiling thing. Just say what you think.'

I take a deep breath.

'I think you need to take time away from these people you employ a little more often. Of course they're going to say yes to your every requirement. It's in their best interests. Then *you'll* do what *they* want you to.'

'How do you mean?' Gabi shades her eyes from the bright sun that is now high above us in the late morning sky.

'The reason you think that everyone recognises you wherever you go is because ninety per cent of them know

152

you're coming before you even get there – they've been primed that you'll be in a certain place at a certain time. That's why there are always photographers wherever you go. Because they've been told where to find you.'

Gabi looks like she doesn't believe this could possibly be true.

'I'm telling you the truth. I'm not saying Madrid and Marcus are bad people. They probably have your best interests at heart, but it's in *their* interest to get you as much exposure as possible in the press and the glossy magazines, and a photo of Gabriella Romero coming out of the spa, or Bergdorf Goodman, is good money to the photographer, and the magazine he or she sells it to.'

I should know – I used to buy that type of magazine for long enough.

Gabi doesn't immediately reply; she looks at me for a moment as if she's fully absorbing what I'm telling her. Then she silently removes her sunglasses, puts her hand up over her eyes again and stares up at Alice and her friends.

'My grandmother used to read me *Alice in Wonderland* when I was little,' she says in a quiet voice. 'It's still one of my favourite stories today.'

I'm reminded of the time my mother and I met at the Peter Pan statue in Kensington Gardens. It seems the stories you have read to you as a child always hold a special place in your heart.

'It was *Peter Pan* for me,' I tell her.

She turns and looks at me, still without the protection of her shades. Her almond-shaped brown eyes are sombre. 'I know I must seem stupid to you, Scarlett, living in this fake celebrity world. But it's all I've known for the majority of my life. My father always courted fame and fortune, and therefore we, as his kids, were brought up under the media spotlight. We've been lucky enough to live a privileged, extravagant lifestyle, and I can't pretend my father isn't the reason I got my first career break. But . . . ' she pauses to gaze back up at the figures on the statue, all intertwined happily with each other, 'it comes at a price. And that price is my privacy.'

'I understand, really I do. But it doesn't have to be that way.' I put my hand gently on her arm. 'You're in control of what you do, Gabi, not everyone else. Yes, I'm sure you have certain responsibilities you have to uphold, commitments you have to honour – that's the nature of what you do – but I'm sure you could attempt to live a more normal life if you tried.'

Gabi looks doubtful.

'Take, for instance, today,' I say, gesturing around me. 'How many people have bothered you since we stepped out of your apartment?'

'There was that guy in Starbucks,' Gabi says, replacing her glasses protectively over her eyes.

'We don't know for sure he recognised you, and even if he did, did he bother you?'

'Well, no . . . but—'

'But nothing. It can be done. You *can* change if you want to. I know you can. We only have one go at this life, you know?'

'Not if you believe in reincarnation – we might have many lives waiting for us. I have this spiritual guru who comes to see me to practise meditation, and he says—'

I cut her off. 'You need to make your own choices about life, Gabi.'

Gabi pushes her glasses up on top of her head and looks at the statue again. 'Yes, you're right. Life is too short to waste. I'll do it,' she announces. 'I'll do it for me, and I'll do it for Nonna.'

'Good girl!' I begin to clap my hands excitedly.

'But,' she continues, 'I need your help, Scarlett. I want *you* to be my new life coach. My new guru.'

I stop clapping, my hands held wide like I'm about to catch a basketball.

'*You* can be the one to help me learn how to live my life to the fullest. What do you say?'

Nineteen

'You're doing what?' Sean asks, when I tell him over the phone the next day about my meeting with Gabi. 'Repeat that again, Scarlett. I thought you said you were going to be Gabriella Romero's life coach then. We must have a bad line.'

'No, you heard right – that's what I said.' I sigh. I'm still not sure about this myself, but Gabi was so keen on the idea and offered to pay me quite a substantial wage. I turned her down at first, but then when I realised exactly what she was suggesting, and what it was going to involve, I agreed to do it for the trust's benefit.

'But how ... why, for goodness' sake?' Sean splutters down the phone.

'She seems to think I know how to live life to its fullest,' I say quietly, knowing how weird that would seem to

156

anyone who knew me well. Or should I say the old me, the quiet me, the me who had barely set foot outside of Stratford-upon-Avon until a few years ago. I mentioned to Sean Gabi's possible involvement with The Dragonfly Trust the other night, but not any of the other stuff she wanted me to do for her.

There's silence on the line.

'Sean ... are you still there?' I ask.

'Yeah, I'm still here,' Sean replies, and I can hear in his voice he's smiling. 'How do you do it, Red?' he asks. 'How do you stumble from one crazy situation to the next, even more wild and totally irrational one?'

'Just lucky, I guess.'

'Hardly. I think it's the people who bump into you and welcome you into their lives who are the lucky ones.'

'Aw, Sean ...' He can be so sweet sometimes.

'It's true.' He pauses to think. 'Well, if this Gabriella thinks you can teach her a thing or two about life, then go for it, I say. You'll get to see how the other half lives, that's for sure.'

'Probably not, actually. That's kind of the idea. I try and show her how to live like a more normal person, within the constraints she has – the fame thing, et cetera.'

'Ah, I see. Well, she's still lucky – at least she gets to spend time with you. I miss you so much already, Scarlett, and you've only been gone a few days.'

'I know, Sean. I miss you too. It's not long before you come over with Oscar for Luke's opening night on

157

Broadway, though, is it? I can't wait to see how he's getting on. Oscar says he loves being here, and the cast have welcomed him with open arms. Hey, you might get to meet Gabi then. I'll have to arrange something if she's in town.'

'There will only be one female I'll be interested in spending time with when I come over. And that's you!'

'Sean, you're so lovely.' On the sofa, I pull my knees up to my chest and hug them with my free arm. 'And as much as I don't want our call to end today, I have to go. I'm meeting Alex for lunch in a little while.'

'So you've bumped into him, then?'

'Yes, we had dinner the other night.' That's funny – I assumed Sean knew about it, the way Alex was talking.

'Good, good. He's OK, Alex, isn't he?' Sean asks, obviously keen to know how we got on after my concerns about Alex in Scotland.

'Yes, he was very charming, and a very good dinner companion. He's even offered to help me out. That's what I'm meeting with him about today.' Damn, I wasn't going to say anything just yet, not until I knew for sure.

'Help you out with what?'

I hesitate. 'Well ... I wasn't going to say anything just yet until I had confirmation, but I went to visit The Plaza the other day.'

'The hotel?'

'Yes.'

'Why?'

'To view it as a future wedding venue.' I wait for Sean's reaction. I expect an explosion down the earpiece of my phone and I automatically hold it a little way from my ear in readiness.

'That's a fantastic idea,' he replies to my surprise. 'I had no idea you wanted to get married in New York.'

'Neither had I until Peter suggested it the other day,' I gush with relief, 'but the more I thought about it, the more it just seemed perfect. I love it over here so much, half my friends and family are here now, and apart from being away from you, I'm always happy when I'm back in the city. It's like my second home.'

'I had noticed,' Sean says. 'I do see these things. I know when you're at your happiest, Scarlett, and you and Manhattan are definitely good for each other.'

I wish Sean wasn't thousands of miles away. Because all I want to do at this very moment is hug his gorgeous body and feel him close to me. He may not always be the best at showing it, but he knows me better than anyone.

'I love you, Mr Bond,' I say simply. 'More than you'll ever know.'

'I love you too, and if the future Mrs Bond wants us to marry in New York, then that is exactly what we shall do!'

Ooh, Mrs Bond ... I hadn't thought about the possibility of changing my name. I kind of liked being an O'Brien. But I don't have time to think about it now as Sean continues, 'So how much are we talking for a wedding at The Plaza?'

'Oh, I'm not sure I remember the *exact* figures that I had quoted,' I say, skirting round what I know will be a tricky subject. I don't want to spoil the mood now Sean has so easily agreed to a New York wedding. 'Perhaps we should just wait and see if Alex can help us. That's the problem, you see – The Plaza was fully booked for this year. But Alex said he knew someone and would try and pull a few favours.'

'A ballpark figure, Scarlett,' Sean insists. 'See what I did there – ballpark?'

I rustle about on the table in front of me to find the piece of paper on which Geraldo had quoted our approximate wedding costs. And as I relay the very cheapest option back to Sean, it's now that I hear the roar I had expected earlier down the phone.

'*How much?*'

'Good news, Scarlett,' Alex announces over the table in a little coffee shop we've agreed to meet in. 'How does the Thursday before Christmas suit for your nuptials?'

'Really?' I ask him, aghast. 'They can fit us in?'

'I told you they'd be keeping some slots free. I know it's not a Friday or a Saturday. There was just no way ... but will it do?'

'Oh, Alex, I could kiss you!' I exclaim with delight. 'It's perfect.'

'I'm not too sure your groom would approve of that,' he grins. 'But I'm glad you're pleased.'

'I really . . . I just can't believe it,' I say, feeling like I'm in a dream. 'Finally, after all this time, we've found a venue, it's somewhere I'm actually happy with, and the best thing of all – it's here in New York!'

'What are best men for?' Alex winks. 'It's all booked. Geraldo will be in touch very soon so you can make the detailed arrangements.'

'You have made my day. No, week. Possibly even my year!' I tell him. 'If there's anything I can do for you any-time, you just let me know, OK?'

'Sure,' Alex nods. 'I'll let you know.'

We continue with our coffees, chatting amiably, but all I can really think about is my wedding. My wedding at the beautiful Plaza Hotel, New York City.

My phone rings just as we're paying the bill.

'Excuse me,' I apologise to Alex. 'I won't be a moment. Hi, Peter,' I say as I take the call. 'What's up?'

Alex pulls some dollars from his wallet while he's wait-ing and tosses them on the table. Then he scrolls through his own phone, checking for messages.

'Great, thanks,' I say in reply to Peter's enquiry about how I'm getting on with Gabi. Aware I can't say too much in front of Alex about Gabi, or indeed to Peter, about the nature of what Gabi has asked me to do for her grandmother, I keep my words as neutral as possible. 'I'll pop into the office in a bit and update you on the situation if you like?'

Alex looks up.

'Sure. See you in a bit, then.' And I quickly end the call.

'Problem?' Alex enquires, returning his own phone to his jacket pocket.

'No, everything is fine.' I smile quickly at him and get up, preparing to leave.

Alex nods. 'Was that Peter Butler you were just talking to, by any chance?'

I glance back at him as I pull on my coat.

'Only you said you knew him.'

'Yes, it was, actually. I need to pop into the office and ... update Peter on some things. Work things,' I add unnecessarily.

'Ah, I see.' Alex nods again and he pulls on his Burberry trench coat over his jacket. 'It would be good to meet Peter Butler one day while I'm here in New York. I've always been an admirer of his work.'

'I'm sure I could arrange that.' I smile at him again. 'It's the least I can do. Leave it with me. We'll have dinner one night, or drinks?'

'Dinner would be spot on.' Alex smiles as he holds the door open for me. 'Thank you, Scarlett – that's just the ticket.'

Twenty

March turns into April and my now almost daily walk across Central Park towards Gabi's apartment has changed from a sometimes chilly one, with winds gusting my hair around my face, to a usually much warmer prospect, with the only threat being the occasional April shower – except this was New York, and this city never did anything by halves, so a shower was more likely to be a torrential downpour that could last all day.

The last few weeks had been a bit manic, with our wedding plans for December now full on. After Sean's initial shock, he'd agreed to us holding our wedding at The Plaza – saying something along the lines of 'If you're going to do something, you may as well do it to your absolute best.' And if The Plaza was *the* best wedding venue in New York, then only the best would be good enough for Sean.

I'd been back to see Geraldo a couple of times at The Plaza, so menus and other ideas for flowers, table decorations and the like had been flying regularly back and forth between Sean and me across the internet. But even though there was still much to do, I felt I could relax a little knowing one of our biggest worries was finally settled. We had a date, and we had a venue.

My next problem – if you can call it that – is what I'm going to wear. But my own Gok Wan – by the name of Oscar – is winging his way across the Atlantic right now, on his way to see his own betrothed, Luke, on his opening night on Broadway tomorrow. Oscar has promised to take me shopping while he's here, with the bold statement 'If I can't find you the perfect wedding dress in the shopping capital of the world, then I may as well retire from fashion and take up a career in taxidermy.'

Oh, how I missed Oscar when I was away from him, almost as much, but in a very different way, as I missed Sean, who was at this moment likely having to deal with Oscar's wonderful ways as he sat next to him on the flight from London.

I smile to myself; Sean would need something akin to strong tranquillisers to calm his nerves after he'd dealt with Oscar in a confined space for that long.

I notice the blossom is just starting to form on the trees of Central Park. It will be a week or so yet before it's in full bloom, though, I think as I continue on my way over to the east side of the park. Gosh, I know New York so well now.

Sean and Peter were right – it really is like my second home. And that thought makes me very happy indeed.

I call a cheery hello to Sylvester, today's doorman at Gabi's apartment block, and I'm immediately let inside. I don't even need fancy passwords to be let in now I'm here so often; I just go straight through and ride up in the elevator to the penthouse.

'Morning!' I sing cheerily to Gabi as I stride through the door into her apartment. 'How are you today?'

'Not as buoyant as you, that's for sure,' she replies, glancing with interest at me. 'What's put a spring in your step today? Have you stopped off at Starbucks already? We always go there together.'

Since our first foray into the green mermaid's lair, Gabi has become quite addicted to the many wonders of the coffee-shop chain. Her favourite is a full-fat grande mocha with whipped cream on top. But most of the time she opts for a slightly less calorific skinny vanilla cappuccino.

'Of course I haven't. Especially not today, remember?'

Gabi pulls a face. 'Do I have to?'

'Yes,' I say firmly. 'You do.'

A few minutes later we arrive outside the same Starbucks Gabi hardly dared set foot inside a few weeks ago, and I deliberately turn my back towards the window and fold my arms. 'Go on,' I encourage her. 'You're ready for this now.'

Gabi sighs. 'All right, but I want it to be known I'm being forced into this against my will.'

'And I bet that never happens, does it?' I smile.

She goes to grab the door handle.

'Ah-ah,' I reprimand before she can go inside. 'Sunglasses?' I hold out my hand.

Gabi testily removes her customary dark shades from her face and hands them to me. 'If Marcus could see me now . . .' she says, rolling her eyes.

'Just as well he's not here, then! Chop-chop.' I wave my hand at her. 'We haven't got all day.'

Gabi shakes her head and mumbles something, which sounds Italian, and I expect is a swear word. Then she pulls open the door of the shop and goes in.

I try not to watch her as she joins the queue. I feel like a mother witnessing her child do something very grown-up on their own for the first time. I don't want to seem overprotective, yet at the same time I feel a need to stay close at hand in case she needs me.

Gabi has come on in leaps and bounds since we started her 'therapy', as I like to call it.

She is happy to leave the apartment 'unguarded' now, and happy to venture further than the wide, open spaces of Central Park into busier, more populated venues such as Bloomingdale's and Fifth Avenue.

This is with me accompanying her, of course. She's not ventured out alone yet. Her foray into Starbucks today is just the first step on her journey to independence.

It wasn't easy at first. It wasn't that Gabi wasn't willing to try all my ideas, not at all; she was very good at embracing the whole concept of stepping out into the real world. It was her 'team' who gave me the most trouble.

Marcus, her manager, a swarthy, raven-haired man with a sharp taste in suits and designer everything, did his best to accompany us the first time I called on Gabi to take her out. Gabi had to physically take him by the hand, push him down onto one of her pristine snow-white sofas and give him a list of people she needed phoning and things she needed doing before we could escape. And even then I kept looking behind us all the time, expecting to be followed by a big, burly security guard.

But the next time I called on Gabi, I was introduced properly to her security guard, Lewis. I'd seen Lewis in Peter's office the first day Gabi and I met, but I hadn't taken much notice of him. He looked nothing like I expected a security guard should – big and brawny with more biceps than brain cells. No, Lewis was quietly spoken, fit – I could definitely see a six-pack lurking under his turtleneck sweater – and above all professional. Instead of giving me a hard time, he simply gave me a few pointers on what to do if we did encounter any trouble. And more importantly his cell-phone number.

Of all Gabi's entourage Lewis was the most down to earth. He reminded me a little of Kevin Costner in *The Bodyguard*, which of course I rather liked. Movies and real life . . . I could always find a link.

I hadn't met the infamous Madrid yet, but from what

Gabi told me about her hotshot New York publicist, she sounded pretty menacing.

Then there was Portia, her PA. I was under the impression that PAs were supposed to be polite, helpful people. Portia obviously hadn't graduated from that school of personal assistance. She made my life as difficult as possible to begin with, by attempting to wreck all outings I planned for Gabi. She blocked my phone calls and didn't pass on messages when I left them. But eventually, after more intervention from Gabi – and probably the threat of being fired – Portia seemed to come around a little, and just about tolerated me taking her beloved employer away from her control for the occasional hour or two.

'*Voilà!*' Gabi announces, appearing from the coffee shop with two steaming-hot paper cups. 'I did it!'

'Congratulations,' I say, taking one from her. 'How did it go?'

'Fine. No one seemed to recognise me at all – and if they did, they never said anything,' she gasps jubilantly, trying to catch her breath as if she's been holding it for the last few minutes. 'I couldn't quite believe it!'

'New Yorkers are usually pretty cool,' I say, sipping my hot coffee and sounding very knowledgeable about such matters. 'This is probably one of the best places you could have tried this experiment.'

'So what next?' Gabi asks excitedly. 'I feel like I can tackle the world now!'

'You better take these first.' I pass her back her glasses.

'One step at a time, and you won't be tackling the world until you can tell the difference between a skinny vanilla latte and a full-fat mocha with whipped cream.'

Gabi looks down at her coffee. 'Oops! I'm just too excited right now,' she says as we swap coffees. 'You're opening up so many new doors for me, Scarlett. I feel so independent doing things for myself without a bodyguard or a PA. I feel so free.'

'Well then, since you did so well this morning, and you're feeling so confident right now, I suggest we step it up a gear . . .'

Twenty-one

'What're our plans for today, then?' Gabi asks as we walk across, then down Central Park, heading for Fifth Avenue. 'More shopping?'

'Nope, we're going to do something a bit more touristy than that. See if you can deal with people from other countries, as well as your disinterested fellow New Yorkers . . .'

'Ooh.' Gabi sounds genuinely excited. 'Where?'

'You'll see when we get there,' I say mysteriously.

'Spoilsport!' Gabi teases. 'You know, I watched one of those movies last night from that list you gave me.'

'Oh, which?' After she'd admitted to never having watched *Notting Hill*, I'd given Gabi a list of some of my favourite movies to watch: rom-coms such as *You've Got Mail*, *When Harry Met Sally*, *Hitch*, *Four Weddings and a Funeral* and *Love Actually*, to name but a few on my very long and detailed list.

'The one at the top of your list – *Notting Hill*. I really loved it. Can't believe I haven't seen it before.'

'It's a classic,' I agree. 'If it wasn't for that movie, I probably wouldn't have met Sean.'

'Really? Did you meet at the movie theatre?'

'No, in the Travel Bookshop – the same one from the film.'

Gabi stops walking. 'You're messing with me, right? I know you guys met in London. But in that actual shop?'

'Yeah, seems a bit mad now. It's quite a story.' I think about Sean, and how my life has changed since we first met in that little bookshop. What if we hadn't? What if I'd never gone to Notting Hill? I probably wouldn't be walking through Central Park with Gabi now. In fact, I know I wouldn't.

'Tell me as we walk,' Gabi insists. 'I want to know it all.'

By the time we get halfway down Fifth Avenue, I've told Gabi everything there is to know about Sean and me. And as we step into the Rockefeller Center, where the famous Christmas tree is erected every year, Gabi shakes her head.

'I don't know about *Notting Hill*, Scarlett, but it sounds like your own story would make a pretty great movie script.'

I laugh. 'Possibly.'

'When are you seeing Sean again?'

'He's on his way over here right now,' I explain. 'With Oscar, my friend.'

'The other guy you met in Notting Hill? The one who held the dinner party for you?'

'That's the chap.'

'Oh, I'd love to meet them. We should so do dinner or brunch or something while they're here.'

'That sounds great. Let's arrange that.' I know Sean will enjoy meeting Gabi, but Oscar will be in seventh heaven. He's a huge fan.

'So why are we here?' Gabi asks, gesturing around at The Plaza. 'I'm not doing an appearance on *The Today Show* or something with NBC, am I?'

The NBC television studios are located just to the left of us in The Plaza, but that's not the reason I've brought Gabi here.

'Ever been up to the top?' I ask, looking up at the towering skyscraper that forms the heart of the Rockefeller Center.

Gabi does the same. 'The Top of the Rock?' she asks. 'Of course. I did a magazine shoot up there once.'

'No, I mean as a normal tourist, not as a private guest.'

Gabi gives me an 'as if' look. 'But won't we have to wait in line?' she asks, already wrinkling her nose.

'No, I have tickets – they have a set time for entering, so it shouldn't be too bad.'

Gabi shrugs. 'Sure. If you think it's a good idea, Scarlett, then I'm all for it! I trust you, you know that.'

172

We enter the vast skyscraper and make our way round to the entrance that leads to the Top of the Rock observation deck.

We hand our tickets over no problem, navigate the security procedures, then follow the queue round to the main entrance and the lifts that will shoot us up to the top.

'Photo, ladies?' A guy with a camera gestures to a bench in front of a backdrop of New York. It's supposed to recreate the famous black and white photo of city workers on their lunch break as they balance precariously over the New York skyline on only a cross-beam.

I'm about to say, 'No, thank you,' when I hear 'Sure!' and before I can do anything, Gabi takes up a professional-looking pose on the pretend cross-beam.

The photographer looks surprised. 'Great! Is your friend joining you?'

'Come on, Scarlett,' Gabi encourages. 'Don't be shy.'

Reluctantly I sit next to Gabi on the beam and the photographer encourages us to pull silly faces.

'Take your glasses off, miss. It'll be a better shot.'

Again before I can advise against it, Gabi does just that.

The photographer is peering through his lens, but he suddenly takes another look at us. 'Hey, aren't you—' he begins before I cut him off.

'Yes, thank you,' I say, grabbing our numbered ticket from his hand. 'We'll be sure to check out our photos upstairs.'

I take hold of Gabi's hand, quickly pulling her away towards the lifts.

'Put your glasses on again,' I hiss as we join the queue. 'Before you're recognised.'

'Sorry,' Gabi says, shoving her shades back over her eyes. 'I got a bit carried away. Have I blown our cover? Hey, that makes us sound like two undercover cops!'

'We should be OK, if he doesn't say anything,' I reply, looking around me to see if anyone else has noticed. 'This isn't a Starbucks on the Upper West Side now. You need to be a bit careful.'

We eventually get to our lift and cram inside with a family from France, who don't give Gabi a second glance. Well, the teenage son glances at Gabi's ample chest a few times when she unbuttons her coat in the stuffy lift, but his eyes don't rise far enough to recognise her face. And then as soon as we've ridden the sixty-nine floors up, we alight onto the first viewing platform.

'Check out your photos, ladies!' a guy at a desk calls.

I just want to carry on up to the seventieth floor – the very top viewing deck. I know how it all works here because Sean and I took a trip up late one summer's evening and admired the stunning views at night.

But Gabi is already heading over to the desk, so I have to follow her as she pushes her way to the front of a very large crowd, many of whom don't seem to be looking at and purchasing their own photos, but appear fixated on one particular picture.

'Your ticket, ma'am?' the attendant asks, looking at Gabi, just as I realise which photo it is they're getting so excited about.

'No, don't worry, ma'am,' he says, suddenly going all coy. 'I . . . I know which is your photo.' He reaches behind the counter. 'And may I say what a privilege it is to have you visit with us today, and what a stunning photo too.'

Gabi simply smiles as if this is the way he treats all his customers.

'Scarlett,' she calls, 'what do you think?'

I manage to weave my way to her side through the throng of people. I glance at the photo. Gabi looks every inch the celebrity. Her hair is immaculate, as though she's just had a stylist run on and touch it up seconds before the shutter closed, and she looks relaxed and happy 'balancing' on the beam above the New York skyline. I, however, do not. I look like I've had to flap my arms and fly up there myself. My face is red and flustered-looking. My black hair, which is tied back in a ponytail today, is sticking out all over the place, making me look like I've got a renegade spider clambering over the top of my head, and my pose is far from relaxed, but looks like I've just been told I have to walk this plank and jump to my doom, instead of jovially enjoy a few lunchtime sand-wiches on it.

'Yes, it's great,' I say, conscious that even more people are looking in our direction with interest now. 'Do you want to buy it?'

'Oh no,' the young man behind the counter says. 'This is with our compliments.'

'It is her!' I suddenly hear someone shout. 'It's Gabriella Romero. She's here at the Top of the Rock!'

Nearly everyone surrounding the photo desk turns and looks our way.

'Ooh, can I get a photo?' I hear someone ask as I get pushed a little.

'An autograph?' another person says as a pen and guide-book are suddenly thrust in front of my nose.

Within seconds I find myself shoved to the floor as the throng of people rapidly descend on Gabi.

I feel helpless as I watch her trying to deal with their demands. And they are demands. There's no queue, no polite waiting in turn. My mind goes completely blank as I sit on the floor. I've forgotten everything Lewis told me to do should we find ourselves in difficulty.

'Do something!' I call to the guy behind the desk, as he looks on in utter panic. 'Do something, please!'

'I-I'll call security,' he shouts back, reaching for a phone.

Gabi could be trampled to death by then.

'Scarlett! What on earth are you doing?' I hear a famil-iar voice call out. I turn round and see my old friend Max walking towards me. He's holding a large bag, which usu-ally means he has a camera stashed inside.

'Max, you've got to help me,' I say as he helps me to my feet. 'I need to get Gabi out of here as quick as.'

I see Max quickly sum up the situation.

'Hold this,' he says, handing me his bag. Which definitely must have his equipment inside: it weighs a ton.

Max pushes his way through the crowd.

'Security!' he shouts in a loud voice. 'Step aside, please. Security. Give the lady some space.'

What Max lacks in height to be the security to a celebrity, he certainly makes up for in brawn and determination, and he quickly manages to pull and then escort Gabi away from her adoring fans.

Gabi looks in shock as she emerges from the throng of people. I'm not sure if it's the sudden onslaught that's caused this or the fact that a strange man is now escorting her confidently away from her troubles.

'This way,' Max says without hesitation, leading us to a door marked 'Private' as the observation deck's security now arrive. 'You'll be safe here.'

Max inputs some digits into the door alarm and quickly we're on the other side.

'Thank you,' I say to him as the door closes behind us and we all breathe a sigh of relief. 'But how did you know the code?'

'I've been filming here today,' Max says. 'They use this place as a dressing room for the celebs when they're shooting stuff at the top. They give me the code so I can stash my equipment here when I need to, to keep it safe.'

I look around the room. It's small, but there are a couple of sofas with a table between them, a large mirror on one wall and a curtained-off area, presumably for people needing to get changed.

'So ...' Max looks with interest at Gabi, 'who's your friend?'

'Sorry!' I apologise. 'Let me introduce you both. Gabi, this is my friend Max. Remember we spoke about him when I was telling you all about finding my half-brother, Jamie?'

Gabi nods and holds out her hand.

'And, Max, this is Gabi, my ... friend.'

Max takes Gabi's hand and shakes it gently. 'I lied just now,' he says. 'I do know who you are, of course.'

Gabi smiles. 'I'm so sorry, Max – I'm forgetting my manners. It's the shock. Thank you so much for what you just did outside. Usually I'd have my security, Lewis, with me, but ...' Gabi looks at me for help.

'We decided on a little adventure on our own today, didn't we?' I try and explain. 'Sadly it didn't go quite as planned.'

'I can see that,' Max says. 'Quite the opposite, in fact. Unless you planned on getting jumped on by fifty bloody tourists firing their cameras off and shouting at you in a dozen different languages. It's bad enough when they're down on the ground – at least you can escape them then.'

Gabi smiles. 'You're English too,' she says. 'Like Scarlett?'

'Yeah, born and bred. Been here a few years now, though. Just don't have the accent yet, and don't plan to either, if I'm honest.'

'Oh, you don't want it,' Gabi insists. 'A British accent is very sexy on a man.'

The only other time I've seen Max flush so red is when I tried cooking him and Jamie a curry one night in my apartment and I misread the recipe book ever so slightly. Let's just say a cup measurement in America is not equivalent to a tablespoon when it comes to chilli powder, and Max, who had insisted up to that point he'd never had a curry yet that was too hot for him, finally met his match.

'Depends where in Britain it's from,' Max quips, covering his embarrassment. 'I've never got on too well with the Welsh.'

'Max!' I admonish. 'Don't mind him,' I explain to Gabi. 'It's just his way. He doesn't mean it.'

But Gabi smiles. 'It's good to have a joke, Max,' she says. 'Life is far too serious.'

Max smiles now too. 'Scarlett's right – I'm only kidding. Some of my best friends are Welsh.'

'Really?' Gabi asks.

'Nah ...' Max shakes his head. 'But I wouldn't turn them away.'

Just then one of the Rock's security guards bursts through the door; his badge informs us he is chief security officer.

'Miss Romero ...' he cries, and for a moment I think he's going to drop to his knees and grab her hand as if she were royalty. 'I cannot apologise enough for the fracas out there just now. If we'd known you were here, we could have escorted you to the top with your own guards.'

'It's fine, Robert,' Gabi says, noting his name. I love how Gabi always uses the person's name she's in conversation with. 'I didn't want to be escorted – that was the whole point. However, I may have been a little naïve in thinking I wouldn't be recognised.'

'Yes, miss. I have to agree with you there,' Robert says, nodding.

'But luckily for me, Max here came to my rescue.' Gabi points to Max.

'Indeed,' Robert says, eyeing Max suspiciously. 'Can I ask how you have access to this room, sir?'

'I'm filming, ain't I?' Max says, fishing a pass from beneath his jacket. 'I use this room to store my stuff.'

Robert nods, accepting Max's explanation and his pass. 'I see. Miss Romero,' he says, turning his attention back to Gabi, 'we here at the Top of the Rock would very much like to make it up to you in any way we can. We will close the viewing deck off for a half-hour while you browse the wonderful views at your leisure. Just give me a few moments and—'

Blimey, I think, so this is one of those celebrity perks in action.

But Gabi cuts Robert off. 'No,' she insists. 'That wouldn't be fair on all the people who already have tickets. If I go out there, I go like anyone would. No special treatment.'

I'm proud of her.

'Is she crazy?' Max whispers to me. 'That would be so cool.'

'I'm teaching her how to try and live a normal life,' I explain. 'She's doing really well right now.'

'Why on earth would she want a *normal* life?' Max asks. 'That sucks.'

'But, Miss Romero,' Robert is trying to persuade Gabi otherwise, 'if you go out there, you will be recognised immediately.'

Gabi thinks about this. 'Scarlett?' she asks, looking at me. 'Any ideas?'

I shake my head.

'I have,' Max says. 'It's a bit of a risk, but I think it might work.'

Gabi smiles warmly at Max. 'I like a risk,' she says, her eyes sparkling. 'Let's do it!'

I feel a right lemon as I stand posing behind one of the big silver viewing binoculars on the Top of the Rock while Max pretends to take photos of me. He says he's only pretending, but knowing Max, he'll have a whole memory card full of snaps of me making a fool of myself.

While he's doing this, and I'm draped precariously over the binoculars, Gabi acts as Max's assistant. She's wearing her dark glasses and is disguised in a baggy Top of the Rock souvenir sweatshirt and baseball cap, under which she has piled up her long mane of dark curls.

Amazingly, this is actually working – no one is taking a second glance at Gabi; they're all too busy wondering why anyone would want to do a photo shoot with me as the model. So under this guise we have been able to make our way around the viewing area completely unbothered.

We do get asked for one autograph, however, just as we're about to leave, and Max and Gabi have to stifle their mirth when it's me who has to sign a young boy's autograph book.

'All right,' I say, joining their laughter now we're safely in one of the private lifts being escorted back down to the ground. 'It wasn't *that* funny.'

'I wonder who he thought you were, Scarlett?' Gabi asks. 'What did you sign in his book?'

'"With love from" and then an illegible squiggle,' I say, smiling. 'He can make up what he likes, then.'

'Thank you, Max,' Gabi says just before we reach terra firma again. 'I had great fun up there today.'

'Really?' Max asks. 'I would imagine you do many more exciting things in your life than take a few snaps with a jaded New York cameraman.'

'Perhaps,' Gabi says honestly. 'But I don't enjoy them anywhere near as much as I enjoyed that.' She takes her baseball cap off now and shakes out her hair.

I see Max swallow hard.

'So how about we all go and get some food together?' I ask, my brain starting to whizz as we step out of the lift. 'Max, are you free?'

Max looks at his watch. 'Sadly no. I have to meet Julie, the correspondent I work with,' he explains for Gabi's benefit, 'in half an hour. We're off to film a story across town. That was a private job,' he whispers, nodding upwards. 'Gotta do the day job now.'

'Well, it was lovely meeting you, Max,' Gabi says, and she gives him a kiss on the cheek. 'And thank you again for being my knight in shining armour today.'

'Anytime,' Max replies, looking like he's been eating my hot curry again. 'My armour might be a bit rusty, but it's always ready for a quick outing.'

'Indeed,' Gabi grins. 'Hopefully we'll meet again, Max. Perhaps you'd like to come to the dinner I'm organising for Scarlett and her friends when they arrive from England?'

Max glances at me and I nod my encouragement.

'I would like that, thank you, Miss Romero.'

'Max!' Gabi admonishes him. 'I told you up there – Gabi, please. I'm always Gabi to my friends.'

Max grins. 'Best not tell you what my friends call me! Yes, Gabi, I would love to come to your dinner.'

I may be a bit out of practice when it comes to these things, now I'm an engaged person, but when Gabi and Max smile at each other, I sense the possibility of something a little special.

Twenty-two

That evening I'm impatiently checking the window of my apartment every few minutes, desperate to see signs of the taxi that will be delivering Sean into my arms once again.

When at last it finally arrives, I rush downstairs to the front steps just as Sean is offloading his bag from the boot of the cab.

'Darling!' Oscar says, climbing out to embrace me briefly, before he continues further uptown to stay with Luke in his apartment. 'How are you?'

'I'm great, thanks. And you?'

'Fabulous, now I'm away from that awful airport and back in this wondrous city again.'

'Did something happen?' I ask, thinking maybe Sean and Oscar fell out on the flight.

'It wouldn't have,' Sean grumbles, walking round the side of the cab, a large holdall slung over his shoulder, 'if *someone* hadn't had two great suitcases to collect from the airport carousel. We had to wait bloody ages until his luminous-pink trunk came tumbling down the chute.'

Oscar tuts. 'It's not luminous pink. As if! It's metallic rose, actually.'

'Whatever,' Sean says, paying the cab driver and instructing him on where he's to go next. 'It's an unnecessary eyesore.'

I smile at them both, used to their constant banter. 'So you had a good trip over, then? You coped ...?' I look at Sean; he looks weary.

'Yeah, just.'

'Seany was most entertaining on the flight, actually,' Oscar says to my surprise. 'Who knew one person could snore in so many different ways! The cabin staff and I had great fun counting.'

'Funny,' Sean grimaces. 'Much as I'd like to stand out here all night and relive that seven hours of joy with you, don't you have someone to go and see, Oscar?'

'I do!' Oscar claps his hands in glee. 'And if I know Luke, this will be a *long* night.' He winks at Sean. Who pulls a disdainful face in response. 'So *adios*, my lovelies, and I shall see you both tomorrow for more fun and japes!' Oscar hops back in the cab and pretends to whip the cab driver as if he's in a horse-drawn carriage. The cab driver – who I guess has dealt with much worse – doesn't even flinch as they pull away down the street and back into the always-busy Manhattan traffic.

'Come on, you,' I say to Sean as I take hold of his hand and lead him up the steps. 'I thought you might be feeling the worse for wear after all that time with Oscar, so I got in some of your favourites.'

Sean stops walking up the steps and looks at me. 'Not the cookies?' he asks, suddenly brightening.

The last time he was here, Sean became just a little bit addicted to some cookies I'd found freshly baked every day just a few blocks from my apartment. The cookies at Levain Bakery were to die for – seriously, I'd never tasted anything like them – and it was hard not to pop by there and buy some every day. But since I didn't want to end up having to be rolled down the aisle in my wedding dress, I'd admirably resisted buying any more, until now.

'Yes, the cookies,' I smile. 'I'll even heat them for you so the chocolate is all warm and gooey inside, just as you like it.'

'Oh, how I love you, Scarlett O'Brien,' Sean says, kissing me on the lips.

'I should hope you do,' I grin. 'And it better not just be for my cookies!'

The next morning I sigh as I stand on Fifth Avenue and look up at the exterior of Bergdorf Goodman. This is the fourth on Oscar's long list of possible places in which to find me a wedding dress.

We've already been to three salons this morning without any luck, including Kleinfeld, down on West 20th Street, which Oscar informed me had one of the largest collections of bridal gowns in New York. Our helpful assistant, Melanie, who tried desperately hard to find me something I liked, also mentioned on several occasions that they stocked over a thousand individual designs, so they simply must have my perfect wedding dress. But like the other two salons we'd visited, they didn't, and I left feeling extremely guilty that I'd let Melanie and her team down by not squealing with joy, as I heard another bride do in the next room, at finding my perfect gown in their establishment.

Oscar is just finishing off a phone call to Luke.

'Okey-dokey, my love, we'll see you later – I can't wait either!' he says, ending the call and putting his phone back in his bright blue Cambridge satchel. He looks up at me, his eyes shining as they always do when Luke's involved.

'Luke was just letting me know about the final arrangements for tonight.'

'Is he excited?' I ask. 'I bet he's really nervous.'

'Very,' Oscar says. 'But I was doing my best to keep him calm last night.'

'Didn't he mind you coming out with me today, when he hasn't seen you for so long? Sean's got a meeting as usual, so he's fine about it. But I thought you and Luke would want to spend the day together.'

Oscar shakes his head. 'No – Luke's better left alone when he's preparing to perform. He prefers solitude to fully get his head round what he's about to do.'

Oscar grins and his eyes light up.

'No, Oscar!' I inform him sternly. 'I know just what you're about to say.' I shake my finger at him as I push open the door of Bergdorf Goodman. 'No ... no ... no! At least *try* to keep your double entendres to a minimum while I'm shopping for my wedding dress!'

Oscar laughs and follows me into the store, and we make our way up to the bridal department on the seventh floor.

The bridal salon has a very beautiful art deco-inspired interior, which, like everything else in the store, looks expensive. We're greeted by the usual immaculate-looking assistant, who tells us her name is Bridget – only she pronounces it Bridg-*eet*!

'Please take a seat, Scarlett,' she says. 'We've been expecting you.'

Oscar reclines on a chaise longue, and I sit down opposite him in a plush chair covered in peach silk brocade.

'Now,' Bridget says, perching just in front of Oscar, 'let's start with a few basics. Do we have any idea of the sort of gown you might like to perform your nuptials in?'

She makes it sound like I'm going into hospital for an operation.

Oscar leans back on the chaise longue behind Bridget and grins at me.

'Er . . . no, not really,' I reply. 'We've been to a few other places this morning and I haven't seen anything I like at all.'

Bridget looks appalled that we could even have thought of trying anywhere else before her own hallowed rooms. But a practised smile appears on her glossy peach lips, which perfectly match the fabric of the chair. 'And that is exactly why you should have come to us here at Bergdorf Goodman first. *We* will find you your perfect gown. Of that I have no doubt.'

She makes it sound like a threat.

'Now,' she continues brightly, 'what style are we looking for?'

I like the way Bridget uses 'we' all the time, like the royal we.

I shrug.

'OK . . .' Bridget notes something down on the clipboard she's holding and I wonder if I'm getting marked out of ten for being the perfect bride. (Or not, as is likely in my case.) 'Let's see, now – would we like an A-line, empire or a ball gown, perhaps?'

'Er . . . I'm not sure,' I hesitate, not wanting to commit myself at this early stage.

'Or we have many styles in trumpet, sheath and mer-maid, too?'

'What's a trumpet dress?' I ask, envisioning some sort of band uniform with gold epaulettes.

'Trumpets fit closely to the body to mid-hip.' Bridget

demonstrates with her hands, obviously pleased to be able to impart her vast dress knowledge. 'Then they widen gradually to the hem. They are so called because they resemble the mouth of a trumpet.'

Oscar pretends to blow on a trumpet behind Bridget.

'They're often confused with a mermaid,' she continues, 'but the trumpet flares from mid-hip, whereas the mermaid flares below the knee.'

'Oh ... right. Thank you,' I say as Oscar on the chaise longue flips his legs together like a mermaid's tail.

Bridget swivels round and looks at Oscar suspiciously.

'So now you know, Scarlett,' Oscar says innocently, his legs still and his hands now placed neatly on his lap.

I narrow my eyes at him. 'Did *you* know the difference?' I demand.

'Of course,' Oscar says, shaking his head now Bridget's turned to face me again. 'Doesn't everyone?'

'Maybe I should take a look at you and suggest some styles,' Bridget says, looking me up and down as though she's measuring me with an invisible tape measure.

'Yes, why not? After all, it can't be any worse than what I've tried already – can it?' I'm joking, but Bridget doesn't get it.

She eyes me suspiciously now. 'And then we can discuss necklines, sleeves and waists,' she continues. 'Have we thought about a train?'

'To take me to the wedding?' I ask, thoroughly confused now. 'I was hoping for a nice car.'

To her credit, on this occasion Bridget humours me. 'No . . . on your dress.'

I flush bright red. 'Oh, of course. Silly me. No, I haven't.'

'Super! Then we have many, many options to explore. This will be so much fun,' she says, standing up. 'Now, you just relax while I go and select some gowns for you. I will get Marcy to bring you over two flutes of champagne. How does that sound?'

'Just dandy, Bridget,' Oscar says, giving her a thumbs-up. 'We'll be here waiting with bated breath. Won't we, Scarlett?'

I nod resignedly. 'Yep, we sure will.'

Over the next two hours Bridget has me wearing nearly every dress that Bergdorf Goodman possesses. Every time I think we must have exhausted her supply of gowns, she disappears again to pull out some more.

Oscar has drunk four glasses of champagne while I've been trying on dresses, and has eaten all the little white bonbons that Marcy brought with the champagne and placed delicately on a glass table next to him, and as a result is now almost nodding off on the chaise longue.

'Oscar!' I hiss, poking my head round the curtain of my changing-room prison while Bridget has gone off to find more dresses. 'This isn't working. I'm not going to find anything here – or in any other shop. They all look the same. They're all hideous on me.'

'Darling,' Oscar says, sitting up and stretching, 'they are quite clearly not all the same – you've been in everything from a Vera Wang to a Jenny Packham today, and every designer in between. How can you not like any of them?'

'It's not that I don't like them. Some of them are lovely gowns. They just don't seem right for this once-in-a-lifetime day. They're just not *special* enough. Oh, am I making sense? I'm feeling very weary now – Bridget is quite exhausting.'

Oscar leaps up, comes over to the curtain and kisses the end of my nose. 'Of course, my darling. If you're not happy, then I'm not. I'm not going to make you choose something you don't absolutely adore.'

'Thank you, Oscar,' I sigh with relief. 'I just didn't want to let you down. I know how hard you tried finding me all these wonderful places to look at dresses.'

'Don't be a silly moo. You're not letting me down. I just want you to be happy. Come on,' he says, looking around him. 'Let's get out of here and go for something to eat – I'm starving.'

'We can't just leave,' I say in horror. 'What will Bridget think?'

'Scarlett, do you want to try on *every* dress in this shop?' Oscar asks. 'Because I have a feeling that Bridget never gives up; she's in this for the long haul.'

'No!' I exclaim, my eyes wide. 'Absolutely not! It's OK for you – you've had a bowl of sweets to keep you going.

I've had one glass of champagne. Let me just get my clothes on and we're out of here. I smell a pizza coming up ...'

Oscar nods encouragingly. 'Ooh yes, that sounds just the ticket! What are you waiting for, missy? Grab your jeans and let's split.'

We don't quite manage to exit the salon before Bridget returns, her arms overflowing with yet more white and cream silk.

'Miss O'Brien,' she calls as we beat a hasty retreat, 'you can't just leave like this. I'm not finished with you yet.'

'Goodbye, Bridg-*eet*!' I call as we run for the escalators. 'Thank you for your time! We'll be in touch if I choose any of your lovely dresses.'

'That's never gonna happen,' Oscar giggles as we ride down to the ground floor together.

'I know,' I agree. 'There's more chance of you wearing one of Bridget's dresses than me!'

Twenty-three

Oscar and I tuck into our slices of pizza and drink our beers.

John's Pizza on West 44th Street is one of my favourite pizza restaurants in the city. The pizzas are delicious, and the restaurant is pretty impressive too. The building is an old gospel tabernacle church and the original high ceiling still houses a beautiful circular stained-glass window. Three levels of tables and chairs jostle for position against a huge monotone mural that covers one of the vast walls. The décor is muted yet chic, and is the perfect backdrop for the mouth-watering multi-coloured pizzas.

'So,' Oscar asks, after he's finished chewing a mouthful of pizza, 'what are we going to do about your dress? I can't have you turning up at the church in any old thing, can I? Plus,' he grins, 'how can we pick what Maddie and I will wear if you don't know your choice!'

'That sounds more like it. What *you're* going to wear to *my* wedding will be top of your priority list. I would have thought right now you'd be more bothered about what you're going to wear to your own wedding.'

'Oh, I know that already,' Oscar says casually. 'Have done for a while.'

'You do?' I exclaim. 'What, and how was I not involved in this decision?'

'Darling, you know I'd have involved you in all my wedding choices if I could, but you've been halfway round the world for the last few weeks, and Luke and I needed to make some decisions fast.'

'But Luke is over here too,' I protest, a bit put out that Oscar has made decisions about his own wedding without me when he's been such a big part of my preparations so far.

'I know. That's why he's left much of the planning to me. Golly, I know just how you feel now, darling. It's such a 'mare trying to plan something like this on your own.'

'Something like what? What are you doing? Do you have a venue, a date yet?' I ask.

Oscar nods excitedly. 'But it was only decided the other evening. It's not like I've been hiding it from you, sweetie,' he says, sensing I'm more than a little upset.

'Well, come on – you'd better tell me, then. I'm dying to know. The last thing I heard from you, you were thinking about London Zoo.'

'Oh, that's old hat. Anyway, can you really see me getting married in a zoo! Imagine the smell.' Oscar wrinkles his nose up at the thought.

'I don't think they actually hold the ceremony in one of the enclosures,' I point out.

'Maybe not, but we decided against it. Luke has an allergy to bird feathers apparently. Who knew?' Oscar holds up his hands.

Oscar had kept me updated on all his wedding ideas over email. Oscar, being Oscar, was determined to do something different for his ceremony with Luke, and we'd been through the Gherkin, London Bridge, even the London Eye as possible venues, until I'd pointed out that Oscar wasn't all that keen on heights. A fact he seemed to have forgotten in the excitement of planning his perfect London wedding.

'So,' I say, 'you seem pretty excited. Where have you finally chosen?'

'The Globe,' Oscar announces with a flourish.

'The Globe? As in the Shakespeare theatre?' I ask in astonishment. 'But you said in Edinburgh you didn't want anywhere old. That it freaked you out.'

'Yes, well, a draughty old castle is a bit different to this!' Oscar justifies. 'We don't get married in the really old part of the theatre up on the stage like we're in a play!' he laughs. 'Heaven forbid!'

'I did wonder. So where, then?' I ask, my earlier annoyance fast disappearing as I sense his excitement.

'They have this huge open space down below the theatre where they hold wedding ceremonies, corporate events, dances – oh, all sorts. It's just fabulous! Darling, you have to see it. It's a glorious venue, and they're going to decorate it however I want them to.'

'Which is how?' I ask. I can't believe Oscar is going to get married at the Globe Theatre. It's just so random, and yet off the wall enough to be Oscar.

'We're having a *Midsummer Night's Dream* theme!' he enthuses, his eyes sparkling with delight. 'It's going to be stunning. The whole venue will be decorated like a fairy grotto, with lights and lanterns and all sorts of twinkliness.'

'And Luke has agreed to this?' I ask, wondering if Oscar's actually explained to him the level of twinkliness that's going to be involved.

'Oh yes. He's an actor, isn't he – it's perfect for him.'

'The venue is – yes, of course. But does Luke really approve of all the other stuff?'

'Oh, Scarlett, don't be such a spoilsport. I'm not going to have him wearing an ass's head, am I?' Oscar grins. 'I thought Sean might like to take on the role of Bottom!'

I shake my head. 'Oscar, stop it. Are you really serious? We all have to dress up like fairies?'

'Only the main wedding party. I'll be encouraging all the guests to at least try and join in with the theme, though. Even if they only wear some wings or a doublet and hose as an absolute minimum! I'm kidding, sweetie,' he says when I look aghast. 'If the guests wish to embrace the theme, they will be more than encouraged to. If not . . . well, they'll be the ones missing out.'

'It's different, I suppose.'

Oscar looks disappointed.

'But I'm sure it will be simply amazing, Oscar, if *you're* organising it!'

He claps his hands together. 'I will make sure of it, and as my chief bridesmaid you will look simply stunning as Titania, Queen of the Fairies!'

'M-me?' I say, clasping my hand to my chest, more in horror than in gratitude.

'Yes, of course you. Who else would I ask? Ursula will also be a fairy attendant, and Luke's young niece.'

'Wonderful!' I say, trying to drum up some enthusiasm at the thought of being dressed in a fairy costume. 'And when is all this going to take place? You said you had a date?'

'Yes, 20th September,' Oscar announces with great gusto.

'So September next year?' I ask, picking up my glass of beer and thinking I must remember to put that date in my diary as soon as I get back to the apartment.

'No, September *this* year.'

'But how on earth have you managed to do that? Everywhere is always booked up.'

'Cancellation,' Oscar says gravely. 'The couple who had that date are sadly no longer.'

'They split up?'

'No, when I say no longer, I mean no longer. Apparently they both died in a strange poisoning accident.'

I look at him, puzzled. 'Poisoning . . . Really?'

'Yes, their families didn't get on apparently, so the couple both drank a poisonous substance from a bottle and died together. It was quite romantic, actually.'

'Gosh, how awful . . . ' I begin to say. Then I think about it. 'Oscar! That's the end of *Romeo and Juliet*!'

'I almost had you!' Oscar grins. 'Well, it is the Globe, isn't it? Actually, the sad truth is, the groom got made redundant from his job at a bank, so they can't afford to hold their wedding there any more. They're still together, though. Caprice at the Globe told me.' He sits back in his chair with a satisfied expression. 'Mine *was* a better story, though – you have to admit it!'

I shake my head. 'You are incorrigible!'

'I know,' Oscar grins. 'But ya still love me! So that's my wedding. What about yours? You said you had some news for me.'

I tell Oscar all about our new wedding venue, and when I mention The Plaza's name, he lets out a low whistle. 'Goodness, Seany is pushing the boat out. I didn't know he had it in him!'

'I'm paying for some of it too, you know. This isn't the 1930s.'

'Of course you are, darling. But your powers of persuasion must be improving. The Plaza will cost you a small mortgage to hire out.'

'It's not cheap,' I agree. 'But, Oscar, you should see it. It's glorious. I can't wait to marry Sean there. Our wedding day will be just perfect, I know it.'

'Then I'm happy for you,' Oscar says, putting his hand over mine. 'In fact, I'm ecstatic for us both. It seems both our wedding days are going to be everything we've ever dreamed of.'

'And more,' I say, smiling happily at him. 'I've a feeling they're both going to be absolutely amazing!'

Twenty-four

'So tell me again, how do you know Gabriella Romero?' Oscar asks as we all ride along in a taxi towards Gabi's apartment for brunch.

I'm sitting between Oscar and Sean in the back seat of the cab, while Luke sits up front with the driver.

'I told you – we met when she came to a board meeting to donate some money to the trust.' I still haven't told anyone the real reason that Gabi sought me out – not even Sean. Gabi asked me to keep it quiet, and so I have, and I never go back on a promise. As far as anyone else knows, we became friends and I'm helping her to 'broaden her horizons' by taking her out and about in the city. I am of course still trying to find her wayward great-aunt for her, but to be honest, it's proving particularly difficult to find out anything about the estranged Evita and I keep hitting brick walls every which way I turn. But I'm determined not to let Gabi down.

'And you became friends with a superstar celebrity just like that?' Oscar puzzles. 'It doesn't seem very likely. You must have done something, Scarlett?'

'Only be me!' I smile cheerily. 'What's wrong with that?'

'Hmm . . .' Oscar says. 'You're up to something, Scarlett. I know you are.'

'Oscar,' Luke says from the front seat, 'you seem to forget the penchant Scarlett has for befriending celebrities. Are you forgetting the rather gorgeous Mr Cooper?'

'Luke, darling, I could never forget Bradley!' Oscar coos. 'And I've seen parts of him that you can only dream of.'

Luke turns round and raises his eyebrows at Oscar. 'It's a good job I know that story or I might just be a tad concerned by that statement.'

On the night I met Bradley Cooper at the charity auction in New York that Peter was hosting, much to my horror Oscar also bumped into him in the men's lavatories . . . It's a story that Oscar has since relished telling on many an occasion.

'No one should ever be surprised at what Scarlett's capable of,' Sean says calmly. 'I gave up years ago and now I just go with the flow.'

I squeeze his hand on the back seat, and Sean smiles at me.

'Ain't that the truth,' Oscar says. He smiles now too. 'I

guess I should just be pleased I'm going to meet Gabriella Romero. In fact, I'm more than pleased – I'm exploding with excitement back here. Do you think there'll be any celebrities at this do?'

'I doubt it. I think it's just us. Gabi said she'd like to meet you all and offered to hold this brunch.'

Gabi actually suggested dinner to begin with, but when I explained about Luke, and him being on Broadway every night, she immediately changed it to brunch. She seemed very keen to meet my friends, and I was happy to oblige.

We arrive at the apartment block and Henry, the doorman, walks forward to open the door for us.

'Scarlett,' he says jovially, 'good to see you again. It's not often you arrive in a cab.'

'No, Henry, I usually walk across the park, but I have friends with me today.'

Henry nods at the others piling out of the taxi cab. 'Miss Romero is waiting for you all,' he says. 'She seems very happy about your meeting today.'

'Good,' I nod, smiling at him. 'OK for us just to go up?'

'Of course,' Henry says. 'Enjoy!'

We ride up in the lift together to Gabi's apartment, and as the door opens, Luke lets out a low whistle. 'Whoa, very nice,' he says. 'Someone has taste.'

They follow me down the little corridor and I press the bell for Gabi's door.

'Scarlett,' she calls enthusiastically, opening the door to greet us. 'So glad you could make it, and these must be your lovely friends you've told me so much about.'

She greets each one of them warmly with a kiss as they walk through the door and I introduce everyone. Even the usually cool Sean flushes a little when Gabi plants a kiss on his cheek, and Oscar clearly bubbles over with excitement.

'Come through.' She gestures for us all to follow her through to the vast living area I was so amazed at when I first visited, and I wait for their reactions.

Sean immediately wanders over to the enormous plate-glass window to admire the view, as I knew he would, while Luke and Oscar busily take in every detail of the exquisite interior.

'Welcome to my little Manhattan home,' Gabi says. 'I'm so pleased you could all come and join me for brunch today.'

'Thank you so much for inviting us,' Oscar gushes. 'I'm a huge fan, Miss Romero.'

'Please call me Gabi,' she says, smiling at him. 'All my friends do, and any friend of Scarlett's is a friend of mine. Now, drinks!'

A waiter suddenly appears with a tray of juices and Buck's Fizz in fine crystal glasses. 'Now please just help yourself,' Gabi says. 'This has been laid on especially for you all today and I want you to enjoy it.'

We each take a glass from the waiter as he drifts around the room.

'My chef is preparing our brunch as I speak,' she says. 'I've requested an international flavour to our little get-together, so I hope there'll be something for you all to enjoy.'

I'm sensing Gabi is a little nervous about this gathering.

'It sounds delicious, Gabi,' I assure her.

She smiles gratefully at me.

'This is a wonderful place you have here,' Sean says, turning away from the window. 'Quite the view.'

'Thank you, Sean. I'm glad you like it. It is pretty amazing. Tell me, how was yours and Oscar's flight over?'

'It was interesting,' Sean says diplomatically.

'Really? How so?' Gabi asks.

'He means it was interesting seeing how long he could put up with me in close proximity,' Oscar replies, grinning. 'Seany and I don't very often see eye to eye. Do we, Seany?'

'I'm afraid he's right, Gabi,' Sean says, grimacing. 'As you can quite clearly see, Oscar and I are cut from a very different cloth.'

'I'll have you know my outfit today is by a very exciting young designer just off the King's Road.' Oscar gives us a little twirl to display his highly unusual patchwork jacket in shades of green, gold and purple. 'It's unique.'

'You might call it that,' Sean says, pulling a face at Gabi.

'We can't all dress like you, Sean,' Oscar replies. 'It must be so difficult choosing which of your fifty shades of blue shirt to wear every morning.'

'That's quite enough from you two,' I command to put a stop to their bickering. 'It's OK,' I assure Gabi, who's starting to look a tad worried. 'They love each other really. It's just an act.'

'Hmm ...' Sean mumbles under his breath, turning towards the window again.

Oscar picks up his glass of Buck's Fizz and grins at Sean.

'Well, it's good you put your differences aside for the sake of our Scarlett,' Gabi says, sounding more than a little relieved. She smiles at them both.

The doorbell rings.

'Oh, that will be one of my other guests,' Gabi says. 'I hope you don't mind but I've invited a couple more fellow Brits to the party.'

She goes off to answer the door and a few seconds later, to my surprise, Max appears.

'Morning, campers,' he says, nodding at us.

'Maxy!' Oscar squeals, rushing to his side. 'I haven't seen you in absolute yonks!'

'All right, Oscar, keep it down,' Max says as Oscar throws his arms around him. But he's smiling as he does.

Max and Oscar formed an unlikely alliance when they first met a couple of years ago, and now every time Oscar is over in New York with me they meet up again. Max always insists they go somewhere manly like a sports bar or a football game; he simply won't entertain Oscar's favoured cocktail bars and fancy restaurants, and Oscar, unusually, puts up with his conditions.

'Max, how are you?' Luke says, offering his hand. 'I must apologise for my overexuberant friend.'

'I'm used to him by now,' Max says, shaking Luke's hand. 'He'll never change. I understand congratulations are in order.'

'Yes!' Oscar cries happily. 'We're to be wed in September!'

'Here's to you both, then!' Max says, lifting a glass of orange juice from the tray being offered to him. 'You deserve a medal, Luke, taking on this one.'

'Less of your cheek, Maxy,' Oscar says, punching him playfully on the arm. 'Now, I'm a little confused – how do you know our Gabi here?'

Just as Max is about to explain, the doorbell rings again.

'Ah, my last guest,' Gabi says, heading for the door once more.

'Another friend of yours, Scarlett?' Oscar asks.

I shrug. 'Not that I know of.'

We all turn towards the hallway to see who will be coming through the door next. I'm not sure who I'm expecting to see appear in the room with us this time, but as he walks in smiling broadly, I realise it's certainly not Alex.

'Hey, all,' Alex says, waving a hand casually in the air.

'Alex, what on earth are you doing here?' Sean is the first to speak.

'Do you guys know each other?' Gabi asks. 'How wonderful.'

'Alex is going to be best man at our wedding,' Sean says, still looking amazed. 'So you could say that. But how do you two know each other?' He looks between Gabi and Alex.

'Alex is on the board of one of my charities,' Gabi explains. 'I've known him for ages.' She smiles at Alex, then looks around excitedly. 'I can't believe you guys all know each other. I invited Alex along because he's the only Brit I know in New York other than Scarlett, and now Max.'

Max lifts his glass.

'It's a small world,' Alex says. 'Scarlett.' He inclines his head towards me. 'Good to see you again. Plans going well for the wedding?'

'Yes, very well, thank you.' I'm as amazed as Sean is by this turn of events. Alex knows Gabi? This is so weird.

'Oscar,' he says, turning to where Oscar is standing sipping Buck's Fizz with Luke. 'Good to see you again, and this must be the infamous Luke you were telling me about the last time we met.'

'It is indeed,' Oscar says. 'Luke, meet Alex.'

'Hi,' Luke says, shaking Alex's hand. 'Good to meet you.'

Alex looks around the room and spots Max.

'I don't think we've been introduced,' he says. 'Alex Woolfe.'

'Oh, I know who you are,' Max says. He shakes Alex's hand, but not very warmly, I notice. 'We worked together once.'

'We did?' Alex asks, tilting his head to one side as if he's examining Max to try and jolt his memory. 'I'm sorry – I work with a lot of people. In what capacity?'

'I was your cameraman when you were reporting on 9/11,' Max says, eyeing Alex warily. 'Don't worry about it, though – I wouldn't expect you to remember me.'

Max turns away from Alex and wanders over to the window.

'Ah ... a little awkward,' Alex says, grimacing at the rest of us.

'So, Alex, let me get you a drink,' Gabi says breezily. She looks over to Max with concern. 'Max, can I get you another one?'

'I don't suppose you've got your wee barista chappie here today, have you?' Alex asks before Max can speak. 'I'd die for one of his cappuccinos.'

'Of course!' Gabi says, looking pleased. 'I was saving him for after brunch, but let's get him busy right now.'

'She has her own barista?' Oscar whispers to me. 'How wonderfully decadent.'

'You wouldn't happen to have a beer, would you?' Max asks, turning round now. 'It's early, I know, but I suddenly feel like one.'

'Yes, I may have.' Gabi looks in the direction of the kitchen. 'I think Lewis keeps some in there for when he's off duty. I'll go and check for you.'

She hurries off to the kitchen and we're all left in an uncomfortable silence.

'Who's Lewis?' Oscar asks, breaking it.

'Her bodyguard,' I tell him.

'Ooh, does he look like Kevin Costner?' Oscar asks. 'I bet you'd love that, Scarlett.'

'No, he doesn't. He reminds me a bit of him, though. He's very quiet and calm, but you wouldn't want to get in a fight with him.'

'I'm surprised Gabi doesn't have more staff flitting about the place,' Sean says. 'She's mentioned a cook, and this barista chap, but that's it.'

'Gabi prefers it that way,' I explain. 'She trying to do things a little more independently these days. I expect she's given them the morning off.'

'Marcus, Madrid and Portia never take the morning off,' Alex laughs. 'If I know them, they'll be working away on some scheme or other to get Gabi even more publicity.'

'I still can't believe you're here, man,' Sean says, patting Alex on the back. 'Gabriella Romero? I knew you had your finger in some pies when you gave up the reporting, but nothing like this.'

'Sometimes it's better to keep quiet about certain aspects of your life.' His gaze flickers towards me briefly. 'They can be more *productive* then.'

'Coffee's on!' Gabi sings as she comes back into the room. 'And look what I found for you, Max!' She holds up a bottle of Budweiser.

'Thanks,' Max says gratefully. He looks at the top. 'I

don't suppose you have a bottle opener?' he asks almost apologetically.

'Oh dear, I'm not very good at this sort of thing, am I?'

'I'll come and look for one with you,' Max offers. 'I doubt you know what one even looks like!'

'How does Max know Gabi?' Alex asks, as they both disappear to the kitchen. 'Through you, Scarlett? You seem to be the key ingredient in this smorgasbord of people here this morning.'

'Sort of.' And I quickly explain how Max came to Gabi's rescue at the Top of the Rock the other day.

'Seems like Max is quite the hero,' Alex says when I've finished.

'He helped us out of a tight spot that day, for sure.'

'And how do the rest of you know Max?' Alex asks now. 'This is all very peculiar and small worldish.'

'He worked with my brother as his cameraman for a while.'

'Your brother is a reporter?' Alex asks with interest. 'Would I know him?'

'I doubt it,' I begin, but just then Max and Gabi return, laughing, from the kitchen.

'Brunch is served!' Gabi sings happily. 'If you'd all like to go out onto the terrace . . .'

We troop out onto the balcony terrace where I stood a few weeks ago and admired the view. There is a huge long table covered with a white cloth, and covering that a vast spread of every breakfast food you can think of, from bagels with smoked salmon to pancakes with jugs of syrup, and eggs, lots of eggs – scrambled, poached, boiled, every possible way you can think of to cook an egg has been catered for. Then just beyond that is another white-clothed dining table, laid with silver cutlery and fine white bone china. There are several big patio heaters running the length of the terrace, so everything is kept warm and cosy for us on this April morning.

'Wow, Gabi,' I say, staring at the table. 'This looks amazing.'

'Thank you,' she says happily. 'I've tried to cater for everyone's tastes. Please help yourselves.'

A queue forms quickly in front of the food table and we all help ourselves to our favoured breakfast foods.

I choose the delicious-looking pancakes with a drizzle of maple syrup, and I'm pleased to find they taste every bit as good as they look.

'So, how're the wedding plans coming along?' Alex asks, taking a sip of his cappuccino, after we've been sitting down feasting on our breakfast delights for a few minutes.

'Good, thank you,' I reply. 'Now we have a venue, things are a little more plain sailing. Still much to do, but we'll get there.'

'I understand from Scarlett we have you to thank for our reception at The Plaza,' Sean says, lifting his own coffee cup as if to toast Alex.

'Ah ... well, sometimes it helps to know a few people,' Alex smiles. 'And I'm pleased to be able to help you both.'

'You're getting married at The Plaza?' Max says. 'Pricey.'

'It's not cheap, Max, no,' Sean says. 'However, hopefully I'll only ever do it the once!'

'I'll make sure you do!' I wink at Sean over the table.

'I think it's romantic,' Gabi says. 'I've been to a few weddings there and The Plaza is simply stunning as a venue.'

'Still,' Max continues, 'it's a lot of money just for one day. Weddings are ridiculously overrated in my opinion.'

'Not a romantic, then, Max?' Alex grins.

'Nope,' Max replies stoutly. 'Never have been.'

'You've never met the right woman, then,' Alex chides. 'Maybe when you do, you'll want to shower her with flowers and gifts, and her ideal wedding.'

Max eyes Alex warily. 'Maybe. Is that what you do, then? Shower your lady friends with expensive presents? Must be costly for you.'

Alex's smile stiffens a little. 'I'm married myself, Max. There's only one lady I shower with gifts, and that's my Charlotte.'

Max eyes Alex for a second. Then he nods silently and reaches for his glass of beer.

'I'm sure Max will make someone a lovely husband one day,' Gabi says brightly, attempting to cut through the awkward atmosphere.

Max looks across the table at Gabi. 'That's kind of you to say, but I don't think so. Too stuck in my ways, me.'

'Well, I think your ways are very endearing,' Gabi replies, still looking coyly at Max. 'I like people who speak their mind. Can't bear people who spin you a load of bull.'

Max's cheeks redden. 'Thanks,' he mumbles, pushing back his chair and standing up. 'Er ... think I'll just get some more food if that's OK?'

I'm really beginning to think Gabi *has* got a soft spot for Max ... And as I watch Max hurry over to the buffet table with flushed cheeks, the feeling might be mutual ... I vow to find out the truth the next time Gabi and I are alone, and if so, help the two of them along a little ...

'Can't bear bullshitters,' Oscar says, continuing the conversation. 'So full of their own pomposity and lies.'

'Me neither,' I agree, turning my gaze away from Max. 'Dishonesty is the thing I dislike most in people.'

'Scarlett is very big on the truth,' Sean says. 'She hates lies. Except when she asks me if her bum looks big in something. Then I find,' he continues over the laughter, 'it's best to tell a few white ones.'

'It's true,' I say, smiling with everyone else.

'Talking of bums looking big,' Luke says, winking at me, 'have you found your elusive wedding dress yet?'

'No.' I shake my head. 'It's proving ... difficult.'

Oscar raises his eyes to the sky. 'Difficult is an understatement. Impossible would be closer to the truth.'

'It's not my fault I can't find anything,' I huff. I look around the table. 'They all look the same to me. I want something different.'

'I might be able to put you in touch with someone,' Gabi suggests. 'I have loads of contacts in that area. I'm sure we could find you the perfect dress.'

I'm about to thank her when I hear Oscar cough loudly.

'That's really generous of you, Gabi, but Oscar has said he'll help me find my perfect dress, and I'm certain he will ... eventually.'

Oscar nods approvingly at me.

'Well, if you'd like any help, Oscar, you know where I am,' Gabi offers.

'Thank you,' Oscar concedes graciously. 'I'll keep you in mind. That's very kind of you, Gabi.'

We finish up our brunch and Guido makes us more coffees, which we take back inside the apartment.

Max is talking to Gabi about places he's filmed. Alex is deep in conversation with Luke about his Broadway show. Oscar has gone to the 'little boys' room', although I know from experience there's nothing little about the bathroom he's using right now. Meanwhile Sean and I stand looking out over Central Park through the long window.

'Glorious, isn't it,' I sigh. 'Gabi is very lucky to wake up to this every morning.'

'Yep,' Sean agrees, 'it sure is. But I wouldn't want to trade places with her, even for this view, would you?'

I shake my head. 'No. Her life is far too controlled and scrutinised to be fun.'

'Did you notice she didn't eat much at breakfast?'

Sean says. 'And when I say not much, I mean hardly a crumb.'

'Gabi is on one of her strict diets right now,' I explain. 'She's put on a few pounds just lately.'

I don't explain that the few pounds are more than likely due to the regular visits we now make to Starbucks, and Gabi's penchant for sweet, syrupy, cream-topped coffees and the odd blueberry muffin.

I've already had a talk from Marcus about restricting Gabi's calorie intake when I'm out with her. I of course listened to him politely, then promptly ignored his advice by taking Gabi to Serendipity 3 for frozen hot chocolate – the restaurant's delicious speciality.

Gabi adored this outing, in part due to the frozen hot chocolate and in part to the fact she'd just watched the movie *Serendipity* the night before. Another on my list of suggestions.

'Must be a nightmare being in the spotlight constantly like that,' Sean continues. 'I'd hate it.'

'Yes, you probably would.' I kiss him on the cheek. I miss Sean so much when we're away from each other it's good to have him by my side again, if only for a short while. I look around the room. 'How odd that Gabi knows Alex, though. Bit of a turn-up for the books.'

Sean shrugs. 'Not really. Like I said, Alex has his finger in many pies. Not always ones as sweet as Gabi, though.'

I wonder what he means.

'A bit like him knowing someone on The Plaza Hotel

board,' I say. 'If he hadn't, we'd still be looking for some-where now. It's a good job you told him all about our problems finding a venue.'

'I didn't tell him,' Sean says. 'I thought you had.'

I think about this. I'd talked with Alex about our wedding problems when we had dinner. But I'm sure he seemed to know all about our issues with a venue before I mentioned trying to book The Plaza.

I shake my head. 'Perhaps it was me then,' I say, still churning it over. 'I've had so much on my mind just lately. But it was you that gave Alex my address so he knew where to find me when he came to New York – wasn't it? He was heading across the park to visit me the day I bumped into him.'

'I didn't do that either,' Sean says, looking quizzically at me.

'My phone number?' I ask. 'Surely that was you?'

Sean shakes his head. 'Today is the first time I've spoken to Alex since we were in Scotland.'

We both turn to look at Alex. 'Well, if you didn't,' I ask, 'then who did?'

Twenty-five

The rest of the morning is very pleasant and enjoyable.

I don't manage to get Alex on his own to enquire how he knew so much about me and my movements in New York because he has to dash off for a business meeting pretty soon after we've eaten. 'With your friend Peter, of all people,' he informs me as he grabs his jacket and heads out of the door. 'Another link to you, Scarlett! It seems we have much in common.'

I don't feel the need to reply, as Alex is escorted to the door by Gabi.

'Who introduced him to Peter?' Max asks. 'Not you, Scarlett, surely?'

I nod.

Max is about to pull a face, but then remembers Sean is here and thinks better of it. 'You really *do* seem to be the lynchpin in all this, don't you?' he says instead. 'What else of yours can Alex get involved in?'

I decide Max and I need to have a private chat about Alex. It's quite clear Max doesn't like him, and I want to know why.

'Ah, Alex is just like that,' Sean says. 'He's one of those people who always seems to know everyone!'

'Possibly ...' Max says. 'Look, I've got to go too. It's been lovely, Gabi, thank you. Well, you can thank your staff.' He winks at her and Gabi goes all coy again.

'I will do, Max, and thank you for coming. Maybe we can do it again sometime?'

'Sure,' Max says, his whole neck flushing this time as well as his cheeks. 'You have my number now, so if you decide you'd like to do something, great. If not, then no worries.'

'Oh, I'll be in touch, Max,' Gabi says, actually fluttering her long eyelashes. 'Be in no doubt of that.'

Max mumbles some sort of goodbye gesture at us and hurries out of the door.

The rest of us decide that it's probably a good time to go now too, so we say our goodbyes and thank yous.

'It's been wonderful to meet you all,' Gabi says as we stand at the door. 'Scarlett is very lucky to have such good friends. I only wish I had half her luck.'

'Don't worry, Gabi,' Oscar says, giving her a hug. 'We can all be your friends now too.'

Gabi hugs him back. 'Thank you, Oscar. That means so much.'

'And . . .' Oscar pauses for effect, 'I'll even let you help with finding the perfect wedding dress for Scarlett if you'd still like to be involved.'

Gabi looks on the verge of tears. 'Oh, I would, Oscar. I'd like that very much.'

I feel quite choked up myself as I say goodbye to Gabi. It's been lovely to see her enjoy the company of many of the people I hold dear to me. And then seeing Oscar offering to share responsibility for my dress was the icing on the cake, because I know how much it means to him.

So as we leave the penthouse and ride down in the lift, I feel an overwhelming sense that all is good in the world. And then I think about Alex, and for some reason the feeling of goodness is replaced by something very unsettling indeed.

The weeks pass, the blossom falls in Central Park, and the weather warms as April turns into May, then May into June. I manage to take a quick trip back to London, but Sean and I spend most of our time doing wedding things – like organising invitations and arguing over what music we might have to waft us up and down the aisle. We finally settle on 'Trumpet Voluntary' for me to walk down The Plaza's promised tree-lined wedding aisle, and 'Spring' from Vivaldi's *Four Seasons* for us both to walk back up it as a married couple.

I think Sean is quite impressed I'm familiar with these pieces of classical music, but I don't let on that I searched for 'the perfect wedding music' on Google and that these were my two favourites when I played them on YouTube.

I manage to catch up with Oscar while I'm in London to find out how his search for my wedding dress is coming along. Surprisingly I find out he's been spending a lot of time on Skype with Gabi and they're working on something 'top secret' right now. It's a good job I trust Oscar. I know he won't come up with anything garish and meringue-like for me. I think of *Four Weddings and a Funeral*, where I first heard this term for a frothy wedding dress. I never thought when I surreptitiously watched that film as a child that I'd one day be organising my own wedding, and in New York, too. I had to sneak that video into the house and watch it when my dad was out one day. My neighbour let me borrow it because I wasn't old enough to buy a 15-rated film at the time. I smile to myself; those were the days – big, bulky VHS tapes on my old Hitachi video recorder. My movie obsession started early.

Oscar's wedding plans are coming along a treat too. He shows me some preliminary sketches for his and Luke's Shakespeare-inspired outfits, and I have to admit they do look pretty special. He measures me for my Titania dress, and even though I'm still not sure about being 'Queen of the Fairies', again I trust Oscar not to make me look a fool.

I try to catch up with Maddie too while I'm in London, but unusually she's away on business. I wanted to check on how things were going for her and Felix. She never really says much about it in her emails, and trying to pin her down to some Skype time is proving almost impossible these days. But she is at last coming over to visit me in New York very soon after I get back, so I am absolutely determined we'll discuss it more then.

I don't see much of Alex either after Gabi's brunch. He sends me a quick text one day to say he is flying back to the UK for a while, but he'll be back in NYC very soon and he hopes all is well. I still haven't discovered how he knew so much about me when we first met up in New York. I attempt to speak to Max about Alex, but he's cagey and doesn't seem to want to say too much. I think because Alex is Sean's friend, Max is trying to be diplomatic, which is annoying, but admirable, I guess.

So although something about Alex still doesn't sit right with me, I have to believe for now all is well.

It's the summer and I'm back in NYC again. It's not so hot right now that I'm complaining about the heat, but I know from past experience just how hot the summer can be in Manhattan. Last year while I was here, the temperature soared into the nineties, almost hitting a hundred degrees on one day. I love New York, but that was seriously testing my loyalty to this great city. Luckily, nearly everywhere you go has fantastic air-conditioning, and I've quickly found the only way to cope with soaring temperatures is to move very quickly from one cool building to another, allowing just enough time for my body temperature to come down before I venture out into the heat again.

But today, as I await Maddie's arrival in the city this afternoon, it's quite a pleasant eighty degrees outside, and a much cooler seventy-two in my apartment.

I'm currently chasing up some leads on Gabi's great-aunt. She really is proving impossible to find. I checked all the obituaries as standard when I first began to look for her, and the mortuary records. It might sound a bit ghoulish, but it's what we have to do at the trust when we search for a missing adult. So I know that she is likely still alive somewhere, but where exactly?

If she changed her name way back when, I'll have virtually no chance of ever tracing her, but I am clinging to the hope she didn't go to quite those extremes when her family turned its back, and that she is just one of those people who hasn't left any trace through life.

The easiest people to find are those who use the internet regularly. Facebook is one of the first places we check when looking for someone. Nearly everyone has Facebook. Even the more mature have accounts these days; it helps them stay in touch with friends and family. But not Evita, it seems – she is one of the few who choose to stay well away. Good for you, I think, even if it makes my job a lot harder!

Evita is such an unusual name. I am very grateful to Gabi's great-grandparents for choosing it, as it made eliminating the wrong people very quick and simple. In this case, however, it doesn't make finding the right one any easier. I am currently investigating some new leads through the other sources we have available to us, like public records and genealogy services, in the hope one of them turns something up.

Gabi is away recording her new album in LA, but I'm keeping her informed of any progress, which isn't very often. I'm determined to crack this one, though. Gabi has become a good friend over the last few months, as well as a client, and I want to do this for her and her family.

I look at my watch. Maddie will be here shortly; the flight landed on time – I've checked – so with passport control and a taxi journey from JFK Airport, I am expecting her anytime now.

I get up and take a look outside my window to see if there's any sign of a yellow cab. As I do, I catch sight of my neighbour opposite. He's sitting at his desk by his window, using his computer. As if he senses me watching, he looks across and waves. I smile and wave back. This is highly unusual; mostly the residents of the apartment block opposite play the game of pretending no one else exists. 'If I don't acknowledge you're there, then you can't see me.' When I first moved into the building, I was fascinated by the comings and goings of the people opposite. You can tell a lot about a person from the short snippets of their life you get to see through their apartment windows. I'd been a huge fan of the television series *Friends*, and although I didn't have an 'ugly naked guy' living opposite me, it was quite surprising what people did in full view of their window with the lights on! But I soon realised trying to interact with the residents of the apartment block opposite wasn't the done thing in New York and I reverted to playing 'the game' with them all. All except for 'Bob', as I like to call him. Bob is friendly and will always wave whenever we happen to be by our windows at the same time. I know nothing about him except he spends a lot of time sitting at his computer, so I assume he must be some sort of writer. We never see each other outside of our apartments, never bump into one another on the street below. Bob is simply my window buddy, and I like it that way.

I see a yellow cab pull up by the kerb down below and Maddie climbs out with a holdall and a handbag in her hands. Not much luggage, I think, looking at her bags, but then Maddie and Felix backpacked round the world together, so she's used to travelling light.

But then the driver steps out of the cab too and walks round to the back of the taxi. He lifts a large black suitcase from the boot and wheels it onto the sidewalk.

What? I think. *How long has she come for?!* This isn't like Maddie at all. She always travels light, and would often tease me about my own 'in case of' way of packing for a trip when we holidayed together in the past.

I hurry down the interior stairs of the brownstone to greet Maddie as she presses on the doorbell.

'Maddie!' I squeal. 'You're here at last!'

Maddie hugs me tightly. 'Exciting, isn't it? I've been looking forward to this trip for ages.'

We carry Maddie's luggage up to my apartment, and I put her bags into the little box room that I usually keep all my junk in, but tidied especially for her visit. I've even bought a little sofa bed to put in there. I don't have many visitors, and I don't think Sean would be too pleased if I suggested the spare room to him! Oscar has come over to stay a few times, but we've always bedded down together in the huge king-size bed I have and had girly chats until late into the night. So I thought it was about time that I got a spare bed for visitors. However, I thought as I purchased the sofa bed that I now had something to threaten Sean with if he should start snoring any more frequently and loudly than he already did ...

'So, do you want to unpack?' I ask her, looking at the big black suitcase ominously. 'You seem to have brought quite a lot of stuff with you.'

Maddie looks at the suitcase. 'Yes, maybe I have come a little bit more prepared than I usually do. It's not full, though. I've left plenty of space for shopping!'

Ah ... so that was it. I didn't think the case felt that heavy when I lifted it up the stairs with her.

'No, I don't want to unpack yet,' she says, her eyes shining with excitement. 'I can do that later. Let me freshen up and we can hit the city tonight. Manhattan, here we come!'

Maddie and I take the subway into the heart of the city, and we're now having dinner in a little Mexican restaurant

I know, not far off Times Square. It's a bit touristy, but this is Maddie's first proper trip here, so she is entitled to be as touristy as she likes. When she came over for Sean's and my engagement, she was only here a day before she had to fly back home.

It's quite surprising considering how much time I spend here in New York that this is Maddie's first trip to see me. But before now she's always been too busy with her job, or jetting off somewhere with Felix, and we've just never got round to synching our diaries so that she could visit while I'm here.

'So what's been happening with you?' I ask her after we've ordered. We're both having fajitas, chicken for me, vegetarian for Maddie.

Maddie shrugs. 'Not much.'

I'm put on guard already. Maddie never says, 'Not much.' She always has lots to say about her life and her job. It's all I can do to get a word in sometimes.

'Not much?' I repeat lightly. 'That's not like you. You must have been doing something.'

Maddie sighs and proceeds to tell me a worthy but dull story about a charity donation that came into her office and how she's deciding the best place for the money to go to be of the most benefit.

'OK . . . ' I say when she's finished. 'Now tell me the real story about what's going on in your life. How's Felix, for instance?'

Our food is delivered at that moment and Maddie is given a reprieve. But once the waiter has left and we've finished spreading guacamole and sour cream on our tortilla wraps and sprinkling sizzling chicken and vegetables into the centre of each one, I ask her again.

'So you were going to tell me about Felix . . . '

Maddie eyes me over her fajita. She chews slowly on the bite she's just taken before speaking. 'Felix is fine.'

'Just fine?' I press. She's not getting away with that.

Maddie puts down her wrap and wipes her hands carefully on her napkin.

'Yes, he was just fine the last time I saw him.'

'The last time you saw him?'

'Scarlett, stop repeating everything I say. Felix has moved out for a while. He's moved in with his brother in Battersea.'

'What! Why didn't you tell me?'

'Nothing to tell. It's happened. I'm dealing with it.'

I watch Maddie open-mouthed while she begins tucking calmly into her fajita again. Something doesn't add up.

'What?' she asks, looking at me. 'There's nothing you could have done about it, if that's what you're thinking. Felix is Felix. He's not going to change.'

'How do you mean?'

Maddie sighs and puts her food down again. 'Look, Scarlett, I don't expect you to understand what I'm about to say because I know you've not had many relationships in the past, and you've only known Sean a relatively short while.' She takes a deep breath. 'Things change when you've known someone as long as I've known Felix. You change as a person, and you hope that your partner will change and grow with you.'

I try and digest this information, along with my spicy food.

'How do you mean exactly?'

Maddie sighs. 'We may have only been *married* a few years, but we've known each other a lot longer than that. We met when I was twenty, and Felix was twenty-three. People change a lot over ten years.'

'But still . . . ' I'm flailing a bit. I knew Maddie and Felix had been having problems, but now Maddie is sitting here opening up to me, I don't know what to say.

'It happens, Scarlett. Couples who seem perfect together when they first meet sometimes grow apart when they have been together a while. They don't want it to happen, and they try everything to make it work again like it did at the beginning. And believe me, we did try! But nothing was working for us. We even had counselling.'

'But can't you try a holiday or something?' I suggest, knowing how weak this sounds. 'You two always loved to travel in the past.'

'Exactly. In the past. We visited almost everywhere we'd ever wanted to go when we backpacked round the world. There's nowhere left to go now.' She pauses, and her face fills with sadness. 'On our travels, or sadly for us as a couple, it would seem.'

'Oh, Maddie –' I grab her hand across the table '– I'm so

sorry. I knew you were having problems, but I didn't realise it was this bad.'

Maddie nods, and her eyes glisten with tears. 'I never thought it would come to this, Scarlett. I thought Felix and I were forever.'

'Maybe you are.' I try and sound bright. 'Maybe this is just a little hitch. All relationships have them. And this trial separation might make you realise how much you love each other.'

Maddie shakes her head. 'I thought that for a while, but now I just can't see a way back for us.'

'Oh, Mad.' I really don't know what to say. I feel awful. I've been so tied up with my own wedding plans that I didn't realise my best friend's marriage was falling apart.

'Anyway –' Maddie blinks back her tears and tries to fake a smile '– I'm here now, and I want to have a whale of a time with my best friend while I am!'

'Yes,' I join in with her optimism. 'Let's forget all about men and just have a lovely girly time while you're here. No males allowed.'

'Yeah,' Maddie replies, not sounding utterly convinced. 'Let's try that.'

Twenty-six

Maddie and I go all over the city the next day, visiting as many New York landmarks as we can without completely exhausting ourselves.

We're just having a quick coffee and a rest after we've ridden all the way to the top of the Empire State Building, and Maddie has had the obligatory photos taken on the eighty-sixth-floor viewing deck, when my phone rings. It's Peter.

'I'd better get this,' I explain to Maddie. 'It's Peter. He knows you're here, so it must be important for him to call.'

Maddie nods as her own phone beeps with a text, and she retrieves it from her bag to investigate.

'Hi, Peter. What's up? ... What?' I ask, shocked by his reply. 'How can that be? ... No, I have no idea how that might have happened … Yes, sure. I'm not too far away from the office. I'll come right over.'

I end the call.

'I'm really sorry, Maddie, but I'm going to have to leave you on your own for a bit. There's been a strange story leaked to the American press about The Dragonfly Trust. They're not publishing it until we can clarify if it's true or not. I have to go across to the office and speak with Peter.'

'Sure, no problem,' Maddie says, not looking too worried. 'I'll be just fine.'

I start to gather up my things from the table. 'So what will you do while I'm gone? I'll text you as soon as I know how long I'll be.'

Maddie shrugs. 'I don't know. A bit of shopping maybe. Should you give me a key to your apartment in case you're gone a while?'

'Er … I'm sure I won't be that long. The story is complete fabrication. Once we clear it up, I'll be out of there.'

'Sure,' Maddie says again. 'If you'd rather not.'

'I tell you what – I have a spare at the apartment. I'll let you have that one when we get back, just in case.'

Maddie nods. 'Just before you go, Scarlett, I was thinking of stocking up on underwear while I'm here. Is there a Victoria's Secret nearby?'

'Yes, there is, actually. Near Macy's on Herald Square. Just head down 34th Street and you're there.'

'Great,' Maddie says, smiling. 'Look, don't rush – I'm sure I can amuse myself while you're gone.'

'OK.' I head out of the door. 'See you in a bit. I'll text you when I'm done!'

Maddie just waves, and the last I see of her she's casually finishing up her coffee.

The press story is really ridiculous. The *New York Times* has been tipped off that we're actually running the trust to cover up a million-pound gambling ring. That's how we make our money, betting on the outcome of football games and other sporting events, not people gambling on us finding their families.

Luckily for us, the *New York Times*, thinking it all sounded a little far-fetched, called Peter, as he is a well-known and highly respected businessman in the city, to warn him and check on the validity of the story.

Peter and I spend the rest of the afternoon showing a journalist from the *Times* our books and records and photos of genuine people we've helped reunite with their lost family members.

To his credit, the journalist does look pretty shame-faced throughout our defence. He says he's only come along because his boss has forced him to. He actually knows someone whose family we've helped, so he's in no doubt that we're genuine.

When the journalist finally leaves the office, happy we're a hundred per cent legit, Peter flops down into my leather office chair and sighs.

'That was too close for comfort,' he says. 'We were very

lucky today, Scarlett. If it had been another newspaper that was tipped off, we might not have been so fortunate. They might have just printed the story and then been forced to issue an apology afterwards when we sued. But by then the damage would have been done, The Dragonfly Trust's reputation ripped to pieces.'

'But who would have made up such a thing?' I ask. 'We don't have any enemies, do we? How could we? We're a charity, for heaven's sake!'

Peter swivels the chair back and forth, pondering this.

'It doesn't add up, that's for sure. I guess we'll just have to be grateful for now that it wasn't a lot worse. But don't you worry, Scarlett – I'll get to the bottom of this.'

'I hope so. I don't want to have to go through that again. I felt like I was on trial.'

Peter nods, then glances at the clock on my wall. 'Hadn't you better be getting back to your friend Maddie? She'll be wondering where you are.'

'Yes.' I follow his gaze to the clock. 'Although, I've left her shopping, so I'm sure she'll be fine.'

On my way down in the elevator, I text Maddie.

All sorted, thank goodness! Where are you at the moment?

I wait for her reply. But nothing comes. *Hmm*, I think as I step out into the warm, muggy afternoon air. *Where should I go and wait until she texts me back?*

234

I decide on Bryant Park. I'll get a drink and sit under the trees in the shade; Maddie can't be too far away.

I buy an iced drink from a vendor and find a free table and chair to sit and drink it. I love Bryant Park; it's a small park by New York standards, dropped right in the middle of the busy shopping thoroughfares. It backs onto the New York Public Library, and in the summer a massive outdoor cinema screen is erected for its summer film festival. They show an assortment of movies throughout the summer months, and more than once I've joined the crowds to view classics such as *Roman Holiday*, *Butch Cassidy and the Sundance Kid*, *The Wizard of Oz* and *E.T.*

I look at my phone again. Maddie still hasn't texted back, so I send her another in case the first one didn't get through.

After another few minutes have passed I'm just about to ring her when my phone beeps.

I'm up on Fifth Avenue near Central Park. Where are you?

Near Central Park? She must have made her way through a good few shops to be all the way up there.

Don't worry, I text back. I'll walk up and meet you. We can walk through the park together to my apartment.

Her reply comes back immediately this time: OK. I'm where the horses and carriages are. I'll wait here for you.

I walk up Fifth Avenue, still turning the fake newspaper story over in my head. Who on earth would have it in for us, a charity? God, there were some weird people about. Thank goodness the *New York Times* was one of the more trustworthy papers. I dread to think what would have happened if it had been one of the more salacious publications they had over here.

I spy Maddie sitting at the entrance to the park on one of the many benches. She smiles when she sees me, and I sit down next to her.

'See that couple over there,' she says, nodding in the direction of an elderly couple sitting opposite us. 'I've just found out they're actually sitting on their very own bench.'

Nearly all the benches in Central Park are dedicated to someone, whether it be a couple or a dearly departed loved one. They all have a little plaque on the back of the bench and are all lovely, and often quite touching to read. They remind me of the bench in one of the locked gardens in Notting Hill, both the movie version and a real one where Sean and I first sat together.

'Really? That's amazing. In all the times I've rested on a bench in Central Park I've never seen that before.'

'Can you imagine being married as long as them?' Maddie asks, watching the couple. 'To Sean?'

I look at the couple sitting peacefully together on the bench. Occasionally one of them will lean across to say something to the other, but mostly they just sit quietly, enjoying watching the people who pass them by and the warmth of the summer sun as it peeks through the trees above.

'Yes, I can, actually,' I say, meaning it. 'I'd like nothing better than to be that happy and content when I'm reaching my twilight years. And I'd like to think that Sean will be the one sitting next to me, making me feel that way.'

'That's so lovely,' Maddie says, nodding. 'It really is. I'm pleased for you. For you and for Sean.'

I glance over at Maddie; her eyes are filled with tears.

'Oh, Maddie, it doesn't have to be the end for you and Felix. You can still try.'

Maddie takes a deep, calming breath. 'I think it does, Scarlett. You see, it's not that simple any more.' She turns towards me. 'There's someone else.'

'Someone else?' I repeat, after a few seconds. 'You mean for Felix?'

Maddie shakes her head. 'No, for me.'

I'm completely thrown by her admission.

'Wh-who? When? I mean, how can there be?'

Maddie smiles now. 'Oh, Scarlett, sometimes you can be so innocent. Sometimes you just meet someone else, some-one new who makes your heart pound and your spirit soar like your old partner used to. I didn't set out to find some-one else; it just happened.'

I don't know whether to feel upset or angry with Maddie. I've been feeling awful since she arrived, thinking

I'd neglected her in her hour of need, and all the time she's been carrying on with someone else.

'It didn't have to happen, though, did it?' I say at last. 'You could have said no.'

'No, you're right, it didn't. But it's happened to me. And I can't go back now.'

'Who is he, then?' I can hardly bear to look at Maddie. I notice the cute elderly couple have now vacated their seat and a down-and-out is now rootling through the bin next to the bench.

'I'd rather not say, if you don't mind.'

'Why? Do I know him?'

Maddie is silent.

'So I do! Who is it? That chap who was at your birthday party last year? The friend of Felix's who wouldn't leave you alone? What was his name? Something beginning with "A"? Alan – that was it! Is it him?'

'No, it's not Alan. As if! Give me some credit.'

I think. 'Who, then? I can't think of anyone else. How can it be someone I know?'

Maddie looks straight ahead. She wrinkles her nose up as she sees the tramp lift a McDonald's carton from the bin, open it and begin to wolf the half-eaten remnants of a Big Mac.

'Why won't you tell me?' I demand. 'I thought we were friends.'

'We are,' Maddie says, looking at me again now. 'Of course we are. It's just this is a *delicate* situation.'

'What do you mean, delicate?' I think about her choice of words. 'You mean he's married, don't you?'

Maddie nods.

'Maddie! That makes it even worse. Has he split with his partner too?'

Maddie shakes her head. 'But they're in a loveless marriage,' she defends before I can speak. 'He's told me all about it.'

'I bet he has,' I murmur under my breath. 'Isn't that what all men say when they're playing away from home?'

'Scarlett –' Maddie is the one getting angry now '– you know nothing about this, OK, so don't judge.'

'I'm not judging. Well, maybe I am a bit. But how do you expect me to react? In the space of a few hours you've told me your marriage is over, Felix has moved out, and now you're having an affair with someone I know.'

'I didn't tell you that. You presumed it was someone you knew.'

'Well, is it or isn't it?'

Maddie sighs. 'You're not going to let this rest until I tell you, are you?'

I shake my head.

She looks up to the sky.

Is she asking for heavenly help? I wonder. *A sudden bolt of lightning that will strike a tree next to us and give her an excuse not to tell me for a while?* But sadly for Maddie none is forthcoming.

She looks at me again. 'Promise you won't be cross.

Promise you'll let me explain before you fly off the handle.'

I nod, wondering all the time what she's going to say. My mind is still racing with possibilities, but none that fit.

Then suddenly, just as Maddie opens her mouth to speak, I blurt out, 'It's Alex, isn't it?'

Twenty-seven

Maddie simply nods.

'Alex!' I exclaim so loudly that a shopper on his way back from a spree in Abercrombie & Fitch – actually, make that tourist if he's been in there and bought that much stuff – turns to look at us on the bench as he passes.

'Keep your voice down, Scarlett,' Maddie hisses.

'Sorry,' I whisper. 'But Alex? Seriously ... *Why?*'

'Why not?' Maddie asks. She's smiling now in that dreamy way that people in a new relationship do. 'He's gorgeous.'

'If you like that sort of thing, I suppose.' *Bloody hell, Maddie is having an affair with Alex? I knew I couldn't trust him.*

'Yes, I do. Very much, as it happens.'

'But how long has it been going on?' I ask.

'Look, let's not discuss this any more here. Shall we go back to your apartment and talk where it's private?'

I nod. 'Yes, I think that might be best.'

We head back across the park towards my apartment. It's a fairly stilted conversation as we walk. There was only one topic I wanted to discuss with Maddie right now, and it wasn't the roller-bladers that passed us, or the tourists having their photo taken by the Angel of the Waters, or the Strawberry Fields memorial.

'Are you hungry?' I ask as we walk along 77th Street and past the Museum of Natural History on Central Park West. It wasn't too often I let myself wander towards this burger house. But this situation with Maddie made me feel like a medicinal trip might be in order.

'Yes, very. Why?'

'Then I know just the place.'

We stop off at Shake Shack, an iconic burger chain in New York. The burgers, fries and milkshakes there are some of *the* best in Manhattan. The calorie count might be off the scale, but the taste of their food is too.

'They sell doggie treats to take away here!' Maddie exclaims with joy as we queue up to order. 'How wonderful.'

'Yep,' I agree, looking up at the menu. 'They absolutely adore their dogs here on the Upper West Side.'

We collect our food and then hurry along with our paper bags to my apartment before it gets cold.

'Right,' I say, when we're sitting down in my living area, food laid out in front of us. 'Let's do this.'

Maddie chews thoughtfully on her burger. 'Mmm, this is fab, Scarlett.'

'I know. I don't venture there very often, but it's good when you're in need!'

'And you're "in need" now?' Maddie asks. 'Have I shocked you?'

I put my burger down and take a sip of my shake.

'Yes,' I reply carefully. 'You have a bit.'

'Why? Because I'm having an affair, or because of who I'm having it with?'

'Both,' I reply honestly.

Maddie doesn't say anything; she looks down and studies the burger in her hand.

'It's just not like you, Maddie. What's happened to make you change?'

Maddie rests her burger back down on its paper.

'The honest answer to that, Scarlett, is I don't know. If you'd asked me a year ago did I think I'd have an affair, I'd have laughed in your face. But things change. Relationships change. New people come into your life and you start to wonder if it might be better with someone else.'

'Like Alex?' I ask, trying to remain calm.

Maddie nods.

'But he's married!'

'So am I!' Maddie says, waving her rings under my

243

nose. 'But it doesn't mean we can't fall for someone else. Especially if we've fallen out of love with our own partner.'

'Oh, Maddie, you don't mean that. You still love Felix – I know you do.'

Maddie nods. 'Yes, of course I still love him, but I'm not *in* love with him any more, Scarlett.'

I sigh. Even though I don't feel like it, I eat a little more of my burger and a couple of fries to give me some thinking time.

'And how does *Alex* –' I can hardly bear to say his name '– feel about you?'

Maddie smiles in that dreamy way again.

Damn, she's got it bad.

'He feels the same way about me as I do about him.'

'You're sure?'

She nods.

I think about this.

'But how is this working? Sorry to sound so practical among all your lovey-dovey stuff, but Alex has been here in New York for most of the year, like me. And the two of you only met in Edinburgh for the first time, didn't you?'

'Yes, but he's been back and forth to the UK a couple of times like you, Scarlett. And we talk on Skype all the time.'

'Skype? You're having an affair with someone over Skype!'

Maddie sighs now. 'No, but that's how we communicate a lot of the time. When we're so far away, it's the only way we can see each other.'

I shake my head. I'm having trouble comprehending all this. Maddie is one of my best friends. I just can't believe this is happening. And with Alex, one of Sean's best friends. It should be the ideal situation, but it isn't. It's just awful.

'But he's not miles away right now, is he?' I ask. 'Is that why you've finally made the trip over to see me? So you can carry on with Alex while you're here?'

Maddie looks up at me cagily. 'I'm not going to lie to you, Scarlett. That was one of my reasons. But not my *main* reason,' she insists when my face falls. 'I wanted to see my best friend again and have some fun with *you*.' She reaches out for my hand, but I pull it away.

'But you're going to see him while you're here?' I hate sounding so disapproving and prudish, but I can't help it. There's something about this situation that doesn't sit well with me, and it's not just the affair part.

Maddie flushes slightly.

'Oh my God, you already have!' I cry. 'Today, when I had to go back to the office, did you see him then instead of going shopping? I wondered why you didn't have any bags when we met.'

The *That Sounds Familiar* bell pings in my head.

'Did you start seeing Alex when we were in Glasgow?' I ask again before Maddie can reply to my first question.

'You said you'd gone shopping the day Oscar and I went to the Rennie Mackintosh house. You came back empty-handed that day too.'

Maddie nods, a little shame-faced.

'It began way back in February! And you've been at it on and off ever since?'

'Well, I wouldn't call it that!' Maddie defends. 'We've not exactly had much chance to see each other, living in different countries. Like I said, we talk a lot online.'

Something else pings now as all the pieces fall slowly into place.

'It was you!' I exclaim. 'That's how Alex knew so much about me when he first came here. You told him.' I shake my head. 'It all makes sense now, how he knew where I was staying, and the problems Sean and I were having with our wedding. Oh my God, it was you that told him everything!'

'Stop this!' Maddie cries, jumping to her feet. 'Stop accusing me like I'm on trial for some horrific crime!'

I open my mouth to reply, but Maddie continues.

'It's OK for you, with your perfect fiancé, your perfect wedding plans and your jet-set lifestyle. You need to remember some of us don't have a perfect life; we have an imperfect one we're just trying to make a little better!' She spins round and stamps over to the window, where she pretends to study the street below.

'I'm sorry, Maddie,' I say in a quiet voice, getting up and going over to the window. I put my arm around her shoulder. 'I'm sorry if I sounded disapproving. It's just come as a bit of a shock, that's all. You were always the one so in control of your life. It was always me who was messing up and needing your help.'

Maddie turns towards me, her face full of distress. 'Well, it's me now, Scarlett. I'm the one who needs *your* help this time. I don't expect your approval, but this isn't just some one-night stand with a guy I've met in a pub. I really care about Alex, and I just want you to be happy for me.'

'I know,' I say, hugging her. 'And I am. If things are really as bad as you say with Felix, then *maybe* Alex could be good for you.' My voice cracks a tiny bit as I say this.

Maddie hugs me back. 'Alex is doing me good, really. I haven't been this happy in a long time.'

I pull back from the hug, and still holding on to Maddie's arms, I look her in the eye. 'Just don't do anything silly, will you?' I warn her. 'Or someone will end up getting hurt.'

She shakes her head. 'I won't. And no one is going to get hurt, Scarlett. I promise.'

As we return to my sofa, and our rapidly cooling takeaways, somehow I find Maddie's promise very hard to believe.

Maddie's time in New York flies by. When we're together, we have a wonderful time enjoying all that NYC has to offer in terms of restaurants and entertainment; it's just like old times, in fact. Maddie is much happier now than on the last occasion I spent time with her, so I guess I have to give Alex some credit for that. But her time with me seems to whizz by even more quickly than it should because Maddie spends so much of it with Alex.

They always meet away from my apartment, at venues Maddie doesn't discuss with me, which I have to assume are various hotels around the city, as I know Alex doesn't have a permanent residence while he's here. Maddie never talks much about Alex when we're together, an arrangement that suits us both. So I don't actually see him at all while Maddie's staying with me, which I'm incredibly relieved about. I don't know what I'd say to him. I just know when we do eventually meet up again, it's going to be very, very awkward.

On Maddie's last night in the city, we have dinner together. She met up with Alex earlier in the day, so at least we get to spend tonight together.

'Does Alex know I know?' I ask Maddie, unusually bringing Alex's name into our conversation.

Maddie nods. 'I told him yesterday.'

'And what did he say?'

Maddie shrugs. 'Not much. He asked how you'd taken the news.'

'And what did you say?'

'What could I say? I told him you weren't exactly over the moon about it, but that you're happy as long as I am. Isn't that right?'

'Yes, yes, of course. And you're right I'm not happy about it, but I'm pleased you are. You're like a different person since the last time I saw you.'

Maddie smiles. She toys delicately with the wine glass in her hands. 'That's what love does to you.'

'You're in love with him?' I ask in surprise. For some reason I hadn't considered this possibility. 'Is he with you?'

Maddie glances up at me. 'I think he might be,' she whispers excitedly.

'But what will you do? About Felix, and Alex's wife? What's her name again?'

'Charlotte,' Maddie says, her dreamy look fading. 'We'll tell them eventually, I guess.'

'You guess? Haven't you discussed it?'

Maddie puts her wine glass firmly down on the table. 'Look, Scarlett, I don't know the exact nature of how everything is going to work out right now. I just know that I love Alex, and Alex loves me.'

'You said he hadn't told you.'

Maddie, looking irritated, pretends to straighten the white tablecloth. She purposefully smooths down the edges, then straightens her cutlery.

'Scarlett, you have to stop doubting us all the time. It's becoming very draining, you know.'

'I'm just trying to help you. I don't want to see you getting hurt.'

'I won't.' Maddie stares defiantly at me over the table.

'I know what I'm doing. I'm a grown woman, not a child. Now, please let's talk about something else.'

'Sure, if that's what you want?'

'It is. Now, more wine?' Maddie lifts our fast-emptying bottle and begins to top up my glass.

I sigh. I have to let it go. There's nothing I can do about this. I just have to let my friend find her own way. I just hope for her sake that Alex is heading in the same direction she is.

Twenty-eight

July and then August roll in and with them bring long, hot days with soaring, sticky temperatures, one of the few things I don't like about New York. But I manage to escape them for a while when I head back to the UK for a week. Apart from spending some much-needed time with Sean, I have a good catch-up with my mother, and we spend a couple of hours excitedly discussing the wedding. Then, while I'm there, I'm measured for my wedding dress, which Oscar and Gabi are apparently very close to finalising.

I guess I should be a little worried. After all, I've watched enough bridal shows to know that when the bride isn't allowed to choose her own dress, it generally doesn't turn out well. But to be honest, with the search for

Gabi's great-aunt taking up such a lot of my time, along with being Gabi's companion on an almost daily basis, looking after three thriving businesses and trying to finalise the rest of the wedding arrangements, allowing Oscar and Gabi, both of whom have impeccable taste in clothes, to choose my dress is actually something of a relief.

'Oh my, it's so hoorrt!' Oscar moans as we walk across Central Park one evening. He pulls his silk lilac shirt away from his chest and wafts it up and down. 'I'll look like a wrung-out sponge by the time we get there. I told you we should have got a cab!'

'It would take longer to get to Gabi's in a cab than to walk across the park,' I try and justify. 'It would be point-less.'

'What's pointless is spending all that time getting ready to go out to a fancy birthday bash, then ruining it by arriving looking like we've just run the New York Marathon.'

Oscar and I are off to Gabi's twenty-seventh-birthday celebrations. She is holding an extravagant party at her apartment, and we've been invited along with lots of Gabi's friends and family. I have a suspicion from what Gabi has told me that there might be a few celebrity partygoers there as well, but I've chosen not to mention this to Oscar in case he gets too excited.

Sean and Luke were invited too. Sadly Sean couldn't

get away at the moment – he'd got some important deal or other going down, and as he put it, 'It simply isn't feasible for me to jump on a plane and fly thousands of miles just for a birthday party.' To be fair to him, he was right. Luckily, though, Oscar was able to fly over, mainly as an excuse to see Luke again, who was coming along to the party later, after his evening performance. I am very glad Oscar is here accompanying me now: as much as I've got used to Gabi's celebrity lifestyle, attending her birthday party on my own is something that would have filled me with dread. Her family will be here tonight, and her 'people'. I don't know about Gabi's family, but her staff certainly don't like me much and I can foresee the evening being a tricky one.

We finally arrive at Gabi's apartment block, and I ask Sylvester, on the door, if there's somewhere for us to freshen up before we take the lift to the party.

He directs us to some opulent washrooms on the ground floor, where we are able to return ourselves to something closer to the fragrant Oscar and Scarlett who left my apartment a little while ago, rather than the two sweaty Bettys who arrived at the apartment block just now.

Then we ride up in the lift together, Oscar eyeing up Lucien, today's lift operator, as we go.

'Oscar!' I admonish as we exit the lift and make our way down the corridor to Gabi's. 'You're an engaged person now. You can't keep flirting like that.'

'Darling,' Oscar says with a flourish of his hand, '*that* wasn't flirting – it was merely showing admiration. I love Luke, you know that. It means nothing. Gabi, my angel!' Oscar cries with delight as the door opens. 'Happy birthday!'

But it's not Gabi standing on the other side of the opened door, but Henry, one of the usual doormen from downstairs, looking particularly smart this evening.

'Hey, Henry,' I say, smiling at him. 'She's got you up here tonight, has she?'

'Bit of extra pocket money, miss,' Henry says, winking at me. 'And a prime view of all the shenanigans ...'

'Of which I expect there will be many,' I say, winking back at him. 'Enjoy.'

'Have a good evening, miss. Sir,' he says, nodding at Oscar as we pass through to the main living room.

'Wow,' I whisper to Oscar as we stand in awe at the sight in front of us. 'Gabi said she was going to put on something special, but I didn't expect this.'

Gabi's apartment, where we sat a few months ago and had brunch in a relaxed, calm atmosphere, has been transformed into a sparkly, glittery wonderland. There are white fairy lights draped from every place they can be; clusters of silver heart-shaped helium balloons are dotted artistically about the room; several huge ice sculptures in the shape of mermaids, fairies and angels stand in the centre of white-clothed tables; and in the middle of everything is a lavish pink and white five-tier birthday cake.

'Hey, guys. You made it!' Gabi calls across the room as she makes her way towards us. 'You look simply stunning, Scarlett,' she says, admiring my long pale blue dress. 'I love your gown. Is it designer?'

'Happy birthday,' I say, kissing her on the cheek. 'I bought it in Bloomingdale's, in a half-price sale.'

'Then we *really* need to go shopping together more often!' Gabi grins. 'That's amazing! And you look fabulous too, Oscar.' She turns towards him. 'Lilac sure is your colour!'

'Thank you,' Oscar agrees, admiring his own shirt. 'I think so too. But look at you, darling. That dress is simply divine on the birthday girl!'

'Do you think?' Gabi says, giving us a little twirl.

'I do!' Oscar says. 'What do you think, Scarlett?'

Gabi is wearing a long, simple gown in pale pink silk. It's sleeveless, very fitted, and is cut to accentuate her ample breasts. There's intricate beading over the bodice, which runs down into a delicate V at the top of the skirt.

'It's very nice,' I reply. 'Suits you.'

'Do you like the style?' Oscar asks casually.

'Yes, of course.'

'And what about the beading?' Gabi enquires. 'Too much or too little?'

Ah, I get what they're doing. They're testing the water to see if I might like this style for a wedding dress.

'I like the fabric,' I tell them, playing along, 'and the cut of the dress. I'm not that keen on a lot of beading, though. I prefer delicate embroidery and—'

'All right, Gok Wan, no need for an eight-page analysis!' Oscar interrupts, rolling his eyes. 'We only asked!'

'But you said—' I'm about to defend my comments when we see Max coming towards us.

'Hey, hey, you two. Beginning to wonder if you were actually coming tonight.'

I see Gabi's eyes light up as Max stands next to her.

I'm one of the few people who knows that Gabi and Max have been seeing each other secretly for a few months. They're getting on very well. Gabi seems to adore Max's down-to-earth style and dry sense of humour, and Max, well, he just adores Gabi.

I feel a bit sorry for Gabi, as it seems that everything she does needs to be kept hush-hush. From me trying to find her great-aunt to her blossoming relationship with Max, it all has to be hidden from the constant glare of the media.

Actually, I've just had some positive news about Gabi's great-aunt. After months of dead ends and no-shows, I'd found out through a friend of a friend that there was a possibility Evita had actually eloped to Scotland when she was very young.

The only reason I'd been able to glean this piece of info was because my contact's friend, Bruce, worked in the office that registered births, deaths and marriages in Scotland. Bruce owed Millie, my friend, a mighty big favour after Millie had discovered that Bruce was having an affair with his boss, and Millie hadn't uttered a word about it to anyone, especially Bruce's wife, Helen, who happened to be Millie's salsa teacher.

It was all a bit convoluted, but things often happened like that for us at the trust: one small piece of gossip or a random event would sometimes turn a case that was proving impossible to solve into one that brought about the required happy ending. And in this case infidelity, which was a huge concern of mine right now, had actually resulted in a positive outcome, as Bruce had been 'politely' asked by Millie if he could search through all of the Scottish records, looking for any Evitas who were listed on the census.

Bruce, surprisingly, had turned up forty-eight different options, but only one that fell in the required age bracket. I nearly fell off my chair when I was told that this particular Evita was not only living in Scotland but had got married at Gretna Green fifty years ago.

I couldn't believe it. Not only another Scottish connection in my life right now, but Gretna again! I started to think about the last time I was there with Oscar, and about the lovely couple we'd met renewing their vows. They'd been married fifty years ago too, just like Evita...

Then it had struck me like a thunderbolt.

That couple had been called *Evie* and Hector.

Evie... That couldn't be short for Evita, could it? No, surely not. That would be just too weird. *Too* much of a coincidence.

But I always say everything happens for a reason. It's my motto in life, and has proved correct many times over the last few years. Why shouldn't my Evie be the Evita I was looking for? Perhaps that was the reason we bumped into each other that day. Stranger things have happened ...

So I'd immediately decided to meet up with Evie and Hector again in Scotland when I was back in the UK for Oscar's wedding in a few weeks. Well, that was the plan, but I hadn't been able to get hold of them yet to try and arrange a meeting. It was early days, though, as this possibly vital piece of information in my search for Gabi's great-aunt had only been passed to me the day before Oscar arrived in New York, so I hadn't had much time to finalise anything.

But now wasn't really the time to be telling Gabi about my latest findings, not here in the middle of her party.

'Doesn't Max look fabulous?' Gabi asks, looking proudly at him. 'I think he looks wonderful in a suit.'

Max certainly does look a little different tonight to the way I'm used to seeing him. He usually wears a T-shirt with long shorts or jeans; comfy casual is definitely Max's style. But tonight he's wearing a smart black suit with a white shirt, open at the neck, and I have to admit that yes, he does scrub up well.

'Why, thank ye,' Max says, smiling at her. 'You don't look too bad yourself in that old number you've found in the back of your closet.'

Gabi grins at him and for a moment it's like the rest of us aren't even there.

'Ahem.' Oscar clears his throat. 'Am I missing something? Is there something going on here people aren't telling me about? I do hate secrets. Especially when I'm not party to them!'

Gabi and Max immediately turn away from each other, a little too swiftly.

'Yes, there is,' Max says quickly. 'Something you'll really like, Oscar.'

'I knew it!' Oscar claps his hands together in excitement. 'Tell me everything and fast!'

Max comes over to Oscar and puts his arm around his shoulder. 'Now, I want you to stay very calm when I tell you this, Oscar,' he says seriously.

'Yes, yes!' Oscar says, almost leaping up and down. 'You can't hide anything from me, you know.'

Gabi looks a little worried, but Max winks at her.

'There's someone here I think you'd like to meet.'

Oscar looks suspiciously at Max. 'Who?' he demands. 'I thought you were going to tell me—'

But Max cuts him off deftly. 'Miss Kylie Minogue.'

Oscar looks as if Max has just told him the Queen is here dressed in a punk outfit. He stares at Max with his mouth open. Then he closes it. Then he opens it again.

I don't think I've ever seen Oscar incapable of speech in all the time I've known him.

'K-K-Kylie. Is. Here?' he asks, looking at us all one by one. 'In this building?'

'No, even better – in this very room,' Max says, whispering into Oscar's ear.

Oscar swivels round on his toes with a pirouette a prima ballerina would be proud of. 'Where?' he gasps, obviously still having trouble with his speech.

'Would you like to meet her, Oscar?' Gabi asks, gently coming over to his other side.

'M-me? Meet Kylie?' Oscar stutters. 'Y-yes ... please.'

Gabi takes hold of his hand like he is a small child. 'I think she's over here talking to some more friends of mine.'

'Kylie Minogue is your *friend*?' Oscar asks, his eyes still wide. 'Scarlett, did you know this?' he demands.

Smiling, I shake my head.

'Come on, then, let's go over,' Gabi says, gently pulling his hand. 'I'll introduce you.'

Oscar nods. 'Wait!' he suddenly says, coming back to life. He lets go of Gabi's hand and quickly checks himself in a mirror on the wall behind us. 'OK, I look good,' he announces confidently, smoothing down his shirt. 'Let's go!'

I shake my head as Gabi leads Oscar away.

'Nicely done,' I tell Max. 'Your distraction technique. He very nearly guessed, you know.'

Max grins. 'Yeah, I can think pretty snappily when I want.'

'So how's it going with you and Gabi? I hear her side of things all the time. But what about you?'

'She's a good kid,' Max says, swilling his drink round in his glass. 'I like her.'

'Kid? She's hardly that.'

'I know.' Max looks at me as if he's considering something. 'Truth is, Scarlett, I like her. I like her a *lot*.'

'I thought you did!' I try not to clap my hands in glee. 'Oh, this is very exciting!'

'But what she sees in me I still don't know.'

'Ha, me neither!' I nudge him. 'But I know she's pretty smitten.'

Max looks secretly pleased. He turns his gaze to where Gabi is now introducing Oscar to Kylie Minogue. Oscar looks like all his Christmases have come at once, and I think for a moment he's going to curtsey when he takes hold of Kylie's hand, but he doesn't; he simply appears to launch into an Oscar-like gush about how wonderful she is. And Kylie, who is even tinier than I imagined she would be, appears to be accepting his compliments with good grace as she tries to retrieve her delicate hand from Oscar's vice-like grip.

'Never really felt like this about a woman before,' Max admits shyly. 'I'm trying not to get too involved, though.'

'Why? Gabi really likes you.'

'Just look at her, Scarlett,' he says, gesturing towards Gabi with his glass of beer. 'Look at the world she lives in. I guess I'm just something a bit different for the time being. A bit of rough in her diamond-encrusted life.'

'No, you're wrong,' I insist. 'Gabi's not like that.'

'We'll see,' Max says, sighing deeply. 'I hope you're right. But things like this don't happen to me. And if they do, they never last.'

'He's right – nothing lasts forever,' we hear a Scottish voice say behind us, and we both swivel round. 'How are you both?' Alex asks, grinning broadly. 'It's been a while.'

Max smiles stiffly at Alex and lifts his glass. 'I'm just going to get a top-up. Can I get one for you, Scarlett, while I'm there?'

'Yes, please,' I reply. 'Something strong.'

Max nods knowingly and walks over to the bar, where a good-looking chap in a white shirt is shaking cocktails.

I turn to Alex. 'Alex, hello. How are you?' I ask as politely as I can.

'Never been better, Scarlett, and yourself?'

'The same, thank you.'

There's an awkward pause.

'So, what have you been up to lately?' I say without thinking, and immediately regret it.

Alex smiles ruefully, and takes a long, slow sip from his glass.

'I think we both know the answer to that, Scarlett, don't we?'

I look around me, wishing Max would hurry up with those drinks.

'Er, yes, I guess so.'

'And you obviously don't approve?'

I look at Alex. I'm not going to lie about my feelings. Why should I? 'No, I don't. But it would seem you're making my friend happy right now. So as long as you continue doing so, I can't really say anything about it.'

'Is that a threat?' Alex asks, raising his eyebrows.

'No, I don't make threats. But Maddie is my friend, and I don't want to see her getting hurt.'

'And you think I'm going to be the one to hurt her, am I right?'

I nod.

Alex sighs deeply and takes another long sip of his drink. Then he leans in towards me. 'Let just say *I* won't hurt your friend if you keep your pretty little mouth shut about our arrangement, OK?'

I stare at him. 'What do you mean?'

'Scarlett, as much as you don't like me, our paths are already linked in far too many ways. I'm one of Sean's oldest friends. I'm best man at your wedding. I'm involved with Gabi's charity. And now I'm pleased to say, thanks to your introduction, I'm about to go into business with Peter in the not-too-distant future. I can't have you blabbing about me into the wrong ears, now, can I? It could be very damaging, for *both* of us. And if you don't realise it already, that *is* a threat.'

I open my mouth to respond, but Max returns with our drinks. He hands me mine and I down it in one go.

'Bloody hell, Scarlett, are you out on a bender

tonight?' he asks, staring at me in part amazement, part awe.

'No,' I gasp. 'I just needed it.'

'Catch you later, guys,' Alex says lightly, as if our conversation never happened. 'Enjoy the party. The shrimp is amazing.' And he wanders off back across the crowded room.

'Did he say something to you?' Max demands, noticing my face as I watch him go.

I shake my head. 'No, it's fine.'

Max growls. 'Smarmy git.'

'You really don't like him, do you?' I ask. 'You wouldn't admit it on the phone, but I can tell.'

'Nah, he's bad news, that one.'

'Why?'

Max looks at me. 'Do you really want to hear me bad-mouth your best man?'

'Yes,' I nod. 'I really do.'

Max looks surprised. 'Right,' he says, lowering his voice. 'You asked for it. He's not liked in journalistic circles for one.'

'Really? I thought he was some super-duper award-winning reporter?'

'Oh, he's award-winning all right. But he had to screw people over to win those awards.'

'No!'

'Yep. I could tell you stories about him that would make your lovely hair curl. If you were lying on the ground, Alex

Woolfe wouldn't stop to help you up unless he thought it was worth his while, or there was a TV camera running close by.'

'Oh my God, that bad?'

Max nods. 'He's not the most popular of people in the TV world. That's why he opted out. No one would work with him any more. It didn't matter so much when it was just people like me, the technical boys, that he was treating like dirt. No one really cared that much then. But when he started screwing over the top bods, the ones who make the decisions, that's when he came a cropper.'

'But I thought he took early retirement to do something else with his life. That's what he told Sean and me.'

'Ha, I don't think so. Not unless early retirement is what you call being fired for sleeping with your boss's daughter.'

My heart sinks. 'He had an affair?'

'Yeah.' Max's voice drops even further. 'It was all kept hush-hush because the poor guy didn't want his daughter getting bad publicity. She was a rather well-known TV presenter at the time. Married too.'

My eyes widen.

'Nope.' Max shakes his head. 'Don't ask me. I can't reveal names. But that's what happened. It's common knowledge in our business that he was caught with his pants down shagging his boss's daughter, and the worst thing was, the boss was his really good mate. He'd invited him to family parties and had even lent him money, so the story goes – that part I don't know so much about.'

'Oh God.' I put my hand over my mouth.

'What?'

'I think I need another drink,' I say, holding out my glass.

'I'll get you two,' Max says, taking it. 'You look like you need it.'

Twenty-nine

I can hardly believe what's just happened.

I knew how *I* felt about Alex; I'd always thought there was something not quite right about him. Until now, though, I wasn't sure what.

But in the space of a few minutes not only has he threatened me to keep quiet about his and Maddie's affair, but also, according to Max, this isn't the first time he's found himself in this sort of situation.

Oh God, I think, *what if he's a serial adulterer? What if there's a trail of women he's slept with and then left to move on to his next conquest?*

Stop it, Scarlett, I tell myself. *You don't know that. Don't let your imagination run wild. Stick to the facts for once.*

But the facts didn't make for very pleasant reading.

Alex was having an affair with my best friend, and my best friend was in love with him. I had to find out if he was serious about her. I couldn't just sit back and wait for him to hurt Maddie. Maddie was all over the place right now; she didn't know what she was doing. Her relationship with Felix was failing, and I didn't know where her head was, but it wasn't screwed on in its usual sensible place, that's for certain.

I had to make sure Maddie didn't lend him any money. Max had said the TV guy had loaned Alex money. I couldn't allow Maddie to do that; she hardly had any of her own as it was. Working for a charity didn't exactly pay a fortune.

I look to see if I can spot Alex in the room and I spy him deep in conversation with a woman. He's obviously flirting with her. I can tell by the way he's standing with his head slightly tilted to the side as if he's completely engrossed in what she's telling him, and by how the woman keeps flicking her hair back and laughing at what he's saying.

Oh ... Oh! That's just how he was at the wedding reception in Edinburgh with Maddie! I remember him reaching out to stroke the hair away from Maddie's face. At least he's not doing— But then he does exactly that.

Right!

I'm about to march over there and demand to know Alex's true feelings for my friend when I feel a tap on my shoulder. I turn round to see Portia, Gabi's PA, standing next to me.

Oh, this is all I need tonight. What grief is she going to give me this time?

'Do you know him?' Portia asks, nodding over to where Alex is moving closer towards the woman every second. 'Alex, I mean. I saw you talking to him earlier. And I saw the look you were giving him just now.'

Portia never says more than three words to me in any one go. I was beginning to doubt she could actually string a sentence together.

'Yes, I know him,' I reply cautiously.

'In an intimate capacity?' Portia asks.

'God, no!' I exclaim. Then a bit more quietly I say, 'He's supposed to be the best man at my wedding.'

Portia looks part surprised at this news, part irritated.

'Damn. Then I'll leave you be. Enjoy the party.' And she moves to walk away.

'Wait!' I say, suddenly intrigued by what she wanted to tell me. Was Portia another of Alex's conquests? 'What is it?'

Portia looks at me. She's obviously debating whether talking to me is a good idea.

'He may be my fiancé's best man, but *I* don't like him,' I tell her, hoping this will help. 'Not one little bit.'

Portia narrows her eyes. Then she nods, her decision made.

'Come with me,' she says. 'I think we need to talk.'

Portia leads me through the party towards Gabi's bedroom. On the way, we pass a number of people I recognise.

Still living it up with Kylie and her gang is Oscar, who from his body movements looks like he's currently trying to get Kylie involved in a rendition of 'The Locomotion'. Max, who seems to have got distracted from his drinks mission, is now deep in conversation with Lewis, Gabi's bodyguard, another of the few people who know about their blossoming relationship. I very nearly stop following Portia and take a diversion to the buffet table when I see Michael Bublé helping himself to canapés. And if I'm not mistaken, I'm sure I spot Jennifer Lopez heading out onto the balcony with a glass of champagne in her hand.

But my mission right now is not to celeb-spot – tempting as that is for me – but to find out what Portia so obviously wants to tell me about Alex. So I ignore my yearning to engage Michael Bublé in conversation, and maybe persuade him to croon us a few tunes, and my just plain nosiness at wanting to see J-Lo up close – could she really be that perfect? Instead, I continue to follow Portia through to Gabi's bedroom, where Portia quietly closes the door behind us.

'You're sure you don't like him?' she repeats for confirmation, once we're safely inside, away from everyone.

'Yes,' I assure her. 'I don't like or trust him one little bit.'

Portia nods. 'Good, then what I'm about to tell you won't come as too much of a shock.'

Waiting here in Gabi's bedroom, with her childhood teddies and dolls carefully arranged on her bed, and some of her make-up still lying on her dressing table, makes it feel like we're two schoolgirls about to exchange gossip at a pyjama party.

'I've suspected for a long time that Alex is embezzling money from Gabi's charity,' Portia says, coming straight to the point. She waits for my reaction before continuing.

That bit of information doesn't come as too much of a shock: after all, Max just mentioned something about some dodgy dealings with money.

'I can quite believe that,' I say, as though it's the most natural thing in the world to be exchanging this sort of gossip in these surroundings. I actually feel a bit like a spy right now, but I'm trying not to let my tendency to romanticise things take over my rational thought. This is serious stuff.

Portia looks surprised. 'I thought that would shock you.'

'No. Someone else just told me something similar not that many minutes ago.' I think about Max. If he finds out Alex is messing around with Gabi in any way, he'll go bananas.

'Oh, really?' Portia says. 'I won't ask who.'

'No, best not to,' I say, thinking I'm going to have to keep this quiet myself. 'Is that it?' I ask. 'Not that that's not enough,' I add hurriedly.

'If only that were it,' Portia says. 'We think there's more.'

'More? More what?'

'More charities he's been involved in and taken money from.'

'How do you know this?' I ask. 'And who's "we"?'

Portia looks around her as though someone might be hiding under Gabi's bed or in her wardrobe, earwigging on our conversation. 'Other PAs for big stars,' she whispers. 'I can't say who, but we all know each other. It's like a little club being a PA in this business. While the celebrities are off attending the big events, we're all hovering in the background. You get to know each other, and gossip travels fast in this business.'

'I can imagine. But how do you know this isn't just tittle-tattle?'

Portia opens her eyes wide. '*Tittle-tattle?* What's that?'

'It's a British expression for "gossip",' I try and explain. 'Like slang.'

'I love that!' she smiles. 'Tittle-tattle. I shall use that one next time I'm tittle-tattling! You Brits have such a great way of saying things.'

'Indeed . . . But getting back to the point. I'm serious, Portia. This information you've given me, how do you know it's true?'

'That's the problem,' she says, turning solemn again. 'It's so difficult to prove. He's a sly one, that Alex. Everyone thinks the sun shines out of his ass. Except those of us who know him better. He uses his connections to worm his way in with a celebrity. Then when he's far enough inside their private circle, he gets involved in their charity, and more importantly their charity's money.'

'So why are you telling me all this?' I ask, not really sure how I'm supposed to respond.

'Two reasons,' Portia says. 'Look, I won't mess with you, Scarlett – when you first became involved with Gabi, we were all completely against what you were doing with her. We didn't like it, and we didn't like you.'

'I did notice,' I say wryly.

'Yeah, I'm sorry about that. I know we tried to make things difficult for you. But Gabi, as well as being our friend, is our job. If she goes off the rails, we go down too.'

I nod. 'I understand that. But she's not going off the rails, is she? She's happy when she's doing normal things like a normal person.'

'Yeah, we know that now. We can see how happy she is at the moment. Me, Madrid, Lewis, even Marcus, we all have to admit that you've done wonderful things with her.'

Gosh, I couldn't imagine them all standing around singing my praises.

'And that's the other thing,' she continues. 'Gabi trusts you – if anyone can make her see what a shit Alex is, you can. He's so sly we can't actually prove anything. It's all hearsay, but very well-founded hearsay.'

I smile at her description of Alex. Yep, he's a shit all right. I've learned so much about him tonight he's like a big heap of dung steaming away in my life. But what am I going to have to do to shovel him up?

'Perhaps I might be able to, but how?'

'I heard him the other day on the phone,' Portia says,

'when he was over discussing a fundraiser for Gabi's charity. While she was using the bathroom, Alex was on his cell talking to some guy named Peter about investing in some trust. Then I heard your name and realised they were talking about The Dragonfly Trust. Scarlett, don't you see? It's your turn next. Alex is gonna screw your charity over, and probably you at the same time.'

Thirty

I spend the rest of the party in a daze. After Portia tells me her suspicions about Alex, I can't think about anything other than what I'm going to do next.

I have a vague recollection of Michael Bublé singing 'Happy Birthday' to Gabi while the other women in the room watch, green with envy. Then Kylie and Michael singing a duet together, and Oscar somehow managing to be involved on backing vocals.

But that's it. I speak to people, I drink the drinks that are thrust into my hand, but the whole time I'm thinking about Alex, and the potential he has for swinging a huge wrecking ball through my life and the lives of the people I hold dear.

When it's time to leave, Oscar and I say our goodbyes,

with Oscar exchanging numbers with Kylie, Michael and J-Lo. I must have missed his escapades with her, so caught up was I in my own turbulent thoughts. But Oscar seems to have made an impression at the party, whatever he's got up to. Which is usually his way.

Luckily for me, as we leave Gabi's apartment block and wait for Sylvester, the doorman, to hail us a taxi, Luke arrives at the party and is able to handle Oscar, who has obviously had a few too many glasses of pink champagne.

'You all right, babe?' Oscar asks, swaying from side to side as we wait just inside the foyer. 'You're awfully quiet. Gabi's party was an absolute blast, wasn't it?'

'Yeah, it was a blast of something,' I reply cautiously. *Something very unpleasant.*

'Scarlett?' Luke asks quietly while Oscar now waltzes round the marble foyer with an imaginary partner. '*Are* you OK?'

I nod. 'Yes, thanks, Luke. I'm fine. Just got some things on my mind, that's all. Nothing I can't handle.'

'Sure, well, you know where I am if you want to talk anytime.'

'Thank you,' I reply, squeezing his hand. 'I really appreciate that.'

'No worries. Great,' Luke calls, glancing through the glass doors, 'it looks like we have a cab at last.'

The three of us pile into the taxi, and it soon returns us safely back to our own apartments. When I get in, I quickly get undressed and ready for bed, pulling on my favourite pair of comfy pyjama bottoms and a Robbie Williams tour hoodie.

The air-con is on full blast in my apartment, so I turn it right down. Suddenly I don't feel very hot at all. Even though the weather outside is still clammy and warm this early in the morning, there's a chill in the air as I curl up in my bed and I feel the need to pull my duvet up around me for the first time in weeks.

But the chill isn't caused by the temperature in the apartment, or by some bug that I've picked up. I know exactly the cause of my shivers.

Alex.

I awake later that morning and find that my chilly feeling has eased and I'm now dripping with sweat because my apartment is way too hot and I'm wearing a sweatshirt.

I fling off my covers, whack up the air-con and jump into the shower. The cool water running over me not only washes away my perspiration but also my feelings of anxiety about Alex.

Firstly, I decide there is no way I'm going to let him do to my charity what, according to Portia, he's already done to others. Secondly, I realise I'm going to have to warn Gabi about him, but without causing too much of a fuss. Even though I'm not going to let Alex intimidate me, I don't want to unleash a tidal wave of problems for myself and those around me. Alex was right about one thing: our lives are intertwined in many ways, and as much as I don't like Alex, he's still Sean's friend and – to my even greater disgust, now I know what sort of man he is – Maddie's lover.

When I've had breakfast, I call Peter's cell phone. It's Sunday, so he won't be in the office, but I know I must speak to him today.

'Scarlett?' Peter says, answering his phone immediately. 'I didn't expect to hear from you for a few days. I thought Oscar was in town.'

'He is,' I say, coming straight to the point. 'But something's happened, Peter, and I need to see you.'

'Of course,' Peter says, sensing the tension in my voice. 'But I'm on my way to visit Sunnyside right now. Fancy tagging along?'

The thought of seeing all my friends at the children's home is tempting, but the way I feel right now, I know I would become overemotional at the thought of someone even considering messing with them.

'No, it's not a good idea. Can I meet you afterwards? How about Brooklyn Bridge Park on the benches that overlook the water?'

'Sure, no problem. Are you OK, Scarlett? I'm sensing something is very wrong.'

'It is, Peter, but I'll tell you more when I see you. Shall we say eleven?'

'Yes. Eleven is fine,' Peter replies, not pushing for any more information. 'I'll see you later.'

There were three reasons I needed to talk to Peter. The first was obviously because he was involved with The Dragonfly Trust, and anything that might jeopardise that was something Peter should know about immediately. The second was that Alex had mentioned something about going into business with Peter, and I knew if Peter had any doubts about a business partner, he would put a stop to further dealings immediately. The one thing Peter put above everything else was trust. If he didn't trust you, he wouldn't do business with you, simple as that. And the third reason was that I just needed to talk to someone about everything, and Peter was my obvious choice.

Peter would listen and advise me on what I should do next. He always had before, and I knew he would again.

I take the subway downtown and across to Brooklyn. I have neither the time nor the inclination today for the fabulous views to be seen by walking across the Brooklyn Bridge. When I emerge from the subway, I head immediately towards one of the many benches that line the side of the East River and face across towards Manhattan.

After a few minutes Peter arrives and sits down next to me.

'What's wrong?' he asks, coming straight to the point. 'It must be bad if you don't want to visit the children.'

Suddenly from nowhere tears start to stream down my face. I don't know if it's only the Alex situation that's causing them to fall or whether it's a build-up of everything: the wedding, Gabi, Maddie ... the list goes on. My life seems to be overflowing with problems to solve and people to worry about right now.

Peter pulls a clean white handkerchief from his pocket, hands it to me, then puts his arm around my shoulders. While people pass us on foot, boats and jet-skis, all enjoying the Sunday sunshine, we sit in silence for a few minutes while I quietly sob and Peter lets me.

Eventually I stop crying and wipe my eyes and nose one last time.

'I'm guessing you don't want this back?' I ask, presenting Peter with a damp hanky covered in tears and mascara.

Peter waves away his hanky. 'You keep it in exchange for telling me what's caused all this.'

I tell Peter everything: about Alex and Maddie, and what happened at Gabi's party. And as I thought he would, he simply listens until I've got to the end of my sorry tale.

'I see,' Peter says when I've finished.

'So what are you going to do?' I ask.

Peter looks at me. 'Nothing.'

I didn't expect this answer. 'What do you mean, nothing?'

'I mean exactly that. I'm not going to do anything. You are.'

'But how? I can't take on Alex on my own. And what about the trust? We can't have him stealing from that. What about the children? What about—'

'Calm, Scarlett,' Peter says, holding up his hand. 'The first thing you're going to do is remain calm.'

'But—'

'Ah-ah!' he says, waving his finger in front of my face. 'Right,' he continues when I'm silenced. 'I don't mean you're on your own. Of course I will help you in any way I can. But if what you say is true, then the only person who *can* deal with Alex's collective misdemeanours is you. You're the lynchpin in all this.'

I sigh. I'd kind of hoped Peter was going to take all my problems away with one big swish of his virtual magic wand. He was usually good like that, but it seemed today his wand was on a break.

'So what do you suggest?' I ask in a small voice.

'First, I will of course be pulling out of any business dealings I was going to enter into with Alex. To be honest, Scarlett, I never really liked him that much either. But I thought because he was your friend, maybe my radar was a little off course.'

'Alex was never my friend,' I point out. 'He was Sean's.'

'Was or is?' Peter asks. 'This is another reason why you need to tread very carefully. Not only could Maddie get hurt here, but Sean too.'

'I know. Everyone thinks that Alex Woolfe is so wonderful. Why am I the only one seeing that he's not?'

'But you're not the only one. What about Max? And Portia? They saw through the wolf in sheep's clothing.'

'Oh!' I exclaim, suddenly realising. 'Yes, that's exactly

what he is, a wolf in sheep's clothing. That's a brilliant description of him, Peter!'

Peter smiles.

'So what next?' I ask eagerly.

'Regarding the business side of things, yes, you're right – Alex has mentioned becoming involved with the trust. But,' he adds just before I explode again, 'I didn't encourage him either way. I said I'd need to talk to you about it.'

'Good.' I breathe out, relieved. 'At least that's something of mine he's not involved in.'

'But, Scarlett, we do have some options. We could still let Alex in and try and catch him at it—'

'No,' I interrupt, shaking my head vehemently. 'Definitely not. I want him as far away from The Dragonfly Trust and Sunnyside as possible.'

'Sure. In that case, then, we'll just block him having any involvement with either of them. If he's already suspicious of you, he might not try anything even if we did let him in.'

'That's a much better idea. We'll just block him and his sly ways from becoming involved with us.' I resolutely fold my arms across my body. 'But what do I do about Gabi? Her charity is already affected.'

'That's a difficult one if what Portia says is correct and they can't actually prove anything. It's just gossip until there's concrete evidence of wrongdoing.'

'But I can't just stand by and do nothing. Gabi is my friend.'

'You may have to, Scarlett. But keep a close eye on the situation. Keep in touch with Portia and Gabi's staff, and make sure Gabi doesn't allow Alex any further access to the charity's funds than he already has. If you want to catch Alex out, the last thing you want to do is raise his suspicions in any way.'

Hmm, I'm not keen on that idea. But Peter is right. I can't just storm in and accuse someone of something when I have no proof. Plus, I'm determined to bring Alex down. He's already messed with too many things I hold dear.

'You should be proud of yourself, Scarlett,' Peter says knowingly. 'Characters like Alex are only wary of foes who are their equal or better. Alex is obviously concerned about you or he wouldn't have threatened you like he did.'

'Really? I can't see that.'

'Trust me. I've been around long enough to know types like him.'

'Perhaps.' I shrug, not really seeing it. 'But I still don't know what do about Maddie and Sean.'

'That I can't help you with,' Peter says, putting his hand over mine on the bench. 'I feel time might be on your side with that one. But something *will* turn up to help you out – just you wait. The good guy always wins in the end.'

I sigh and place my other hand over Peter's. 'I do hope so, Peter. This Red is definitely going to defeat the Big Bad Wolf, riding hood or not!'

Thirty-one

September arrives and I find myself back in London for Oscar and Luke's wedding. First, though, there's Oscar's stag night, which is sure to be a hoot. Oscar and Luke have decided that they don't want separate stag nights, and Oscar has always declared that he wants a hen night anyway. So instead they have a joint 'hen and stag' party at their house in Notting Hill.

Even though Oscar insisted he was going to 'tone it down' for Luke's sake because he'd got his way with the wedding theme, Oscar's version of toned down involves having a pyjama party, with Oscar and the main wedding party looking like extras from the sleepover scene in *Grease*. We are made to wear baby-doll nighties, which Oscar supplies, and put our hair up in curlers, and Oscar hires a trained beautician to provide face packs, manicures and pedicures.

It turns out to be a lot of fun, though; some of the other guests show up wearing their own nightwear, including all-in-one sleepsuits, and even Sean, who hates dressing up, joins in the fun and goes to the party in a pair of slippers suitable for an old man, matched with some traditional blue and grey striped pyjamas – even though I know he usually wears nothing in bed.

'Hey, sexy,' I say to him, when he brings me over another glass of Oscar's homemade 'snoozy' cocktail. I run my hands over the fabric of his pyjama top. 'I quite like you in those PJs.'

'Oh, really?' Sean says, pulling me to him. 'Well, I quite like you in that baby-doll nightie Oscar has made you wear tonight. Maybe we should keep our outfits on when we get home later. You might lose the curlers, though,' he winks, looking up at my hair, which is rollered on top of my head.

Lovely though that sounds, I'm pretty sure that given the strength of the cocktails we've been downing all night, neither of us will be capable of anything other than sleep when we get home. If we manage to stagger home, that is. I'm already starting to feel a bit giddy on my feet.

'Hey, you two, put each other down,' Maddie says from her space on the sofa. Maddie is wearing her own baby-doll nightie 'direct from Victoria's Secret in New York', as she informed us when Oscar offered her one of his own. (Not Oscar's actual own. The ones he'd purchased especially for tonight!)

Even though I'm pleased to see Maddie still looking just as happy as the last time I saw her in New York, when I see her wearing her nightie, it makes me wonder if she's worn it when she's been with Alex. Actually, scrub that – I know she will have done, and the thought makes me feel quite nauseous.

Nothing much has happened regarding Alex in the few weeks since I sat in Brooklyn Bridge Park with Peter. Peter pulled out of his deal with Alex – luckily he hadn't signed any actual contracts – and told him he felt The Dragonfly Trust was turning over a healthy profit right now, especially with Gabi's help, so even though we were most grateful for his offer to become involved, his services would not be required.

As far as I was aware, Alex had taken this all quite well. Peter said there appeared to be no animosity on his part, even though Peter had prepared himself for it, and that I shouldn't worry – The Dragonfly Trust was perfectly safe.

With Portia, Marcus and Madrid's help, I was keeping a close eye on Alex's dealings with Gabi. He didn't appear to be trying to get closer to her, or further involved with her charity. So for now we just waited like fishermen, hoping we might get a bite on our line. But it wasn't a little fish we hoped would take the bait. We willed it to be the shark, so we could reel him in hook, line and sinker.

So that just left what I was going to do about Maddie and Sean. And I decided nothing for now. What was I supposed to say? 'Hey, Maddie, your married lover is a bit of a shit? I and a few other people don't like him.' It was hardly grounds for them to split up, was it? If I said anything to Maddie right now, it would only cause friction, and I didn't want to do that before Oscar's big day. No, I needed to wait until I had actual proof, not just gossip.

The same applied to Sean. So what if Max and I didn't like Alex? It wasn't a rule that you had to like all your future spouse's friends. I could have done without Alex being our best man ... but he *was* the person who got us my perfect wedding venue – I couldn't forget that. Perhaps I was overreacting a little. Maybe he wasn't quite as bad as I had originally thought. Yes, he threatened me at Gabi's party, but maybe that was because he truly did care about Maddie and didn't want anything to come between them.

Nah, I didn't really believe that either. But it was all I had to cling to right now until I knew otherwise.

The party is in full swing and everybody seems to be having a great time. I have to hand it to Oscar – he sure knows how to throw a hen and stag night!

Right now we're in the middle of a game of spin the bottle – truth or dare. Oscar has already been dared to run up and down the street in his baby-doll nightie, which he immediately did without any fuss, pirouetting and skipping all the way. Luke was asked to tell the truth about any tales he knew of the infamous 'casting couch', which, after some cajoling, he did. Most of us sat open-mouthed when he revealed to us some of the stars who had landed their major TV roles in this way. I chose truth too and was asked just exactly what had happened when I met Bradley Cooper for the first time – even though many of the guests already know the answer to this question, they never seem to tire of hearing about it, or of trying to press me for more details.

The bottle has just been spun by Luke again and has finished up facing Ursula, Sean's sister, when I hear my phone ringing in my bag. *That's odd*, I think, leaving it. *Who's calling me at this time of night?* I glance at the clock on Oscar and Luke's mantelpiece – it's gone eleven. Ah well, I'll take a look at the number when I visit the loo in a bit to freshen up. But then it rings again.

'Is that your phone?' Sean asks, seeing me look with concern towards the empty sofa where my bag rests. 'Who's calling you now?'

'I think I'd better check,' I say, standing up. 'Be right back.'

I leave Luke trying to choose a dare for Ursula – knowing those two, it will probably be quite tame anyway – and head over to my bag, but I don't get to it in time before it cuts to voicemail. I take a look at the number. It's international, a US number to be precise. Then a message beeps through.

Gesturing to Sean that I'm going to listen to the

message outside, I walk through the hall, open the front door and stand at the top of Oscar's front steps. I press the voicemail button and lift the phone to my ear.

'Good evening, Miss O'Brien,' a clipped American voice says. 'This is Raoul calling from The Plaza Hotel. I'm terribly sorry to be the bearer of bad news on this sunny New York evening, but I'm afraid there is a problem with your booking with us for December. It seems your wedding planner, Geraldo, has double-booked you with another couple – it's all a terrible misunderstanding, and as such I can assure you that Geraldo's services will no longer be welcome here at The Plaza Hotel. But unfortunately it means we are no longer able to accommodate you and your wedding here at the hotel. I realise this must inconvenience you terribly, and if there's anything I can do to be of assistance in rearranging your plans elsewhere, please don't hesitate to get in touch. Your deposit will, of course, be immediately refunded. Again we send you our most heartfelt apologies, Miss O'Brien, and hope you'll choose The Plaza again for any future event you may wish to hold.' And the message ends.

I stand on Oscar's steps completely motionless. Passersby might have thought I was a statue were I not wearing a baby-doll nightie and slippers. But I feel as hard and cold as a statue right now as I try to digest the message I've just heard on my phone.

No, this simply can't be happening, I tell myself. *Not after we've spent so long looking for the perfect venue. What will we do now? The wedding is only a few months away; I've already sent 'save the date' notecards out – just like I was advised to in all my bridal magazines. I've organised flowers and menus and … Oh, the list goes on and on. I can't just start all over again.*

I realise my phone is still held to my ear, so I slowly lower it to my side and look up into the night sky. *Why?* I ask it silently. *Why is this happening to me?*

If everything happens for a reason, why is this?

After I've taken a few deep breaths outside on the steps, I head back into the house.

'Darling!' Oscar calls down the hall as he heads back to the lounge with a large jug of something dangerous-looking. 'What have you been doing outside dressed like that?'

'Just a phone call,' I say, holding up my phone.

'Anything important?' Oscar asks, coming over to me and putting his arm around my shoulders. 'Isn't this just *the* best party ever, sweetie? I'm just so happy tonight I could burst. Goodness knows what I'll feel like at the wedding on Saturday if this is anything to go by!'

I turn to Oscar. He really is radiating happiness tonight. Both he and Luke look like they're wearing coat hangers in their mouths, their smiles are that wide. 'No, it's nothing important. Nothing that can't wait, anyway.'

'Good, good,' Oscar says, kissing me on the cheek. 'I can't have my chief bridesmaid stressed in any way, now, can I?'

I shake my head and take a deep breath as we head back into the lounge together.

No, the stress will have to wait until tomorrow. Tonight is Oscar's night, and I won't have that spoiled by anything or anyone.

Thirty-two

The next day I'm up early, but Sean, as I suspected he would, sleeps late.

We rolled in in the early hours of the morning, quite the worse for wear, and Sean fell asleep straight away.

I was glad. I'd spent enough of the night faking happiness after I'd listened to my phone message, so I really didn't want to have to fake anything else.

I hadn't told anyone about the voicemail from The Plaza, not even Sean. I knew if I did, I would only burst into tears, and I didn't want the whole story to come out at the party and ruin Oscar and Luke's night.

But now, as I sit in our kitchen drinking a mug of coffee, I can't wait for him to wake up so I can share my awful news. What do they say? 'A problem shared is a problem halved.' I highly doubted it in this case. This problem shared would just mean two of us stressing about where our wedding would now be held.

'Is there any of that coffee for me?' Sean asks, standing with his head pressed against the kitchen doorframe. 'I'll need about a gallon to make this hangover go away.'

'Teach you for drinking so much,' I say, standing up to get him some, as he slides onto a kitchen chair and rests his head in his hands on the table.

'You were drinking too,' Sean says. 'How come you don't feel like this? What the hell does Oscar put in that punch of his, anyway?'

'You don't want to know,' I reply, pouring him a mug of black coffee and passing it to him at the table. 'It will only make you feel worse.'

Sean takes a sip of the coffee and sits back in his chair. 'So why *aren't* you looking like me, then? You seem remarkably wide awake this morning.'

I sit down in the chair opposite Sean. 'I had some bad news last night. That phone call I took outside Oscar's house.'

'What? But you said that was just work.' Sean sits bolt upright, his expression suddenly much sharper. 'What bad news?'

'Our wedding at The Plaza has been cancelled,' I tell him, not pulling any punches. 'Apparently they double-booked us.'

'What?' Sean says again. 'How? I mean, I know how, but how can The Plaza have let that happen? They're a

293

top-notch hotel; they don't just double-book people. A dinner reservation maybe, but not a whole bloody wedding!'

Sean's voice has risen steadily throughout his speech to a loud roar. He winces now as his hangover cuts in again.

'It's not the best news to wake up to this morning, I know. But what can we do?'

'I'll tell you what we can do. We'll ring them up straight away. We can't just be let down like this. They need to sort out their priorities. Where's your phone? Give me the number.'

'Sean, calm down. There's no point.'

'There is a point. I'm going to sort this out right now.'

'No, you're missing my point. You can't – the time difference?' I remind him. 'It's too early there yet.'

Sean nods. 'Fair enough. But as soon as it is an appropriate time, I'm straight on the phone. Who do I need to speak to?'

'Our wedding was arranged by Geraldo, but apparently he's been fired as a result of what's happened. My message last night was from a Raoul.'

'Right,' Sean nods. 'Raoul it is. I'm going to get to the bottom of this, Scarlett. No one is going to mess with our wedding day, do you hear? No one.'

But as hard as Sean tries later, remonstrating and arguing with Raoul for some minutes, even he can't sort this one.

'I'm sorry, Red,' he says, shaking his head as he hangs

up his phone and comes over to me. 'They won't budge.' He puts his arms around me and pulls me close. 'I've even threatened them with legal action, but they say it will make no difference; there was a clause in the contract you signed, apparently. Was there?'

I look dismally up at Sean. 'I don't know,' I answer in a voice that I can hardly stop from breaking. 'I was just so pleased we'd actually found somewhere to get married at last that I simply signed my name. I assumed it would be OK.'

'And it will be, Red,' Sean says gently, seeing how upset I am. 'We may not be able to get married in some poncey hotel, but we'll still have our day.'

'How will we when we don't even have a venue now? We can't just get married in a field somewhere.' I pull away from Sean's embrace and begin to pace the kitchen as my upset swiftly turns to frustration. 'Oh God, what about all the people we've invited? What are we going to tell them? That I've ballsed it all up yet again?'

'Scarlett ... listen to me.' Sean grabs me again by the arms and holds me still, so I have no choice but to look him in the eye. 'This is not your fault. It's all going to be fine. I'll make sure it is, I promise you.'

'But how can you?' I'm beginning to sob now. 'We've organised everything around The Plaza. We can't just change all our arrangements now.'

'Who says we can't?'

'There isn't time to. I definitely don't have the time to

organise a wedding all over again. There's the businesses, the trust, my project with Gabi. Then there's—' I'm about to tell him about Alex and the trouble he's been causing me, but I stop myself just in time.

'There's what?' Sean asks.

'Nothing. It's nothing.'

'It's obviously something if it's stressing you this much.'

I want to, but I just can't tell him about Alex. Not yet. Not until I know for sure.

I think quickly.

'There is something else,' I improvise. 'But I can't tell you about it.'

Sean's forehead wrinkles. 'Why? We never have secrets from each other.'

I take a deep breath. 'I'm not just helping Gabi in the way you think I am.'

Sean waits for me to continue.

'She's asked me to search for her relative too,' I say truthfully. This isn't a lie. I *am* doing this. It just isn't the thing that's my *main* source of stress right now.

'And so?' Sean asks.

'It's complicated. She doesn't want any press involved. She wants to keep it a secret.'

'And you think I'm going to go running to the press?' Sean asks, stepping back from me a little.

'No, of course not. She asked me not to tell anyone, that's all, and so I haven't. But it's taking up so much of my time, Sean. Her great-aunt is proving impossible to find.

Even though I'm happy to do this for Gabi, it's another thing I'm trying to squeeze into my already manic life.' I look up at him. 'I'm so sorry I couldn't tell you before. I felt really bad if it's any consolation.'

'Nah, you did the right thing,' Sean says, relaxing a little. 'If she asked you not to share, then you were only keeping a promise.' He takes me in his arms again. 'I can see why you're getting so stressed at the moment, now you've told me all that, though. But no more secrets from now on, OK?'

'Sure.' I try to sound convincing.

Sean looks over my shoulder into the distance, his eyes slightly glazed.

'What? What are you thinking?' I ask, worried.

'Scrub what I just said,' Sean says, a smile spreading across his face.

'Which bit?'

'About no secrets. I want to keep a very big secret from you, Scarlett – for the next few months, anyway. I know you didn't want this before, but now it's the perfect solution.'

'What do you mean?'

'I'm going to take all your stress away,' Sean says, his eyes shining with excitement. 'Well, some of it, because *I'm* going to organise our new wedding. Just me, no one else. And you, my beautiful bride, you are simply going to turn up on the day – radiant, without a care in the world.' He looks down keenly at me for my reaction. 'What do you say, Red? Do you trust I can do it?'

I think about everything that's happened, and everything that's still going on right now. Things I need to do, and things I'll have to do if I'm to organise a whole new wedding ...

'Come on, Red?' Sean encourages. 'Do you trust I can organise our wedding or not?'

His enthusiasm is infectious. 'I do,' I say, smiling up at him. 'Of course I'm going to say I do!'

Thirty-three

I look at myself in the full-length mirror that hangs in Oscar's bedroom and I have to admit that actually I don't look too bad.

When Oscar first told me about the *Midsummer Night's Dream* theme for his wedding, I was very concerned. I knew Oscar, and I knew what he was capable of dress-wise. I didn't really get a proper idea of our outfits when I went for my fitting because the costumes we tried on (and they really were costumes, not just dresses) were just pieces of fabric loosely stitched together to form a cloth pattern, a bit like the sort tailors make as a template before the final suit. But now, as I stand here admiring my final costume, it really is quite something to behold.

All Oscar's female attendants are going to be dressed as fairies – but not the sort of fairy you stick on the top of a

Christmas tree, or a pink sparkly doll that a little girl might carry around. No, we are very definitely the mystical sprites and nymph-type fairies that Shakespeare created for one of his most beloved plays.

My outfit, supposedly based on Titania, Queen of the Fairies, is in the main made of a dark green silk. My dress has a boned bodice that laces at the back, with gold leaves and flowers embroidered all across the front. The skirt is three-quarter-length and loose, and my billowy sleeves are made of delicate green gossamer. Wound like a snake round my bodice are long silk strands of green ivy. I am wearing large fairy wings, but they are so light and translucent that I hardly know I have them on. In my long, dark hair, which I'm wearing loose at the back and pulled up at the sides, I have more strands of ivy intertwined with delicate old-fashioned white roses.

'Looking good, Scarlett,' a voice says behind me. 'Who would have thought we could pull off fairies at our age!'

I turn round to see Ursula, who is wearing a similar outfit to mine, but in a dark ruby red, and where my roses are white, hers are deep red.

'I know. I can't say I wasn't a little worried when Oscar said what he was thinking of for us, but that guy Jonnie has done a fantastic job.'

Jonnie is a friend of Luke's who works in theatre costume design. Oscar and Luke asked him to design them some wedding outfits as a favour. Not only had he designed and made our outfits, but he'd made Oscar and Luke's too.

'Hasn't he just,' Ursula says, spinning round so her light skirt billows out. 'I really do feel like a fairy princess.'

'Me too,' I agree, taking another quick look in the mirror. 'They truly are exquisite.'

We were also going to be joined by Beth, Luke's niece. Beth was being dressed by her mother right now in the living room as she was only four years old. Her outfit was similar in design to mine and Ursula's, but was in gold.

'Hey, my two best girls,' Oscar calls at the door. 'How's it going? Whoa!' he calls as we turn round. 'You two are going to steal my thunder looking like that!'

'I hardly think so!' I reply, taking in Oscar's outfit. 'You look amazing!'

Oscar looks like autumn has just exploded all over him. His trousers are covered in burgundy, green and gold feathers, so his bottom half looks like an exotic bird of paradise. He has a matching feather sash leading from his trousers to his fitted tailcoat jacket, which is black velvet, with green, red and gold embroidery to match our dresses. On his head, he wears a simple garland of ivy, with no flowers this time, but a few more feathers, and if you look closely, you can just see two tiny horns peeking out of his dark brown hair.

'Do you think?' Oscar asks, doing his usual spin. 'It's not a tad over the top, is it?'

I look at Ursula.

'Of course it is, you fool,' she says, trying to hug him without getting into a tangle of feathers and ivy. 'But it wouldn't be you if it wasn't!'

'Scarlett?' he asks, looking at me for approval.

'It's just perfect for today,' I reply. 'Luke will adore you in it!'

'Oh, I hope so,' Oscar says, looking worriedly in the long mirror. 'His outfit is a tad more traditional than mine. I hope he doesn't think I've gone too far. I'm supposed to be Puck to his Oberon, you see?'

'Oh, now I get the horns. I did wonder,' Ursula says, examining his hair again.

'Oh God, oh God, what have I done?' Oscar suddenly squeals. 'Everyone is going to laugh, aren't they?'

'Oscar,' I try and say in a reassuring voice, 'no one is going to laugh. They will all be here because they love you and Luke. They know exactly what you're like. And that is *why* they love you.'

Oscar smiles now. 'Yes, I know, and you're right of course. I'm just really, really nervous.'

'You are simply behaving like any bride on her wedding day,' I wink. 'You did tell me you were going to be a bride one day, remember?'

'Of course I do! I never thought I'd be one before you, though, sweetie.'

My heart sinks as I'm reminded of the chaos surrounding my own wedding right now. But I'm determined my problems aren't going to cast a dark cloud over today. This is Oscar and Luke's special day, and no one is going to ruin it.

Our mode of transport to the Globe Theatre isn't quite so Shakespearean; it's a VW camper van decorated with yet more ivy and white flowers to tie in with the theme. The cream and white model that arrives to collect the wedding party from Oscar's house in Notting Hill is absolutely pristine, and its chrome gleams in the bright September sun as we make our way across London to the Globe.

As we all sit in the back of the van, Oscar looks more nervous than I've ever seen him. In fact, I can't remember seeing Oscar look nervous about anything before.

'It's going to be fine,' I assure him. 'It's all going to run smoothly.'

Oscar just nods and clutches his bouquet even more tightly. His and our bouquets consist of a few stems of the same white and deep red flowers that Ursula and I have in our hair, bound simply by a few strands of gold and green ivy.

'You look lovely, Uncle Oscar,' little Beth says from her seat next to me. 'My uncle Luke loves you very much.'

Oscar smiles down at her, his paralysing nerves suddenly banished by a few perfect words from a little girl.

'Thank you, Beth,' he says, leaning across to squeeze her hand. 'I'm really glad you think so.'

*

Luke has already arrived when we get there. He's been driven to the Globe in his best man's Aston Martin.

I love how even though this is a civil ceremony between two gay men, they are both playing their parts as if it were a ceremony for a straight couple, Oscar carrying out the traditional role of the bride, with us as his attendants, and Luke arriving separately, with his own groomsman.

Although Luke is wearing a much more traditional outfit than Oscar, he is still following today's theme. He wears a pair of black velvet trousers with a matching long tailcoat, which, like Oscar's, is edged with the red, green and gold threads that link all the outfits. He also wears smart black patent shoes, a crisp white wing-collared shirt and a thin belt of ivy and feathers round his middle to tie in with Oscar's more flamboyant outfit. The lining of his suit, I notice as he moves, is a red and green tartan print.

He looks elegant and very handsome as he comes over to greet us all.

'You look fabulous, Luke,' I tell him. 'Your friend Jonnie has done a fantastic job on our outfits.'

'Hasn't he just,' Luke says, but his eyes dart over towards Oscar, who is just alighting from the camper van.

'Well, what do you think?' Oscar asks, striking a thespian-style pose in his outfit.

Luke simply goes over to Oscar and whispers in his ear.

I don't know what he says, but it must be good because Oscar flushes red, and his nervous smile turns into one of the broadest, happiest grins I've ever seen.

'Right, let's do this!' he calls to the rest of us. 'It's time for us to go get wed!'

The area of the Globe where the wedding is being held is called the UnderGlobe because, funnily enough, it's situated under the Globe Theatre. I've visited once before, with a business contact of Sean's from Seattle who was a huge fan of Shakespeare. We had the full tour of the theatre while we were there; we sat in the wooden stalls trying to imagine what it would have felt like to be watching a Shakespeare play hundreds of years ago, and we visited the Globe exhibition, which was what the UnderGlobe area usually housed, so I think I know what to expect as we walk through the entrance doors to join the rest of the wedding guests today.

But how wrong I am. The UnderGlobe has been transformed into an enchanted wonderland full of glitter and magic. It's like I've stepped into another world. A world in which dreams become reality, and fairy tales become truth.

There are huge swathes of tulle and net fabric hanging from the ceiling, creating a shimmery, cloud-like effect when you look up. Twinkly white fairy lights have been twisted round tables and pillars with more strands of ivy. Tall trees in pots, similarly decorated with lights, and the elegant white marble statues that have been placed around the room add a sense of serenity and calm. Tables cover most of the floor, beautifully laid with cloths in burgundy and deep green. There are swags of the same tartan fabric that Luke has in his tailcoat tied to the backs of gold chairs, which in turn match the gold cutlery that marks each place setting. A single tall gold pillar candle stands in the centre of each table inside a long glass vase, with graceful lilies appearing to grow up around them.

The wedding guests are all sitting in front of a stage area, waiting patiently on rows of gold chairs, with swags of yet more ivy and white flowers linking each row to make an aisle down which the happy couple will walk in a moment. At the end of the aisle, on top of the stage, there are yet more flowers and lit candles, of varying sizes this time, standing on two tall columns draped in white tulle and gold silk. The whole effect is quite breathtaking.

'What do you think?' Oscar whispers to me. 'I helped them design the entire thing.'

'It's just beautiful, Oscar,' I gasp. 'I can't believe how wonderful it all looks.'

Oscar nods. 'Yep, it's come off a treat.'

'Ready to rumble, Oscar?' Luke asks, taking Oscar's arm.

'Of course,' Oscar says. 'Lead on, Macduff! Wrong play, I know,' he winks at us, as we gather in front of them to walk down some steps and along the aisle.

'Actually, that's the wrong quote,' Luke says. '*That* character actually says, "Lay on", not, "Lead on". It's heavily misquoted.'

'See, this is why I'm marrying you,' Oscar says, smiling

adoringly at him. 'So very clever. You can even correctly quote from *Mac*—'

'Nope!' Luke says, placing his hand over Oscar's mouth. 'This *is* a theatre, you know. We can't mention the Scottish play before a performance, or even quote it fully! Which, you'll note, I didn't,' he says proudly to us.

'Oops, sorry, babe!' Oscar says. 'We don't want any bad luck today, that's for sure.'

'There won't be any,' I promise him. 'Today is going to be absolutely perfect, Oscar. Of that I have no doubt.'

Thirty-four

The ceremony of course goes wonderfully.

Oscar has hired a harpist, and she plays 'The Flower Duet' by Delibes as we walk down the aisle.

Beth is the first to walk along the flower-filled aisle; she scatters rose petals from a tiny basket to 'ooh's and 'ah's from the guests. Ursula is next, accompanied by Luke's groomsman, Paul. I then follow, holding the arm of Luke's best man, Zachary.

I can barely keep back my tears and emotion as I reach the top of the aisle, climb up on the stage with Zachary and then watch Oscar and Luke follow us down the aisle. They both look so happy.

I've heard Oscar's personally written vows already – he ran them past me the other evening before his hen and stag night – but I'm in bits when I hear him recite them to Luke, who in turn recites his own tenderly back to Oscar. Zachary has to remove his green handkerchief from his top pocket for me to dab my eyes with, my tears run that heavily.

When we have a break in the ceremony for Oscar and Luke to sign the register, the harpist plays another song, and then a quartet of musicians play Elizabethan music on traditional instruments that would have been around in Shakespeare's time – a lute, a flute, a harpsichord and some bagpipes – yes, they even managed to bring a Scottish twist to the music.

Then it's time to walk back down the aisle to 'The Trumpet Voluntary'. I feel quite cultured knowing the names of these classical pieces of music, but it's only because Oscar sent an email of YouTube links for me to listen to when he was choosing them. In fact, this whole wedding has so much of Oscar written all over it that I begin to question just how much Luke actually had to do with it. *Will my own wedding be like this?* I wonder, as I walk back down the aisle behind the happy couple. I catch Sean's eye as I pass him and he gives me an approving wink.

And would it be all that bad if it was? Sean, for all his often staid, practical ways, was very inventive in both the manner we finally got together at the top of the London Eye and in his proposal to me on the Brooklyn Bridge in New York. Would he really make such a bad job of organising our wedding? I was beginning to think he might make a much better job of it than I ever could.

*

After the ceremony we all mingle, glasses of champagne in hand, while the wedding photographs are taken. Then we get the chance to stand upon the hallowed Globe stage while the photographer sets up some atmospheric shots of the couple and the wedding guests. Afterwards we all return to the UnderGlobe and back to the party.

'Hey, Scarlett. You look divine!' Gabi says to me as I help myself to another glass of champagne. 'I'm so glad I flew over for this. I wouldn't have missed it for the world.' Gabi is looking stunning as always today. She has a ring of purple and pink flowers delicately placed in her hair, and she wears a long deep purple mediaeval-style dress. I knew she'd surreptitiously flown over with Max from New York a couple of days ago, but since their relationship is still a secret, I am the only one who knows they came over together.

Oscar and Gabi have grown quite close since her party. The common ground they found initially in their search for my perfect wedding dress, which I'm still to see, has now turned into friendship through their many messages and sessions on Skype. So it was no surprise when Oscar said he was going to invite her to his wedding.

'Why, thank you.' I give a little twirl. 'Do you think wings suit me?'

But as I spin back round to face her, I find someone else by Gabi's side passing her a glass of champagne, and it's a face I don't find as welcoming.

'I think they are very becoming,' a deep Scots voice replies. 'You look beautiful, Scarlett.'

'What are *you* doing here?' I demand, shocked to see Alex's sly face before me. 'You weren't invited.'

'Scarlett!' Gabi says, looking a little surprised at my outburst. 'Alex came with me today. We have some business to attend to while I'm here, and since Alex knew Oscar a long time ago, it didn't seem inappropriate he should attend as my guest.' She gives me a look to suggest she couldn't exactly arrive with Max.

He didn't seem to know Oscar all that well when we were in Edinburgh, I think. *What was Alex up to this time? Or was this simply so he could see Maddie while he was here?*

'Yes, of course. I'm sorry,' I reply, trying to get my thoughts together. 'I'm sure you'll be most welcome, Alex.'

I look him in the eye, but I can't go as far as faking a smile.

'I'm enjoying what I've seen so far,' Alex says. 'And I'm liking the Scottish theme running through everything. I've even got a little of that going on myself.' He holds out the side of his black tuxedo jacket to display a tartan waistcoat.

How can I love one Scotsman so much and yet hate another with the same intensity? I wonder. Luke is a lovely, gentle man who wouldn't hurt a fly. And Alex ... Well, Alex Woolfe just makes my skin crawl.

'Yes,' I reply, trying to continue a polite conversation as best I can, while my mind still churns over Alex's presence. 'Oscar has tried to include Luke's heritage as much as possible. So what sort of business are you two doing?' I ask suddenly. I'm concerned for Gabi's welfare if what Portia,

311

and now Peter and I suspected turned out to be true. Gabi's charities are all based in the US, so it can't be anything to do with them. This must be something new.

'Oh, nothing we need discuss now,' Gabi says. 'This is a wedding – it's bad form to discuss business here.'

I mustn't look too satisfied with that reply because she adds, 'Alex has had someone drop out of an investment deal recently and he wants me to come in with him, that's all.'

Alex gives me a knowing look.

Peter's cancelled deal. Of course.

'Hey, gorgeous.' I feel two arms try and wrap round me from behind, but they get tangled in my wings and so Sean appears at my side instead. 'How's my little Tinker Bell?'

I give him a scathing look. 'I am not Tinker Bell, as well you know. I'm supposed to be Titania, Queen of the Fairies.'

'Yes, of course you are, my love,' Sean says, winking at Gabi and Alex. 'Hey, man. How are you?' Sean gives Alex a manly hug.

'Good, Seany, good. Your turn next at this wedding lark, eh?'

'Yep, I reckon so,' Sean says. 'Although, we have had a slight hitch with the venue ... so we're not getting married at The Plaza now.'

'What?' Gabi exclaims. 'Why not?'

'There was a mix-up with the booking,' I explain. 'It's fine – we'll sort something out, won't we, Sean?'

Sean smiles at me. 'Of course we will!'

'If you need any help,' Gabi says, looking worried, 'you only have to shout – you know that. I have a few contacts.' She gives me a little wink.

'I wouldn't normally encourage another woman to wink at my fiancé, but on this occasion it's Sean you should be winking at, Gabi. He's the one organising our wedding from now on. I'm having nothing to do with it. It's all going to be a lovely surprise on the day.'

Well, I hope it will be a lovely one . . .

'Really?' Gabi exclaims again. 'How wonderfully novel.'

'Yes,' Alex agrees. 'Very *new man*, Sean.'

'That's because I am,' Sean says proudly. 'And I'm going to make it the best wedding ever since nuptials began.'

I squeeze his hand and he smiles at me again.

'Well,' Alex says, 'good luck to you. I can't believe The Plaza let you down like that. They're usually so good. I'm sorry – I hope it wasn't anything I did.'

'No, mate, of course not,' Sean says, patting Alex on the shoulder. 'Thanks for trying to help us in the first place, though.'

'It was nothing,' Alex replies. 'Oh dear, it's *awful* what can happen when people become slack, isn't it?'

I glance at Alex when he says this. He's looking at me.

'As Scarlett always says, everything happens for a reason, so I'm sure it will be for the best,' Sean says perkily. 'Whoever was the cause of the cancellation will no doubt have done us a favour in the long run.'

A man with a loud Shakespearean voice, wearing a ruff

313

and doublet and hose, instructs us it's time to take our seats for dinner, so we dutifully go over to inspect the seating plan, which is written in ornate black calligraphy. Sean and I are at a round table with Oscar, Luke, Ursula and Paul, and Zachary and his partner.

As I wait for my first course to be served, I inspect the other wedding guests in more detail. Many of Oscar and Luke's friends have really made an effort with their outfits, either embracing the *Midsummer Night's Dream* theme by wearing fairy-inspired costumes or by going the full Elizabethan, with a ruff and doublet and hose, like the master of ceremonies, who I discover during dinner is an acting friend of Luke's.

Then there are the older guests, who I suspect are mainly relatives. They have gone the more traditional route and the men are wearing suits or, in the case of some of Luke's family, kilts, while the women wear the usual wedding attire – a mixture of dresses and skirt suits, with the odd hat thrown in.

I have to admire the woman who has come as the character Bottom from the play. She has a full mane of ragged black donkey-like hair, big pointy grey ears and a really long— Oh, I realise as she turns fully towards me, that's her *real* face and hair. It's just the donkey's ears she's added as a nudge towards the play.

Now I'm the one feeling like an ass, as I hurriedly turn back towards my own table, glad I haven't pointed her out.

I'm pleased that Oscar and Luke have placed us on the

main table with them. Not because I want to feel special or more important than any of the other wedding guests, but because I know that Oscar's family is a lot sparser than Luke's and if Luke's parents had sat at the top table, it would have been very obvious that Oscar was sadly missing his. But I am pleased to see Oscar's grandmother has made it today. I've met her a few times when she's visited Oscar in Notting Hill. She's a wonderful woman, full of spirit and joy – in fact, she reminds me a lot of Oscar.

The dinner, just like the rest of the wedding, is absolutely perfect, and soon it becomes time for the speeches.

Luke makes one first about Oscar and then goes on to thank us all for coming and joining them here today – he delivers it in a very professional, actory-type way. But when he's finished there is no doubt in anyone's mind how genuine his love for Oscar is.

Then Oscar stands up. 'Darlings,' he begins, 'I can't thank you all enough for coming here to join us on our very special day. When I first met this man –' he turns to Luke '– I had no idea that first meeting would one day lead to all this.' He gestures out into the room. 'Luke and I didn't really see eye to eye to begin with – on many levels!' Oscar lifts his hand over his head and pauses while the guests laugh at his joke. Luke, at six foot two, towers over Oscar's petite five-five frame. 'He was cool, calm and collected, and I'm … Well, you all know what I'm like.' He gives us his usual Oscar-like twirl and his audience laugh at him again. 'So really we were two complete opposites. But given the right circumstances, opposites attract. And I'm very pleased to say we did too – to magnetic proportions!' Luke reaches up and takes Oscar's hand. 'So much so that now you can't keep us apart ... Well, except when his pesky acting gets in the way!' There're a few polite titters. 'But even then I'm always with you in spirit.' Oscar looks down at Luke. 'You know that, don't you?' he says almost in a whisper.

Luke nods.

'So now I want you all to raise your glasses to my one and only – and many of you never thought you'd hear me say that!' He winks at the guests. 'My darling, gorgeous, handsome new husband, Luke!'

We all raise our glasses to Luke, who in his usual modest way looks a little embarrassed.

'Now, I believe Zachary, Luke's best man, will say a few words.' Oscar sits down and we wait for Zachary to stand.

'What a lovely speech,' I say to Sean. 'Oscar's really matured since he met Luke.'

'Hasn't he just?' Sean replies. 'This whole wedding has been very elegant and restrained. I'm impressed – it's not at all like Oscar!'

I grin at him and turn to where I expect to find Zachary already standing, about to begin his speech, but he's not – he's frantically feeling in his pockets and looking extremely worried, while Luke talks to him.

'What's wrong?' I ask Oscar, next to me, tapping on his shoulder.

Oscar turns round. 'Zachary's only lost his bloody speech!

I knew Luke should have asked someone more reliable – Zachary is a fruit loop at the best of times.'

'Zachary's lost his speech,' I report back to Sean.

'Uh-oh,' Sean says, grimacing. 'That's not good. Can't he wing it?'

'Can't he wing it?' I ask Oscar again, who by the look on his face is ready to leap on Zachary himself and turn out his pockets.

'He says he can't. He's panicking, just like I told Luke he would.'

I look around at the guests, who are beginning to shuffle awkwardly in their chairs. Oh dear, this isn't good; it's all gone so perfectly up until now.

'Can't you say something?' I ask Sean.

'Me?' Sean says. 'Why me?'

'Because you're good at all that speech-making kind of thing. You do it all the time when you're at work.'

'That's not a speech; that's a presentation. It's different – I've prepared for it. I feel quite sorry for poor Zachary there.'

'Please, Sean! Help them.'

Sean rolls his eyes at me. 'OK, OK!'

He stands up and clears his throat. 'Ladies and gentlemen, if I could just have your attention for a moment. I'm afraid we have a slight technical hitch to the proceedings – in the name of a missing best man's speech.'

There's laughter, then the scraping of a chair as Zachary now flees from the room red-faced.

'And, it would seem, a missing best man now too,' Sean continues. 'So I guess that's a change of plan, then?'

I look around the room at all the people now smiling and whispering between themselves, and then my eyes rest on Alex. He's looking at us all sitting at the top table, but his isn't a smile; it's very definitely a smirk. 'Slack,' he mouths to me. 'Very slack.'

I pull on Sean's arm. 'Announce me,' I beg him.

'What?' he whispers.

'Tell them I'll be making the next speech.'

'Are you sure?'

'Yes, just do it.'

'Ladies and gentlemen,' Sean says, tapping his dessert-spoon on a glass to gain their attention, 'the next speech will be made by Miss Scarlett O'Brien.'

I stand up to silence. There are curious and, in some cases, judgemental eyes glaring at me now and I feel myself start to shake. But then I hear a whoop and some clapping, and I spy Max sitting across the room. He's managed to squeeze himself in next to Gabi – no doubt changing the name cards around, I think, smiling gratefully at him. Gabi joins in with the clapping with a shrill whistle, and then Maddie, Ursula and all the guests who know me are encouraging me.

I hold up my hand to think for a moment and there's silence again when I bring it back down.

'Many of you won't know who I am,' I begin quietly, 'but my name is Scarlett, and I'm Oscar's friend.' I don't mean to, but I can't help glancing over at Alex. He's yawning in a very conspicuous manner. 'When I first came to London,' I continue in a louder, more confident voice, 'I didn't know anyone. I was a bit of a lost soul, both inside and out. But then I met Oscar and he befriended me. He took me, a complete stranger, into his home and made me feel welcome. He introduced me to his friends, many of whom are in this room today, and they too made me feel welcome and part of their unique family.'

Ursula, along with Lucien and Patrick, and Brooke and Vanessa, who attended the dinner party that Oscar held for me when I first arrived in Notting Hill, wave and clap.

'But Oscar did more for me than simply make me feel like I belonged; he helped me find the love of my life too, who, I'm pleased to say, is the man sitting next to me right now.'

I look down at Sean; he winks quickly and nods his encouragement.

'So all I've ever wanted for Oscar is to find the same sort of love that I have in my life.'

There are a few 'aw's.

'Let's just say Oscar tested the water very thoroughly before finding Luke—'

I'm surprised to find myself having to wait for laughter to die down before I can continue.

'But when Luke came along, Oscar's gaydar was well and truly put into retirement.'

More laughter. I'm beginning to quite enjoy this. I

hadn't meant to be funny at all. I hadn't meant to be anything; I was just telling them exactly what came from my heart.

'I think I knew Luke was the man for Oscar before even he did.'

I turn and look at Luke now. He's smiling.

'Luke, you are everything that Oscar isn't. You're calm, restrained, eloquent and handsome too.'

More laughter. *Oh, was I making a joke again?*

'But my Oscar, he's vibrant, loud and full of life. He also has the most garish dress sense that I've ever seen!'

Whoops with applause this time.

'But he manages to make all this work to his advantage and with great aplomb. And that's what's so wonderful about the two of you: it's your differences that make you the perfect couple, along with your unbreakable love for each other, which we've all seen demonstrated so clearly today.'

More applause.

'So now, instead of one fabulous friend, I have two wonderful people in my life who I am lucky enough to be able to call my very good friends. So, ladies and gentlemen, I ask you to raise your glasses to the perfect couple. To Oscar and Luke!'

'Oscar and Luke!' everyone repeats as they stand, and it's then that I look at Oscar for the first time. I haven't dared to look at him the whole time I've been speaking, for fear I might break down with emotion. But now, as I look at my friend, I see his face awash with tears. And it's then that I start crying too.

'I love you, Scarlett,' he mouths at me among all the cheers and clapping, which, I suddenly realise now the toast has finished, are for me and my speech.

'I love you too, Oscar,' I manage to reply, before I flop back down into my chair in relief.

Thirty-five

Later, the tables have been cleared, and the atmosphere has become much more relaxed.

A disco has been set up, and we are just getting ready to enjoy some music, dancing and a few more drinks from the well-stocked bar that has appeared in a far corner of the room.

'Ladies and gentlemen,' our Shakespearean master of ceremonies announces, 'please gather round for your newly-weds' first dance together as a married couple!'

We all form a circle round the dance floor and await Oscar and Luke's appearance.

'Will their first dance mirror the rest of the day so far and be elegant and refined?' Sean asks me as we wait.

'I really don't know anything about this part: Oscar hasn't told me a thing. It's a closely guarded secret.'

Just then the lights lower and a spotlight is shone on the centre of the floor, and suddenly it seems like Oscar is not only about to reveal his and Luke's first dance but a whole lot more besides, as he struts onto the floor in a pair of skintight black leather trousers and a tight black shirt. He takes up a John Travolta 'Staying Alive'-style pose under the spotlight, then we hear the first notes of 'Vogue' by Madonna, to which Oscar goes on to expertly perform all the movements with great relish. The music then does a smooth transition into 'Always' by Bon Jovi and Oscar performs the first verse with much gusto, acting the part of a lost, heartbroken soul, until the chorus, when suddenly from across the floor Luke, like his knight in shining armour, appears and they come together to dance a slow, loving waltz to the chorus.

The guests love it. They clap and whoop, as Oscar and now Luke dance for them. Then the music changes again and the first beats of '(I've Had) The Time of My Life' from *Dirty Dancing* are heard. They now perform a wonderful and quite complex rhumba to the song (yes, I've watched enough *Strictly* to know my dances!), with Luke even lifting Oscar at the end, just like Johnny does to Baby in the film, much to the delight of the guests, who clap, shout and whistle their approval.

At the end of the song, Luke and Oscar take their bows, Oscar milking the attention and applause for all he's worth and Luke simply giving a small nod to his guests in gratitude for their appreciation.

Then we are encouraged onto the dance floor by the happy couple, and Sean and I dance in each other's arms to 'She's the One' by Robbie Williams.

'I'm pretty sure old Will Shakespeare never saw dancing like that at the Globe in his day,' Sean says, whispering into my ear while we dance. 'But they made a good job of it, I thought.'

I look up at Sean. 'Shall we do something like that for our first dance?' I ask, batting my eyelids innocently at him.

Sean looks panicky, until he sees my eyelashes fluttering. 'Er ... I think not, no. We'll leave the showman stuff to Oscar – *he* suits it!'

I laugh. 'Yes, he does. I'm pleased he did that, though. I was beginning to feel this wedding was a little too one-sided.'

'How do you mean?'

'Even though it's been the most beautiful wedding, and I know Oscar was the one who did most of the organising and preparations, it just felt a bit too thespian. A bit too Luke. Am I making sense? That little display there brought some of the real Oscar into the proceedings. The one I know and love.'

Sean nods. 'Are you worried that might happen with our wedding, now I'm in charge of the preparations? It might be too one-sided?'

'Perhaps, a little bit.'

'Scarlett, don't you worry,' Sean says, holding me at

arm's length while we spin round. 'I will make sure our day is as much a part of you as it is me. You have my word!'

He pulls me back in towards him and we're about to kiss when I feel a tap on my shoulder.

'Would you mind awfully if I cut in?' Alex asks. 'I'd like to take the future bride around the dance floor, if I may?'

'Of course you may,' Sean says at the same time as I call out, 'No!'

Sean looks at me with a puzzled expression.

'I mean, listen –' I hold my hand up in the air '– the song has finished now.'

But of course another one immediately starts up.

'Wonderful,' Alex says, grabbing me. 'I'll bring her back safe and sound, Sean, don't you worry!'

And then before I can argue further, Alex whisks me out into the middle of the dance floor, away from Sean.

Having Alex this close makes me feel quite nauseous, and as I glance up at him now – through necessity rather than choice – I see he's smiling.

I remember the first time I saw his smile; it reminded me of a shark. Even though Alex's bright white teeth are carefully polished like an antique mahogany table, his smile isn't anywhere near as genuine.

'So, have you enjoyed yourself today, Scarlett?' he asks as we dance to Christina Perri's 'Jar of Hearts'.

'Yes, it's been an amazing wedding. As near perfect as you can get.' I decide I'll be polite. Sean, although now in conversation with Maddie, is watching us from the sidelines.

'Indeed. Even the slight hitch with the best man hasn't precluded it from being in the amazing category. I imagine you hope your day will be just as wonderful.'

'It will be.' I look him directly in the eye. 'Now Sean is organising it, nothing can go wrong.'

'Ha,' Alex laughs. 'Never say that, Scarlett – you're just tempting fate. After all, look what happened with The Plaza. I've known the people who work at that hotel for years and I don't remember anything ever going wrong before. Funny how when *you* get involved, it does, though.'

'What's that supposed to mean?' I demand, stopping still in the middle of the floor. I see Sean glance our way, so I begin dancing again.

'I mean it's odd how things can get slack and suddenly fall apart. Are you usually the cause of trouble for people, Scarlett?'

What is he saying? I try and think as the room now begins to spin a little, partly from the dancing and partly from all the champagne I've had today.

'I'm not sure what you mean. If you're trying to imply that was my fault, then you're wrong.'

'Ah, but it *was* your fault, Scarlett,' Alex now whispers in my ear.

'How … how could it be?' I ask, struggling with him so I can get my face away from his, but Alex's grip on my arms tightens.

'Because you messed in my business, Scarlett,' he whispers in a more forceful voice this time. 'You meddled in my deal with Peter, didn't you? And spread all sorts of vicious rumours about me and my business dealings.'

'No, I didn't. I just tried to protect my own charity from you and your dodgy ways. But I don't see . . .' I pause as the realisation of what Alex is telling me finally dawns. 'You!' I exclaim. 'You did it!'

'Keep your voice down,' he hisses. But no one hears us, as the music from the disco easily drowns out our voices. We're close to the edge of the dance floor, which is now absolutely packed with people. Suddenly Alex jerks me to the side and pulls me through a fire exit. We find ourselves in a corridor not far from the kitchens; a waitress looks with interest at us as she hurries towards the kitchen with an empty tray. Alex swiftly looks around him, then suddenly frogmarches me up some stairs and through another door so we find ourselves outside lit only by the light from the emergency exit sign.

The cool air outside clears my foggy brain as quickly as the door closes behind us.

'Why would you ruin our wedding?' I demand. 'Sean is supposed to be one of your best friends, for heaven's sake! What did you do, pay someone off?'

Alex smirks. '*That* is none of your business. I warned you, Scarlett, I warned you at Gabi's party that if you meddled in my business, things would get messy for you. But I thought it would be my rather lovely business with your good friend Maddie that you'd try and ruin. Not my financial business. I don't let anyone do that.'

'But you can't just go around wrecking people's lives like this.' I run my hands through my hair in exasperation. 'You ... you won't get away with it.'

'And why would you think that?' Alex asks, his eyes wide with apparent innocence.

'B-because I'm going to tell Maddie and Sean just what you've been up to,' I gush suddenly. 'Maddie will never want to see you again, and ... well, I don't know what Sean will do. But you'd better be prepared to be very, very far away when *he* finds out!'

'You won't do that,' Alex says, not appearing in the least bit rattled by my threat.

'Yes, I will.' I jut out my chin defiantly, trying to find some inner strength. 'You don't know me at all well if you think I'm just going to let you walk all over me like this.'

'I know so much more about you than you realise,' he says, smiling in that horrible way he has, like a predator toying with its prey before it goes in for the kill. He grabs my arms tightly again and pulls me towards him. 'You, my dear Scarlett, won't say anything to anyone. Because if you do, I'll spread yet another of your little secrets.'

'Wh-what secrets?' I'm starting to shake now. He's really beginning to scare me. I feel his breath on my face as his piercing blue eyes, which I once thought handsome, burn fiercely into mine.

'Your good friend Gabi's little secret – the one about her and David Bailey out there.'

'You mean Max?'

'Yeah, that little shit. He should have kept well away from Gabi – she's way out of his league.'

'But they love each other.'

'No such thing. Lust, yes – I know exactly what that is.' He smirks. 'I feel it every time I see Maddie. And she's very good at satiating it for me.'

I turn my face away. I was nauseous before, but I think I might actually vomit in a moment. Just then, though, something in me stirs – a little bit of the fighting spirit I still have left.

'You know who I feel the most sorry for in all your sordid little games?' I turn my face back towards him and shake his hands away from my arms. 'Your wife!'

Alex flinches. *Ah, hit a nerve, have I?* I wonder. So I take my chance.

'Yes, your wife when you have affairs, of which I bet there've been plenty. I know Maddie isn't the only woman you've used in your time.'

Alex is for once silent as he listens to my accusations.

'Your wife when you spend weeks, sometimes months away from home concocting your sordid little business deals. Screwing people over, and worse – charities. Oh yes, I've heard all about that from some very interesting sources.'

Alex opens his mouth to object, but I don't care. I'm not finished; I'm on a roll now.

'And your poor wife when you say there's no such thing as love.' I shake my head. 'How sad is that? I feel nothing but sorrow for her, and pity for you!'

Alex's face is reddening as I speak. 'Leave my wife out of this,' he says in a steady voice that's far too cool. 'She is nothing to do with any of it.'

'Oh, but she is. The poor woman is living a lie, and no one should have to do that. She's probably just innocently going about her daily business up in Scotland, thinking her husband is quite the heroic reporter turned successful businessman. But you and I know the truth, don't we, Alex? That you're nothing but a lying, cheating, devious bastard!'

I feel quite exhausted at the end of that speech, but it's difficult to know what Alex is thinking. His face is impassive.

I wait for him to say something, but he just turns away and pulls a packet of cigarettes from his pocket. He casually lights one, then watches me as he takes a long drag on it.

'You think you know it all, don't you?' he says, puffing dirty, filthy smoke into the already toxic air. 'You live in your perfect little jet-set world with oh-so-perfect Sean and your perfect little Dragonfly charity, coming to the aid of those who need help – like some new-age superhero, aren't you? Look –' he waves his cigarette towards my shoulders '– you already have the wings!' Then he shakes his head. 'People like you know nothing of the real world.'

'I know more than *you* think! I know what's important in

life. I know about truth and honesty, and about *real* friendship. Things *you* will never know.' I'm defiant now as I stand in front of him with my arms folded.

Alex simply regards me while he slowly puffs some more on his cigarette.

'But more than any of that,' I continue, my arms now dropping to my sides, 'I know what it feels like to love, to give love freely and be lucky enough to receive it in return. Something you will sadly never, ever experience.'

Alex puffs a plume of smoke directly into my face. It makes me cough.

'Quite the little speechmaker tonight, aren't we, Scarlett? Have you finished now?' He throws his cigarette to the ground and stubs it out with his shoe. 'Look, I'm going to keep this so simple even you'll understand it this time.' He presses his face into mine again. 'Keep your pretty little nose out of my business. Keep it out of my business with Maddie. Keep it out of my business with Gabi. And keep it out of my financial dealings. Or you *will* pay the price next time.'

'I'm not scared of you,' I say bravely. 'Max and Gabi's relationship will come out sooner or later anyway.'

'I'm not talking about them now. I know something much, much worse that the press would have an absolute field day with.' He pauses for effect. 'The search for a certain Gabriella Romero's long-lost great-aunt?'

He waits for my reaction, and gets it as I freeze in disbelief.

'How ... how do you know about that?'

'I have my sources. And I also know that a certain Vincenzo Romero wouldn't want it known that his fortune was inherited from his wife all those years ago and that he wasn't ever a self-made man. He has quite a weak heart, if I remember. I'm sure the crushing humiliation wouldn't be good for his condition.'

I can only stare at him in amazement that someone could be so cruel.

'What would that do to your relationship with Gabi if the press got wind of your search, hmm? She wouldn't be very happy if you put her father's health in danger – her grandmother's is bad enough, I hear. And what would it do to The Dragonfly Trust's reputation if it got out that you couldn't keep your client's identity a secret? The press would go to town with the whole thing. I understand they were pretty interested last time in the gambling suspicion.'

I stare at him. 'That was you!' I exclaim in disbelief as I realise. 'You set that up just so you could spend the afternoon with Maddie?'

He nods. 'You see, Scarlett, when an obstacle gets in my way, I remove it. By whatever means necessary. So that is why you are going to keep this –' he puts his finger on my lips '– permanently shut this time. Do you understand?'

I can only nod. I can't believe what I'm dealing with here. This man – I can hardly bear to call him that – seems willing to put at risk so much of what I hold dear just to get his own way.

'I can't hear you, Scarlett.'

I bat his finger away with my hand. 'Yes, yes, I understand you.'

'What do you understand?' a voice asks, joining the conversation.

Sean!

I run to him through the darkness as he appears before us with his hand shielding his eyes from the light he's suddenly exposed to. He immediately puts his arm around me.

'What's up, Red? You're shaking.'

'It is a bit nippy out here,' Alex answers for me. He pretends to rub his own arms.

'What *are* you two doing out here, anyway?' Sean asks, walking me back in exactly the opposite direction to the one I want to go in, so we're all now fully lit up again under the fire-escape door. 'You were on the dance floor one minute and the next I find you out here. I wandered around the whole place looking for you.'

'We were discussing your stag night, of course!' Alex says, as if he has every answer carefully prepared. 'I just wanted to check a few things with Scarlett. We don't want the bride upset just before her big day, do we, now, Scarlett?'

I shake my head and pull Sean even closer to me.

'So, Scarlett, just remember what I said,' Alex says lightly, as if he's repeating an earlier instruction about the stag night. 'And everything will be just fine, OK?'

I nod meekly.

'My God, Alex, you've managed to silence Scarlett,' Sean jokes. 'I don't think I've ever been able to do that in all the time I've known her. How d'you do that?'

'Let's just say I have a way with words, eh, Scarlett?'

And all I can do for now is agree with him.

Thirty-six

The journey up to Glasgow today seems particularly long, even though I'm on a super-fast train that hardly stops as I whizz my way up the country from London.

Sean is the only one who knows why I am heading up here. Now he knows about my search for Gabi's great-aunt, I could at least share that with him. He's in Chicago right now, attending to his own business affairs, so couldn't make the trip with me. But for once I was pleased – I had a lot to think about right now. Especially since my run-in with Alex at Oscar and Luke's wedding.

After we went back inside that night to the wedding and the other guests, for the rest of the evening Alex behaved as if nothing had happened. I watched him while he laughed and danced, and spent far too much time canoodling with Maddie. They didn't make anything too obvious, though: Alex may be many things, but he isn't stupid. There were far too many people at the wedding who knew he was married, but only one other who knew about him and Maddie.

Me.

I'd wondered where his wife was that evening. I knew that Gabi had only really invited him along to try and conceal her own relationship with Max. But even so, considering Alex was actually *in* the country for once, surely it was odd for him not to be spending time with his wife.

I shake my head. I'm behaving as though Alex is a normal human being, with the usual values of decency and loyalty. He is, as I've discovered to my cost, far from that.

Alex really shook me up that night. When Sean and I returned to the wedding, I barely allowed him to leave my side all night. Even when he wanted to visit the little boys' room, I clung on to him to the very last moment.

'What on earth is with you tonight, Scarlett?' Sean joked. 'It's lovely to have you by my side being this attentive, but this is bordering on fiancé abuse.'

I shook off his comment with a jibe about me not being allowed to show my fiancé any affection, and I tried to behave normally for the rest of the evening, but the truth was, I was frightened. I was frightened of Alex, and I was scared of what he could do to me, and those around me.

Luckily, except for Sean's comment, no one else

seemed to notice that anything was wrong. They were all too busy enjoying themselves. Which was just how I wanted it to be. There was no way Alex was going to ruin Oscar and Luke's special day. I wouldn't allow him to.

Aside from my issues with Alex, the rest of the wedding was wonderful, and Oscar and Luke had an absolute blast with their guests for the rest of the evening, dancing, singing and looking happier than any newly married couple I'd ever seen.

Oscar almost fainted when I presented my gift to him during the evening. I say presented – the truth was, his 'gift' suddenly appeared on the stage in front of us. She was wearing a tiny but exquisite sequinned gold dress, carried a microphone and began singing 'Spinning Around', followed by 'Can't Get You Out of My Head'.

Kylie had been an absolute gem when I'd contacted her through Gabi about Oscar's wedding. I didn't imagine she said yes to many freebies, and I'd wondered if she'd even remember him from the party, but I should know by now that no one ever forgets Oscar! And amazingly, in one of those 'you never know unless you ask' moments, she'd checked her diary, found she was in London that day and had said she'd love to sing at Oscar's wedding in return for a small donation to her favourite charity.

She followed her first two songs with 'The Locomotion', which we were all coaxed to join in with and perform the movements to, and a fabulous rendition of 'Especially for You' in which Jason Donovan's vocal was enthusiastically covered by Oscar with a second microphone.

He was in seventh heaven, and I was ecstatic for him. For that short time I was able to forget all about Alex and his threats. But no sooner had Kylie finished her set with 'On a Night Like This', which she dedicated to Oscar and Luke, I was dropped right back into my pit of worry and fear.

Now, sitting on the train, I try and clear my head of all thoughts of Alex. I need to concentrate on the matter at hand, the reason I'm heading all the way up to Scotland – to see if Evie is by some remote chance the long-lost sister of Gabi's grandmother. I know it's an incredibly long shot, but stranger things have happened in my life. In fact, strange things are happening again right now. But they're things I'm determined not to think about currently.

I arrive in Glasgow Central Station and am immediately reminded, as I drag my small suitcase along the platform, of the time Sean and I came up here for his cousin's wedding when we weren't even a couple. In fact, we were virtually strangers.

How long ago that all seemed now. So much has happened since then that I hardly feel like the same person. In fact, I know I'm not the same.

The Scarlett back then would definitely have panicked if someone like Alex had threatened her in the way he had the other evening. She would have immediately retreated into herself and hidden from the world like a scared little mouse. *But I'm not that Scarlett any more*, I think, as I confidently hail a taxi. I may be extremely worried about Alex and what he's capable of, but I won't allow myself to be scared of him. No way.

My taxi drops me off at my hotel in Glasgow, and I don't even bother unpacking my overnight bag when I check into my room. I quickly freshen up and head straight back out again. I have an appointment, and a strange feeling in the pit of my stomach tells me it's going to be an important one.

Another short taxi ride and I'm pulling up outside a very nice-looking detached house in an upmarket area of Glasgow called Thorntonhall.

Evie and Hector have asked me to meet them here. Apparently, they're staying with their granddaughter at the moment for a short holiday.

'Hello, dear!' Hector says cheerily, opening the door. 'How lovely to see you again.'

'And you too. Thank you so much for agreeing to see me today.' I walk through the opened door into a large hall with pale wooden floorboards and white walls, with abstract paintings carefully mounted in appropriate spots around the room.

'Scarlett,' Evie says, appearing from another room. 'I do hope you've had a good journey up here. I have no idea why you'd want to travel all the way from London to speak with us, though. You made it sound quite intriguing over the phone.'

I smile nervously at them. 'My journey was fine, thank you. And it's not really that exciting.'

Well, it could be . . . Only the next few minutes will tell.

Once Evie has fussed about making us all some tea, brought it to the living room on a carefully laid tray, poured us all a cup and insisted I take a biscuit, I can begin.

The living room is similar in style to the hall: simple clean lines, broken only by the odd accent of colour here and there in a cushion, throw or fancy piece of artwork or wall hanging. There are a few elegant trophies on a shelf, but aside from them, everything in the room coordinates beautifully.

I sit facing Evie and Hector on two caramel-coloured leather sofas, with the tea tray on a low coffee table between us. Under the coffee table, I notice, are interior-design magazines and a copy of *Vogue*.

'Those are my granddaughter's,' Evie says proudly when she sees me glance up at the trophies. 'She's an interior designer. A very successful one too.'

'My friend Ursula is an interior designer,' I tell them. 'Down in London. Her house is just as immaculate as this one.'

'You mean a devil to live in,' Hector winks, and as he smiles, he reveals a perfect set of white dentures.

'Yes, exactly! I hardly dare touch anything when I'm there for fear of ruining the perfect lines and feng shui.'

'We're just the same when we come to stay here,' Evie says. 'Which sadly isn't as often as we'd like these days.'

She exchanges a glance with Hector and he pats her hand.

I want to ask why, but I know it's not my place, so I decide to dive in with the real reason I'm here.

'I really appreciate you agreeing to meet with me again,' I tell them. 'I know over the phone I was a little hesitant at revealing just why.'

They both look keenly across the coffee table at me, and I take another sip from my Orla Kiely cup, stalling for a minute longer.

'Look, I'll just come straight to the point,' I have to say eventually. 'Evie, you remember when you told Oscar and me that you ran away from home when you were very young?'

'Yes?' she says, looking puzzled.

'And that you got married at Gretna Green because your family disapproved of Hector?'

'Yes,' she repeats, a little more hesitantly this time.

I sigh. How can I put this? It's going to sound mad however I say it.

'Is your real name Evita?' I suddenly blurt out. 'And was your family Italian by any chance?' There – I've said it.

Evie looks completely baffled now. 'No, dear. My family originally came from Suffolk, not Italy, and my full name is Evelyn Jane.'

My heart sinks. I knew it was a long shot.

'They're some odd questions to be asking,' Hector says, putting his cup and saucer down on the glass table. Evie hurriedly scoops it up and onto a coaster. 'Are you going to explain further?'

I take a deep breath. All of a sudden I feel close to tears. I try and blink them away. 'It really doesn't matter,' I reply, attempting to raise a smile. 'But thank you for your time and honesty.'

'Whoa there, lassie,' Hector says. 'I think we deserve a bit more than that. And it must matter a lot for you to have come all the way up here to see us today.'

He's right – I can't just leave it at that. It's not fair to them.

I explain to Evie and Hector as simply as I can without naming names who I was looking for and why.

'But why me?' Evie asks when I've finished. 'Apart from the slight similarity in name, and the fact we got married at Gretna, it's a very loose connection, surely?'

'You told Oscar and me that you were estranged from your family at an early age, just like the Evita I'm looking for, and you fitted into the right age group. There were just too many coincidences to ignore. I've been doing this job long enough now to know that coincidences usually add up to something.'

'Sadly not this time, though,' Hector says, picking up his tea again and helping himself to a biscuit.

'Indeed,' I reply dismally.

'Oh, how disappointing for you,' Evie says. 'I kind of *wish* I was her, just to fit your missing pieces together. I often wish I'd traced my family when I was younger now.'

'It's never too late,' I tell her. 'You have my number if you ever need help. You know that.'

'No, no,' Evie says dismissively, waving her hand. 'We have enough problems with our family now, let alone adding to them with more relatives.'

'Really? I hope it's nothing serious,' I say, trying not to sound too curious.

Evie glances at Hector. 'Bad enough.'

Hector tries to reassure her with a smile. 'Families are never easy,' he says, looking at me now. 'Take, for example, our granddaughter here. We only get to see her when her husband is away.'

'Why?' I demand, feeling for the two of them. I don't really know Evie and Hector all that well, but I know they are good people. And I like them, a lot.

'He's very controlling,' Hector continues, while Evie tries to hide her distress. 'You wouldn't know it if you met Lottie, though. She's a confident, successful business-woman. But when it comes to that man –' he grimaces '– her brain seems to go completely to mush. It's the same with all her family. He hates her seeing them, so she has to make up stories to visit, or sneak us in here when he's away from home, which thankfully is much of the time.'

'I don't know what will happen when the baby comes, though,' Evie says, not aiming her comment at anyone in particular, simply a general observation. 'She's going to need her family around her then ...'

'Oh, she's pregnant. Is she due soon?' I don't know why I ask this. It just seems relevant.

'Yes, lovey, very soon. That's why we're here at the moment. We don't know when we'll be able to see her again after the baby is born.' They look at each other again with anguish. This is obviously something that's distressing them both greatly.

'Depends how much time the bastard can spare in his *hectic* schedule, I suppose,' Hector laments sarcastically. 'I mean, it's only his *first*-born child.'

'Hector!' Evie admonishes. 'It's our first great-grandchild,' she explains to me. 'That's why it means so much to both of us.'

I'm not sure what to say. *Men*, I think, reminded of Alex again. *They can be such bastards to women, and women can be such idiots when it comes to men.* From what little knowledge I've gained of Evie and Hector's granddaughter, she must have her head fairly well screwed on to be as successful as she's obviously been with her own business. Why would she let her husband dictate to her who she can and can't see? It doesn't make sense.

'Relationships can be very complex,' I suggest. 'Perhaps when the baby's born, things might be different.'

'I doubt it,' Hector says. 'If he has his way, we'll probably never get to see the little mite until it's old enough to go to school, probably even university.'

Evie suddenly breaks down and begins to sob. 'I'm sorry, Scarlett,' she tries to apologise, dabbing at her eyes

344

with a tissue. 'This isn't your worry, lovey. We shouldn't be troubling you with our problems.'

'No, it's totally fine, honestly. Look, can I make you another cup of tea?' I offer.

'More tea would be lovely. I'll get it,' Evie says, trying to stand up, but she wobbles and holds her head. 'Oh, I feel a little dizzy . . .'

'Sit down, woman. It'll be your blood pressure again,' Hector instructs her, easing her back down onto the sofa.

'Let me get you some water,' I insist. 'Then I'll make us that tea.' I stand up. 'It's the least I can do.'

I feel absolutely awful knowing that arriving at the couple's granddaughter's house like this today has made Evie so miserable, and now, it seems, ill too. I quickly whisk myself off to the kitchen to fetch her that glass of water.

The kitchen is much like the rest of the house: sleek and understated. I quickly fill the stainless-steel kettle and put it on to boil. Then I look through the cupboards for a glass. I find a small green tumbler and am about to fill it from the tap when I notice they have the same fridge as Sean and I have at home. It's one of those large double-door American ones, with filtered water and an ice dispenser. So I go over and begin filling Evie a nice cool glass of water from there instead.

I notice that the fridge is one of the few places in the house that *is* a little cluttered. There are numerous rainbow-coloured magnets attached to the door of the fridge holding

345

up reminders to do various things like buy milk and Quorn. A vegetarian, then, I think, my mind randomly wandering. While I fill the glass, I scan the rest of the notes and pieces of paper. There are doctor and hospital appointments – presumably for pregnancy check-ups – and a Sainsbury's voucher.

It's then that I spy something familiar pinned to the fridge, and it's as I begin to read the black calligraphy over and over again in my head in case I've made a mistake that I feel the cool water begin to splash over the side of the glass and down onto the floor below. But I don't stop to pull the glass away; I keep filling it. My mind has suddenly become incapable of thinking about anything other than this simple piece of cream-coloured card.

The card asks the addressee to kindly 'save the date'.

The special date asking to be saved is for a wedding in New York in December.

The couple requesting that the date be saved are Sean and me.

And the two people who are requested to keep this special date free are . . . Charlotte and Alex Woolfe.

Thirty-seven

The next day I hardly notice the countryside flashing past my train window. I can't stop turning over and over in my head what I've done and what I'm about to do.

After I saw our 'save the date' card pinned up on Charlotte and Alex's fridge, I went into a kind of shock, and when I'd not returned with their tea and water, Hector eventually came and found me still standing in the kitchen with a pool of water at my feet and the green glass held limply in my hand.

Without making a fuss, he quietly escorted me back to the lounge, sat me down with a new glass of water, which he told me to drink, then went and made us all another cup of tea while Evie sat with me. I think they thought I'd had some sort of fit, with my vague behaviour and dazed face.

'Are you feeling any better now, dear?' Evie asked me gently while Hector poured us some more tea from the freshly brewed pot, tipping several medicinal spoonfuls of sugar into my cup.

'Yes, yes, I am now, thank you.' My senses were starting to work again, and I accepted the cup of tea gratefully.

'Did you have a little episode in the kitchen back there?' Evie asked. 'Don't worry, dear – it's nothing to be ashamed of. My friend Maureen has something similar – petits mals, they're called, aren't they? Like a little epileptic seizure. Is that why you had to get the train up here, because you can't drive?'

'No ... no, I don't have epilepsy.' Oh Lord, how was I going to explain this? 'Hector, Evie ...' I looked at them both and then took a deep breath. 'I have something to tell you.'

The train finally pulls up at Euston Station, and I hail a taxi immediately. It's not to my home in Notting Hill that I ask the driver to take me, but Maddie's house in Putney.

I have to do this quickly before I change my mind.

When I took that trip up to Scotland, I sensed it would be significant, but I'd no idea it was going to be significant in this way.

Alex was a lowlife – I knew that – but I didn't think even he would stoop this low. All the time he'd been having an affair with Maddie, his wife had been pregnant.

I just couldn't believe it. He'd told Maddie that he and Charlotte didn't really get on any more – the age-old story – and he'd pounced on my Maddie with all his charm and good looks when she was low and vulnerable in her own relationship with Felix.

My fist curls into a tight anger-filled ball as I sit in the back of the cab. But I know I have to keep calm right now – for Maddie.

I try not to think about the consequences of my actions . . .

When we arrive at Maddie's house, I don't even know if she'll be in. I just hope she is. She often works from home when she's organising her charity stuff. This wasn't a matter I wanted to talk to her about over the phone, and Maddie would become immediately suspicious if I informed her I was popping over in the middle of a week-day afternoon.

I pay the cab driver and ask him to wait for a moment while I see if my friend is in. Then I climb the small step in front of Maddie's terraced house, push the doorbell and wait.

Nothing.

I roll my eyes. *Please be in, Maddie*, I pray. *I need to do this now, not when I've had time to think about it. I might chicken out.*

But I know I'm not going to do that. Alex has taken it just that one step too far this time.

I press the doorbell again and smile awkwardly back at

my cab driver, but he's already opened his newspaper and is happily involved in the world as seen through the eyes of the *Daily Mirror*.

I'm just about to give up when I see a curtain flicker upstairs. I take a step back from the door, then see Maddie's head poke out of the curtains. She sees me, waves and indicates she'll be right down.

'Thank you!' I call to my cab driver. 'She's in,' I say, gesturing at the door. 'You can go.'

The driver gives me a thumbs-up, folds his paper in half, then moves off down the road, just as Maddie appears at the front door.

'Scarlett, what are you doing here?' she asks, as I walk past her through the open door.

Maddie is wearing a flimsy sort of dressing-gown thing, which she adjusts as she closes the door behind me.

'Were you about to take a shower?' I ask.

'No. Why? Oh, my robe ... I was about to take a nap, actually.'

'Oh, right. Sorry if I've disturbed you, only I need to talk to you about something.'

'This is going to sound very rude of me, Scarlett, but can it possibly wait?'

I hadn't expected this reaction.

'No, not really. I need to tell you now.'

Maddie nods. 'OK, then. You'd better come through.'

We walk through to Maddie's kitchen, where I've sat with her many times before since she moved to London, drinking coffee and often wine, having girly chats and putting the world to rights.

'Shall I put the kettle on?' she asks.

I've a feeling she might be wanting something a bit stronger than tea in a moment, but I nod.

'Right, then,' Maddie says when she's satisfied that the appropriate beverages will be served shortly. 'What's up?' She slides onto the kitchen stool opposite me and we look at each other over the little breakfast bar.

'Hmm,' I stall. 'I don't know how to begin, really.'

'At the beginning is usually a good place,' Maddie smiles. 'Scarlett, seriously, what's up? You look like someone's just put you in charge of the country and you're about to press the big red button!'

I was, virtually. But the big red button on her life.

I take a deep breath and tell Maddie all about my trip and why I really went up to Scotland – I don't mention Gabi by name, and especially not Charlotte just yet, but then I tell her what happened when I went through to the kitchen.

'You were in Alex's wife's house!' she whispers, her eyes wide.

I wonder why she's suddenly whispering.

'Yes,' I continue in my normal voice. 'But it doesn't end there, you see—'

'Oh, I think it does end there, Scarlett.'

I turn to the new voice at the door and am horrified to see Alex standing there. He's wearing jeans and an unbuttoned blue shirt that he's obviously just pulled on. His feet are bare, and his hair is dishevelled.

I suddenly realise what's going on, and why Maddie is in a robe.

'Oh God, were you two at it when I arrived?' I cry, looking at Maddie.

'You could say that.' Maddie smiles seductively at Alex.

I close my eyes for a moment to try and compose myself. 'I guess you heard all that?' I ask Alex.

'Enough to know you're poking your nose into my business again.'

'No, Scarlett didn't know it was your house when she arrived, did you, Scarlett?' Maddie says, trying to defend me.

Alex and I eye each other, like gunslingers at dawn waiting to see who is going to pull the trigger first.

'No, Maddie,' I say, smiling at her. 'You're right, I had no idea. But it was a very *interesting* visit,' I say now to Alex, with a different intent in my voice. '*Very* interesting indeed.'

'Why?' Maddie asks now, starting to sound worried. 'What's going on, and why are you two looking at each other like that?'

'Alex, would you like to share?' I ask him, my eyebrows raised.

'Don't do this, Scarlett,' he warns. 'I've told you before.'

Maddie looks between the two of us again. 'Why are you speaking to Scarlett like that, Alex? Will someone please tell me just what's happening here?'

'I didn't think you'd have the balls,' I tell him. I glance down at his jeans. 'Aren't they too weak?'

Alex's face is dark and threatening. 'Don't,' he repeats.

'Did Alex tell you his wife is pregnant, by any chance?' I ask Maddie in a much brighter voice than was appropriate to deliver news like this.

The look on Maddie's face suggests not.

'And not just a *little* bit pregnant, but actually very heavily pregnant. The baby is due very soon if its great-grandparents are to be believed.' Now it's my turn to look darkly at Alex. 'And I *do* believe Evie and Hector. I believe *everything* they've told me about you.'

Alex looks like he wants to strangle me right now in the kitchen.

'Which, if you haven't worked it out already, Maddie, means that Charlotte has been pregnant the whole time Alex has been having his sordid little affair with you. He's been using you the whole time to get his kicks while his wife was … How can I put this kindly? Not her usual self?'

I look at Maddie now and immediately feel awful. I took that speech just a little bit further than I meant to. But I was angry: angry for Maddie; angry for Hector and Evie; and angry for myself, and the way Alex has made me feel and behave.

Maddie looks as if her whole world has just imploded, and she's the one carrying all the broken pieces around inside her.

And the person who's done that is me.

'That wasn't supposed to come out like that, Maddie. I'm sorry. But I had no idea *he* was going to be here when I told you all this.'

Maddie, her face pale, puts her hand out to me over the breakfast bar. I take hold of it, but she just squeezes my hand quickly before letting it go and standing up.

'Is this all true, Alex?' she asks quietly.

Alex's face, which has looked dark and hostile up until this moment, softens, much to my surprise. He moves towards Maddie, but she steps back and shakes her head.

Alex nods, understanding. 'Yes, Maddie. I'm not proud of it, but it is.'

'But why?' she asks, her voice trembling. 'Why would you do that to me? To your wife? You told me you were virtually on the point of breaking up, that the two of you hardly ever spoke, let alone did anything else. You said you loved me, Alex.'

Alex's body stiffens. 'I think you'll find I didn't actually say *those* words.'

'As good as!' Maddie cries now. 'And all the time you had no intention of us ever being together, did you? What was the real reason you wanted me, then? Was your poor wife not performing as you liked in bed because she was pregnant! Or was it her body that repelled you, hmm? Her beautiful, natural, pregnant body? Or worse still, were you still doing her while you were with me!'

Maddie charges at him and begins beating her hands fiercely against his bare chest. Alex pushes her away and holds her at arm's length.

'Stop it! You're making a fool of yourself. There never was an *us*. You, Maddie, are a very attractive woman; you simply came into my life at a time when I needed a little *extra* company, that's all. It was never going to be anything more. And I think if you look back, you'll find I never promised you anything.' Alex looks over Maddie's head at me. 'Get her away from me now,' he instructs. And for once I listen. I carefully peel Maddie off Alex and cradle her in my arms while she begins to sob.

'I'm going to go upstairs and get my things,' he tells us coolly. 'I won't be returning to say goodbye. But, Scarlett, you should know that as much as I'm finished with your friend there, I'm very definitely not done with you!'

We listen while Alex gets his things and returns downstairs. Then we hear the front door open and close.

Maddie and I stand silently in the kitchen; I'm still holding her protectively in my arms.

'Oh, Scarlett,' she sobs against my chest, 'how could I have been so stupid?' She wipes her nose on a tissue from the pocket of her robe. 'You warned me, didn't you? You tried to tell me he'd hurt me. And you were right. Just like you always are.'

'Not always,' I say quietly. 'Sometimes I do things a little too impulsively and then have to face the consequences afterwards.'

'Like what?' Maddie lifts her head and looks up at me. I stroke her hair away from her tear-stained face.

'Like telling Hector and Evie just what sort of man their granddaughter is married to.'

'You didn't?' Maddie asks, her red, puffy eyes now wide. 'What, *everything*?'

'Everything,' I repeat, grimacing.

'Will they tell her, do you think, about me?'

I shrug. 'I don't know. They might, after the baby is born. They were no great fans of Alex before, but this has given them the ammunition they need to bring their granddaughter back to her family.'

'You are something else,' she tells me. 'I can't believe you did that.'

'Neither can I. I just hope I've done the right thing.'

'You have,' Maddie insists. She stands up straight now, facing me. 'You always do the right thing, Scarlett.' She manages to raise a tiny smile. 'It's just the rest of us who mess up. Oh . . . ' she says, running her hands through her damp, messy hair. 'Thank God I never have to see him again. Thank God it's over.' She wraps her arms around me.

But as I hug Maddie back, I know it's not over for me yet.

It's only just begun.

Thirty-eight

I spend the next few days with Maddie in Putney.

I hadn't intended to stay when I'd originally arrived outside her door, but after what had happened with Alex, and the way it had happened, I felt partly to blame, and Maddie was in such a state I could hardly leave her on her own.

Her emotions would veer from full-on sobbing – on the sofa, on my shoulder or just anywhere that the hurt and misery caught up with her – to anger, when she would scream and beat her fists into a cushion, pretending it was Alex's head or maybe even his testicles.

I nearly joined her a couple of times. I could only imagine what Alex was in the process of doing to me and my life right now, and the thought of pounding his smug face into obscurity was very tempting indeed.

It's three days since our showdown with Alex. I was supposed to fly back to New York two days ago, but I cancelled my flight. This is partly so I could spend time with Maddie, and partly because I'm scared about what I'm going to find when I get back there. My mobile phone has already had three missed calls this afternoon from Gabi, with a voicemail, plus two calls from Max and one from Peter.

It's happening already.

I look at my phone while I wait for the kettle to boil in Maddie's kitchen. How long could I realistically ignore them for? Long enough, I decide, and I switch my phone to silent and shove it back in the pocket of my jeans.

'I've found *Bridget Jones* for us to watch,' Maddie says from beneath the blanket she's been almost permanently cuddled under for the last few days. I hand her a mug of tea. 'A bit of Colin Firth will cheer us up! Never fails.'

She presses play on the DVD player and we are immediately involved in Bridget's wonderful world of singletons, Christmas jumpers and of course Mark Darcy. Under different circumstances, the last few days would have been quite good fun. Maddie and I used to do this sort of thing all the time when we lived in Stratford-upon-Avon. That was before she met Felix, and way before I'd even known Sean existed in this world. If one of us had a problem, often related to the latest male in our lives, we'd have one of our 'duvet days' of just watching movies and pigging out on ice cream, and fish-finger sandwiches, which only Maddie could make just right. We've eaten a lot of fish fingers over the last couple of days, and I've had to pop down to the local newsagent's to buy copious white Magnums after the tubs of Häagen-Dazs ran out. Now we're older, we've extended our heartbreak menu to include wine, and we've been fairly – actually, make that *very* – intoxicated for the last couple of nights.

But today all is well in the world of Bridget Jones, even without any calorie-laden snacks to keep us company. We got through the part where Bridget sings 'All By Myself' with only minimal tears from Maddie, but it's when we're at the part where Bridget is dressed as the Playboy bunny and Daniel cheats on her that I suddenly hear Maddie begin to sob again from beside me on the sofa.

'Oh, Maddie,' I sigh, passing her a tissue for what seems like the hundredth time today. 'I know you're upset, but he's really not worth it, you know.'

Maddie nods and wipes her permanently red-rimmed eyes. 'I know he's not,' she agrees. 'I've realised that now. But it's not so much him I'm crying about; it's the fact I let him take me for a ride.' She winces. 'Bad choice of words.'

'I bet you're not the first person he's screwed over.' I roll my eyes. 'Oh God, I'm doing it now too.'

We both smile at our unintentional faux pas.

'Yeah,' Maddie agrees, 'but I always thought I was

smarter than that, that I'd never fall for a man's charms in that way. Oh God, Felix would never have treated me like this. What have I done?' Her face crumples in distress again.

'It's not your fault, Mad. Alex is sneaky like that. He makes you think he's Mr Wonderful so you're lulled into his lair. Then the next minute he's shafting you left, right and centre. No pun!' I call, before she can say anything. 'Even Peter said he was your typical wolf in sheep's clothing.'

Maddie sniffs and forces another smile. 'I like that analogy. Peter is very wise. He's quite right, of course – that's exactly what he is. But what made Peter say that about him? Does he know Alex well?'

Damn, I didn't want Maddie to know about all the other stuff just yet. It would only upset her more.

'He's come across him in a business sense, I believe.'

'Scarlett … what are you not telling me?' Maddie demands. 'I know you're hiding something – I can tell by your face.'

'Nothing!' I try innocently. 'Nothing you need worry about just now, anyway,' I add when Maddie throws her blanket off and pauses Bridget just as she's telling Daniel Cleaver where he can stick his job.

'What do you mean, "just now"?' Maddie is sitting bolt upright. She looks more alert than I've seen her in days. Maybe now *was* the right time.

I tell Maddie everything, from my initial suspicions

about Alex to his threats at Gabi's party. Then I move on to The Plaza being cancelled and Alex's final intimidation at Oscar's wedding.

'And you know the next part,' I finish, 'when I went up to Glasgow to see Hector and Evie. That takes us right up to the present moment.'

Maddie, who's sat perfectly still with a neutral expression on her face while I've been telling her all this, says nothing; she simply slides further across the sofa and puts her arms around me. 'Scarlett, you are the best friend anyone could ask for, do you know that?'

'Hardly.' I shrug under her embrace. 'I've let *you* down by not telling you about Alex sooner, and Gabi down by allowing someone to spill her secrets to the press. I've even let the children at Sunnyside down by probably preventing us from raising any more money for them. No one will want to be involved with The Dragonfly Trust after this.'

Now it's my turn to begin sobbing as all the pressure and stress of the last few weeks comes flooding out along with my tears.

Maddie pulls several tissues from her box and passes them to me. She lets me cry it out on her shoulder for a couple of minutes before she tries to intervene.

'Feeling any better now?' she asks when my tears begin to subside a little.

'No.'

Maddie pulls her shoulder away. 'Now you listen to me,

miss. Just like you've been telling me for the past few days, none of this is your fault. None of it, do you hear?'

I nod, mainly to appease her.

'Alex is obviously a law unto himself. It seems like none of us really knew what he was like until now. But you've exposed him, Scarlett. Don't you see? Now everyone will know what he's really like.'

'No, they won't – he's too clever for that.'

'The people that matter are already finding out, thanks to you.'

I think about this.

'Have you told Sean yet?' she asks.

I shake my head.

'Well, you must. He needs to know.'

'He's away at the moment, in Chicago.'

'As soon as he gets back, then.' Maddie stands up and begins to pace about the room. This is livelier than I've seen her in days. 'And what about Gabi and Max? They should know too, be forewarned at least.'

'I think it's too late for that.' I pull my phone from my pocket. More missed calls, another from Gabi with a second voicemail, and a missed call with a voicemail from Sean. 'Look at all my missed calls.'

'Scarlett, you can't hide from this forever,' Maddie says, glancing at my screen. 'If Alex has already gone to the press, then you have to face the music. Gabi will understand – she's your friend, and so is Max.'

'What about Sean?'

'Do you even have to ask me that? Sean loves you. He'll stand by you no matter what. I wouldn't want to be Alex when he finds out, mind.'

She's right, of course – I have to go back to New York to deal with this sometime.

But did it have to be just yet?

Thirty-nine

I disembark from my flight at JFK and get my usual yellow cab back to the city.

As the houses we pass on the way back to Manhattan gradually turn into skyscrapers, I know I'm home.

Home. Did I really just call it that? Is this what I subconsciously think of Manhattan as now? Well, if it is, it certainly doesn't feel like the most hospitable place right at this very moment. It's absolutely tipping down with rain, so heavily that I can barely see through the cab windows.

I sit back and let my thoughts entertain me for the rest of the journey. Even after Maddie persuaded me to return to New York, I didn't return anyone's calls. Only Sean's.

His message had asked me to call to let him know I was all right. Apparently when they couldn't get hold of me, both Peter and Gabi, worried, had phoned Sean to check if I was OK.

I told Sean briefly that I'd been looking after Maddie because she wasn't feeling too well, and strangely, even though it was London, my usually good phone signal in Putney was very weak and I hadn't been getting many calls through. Luckily Sean seemed to believe me.

I wasn't going to tell him about Alex over the phone. I needed to be face to face with him for that.

I arrive back at my apartment building and notice as I put my key in the external door that a light is shining from my window upstairs.

That's odd, I think. *I'm sure I didn't leave one on before I left for Oscar's wedding celebrations.* It's just over three weeks ago that I left for London, yet it seems like a lifetime, so much has taken place while I've been gone.

As I reach the top of the stairs, I put my second key in the door to my apartment and open it cautiously. When I moved in, the supervisor of this building proudly told me he hadn't had a break-in in any of his apartments in over fifteen years, but this was New York – you could never be too careful.

Thankfully the only thing waiting to greet me as I step cautiously inside is friendly.

'Scarlett, you're back at last,' Sean says, appearing in the hall to take my bags. He hugs me and I don't want to let him go. Everything always seems so much better when Sean is with me.

365

'But what are you doing here?' I ask, astonished to see him.

'Don't you remember? I said I'd fly across to see you when I'd finished in Chicago.'

'Oh, that's right, so you did.' I have totally forgotten with everything else that's been going on.

'How's Maddie?' he asks. 'Is she feeling any better? You were a bit cagey when I spoke to you on the phone. Is it women's troubles?' he asks delicately.

'Er, you could say that . . .'

Sean makes us both some supper, and then I tell him everything that's been going on, not stopping at any part. I totally ignore whatever face Sean pulls or exclamation he makes during my story; I just carry on until I've finished with the whole sorry tale.

'Is that it?' he asks at the end. 'Everything?'

I nod.

'I'll kill him!' He leaps up in the air, punching his fist into his hand. 'I'll bloody kill him. Is he here in New York at the moment?' he demands. 'If so, I'm going straight round there.'

'Sean –' I stand up to try and calm him '– I have no idea if Alex is here or not. But I know one thing: you running over there with your boxing gloves on isn't going to solve any problems.'

Sean doesn't look in the least bit convinced. He paces about the room looking so angry I'm worried he might actually smash his fist through the wall at any moment.

'Why didn't you tell me all this was going on?' he demands, turning his anger on me.

'I couldn't.'

'Why not? I'm your fiancé, for God's sake. I should have been there to protect you.' He runs his hands through his hair, almost ripping it out in his frustration. 'Jeez, that night outside Oscar's wedding – I was there. I was there, Scarlett, and I let it happen.'

'No, no, you didn't.' I go over to him and place my hands firmly either side of his face. 'Sean, look at me,' I command, trying to look into his eyes, but he won't let me. 'Sean!'

Sean allows himself the briefest of eye contact with me.

'None of this is anyone's fault, do you hear? Not mine, not Maddie's and especially not yours. Do you understand me?'

Sean's eyes still hold anger, but he nods reluctantly in my hands. His body, so taut and ready to explode, visibly softens against me. Then we kiss, and for a few seconds I let myself be totally in the moment. I allow myself the confidence of knowing that however bad things get, no one is ever going to come between us. We're too strong for that.

'I can't let him get away with this, though,' Sean says moments later with quiet determination, his eyes now focused fully on mine. 'You know that, don't you?'

I nod. 'Don't worry, Sean – I have no intention of letting that happen either.'

'That's my girl.' Sean smiles. 'That's my Scarlett.' Then he wraps his arms tightly around me and we strengthen our unbreakable bond even more.

Forty

The next morning I'm up early, considering the jet lag, and I begin making my dreaded phone calls.

Gabi first. 'Scarlett!' she cries down the phone. 'Where have you been? I've been trying to get hold of you for days. Are you OK? Sean said you were staying on with Maddie in London for a while.'

'Yes, Gabi, I'm fine now, thank you, and I'm back in New York. I flew in last night.'

'That's wonderful news,' she says, sounding a lot brighter than I expected. 'Shall we meet for brunch somewhere? I have so much to tell you. You've no idea what's been going on while you've been away.'

'Er … sure, OK.' This is not what I expected at all. I thought Gabi would be gunning for me.

'Our usual place? Say about eleven?' Gabi asks. 'I have

to dash – Max and I are going running in the park in a few minutes and I'm not even dressed!'

'*Max* is going running?' This on its own is amazing enough: Max never runs anywhere unless it's to chase a twenty-dollar bill down the road. But the two of them together?

'It's his first outing today. I've bought him new running sneakers and everything. Oh, there's my doorbell. Have to dash. See you later. Bye!'

And she's gone.

Hmm, I think, looking at my phone, which is still in my hand, *that went much better than I expected. Maybe Alex didn't go through with his threat after all. But why would everyone have been phoning me if he didn't? I'll call Peter next. He will know.*

But all I get is voicemail on Peter's phone, so I phone his office and find out he's in an early breakfast meeting.

I sigh. I have to remain positive. Things aren't as bad as I thought they might be when I woke up first thing this morning. But I'm still no clearer as to what's going on.

Later that morning I wait in the little coffee shop that Gabi and I often frequent these days, a cappuccino already sitting on the table in front of me. It is almost the end of September. Next month shops like this one will be proudly displaying pumpkins and other Halloween décor in readiness for the night so beloved of Americans. *Just where has this year gone?* I wonder as I sip on my coffee. It started well enough, with us all celebrating Burns' Night with Luke and Oscar at that restaurant in London, but since then the year has been like a rollercoaster ride for me, with so many emotional highs and lows. Plus, more worry, fear and anger than I ever want to experience for the rest of my life, let alone in the course of nine months. And the driver for the majority of my rollercoaster ride has been Alex.

Sean worried me with his initial reaction to my news last night. But his anger was to be expected given the circumstances. It is a primeval instinct in men – however mild and calm they appear on the surface, their natural reflex is to feel the need to protect their woman and family. In a way, it was quite nice to know Sean feels that strongly. What woman, however tough and independent she may seem, doesn't want a man trying to defend her honour? I guess they'd have duelled with pistols at dawn if this were the olden days. But this is the twenty-first century, not the eighteenth, and I'm not wearing a long dress and waving a white handkerchief, and thankfully for Alex, Sean doesn't own a pistol.

But whatever the time zone, I know if I don't come up with a plan to satisfy Sean that Alex has been well and truly dealt with, he'll feel the need to deal with him himself.

Gabi and Max come bundling into the coffee shop looking flushed, so I assume they've not long finished their run. Max goes up to the counter, while Gabi comes straight over to me and hugs me, as she always does when we meet.

'It feels like ages since I last saw you,' she gushes as she positively bounces into the seat opposite. 'But it was only at Oscar's wedding!'

'Yes,' I smile warily. I'm not sure what it is, but something isn't right.

'Oh, Scarlett, I have so much to tell you,' she says, taking my hand over the table. 'And so much to be grateful to you for.'

'You have?'

'Where do I start?' she begins, as Max slides into the seat next to her.

'Great here, isn't it?' he says, looking back at the counter. 'They said they'd bring our coffees over; they don't do that in Starbucks. I ordered you another one, Scarlett. Hope that's OK.' He looks me over. 'You look like you could do with something more substantial, though. Have you lost weight? You're a bit gaunt.'

'Max!' Gabi reprimands. 'What have I told you about being polite – especially to ladies?'

'But it's Scarlett,' Max says, grinning at me.

'Don't you dare say it.' I waggle my finger at him. 'I know exactly where you were going with that one, Maximilian!'

'Only my mother is allowed to get away with calling me that! Touché, my friend.'

So they obviously don't hate me, then . . .

'Now, as I was saying,' Gabi begins again, 'it's all been happening here while you've been away.'

This is it. I brace myself.

'Somehow the press found out about your search for my great-aunt,' Gabi says. 'It was all over the gossip columns of the papers. Hmm ... what day was that, Max?' she asks.

'Er ...' Max thinks. 'Wednesday? Yes, that was it because I was filming some footage down in the Village when I saw the headlines on a newsstand.'

That would make sense. I saw Hector and Evie on the Monday, and then Maddie and Alex on the Tuesday afternoon. With the time difference, it would have just given Alex enough time to alert his contacts in the press to the story and for them to turn it round for the papers the next day in the US.

'I'm really sorry,' I tell them both. 'If I could have prevented it, I would have.'

Gabi shakes her hand at me. 'No, don't be. I mean, I was fuming with you to begin with, Scarlett, don't get me wrong. This was just what I'd asked you not to let happen. That first voicemail I left for you was pretty nasty. So I'm the one who should be sorry.'

I deliberately haven't listened to any messages. I'm glad now.

The waitress brings over three coffees, and a large slab of pie for Max.

'Max!' Gabi says, astonished. 'I thought you were on a health kick!'

'I am,' Max says, already pushing a fork into the pie. 'But you made me run around Central Park today – the exercise, and the embarrassment,' he says, winking at me, 'have given me a massive appetite. Besides, it's apple, isn't it? It's virtually a health food!'

Gabi shakes her head and reaches for her coffee. 'There's no telling him,' she says. Then she smiles lovingly at Max. 'It's just as well I adore your little love handles.' She kisses him on the cheek, while poking his stomach.

I look around the coffee shop to see if anyone's noticed.

'What's going on?' I ask, suddenly realising what's wrong – the two of them are displaying affection for one another in public. 'How come you can kiss Max in a public place all of a sudden?'

'That is what I'm coming to next,' Gabi says. 'When the story came out about my great-aunt, it was of course centred round me.' She rolls her eyes. 'I'm the one who sells the papers, apparently. So at the same time as trying to bring humiliation to my father and the rest of my family, they decided to out Max and my relationship too.'

'Oh God, again I'm so sorry!'

'Stop apologising, Scarlett. That wasn't your fault, was it?'

I'm about to hold up my hand and confess when Gabi continues, 'Whoever discovered our relationship and then sold their sad little story to the press did us a favour.'

'They did?'

'Of course. Now Max and I can declare our love for each other in public, can't we, Max?'

Max just nods, his mouth full of his fast-disappearing pie.

'We can go out together for meals, run together in Central Park … do anything we want without fear of someone discovering our secret. It's wonderful, isn't it, Max?'

'I could do without the running part,' Max says, putting his fork down on his empty plate.

Gabi just tuts good-naturedly.

'But what about everything else?' I ask. 'Your father, your family, how did they react to the news?' I can't believe this is happening. Everything seems to be fine. My friends don't hate me, and the press and Alex haven't ruined all our lives.

'Badly at first,' Gabi says soberly now. 'My father, particularly, hit the roof when he found out about Max.'

Max squeezes Gabi's hand.

'But in a way that was good,' she continues. 'He was so busy worrying about my love life, he didn't have much time to worry about the press trying to sully his reputation. And now he's met Max, he's OK with him. Max makes him laugh, and believe me, that's not easy with *my* father.'

Still holding hands, they look at each other adoringly.

'And your grandmother? How is she doing?' I ask.

'She's still much the same health-wise,' Gabi says gravely. 'That's not going to change now at her age. But,' she says, brightening, 'I haven't told you the absolute best part about any of this yet!'

'There's something better?' Compared to what I've been imagining, this is already too wonderful for words.

'Yes!' Gabi says, excitement radiating from every pore on her face. 'After the story was in the papers on Wednesday, I had a call on Thursday. You'll never guess who it was.'

The way this story is progressing, it could well have been from Barack Obama.

I shake my head. 'No idea.'

'My great-aunt Evita!'

I feel my mouth literally drop open.

'I know!' Gabi says, seeing my shock. 'I felt pretty much the same when she called. She said she'd seen the story in the papers and she'd like to come and visit my grand-mother again. Before it's too late,' she adds sadly. 'She's flying in from Boston next week to visit with us all. Can you believe it, Scarlett?'

Gabi's eyes are shining with joy, and her face is glowing with happiness.

'That's what I was trying to call you about when you were at Maddie's.'

I shake my head. This, after everything else, is just too much. I was dreading coming back here to New York to see what carnage Alex had caused, and now instead of darkness and despair, I only find love and light surrounding those I hold dear.

Unexpected tears begin falling from my eyes.

'What on earth is wrong?' Gabi asks, her hand taking mine across the table.

'Scarlett?' Max asks with concern. 'What's up?'

'Nothing. Nothing bad, that is. I'm just so happy that everything has worked out OK. I thought I was going to come back here and you'd all hate me for what's happened.'

'Why would we all hate you?' Gabi asks in distress. 'We love you, Scarlett. It's not like any of this was your fault.'

'Oh, but it was,' I tell them. 'Whatever the end result was, it was my fault it all came out in the first place.'

Max puts his hand up to the waitress. 'Three more coffees, please,' he says, when he has her attention. 'And three more pieces of that delicious pie, too, if you have some. I think we're gonna need them.'

When I've finished telling them all about Alex and what's been going on over the last few months, as always I feel wrung out and exhausted. Every time I have to tell this sorry tale to someone new it feels like I'm living the whole horrid experience all over again.

I look at their faces over the table while I dig into my pie; I'm suddenly quite ravenous. Gabi's expression is one of shock, like she can hardly believe all this has been going on, and with someone she knows, too. Max has quite a different expression. It's knowing, like he's not in the least bit surprised to find Alex has been doing all this. At the same time, though, I can see anger bubbling under his cool exterior.

'Have you told Sean about this?' he asks matter-of-factly.

'Yes, of course, but he only found out the full story last night when I got back to Manhattan.'

'And what does he say?'

'It was all I could do to stop him rushing out to find Alex to beat him to a pulp there and then.'

'I bet,' Max says darkly.

'I just can't believe it,' Gabi says. 'Not Alex. He seems so . . . so . . .'

'Smarmy?' Max suggests. 'Slimy, nauseating, smug, arrogant . . . ? Take your pick.'

I smile at Max in agreement.

'I'm so glad I didn't persevere with that business deal he wanted me to come in on now,' Gabi says thankfully. 'I was going to, but Portia seemed so against it that I decided not to in the end.'

Good old Portia, I think. *Always looking out for Gabi.*

'So,' Max says, 'we've all discovered what I long suspected – Alex is a nasty little parasite the world really could do with eradicating.'

I'm surprised at Max's terminology.

'And I might just have an idea how we can go about that . . .' He violently stabs his fork into a piece of pie crust still lingering on his plate.

Gabi and I open our eyes wide.

'Nah ...' he says, seeing us. 'This isn't *The Sopranos*. I mean I think I might know a way we can take our Mr Woolfe right back down to where he came from – the sewer. And,' he adds when I begin to look interested, 'your brother could be just the one to help us out.'

'Jamie?' I say in surprise.

Max nods. 'Yup, me old mate Jamie.'

Forty-one

I wait nervously in the audience for my category to be announced by our host for the evening, Ted Dawson, a favourite daytime chat-show host here in the US.

Then I adjust my evening dress for about the tenth time in the last few minutes, take another large gulp from my glass of white wine and look around me again. Currently I'm surrounded by the cream of the American press industry; there are TV reporters, producers, directors and technical bods who work on TV news. Then there are those who report the news through the medium of print: newspaper journalists, editors and the staff who work with them.

The annual United States Media Awards is one of the

most prestigious nights in the media industry, and the whole event is being broadcast live from the ballroom of the Waldorf Astoria Hotel in New York. We've all been treated to a sumptuous four-course meal, and now we're supposed to be relaxing as award after award is announced and the lucky recipient is applauded up onto the stage to receive their trophy.

Thankfully, I've spent the evening in the company of Peter and some very nice people who work with him at his production company, TVS, so I haven't felt completely out of my depth in among all these media-savvy types. But now as my time grows ever closer, I'm finding myself veering between feeling extremely hot one moment to cold and shivery the next.

'You'll be just fine, Scarlett,' Peter says, leaning across in the seat next to me. 'I know you can do this.'

'But what if he doesn't win?' I ask Peter. 'This is all going to be wasted.'

'He'll win,' Peter says confidentially. 'His exposé on that appalling child labour racket in India is enough to win on its own, let alone all the other fine reports he's filmed over the last year.'

'There's part of me that really hopes Jamie wins for his sake,' I tell Peter honestly. 'He truly deserves it. But for my own sanity, the other part of me would be quite happy if I was still sitting here in this seat when the winner is announced.'

Jamie, much to all our delight, has been nominated for

'Best Foreign Correspondent in TV News' tonight, but because he's in Pakistan right now working on a story, he hasn't been able to make it back to New York for tonight's ceremony.

Which is where I come in.

Jamie told his old friend Max about his nomination before it was even announced to the general public, and also how he feared he wouldn't be able to fly back for the ceremony. He asked Max if *he* would attend tonight on Jamie's behalf and, if he won, accept the award for him.

But Max subsequently asked Jamie if I could replace him. When he explained why, and enlightened him on his plan, Jamie, after a few choice swear words aimed in Alex's direction, heartily agreed to the substitution.

So here I am, waiting to see if my quivering legs are going to be required to walk me up to that stage in a few moments and make the speech of my life live on American television.

'I'm going to the ladies' room,' I tell Peter. 'I need to check my legs are still working OK.'

Peter just smiles. 'Sure, but don't be too long. Jamie's award is coming up really soon.'

I manage to walk to the ladies' room, and when I get there, I wash my hands in the cool running water, then splash a little on my face in an attempt to sharpen my senses.

To try and will some courage into my quaking bones, while I brush my hair and freshen my make-up I think about the children at Sunnyside, and some of the families The Dragonfly Trust has helped to reunite in the past. Alex put everything we've worked for over the last few years at risk. He went to the press knowing that his story could ruin my charity's reputation, simply to take revenge on me.

I stare at myself in the mirror, oblivious to the other women coming and going at the sinks next to me, and I smile.

As it's turned out, in another wonderful twist, and just proving that there really is no such thing as bad publicity, Alex's plan has backfired, and since the story of Gabriella Romero's search for her great-aunt hit the newspapers, the number of people contacting The Dragonfly Trust for help has trebled. We are going to be taking on four more staff next week to cope with all the new cases that are arriving at our offices.

So however much he tried, Alex hasn't been able to hurt me, my business or my friends – except for Maddie, that is.

It's just over a month since Maddie found out about Alex's wife and his unborn baby, and she's still hurting. I speak to her nearly every day to check how she's doing. It seems Maddie had cared a lot more about Alex than he'd cared for her and now she's paying the price, with the heartache and humiliation of knowing that someone she trusted could be so cruel not just to her, but to others too.

I take a deep breath. 'I have to do this, and I have to do it well,' I whisper to myself in the mirror. 'For Maddie, for me, and for all the other charities and people who have been unlucky enough to be touched by Alex's vile ways.'

Since I returned to New York after that fateful day in Glasgow, I've also discovered just how many charities Alex has been suspected of stealing from, or 'misappropriating funds', as Peter called it.

Peter has been fantastic. Once he found out the full story about Alex and what he'd been up to, he reached out to all his contacts in the business world and found out just how many times Alex has been suspected of wrongdoing with charities. The problem was, no one ever seemed to be able to prove it, and if they did, Alex always seemed to find some way of keeping them quiet.

'But not me, Alex Woolfe,' I whisper to a face in the mirror I barely recognise. This face looks confident and determined, as if nothing ever fazes it. That couldn't possibly be me, could it?

But as I walk back to my seat in the ballroom, I feel an air of self-confidence surrounding me that I've never felt before. Maybe I've borrowed it from the same place I borrowed my dress from tonight. Maybe when I return this designer gown, my confidence will drop to its usual level.

Just as long as it stays put for the next few minutes I don't really care.

Ted Dawson finally announces to the audience in the room and the viewers at home that the next category is for 'Best Foreign Correspondent in TV News'.

I hold my breath. *This is it*.

'And to present the award,' he says, 'a multi-award-winning foreign correspondent. We all remember his spectacular yet gritty reports from Iraq during the Gulf War. But these days he's more likely to be found raising much-needed dollars for charities throughout America . . . I give you Mr Alex *Grrrowler* Woolfe!'

Loud applause from around the room as Alex walks confidently onto the stage. He holds up his hand to acknowledge his appreciation of the audience.

My mouth has gone very dry, I suddenly realise as I try to swallow.

Alex, with great aplomb, announces all the nominees, and then a short snippet of their reports is played to the audience here and at home. The screen on the stage behind Alex then shows live pictures of each nominee in the room – all except Jamie: in his quarter of the screen is a still photo. He looks very handsome, though, as he smiles back at the audience.

My brother, I think proudly. *I'm doing this for you too*.

'And the winner is . . .' Alex announces, pausing for dramatic effect. He opens the envelope, and as he does, I see his face twitch.

I know before he even says it.

I know as the applause begins, and the guests in the room look around to see where Jamie is.

I know as Ted whispers in Alex's ear and Alex's face darkens.

I know I can do this now.

Alex holds up his hand and the audience quietens.

'Apparently Jamie can't be here tonight to collect his award,' he says through a smile faker than most of the D-cups in the room. 'I guess he's off reporting on something a little more special than us.' He chuckles, but not many people join in. 'So, to collect the award on his behalf, I'm told his sister, Scarlett, will do the honours.'

Peter gives me a little shove as the audience starts clapping again, so I stand up and begin to make my way up to the stage.

I don't look at Alex until I'm standing right next to him at the podium. Then, as I accept the award from him, I allow my eyes to connect with his for the first time.

'Thank you so much for this opportunity,' I say, smiling at him but avoiding speaking into the microphone. 'I'm going to enjoy this.'

Alex looks at me quizzically, not understanding.

'Thank you!' I say into the microphone, as the crowd quietens to listen to me. 'As you all know, my wonderful brother, Jamie, can't be here tonight because he's in Pakistan filming. But he sends his love and thanks to you for this wonderful accolade.' I hold up the trophy and the audience applaud, thinking that's the end of my speech. Out of the corner of my eye, I see Alex begin to back away too.

'There are so many other reporters out there working in the same area of journalism,' I continue. 'Brave, bold, intrepid men and women whose search for truth and justice in the world is brought into our homes through our television screens. People like you, Alex,' I say, turning round and gesturing to him.

Alex has to turn round now too, having almost made his escape out into the wings. He smiles awkwardly as a spotlight is thrust upon him.

'Of course everyone remembers Alex Woolfe's wonderful reports,' I continue, turning back to the audience and the cameras. 'You even won awards for many of them, didn't you, Alex?'

Alex nods, his face reddening.

'Come up here so the audience can see you properly, Alex,' I encourage.

Alex shakes his head, the redness in his face beginning to stem from anger now, rather than embarrassment. But I hear a shout of 'Go on, Alex!' from someone who sounds very much like Peter, and then a few more people join in too, mostly spurred on by the copious amount of free alcohol they've downed throughout the evening, rather than by a longing to see more of Alex.

While Alex makes his way back up to the podium again, I notice the floor manager lift her hand and begin to do the wind-it-up signal, but then she lowers it immediately and instead frantically presses her finger to her ear, as if she's trying very hard to hear what someone is saying in her earpiece. She looks shocked by what she hears.

Alex's face is very dark as he stands next to me now; I think he might have twigged where all this is leading.

'So, Alex,' I ask him, smiling brightly, 'what would you say are the most important attributes in a good correspondent? You know, the type of thing viewers would want to see in a person they let into their homes on a daily basis.'

'What is this, an interview?' Alex asks, trying to act glib. 'This is an awards ceremony, Scarlett.' He pulls a comic face at the audience. 'I think someone's thirty seconds in the spotlight have gone to her head!'

There are a few polite chuckles.

'Would one of them be honesty?' I ask, ignoring him. 'Come on, Alex – I'm sure the people at home want to know.'

Alex, realising that this isn't all going to go away, that the cameras are still rolling and people are still looking at him, has no choice but to play along.

'Yes, of course it is.' He beams out into the audience.

'Excellent. That's good to know. Honesty is a wonderful attribute to have.' I pretend to think. 'What else would you need to be, I wonder? Trustworthy, perhaps? I expect people want to see someone like that on their TV screens. Someone honest and trustworthy.'

Alex just nods quickly; he looks desperately around to see why no one is putting a stop to my nonsense. But the intrigued production crew just stare up at us on the stage along with the audience, and the red light on the camera stays lit.

'Do you have both those assets, Alex?' I ask now. 'Are you honest and trustworthy?'

Alex swallows hard. 'Of course I am.'

'Really?' I ask, sounding surprised. 'So would that be why I've heard from very reputable sources that many of your reports were faked for the cameras, and you treated your fellow crew members pretty badly much of the time? In fact, in certain sectors of the industry you're actually known as "Wanker Woolfe", rather than your favoured "Growler". Isn't that right, Alex?'

The audience find this hilarious.

Alex glowers at me with loathing. It's actually quite frightening to see so much hatred in one person.

'I have no idea where you got that information from,' Alex says lightly. 'What is this, some sort of joke?' He's desperately trying to find a way out of this corner I have him pinned in. But sadly for him, there is no way out, and I carry on mercilessly.

'And being honest and trustworthy must come in so handy with all your charitable work too?'

Alex nods warily.

'If that's the case, just why have you been removed from several charities' boards over the years for misappropriation of their funds?'

If looks could kill, I'd be in a crumpled heap on the floor right now. But unfortunately for Alex, they can't, and I'm still on the stage in front of a microphone.

The audience are completely silenced now.

'Shall I go on?' I ask him. 'Because you and I both know that there's *so* much more the audience should know about this particular *Woolfe in sheep's clothing*!'

Alex can control his temper no more. He lifts his hand as if he's going to strike me, but I manage to swerve so he catches it hard on the podium, and as Jamie's award goes crashing to the floor, and Alex jigs about in pain, two security men rush onto the stage to try and escort him away.

'You won't get away with this, Scarlett,' he cries in true villain style as they drag him from the stage.

'Alex, are you threatening me *again*?' I ask as he disappears from sight.

I turn to the audience for the last time and notice the floor manager below me once more anxiously rolling her hands to try and wind me up.

'Thank you for your time, ladies and gentlemen,' I say, reaching down to pick up Jamie's award, which amazingly is still in one piece. 'I'm so sorry you had to witness that. Yes, yes, I know,' I say to the now quite frantic floor manager. 'Let me just say this one thing.' I look out into the audience. 'Martin Luther King once said, "Darkness cannot drive out darkness; only light can do that."' I lift Jamie's award in the air one last time, and then I'm carried back to my seat on a wave of whoops, whistles and applause. Which is just as well, because my legs now seem to be quite incapable of functioning on their own.

Forty-two

People begin swooping on our table the moment I sit down. This is a press awards, after all, and they want the scoop on what's just taken place. But Peter quickly whisks me away from the ballroom to a private room at the hotel; he sits me down on a plush velvet sofa and thrusts a stiff drink into my now shaking hand.

'Was I OK?' I ask him after I've had a few sips of the whisky.

'Were you OK?' Peter exclaims. 'Scarlett, you were an absolute star out there.'

'Really?' I ask, looking up at him. 'I can't really remember what I said – it's all a bit of a blur.'

'Well, I can tell you that speech you've been working on was just the ticket – absolutely perfect.'

I think about the speech I wrote a few days ago. It's still hidden in my evening bag, so I delve inside and pass the piece of paper to Peter.

Peter opens it and reads what I've written.

'But this isn't what you just stood on the stage and said a few moments ago,' he puzzles. 'Nothing like it. I thought including the whole Martin Luther King quote was absolute genius, but it's not even mentioned here.'

'I quoted Martin Luther King?'

Peter nods and passes me back my speech. 'Sounds like you winged it, Miss Scarlett, but in a most successful way!'

Max bursts through the door.

'Scarlett, you were bloody brilliant!' he cries, rushing over and hugging me in a most un-Max-like way. 'You really made that worm squirm.'

'Did I?'

'Scarlett can't really remember what she said,' Peter explains. 'I think she's in shock.'

'You can ditch that nonsense,' Max says stoutly. 'You're the talk of the town out there. Everyone is gossiping about Wanker Woolfe!'

I look at Max. 'What?'

'That's what you called him,' Max grins. 'Absolute genius. I thought it was only me who called him that.'

I pull a face. 'It probably is. I have no idea where that came from. Oh God.' I bury my face in my hands. 'I really said that?'

'Yep!' they both reply, grinning at me.

The door bursts open again. But this time the person entering does not look as gleeful. It's Alex.

'Alex,' Peter says, stepping in front of him. 'I thought you'd been removed from the premises.'

'I had.' Alex tries to get a look at me over Peter's shoulder. 'But it's amazing what can happen if you float a few dollars under someone's nose.'

I put my glass down on a nearby table and stand up. 'It's OK, Peter. I can handle this.'

Peter looks over his shoulder, then steps aside.

Alex regards me for a few moments.

'You play a tough game, Scarlett,' he says. 'Dirty. Under normal circumstances, I'd quite like that in a woman.' He looks me up and down, and I feel my skin prickle with revulsion.

'And *you* play the foulest game of all,' I reply. 'You mess with people's lives and emotions in the most horrible of ways.'

Alex smiles ruefully. 'You've done the same,' he replies. 'You've ruined my life now, haven't you, with tonight's little pantomime. My reputation is ruined forever.'

I hear Max's fake laughter behind me.

'But don't think it ends here,' Alex continues. 'I always come out on top. Peter,' he says, turning to where Peter is attempting to control his anger, his hands curled into tight fists by his sides. 'I don't know who gave permission in your corporation for that witch hunt to take place tonight,

393

but I shall be suing your television company for defamation of character.'

'Oh, really?' Peter says calmly.

Alex nods. 'Yes. You can't broadcast those sort of lies over the air and expect to get away with it.'

'No,' Peter agrees. 'Indeed I can't. Even if everything Scarlett said was true, I still wouldn't be allowed to broadcast it. Which is exactly why I didn't.'

'What?' Alex and I both ask together. We look between Peter and Max for an explanation.

'Yep, sunshine,' Max says, standing up, 'you weren't going out live on air. Everything Scarlett said after accepting the award was said during a commercial break. It was only your peers who heard what a lying, cheating little snake you really are.'

This is news to me. As far as I was aware, I was broadcasting to the whole of America. The news that I wasn't actually comes as something of a relief.

Alex, having absorbed all this information, smiles.

'Touché, *amigos*. You play a good game. You may have ruined my reputation within the industry, but at least my family still thinks I'm a good guy! Even you can't ruin that, eh, Scarlett?'

'Oh, Alex, if only that *were* the case.' I fold my arms and sigh heavily for effect. 'You see, I'm not quite as cold-hearted as you. It wouldn't have been fair on your poor wife to let her know what sort of man she's really married to, not in her delicate condition.'

394

'Exactly,' Alex says, smirking.

'So I told her grandparents instead,' I smile sweetly. 'I gave them the option of telling Charlotte when she's had the baby or keeping quiet about it. They have the upper hand now, Alex, not you. So I suggest you better start playing nice with Charlotte's family in the future, hmm?'

Alex is for once lost for words.

'And,' Max says, joining in, 'just because your little performance out there tonight wasn't broadcast live, don't think you've got away with it. The big boys with the cameras may not have been filming you, but I was.' He holds up his own video camera. 'I just love a bit of YouTube, Alex, don't you? I hear you can get away with so much more on the internet than on television.'

Alex gives a derisory shake of his head. 'You all think you're so clever, don't you?'

'Yep, pretty much,' I say, grinning. 'We make a great team. You worked in the media industry for long enough, Alex. You should know how much they love a happy ending. And *this* ... is it!'

Alex swivels on the heels of his perfectly polished shoes and is just about to exit though the door when it opens.

'Sean,' Alex says, immediately backing away.

'Alex,' Sean says pleasantly. 'I've got something for you, something you really deserve.'

Alex looks puzzled. 'W-what?'

'This,' Sean says as his fist lands hard in the centre of Alex's face and Alex crumples on the carpet below.

I rush over to Sean and he wraps his arms around me. '*Now* it's the end,' he says, kissing me on the forehead. 'You can't have a happy ending without your hero rushing in to save you!'

I kiss him. 'You'll always be my hero, Sean. But I have to disagree with you on one point.'

'What's that?' Sean asks.

'I think this is just the beginning …'

Forty-three

'It's absolutely perfect, Oscar,' I say, looking at myself in the mirror.

'Did you ever doubt it would be?' Oscar replies as we both stare back at the reflection of me in my stunningly beautiful wedding gown.

It's finally here at last, the day I'm going to be married to Sean, and I know nothing of what's about to happen.

True to his word, Sean has kept our entire day a closely guarded secret since he agreed to organise the whole thing. It was fine at first – with everything that has gone on over the last few months, I didn't have time to worry or fret about what he was doing – but after the awards and my now quite famous (in certain circles) speech, I began to think about what he might have planned. But try as I may – and believe me, I have, in every sneaky way possible – I just couldn't find out anything about what was going to happen.

I had a feeling it was going to be one of those occasions when everyone else knew what was going on except me. I knew Sean had enlisted help from Oscar and Gabi, because I'd often walk in on them discussing something and they'd hurriedly change the subject. In fact, it had happened with so many different people over the last month that if I hadn't known Sean was planning our wedding day, I'd have begun to get quite a complex.

'I just can't believe this is my wedding dress . . . ' I say to Oscar again. I can't take my eyes off what I see in the mirror. 'How did you know this is what I'd love when I didn't even know what I wanted myself?'

The wedding dress Oscar has designed for me is based upon the Charles Rennie Mackintosh panels we saw together at the House for an Art Lover up in Glasgow. He remembered how I stopped to admire the long, fluid lines and linear designs inspired by the natural world, and the women who were wearing long Pre-Raphaelite-style dresses encompassing the look, and he created a dress for me that mirrored that whole art nouveau style.

My dress is in raw ivory silk. It has beautifully delicate, long, billowy sleeves with tiny fitted silk cuffs, which make me feel like wafting my arms around like a ballerina. The rest of the dress is very fitted, quite reminiscent of the flapper-girl style of the 1920s, except it extends all the way down to my toes. But what makes the whole thing so special is the matching silk ivory embroidery, dotted with occasional tiny iridescent beads, that extends over the entire dress.

The embroidery is exactly like the designs we saw in Glasgow; long, formal Mackintosh-style lines spread over the whole gown, stitched to accentuate my figure in all the right places. Stylised rosebuds with long, curvy stems wind their way up my gown from the base, their leaves intertwined with the more formal lines, softening the whole effect. There's even a tiny dragonfly perched on one of the stems, a detail that almost makes me cry when I discover it.

It's perfect.

'But that's not where it stops,' Oscar says now, producing another hanger with a protective bag over it. 'Someone was silly enough to want to get married in New York in December! So we can't have you freezing yourself to death before you've even become Mrs Bond.' He carefully unzips the bag and from it pulls the most gorgeous long, flowing cape I've ever seen. It's in exactly the same fabric as my dress, with the same stylised flowers growing up all around the base and around the edge of the hood, except this time the leaves are picked out in ivy green and the flowers a gorgeous shade of scarlet.

Oscar places it gently over my shoulders and then carefully does the little clasp up round my neck, arranges my hood, then stands back to view the whole effect.

'Oh, Oscar,' I say, desperately trying to keep my tears at bay. 'No words can describe how much I love this whole outfit. And,' I say, turning away from the mirror to face him, 'how much I love you.'

As Oscar and I hug each other, there's a knock at the door and Gabi comes into the room with Maddie.

We've all been getting ready at Gabi's apartment since early this morning. In fact, the three of us stayed over here last night and had our own impromptu pyjama party, in which lots of milkshakes and hot chocolate were drunk, and many slices of pizza were ordered and then eaten with great relish.

In typical Gabi style, this morning experts in beauty, hair and nails had all arrived at Gabi's apartment, while we were still wandering around bleary-eyed, to knock us into shape for my big day – and that's exactly what they've done, with manicures, pedicures, facials, conditioning hair treatments and even on-the-spot massages.

The hairdresser Gabi has hired has done a wonderful job. My long, dark hair hangs in loose bohemian-style waves down one side of my face; the other side is pinned up loosely in a coiled bun, with some delicate strands of iridescent beading that match my dress winding their way round the outside. The bun is completed with three tiny red rosebuds pinned in the middle.

Now, as we all stand here inside Gabi's dressing room with its full-length mirrors covering the whole of one wall, we look like we've stepped off the shoot of an upmarket bridal magazine, or even a new period drama.

After consultation with both Maddie and Oscar, I asked

Gabi to be my third bridesmaid (we all counted Oscar as one!) and Maddie and Gabi are wearing dresses that mirror mine, bohemian art nouveau-style gowns in the same shade of red as the rosebuds on my cloak. Their dresses have similar, though less detailed, embroidery to mine, and they too are wearing capes that match their gowns, with a single red flower in their hair.

Oscar, looking very dapper, has on a pair of matching red velvet knickerbockers, an ivory shirt with a ruffle, a fitted waistcoat with matching rosebud embroidery and a tailcoat in a fine black velvet. His feet positively gleam in shiny black patent-leather ankle boots.

'Well, don't we all scrub up well!' Oscar says, making everyone laugh, which is just as well, as we all look quite emotional right now and likely to burst into tears. 'No one who saw the state of us on your hen night would have believed we could look like this!'

My hen night was not a night I wanted to recall in a hurry . . .

Sean and I both chose to spend the evening in London to balance the fact our wedding was going to take place in New York.

Sean's night, I later found out, was fairly uneventful – a nice meal at an expensive restaurant, followed by some drinks in an exclusive Soho bar. In fact, the worst thing his friends did to him all night was make him pay the bill at the end of the evening. My night, on the other hand, was a riotous affair from start to finish.

Oscar and Maddie had gone the whole hog and had tacky bright red T-shirts printed with 'Scarlett's Hen Night' on the front and 'We're gonna paint the town Red!' on the back. Plus, to add to my embarrassment, I was made to wear a bridal veil all evening, so no one was in any doubt as to who the bride was in our party.

It all started fairly tamely: a very nice meal at a restaurant in Covent Garden to begin with, and then we took taxis to a trendy nightclub in Mayfair that apparently many celebrities frequented when they were in town. Gabi had made arrangements with the management for us all to be allowed in tonight as her special guests.

'T-shirts off!' Oscar instructed as we piled out of the taxis and gathered outside. 'We'll not be allowed in wearing these.'

So we all temporarily removed our hen-night shirts to reveal our original party outfits, and Oscar stuffed the T-shirts in a carrier bag until we got inside.

This particular club was apparently very famous for its cocktails, and it was when I started sampling some of these that my problems began, and where my memory of the evening becomes somewhat hazy.

I vaguely remember telling an ex-*EastEnders* cast member how much I loved him, and how it was a tragedy that his character had been killed off in a freak washing-machine accident in the launderette. Then, I'm told, I happened upon one of the *Strictly Come Dancing* pro dancers and proceeded to try and make him tango me around the dance floor. But my biggest embarrassment, which Oscar recalled with great delight to me the next morning, was that I'd barged my way through a crowd surrounding *X Factor* guru Simon Cowell and attempted to audition for him there and then. Apparently my chorus of 'I Will Always Love You' did not put me in the running to be the next Whitney Houston. But I did cause Simon much amusement when I told him I could audition for *Britain's Got Talent* with my belly-dancing routine and had hitched my now replaced red T-shirt up round my waist and begun gyrating in front of him still wearing my veil . . .

'The less said about that night, the better,' I say now as we all admire each other's much more elegant reflections in the mirror. '"What happens in Mayfair stays in Mayfair" I believe is the saying!'

Everyone laughs.

'So what happens now?' Maddie asks. 'It's not long now until all the fun begins!'

'I don't know,' I wail, looking at the clock on Gabi's wall. 'No one will tell me anything!'

They all smile knowingly at each other.

'That's the best way!' Gabi says, grinning. She claps her hands together. 'Oh, Scarlett, you are in for such a treat today. This is going to be so much fun!'

Forty-four

Everyone else has left for the wedding, so I'm here all alone waiting in Gabi's apartment.

I don't know where they've gone or how they're getting there; all I know is that everyone disappeared about ten minutes ago and I'm to wait for my call from downstairs.

I sigh. Usually I quite like being on my own – it gives me space to think – but right now I'd be much happier surrounded by those I love. This is my wedding day – I'm nervous enough, but not knowing what's going to happen to me is starting to feel very scary indeed.

The doorbell rings, so I collect up my bouquet – a small posy of rosebuds to match my dress – and go to answer it.

It's Henry, my favourite of all Gabi's doormen.

'Miss Scarlett,' he says, giving a little bow, 'I believe your carriage is awaiting you downstairs.'

Henry escorts me down in the lift and through to the front entrance of the building; we go through the glass doors out onto the sidewalk.

But rather than seeing a stretch limo or a horse and carriage with my father waiting inside, I can only see a black motorbike, and a biker dressed from head to toe in black leather.

I look around, wondering what's going on.

The biker leaves his bike and walks across the sidewalk towards me. He stands so close that I begin to feel a little apprehensive.

Then he removes his helmet.

'Bradley!' I cry in delight, as I find a grinning Bradley Cooper standing in front of me. 'What are you doing here?'

'I couldn't miss your big day, could I?' he says, kissing me on the cheek. 'I was part of your proposal and I wanted to be part of your wedding.'

'But—'

'No time to explain,' he says. 'Come on.'

I look at the bike. On any normal occasion, I'd jump at the chance of riding on the back of a motorbike, holding on to the waist of a leather-clad Bradley Cooper while we zip through the streets of Manhattan. But this is my wedding day, and there is no way I am putting a motorcycle helmet on top of my beautifully coiffured hair and hitching up my skirt to get on that thing.

'Don't worry,' Bradley says, unzipping his leathers to reveal a smart black suit and a white shirt. 'We're not going on that. We're going in this!' Bradley walks towards a gleaming white Jaguar sports car, throws his leathers in the back, then opens the door for me.

'Thank goodness,' I smile, climbing into the passenger seat. 'You had me worried for a few moments there. Although,' I say, looking back at the bike, 'a ride on the back of that would have reminded me of a time Sean and I rode on motorbikes to a wedding.'

'I know,' Bradley says, climbing into the driver's seat next to me. 'Sean said it would. That's why I arrived on it.'

I look wistfully back at the motorbike as Bradley starts the engine and we pull out into the Manhattan traffic.

'Where are we going?' I ask. 'You do realise I know nothing about today?'

'I do indeed!' Bradley says, slipping on some shades. It may be mid-December, but thankfully it's a bright, sunny day for my wedding. 'That's why I'm sworn to secrecy like everyone else!'

Usually I hate to take a car anywhere in New York – the traffic is always horrendous and it takes you ages to get to your destination – but today is an exception. I'm driving through downtown Manhattan with Bradley Cooper in an open-top sports car! Fantasies do sometimes come true.

But Bradley is only the first of many surprises today . . .

After an unusually enjoyable slow drive across the city, Bradley pulls up at one of the piers that overlook the Hudson River on the west side of Manhattan.

'Now what?' I ask him as he jumps from the car and hurries round to open my door for me.

'Please accompany me,' Bradley says, holding out his arm for me to take, 'to the next stage of your journey.'

We walk down to the edge of the pier to find a large white speedboat covered in red ribbons moored and waiting for us to board, and on it, waving madly, is Oscar, along with Maddie and my father, who's looking very smart in a black tuxedo, white shirt and black bow tie.

'Dad!' I cry in delight, hugging him after he's helped me down into the speedboat. 'You made it back. You look fantastic, and so tanned too!'

He stands back to look at me. 'Oh, Scarlett,' he says proudly, his voice breaking. 'You look absolutely beautiful.'

'Of course she does!' I hear Oscar pipe up. 'And I take most of the credit for it!'

I turn round and grin at him. 'Did you know about all this?' I ask. 'He –' I point to Bradley, who's just climbing down into the boat to join us '– nearly had me on a motorbike this morning. It would have ruined my hair!'

Oscar pretends to fan himself. 'That, darling, is one of my own personal fantasies! Hi, Bradley!' He waves, rushing over to him as quickly as he can in the boat.

Maddie smiles at me. 'Just enjoy it,' she says simply. 'Go with the flow, because it gets even better than this.'

The speedboat is soon whizzing along the Hudson River, past all the piers that line that side of Manhattan, and I have to pull the hood of my cloak up to protect my gorgeous hairstyle. No sooner have we got going, though, than we seem to be slowing down again.

'What's happening now?' I ask. But as always no one will tell.

The speedboat pulls up alongside a much larger boat. I've seen this vessel sailing around this part of the bay many times when I've been down here. It's a schooner, with three huge billowing white sails, and as I look up, I can see Sean's sister, Ursula, his dad, Alfie, and his step-mother, Diana, waving at me.

Some steps are lowered from one boat to the other and I manage to climb aboard. I wonder when Sean has been planning all this if he's taken into account the fact I'd be wearing a floor-length dress today. It's just as well I don't have a long train to contend with too! But knowing Sean, I'm sure he would have consulted with Oscar about the mechanics of my outfit beforehand.

'Ahoy there, me hearties!' Alfie calls, coming over to greet the newcomers to the ship. 'Welcome aboard!'

I greet Alfie, Diana and Ursula, and then suddenly I understand.

'Are you all joining this Pied Piper tour in the order I met you?' I ask. 'Is that what's going on?'

Ursula nods. 'You've got it. All except Bradley, who we agreed was the perfect person to collect you in the sports car.'

Bradley winks at me.

I think about this. 'So my mother is next?'

'I'm already here, darling,' she says, stepping out from one of the cabins. She looks gorgeous in a purple and scarlet red silk suit, with matching hat.

'Mum!' I cry, rushing to her. 'I wondered why you weren't at the apartment earlier.'

'I wanted to be, but Sean has put so much thought into this that I wanted it to be just perfect for you.'

'It is, it is!' I cry, excitedly looking around at them all as a glass of champagne is thrust into my hand. 'Now, where are we sailing to next?'

The schooner sails away from the banks of Manhattan out to Ellis Island, and then round Liberty Island too, so we all have some fantastic views of Lady Liberty on this bright winter's day.

We sail round to the southernmost point of Manhattan and moor close to Battery Park. Everyone then disembarks onto dry land, while I look around me to see what's happening now.

'This way,' Bradley calls, as everyone files behind him. 'Hurry up, Scarlett. Don't you want to know what Sean's got planned for you next?'

Forty-five

This is not at all what I was expecting to be doing on my wedding day: standing in a grubby subway station waiting for a train.

But that's exactly what all nine of us are doing right at this very moment.

Maddie smiles reassuringly at me. 'Don't worry,' she says. 'I know this seems very odd, but this is Sean. All will be fine.'

Suddenly over the subway tannoy there's an announcement. 'The next train to arrive on platform one is the number four express to Yankee Stadium. Please be aware that the first carriage is for members of the O'Brien/Bond wedding party only. I repeat – the first carriage is for members of the wedding party only. Have a nice day, Scarlett!'

I look up at the tannoy and laugh. No way has Sean hired a subway train!

But Sean has, and as the train now pulls into Bowling Green Subway Station, the first carriage looks much brighter than all the others. It's been decorated inside with balloons and streamers, and as much wedding paraphernalia as possible. And standing in the centre of it all are of course Jamie and Max.

'Jamie!' I cry as the doors open and we climb aboard. 'You came!'

'Of course!' he says, hugging me. 'You don't think I'd miss my own sister's wedding!'

'Max,' I say, hugging him now too. 'This is all such madness!'

'It's your future husband who's mad,' he says. 'Why couldn't we all just have arrived at the wedding in cars like normal people? We've been riding up and down on this subway for hours now.' He kisses me on the cheek. 'But you're worth it,' he whispers. 'Just don't tell anyone I said so!'

Our subway carriage takes us north again. *We can't really be going to the Yankee Stadium, can we?* I wonder as the train rattles along and everyone sits chatting amiably with each other.

But when the train pulls up at Grand Central Station, apparently it's time for us to disembark again.

I wonder what we must look like as we all walk through the station together. But this is New York and no one even

411

blinks twice as we troop through the station out onto 42nd Street.

'No way!' I say again, as an open-top tour bus with yet more balloons and streamers is waiting to collect us outside. Up on top, I see Peter, and Jamie's mother, Eleanor, beaming down at us.

We drive through downtown Manhattan like a winning soccer team, or a group of Olympic gold medallists, waving to passers-by below. Just like a tour bus, we go down Park Avenue and then along 34th Street, past the Christmas shoppers heading in and out of Macy's, and the tourists heading for the Empire State Building, then up Fifth Avenue, passing the New York Public Library, the Rockefeller Center, with its huge Christmas tree, St Patrick's Cathedral and, finally, Tiffany's.

'We've been past everywhere today that's special to me in New York,' I say to Jamie, who's standing next to me just now on the bus.

'I think that was probably Sean's idea behind all this,' Jamie says, waving to some Japanese tourists. 'He wanted it to be special for you, to bring back some good memories. He's a pretty decent guy, is your Sean.'

'I know he is. I'm so lucky to be marrying him.'

We pull up at the southeast corner of Central Park, almost back where I started this morning at Gabi's apartment, and I'm instructed to climb down from the bus with everyone else.

Luke and Gabi come rushing over.

412

'Have you had an absolute blast?' Gabi asks excitedly. 'I'm so sad I missed it all, but I'm one of the last special people to come into your life since you met Sean.'

'You may be last, but you're definitely not least,' I say, hugging her. 'I know you've been a part of organising all this today, Gabi. Thank you so much.'

'Ah, I only helped a little. It was all Sean's idea.'

'Scarlett,' Luke says, hugging me now too, 'you look stunning in that dress.'

'I have your husband to thank for that, as you well know!'

'You're very special to him, Scarlett, as you are to me now too.'

'Aw, Luke, don't start me off – I'm holding it together right now. I can't cry or my make-up will run.'

Luke winks. 'I'll say no more.'

'So what happens now?' I ask as one of the Central Park carriages pulls up next to us.

'This!' Gabi says, gesturing to indicate a whole line of horses pulling decorative carriages. 'There's one for all of us!'

My father helps me up into the first, very ornate cream carriage and sits down next to me. Then the other three are filled with Maddie, Oscar, Gabi and my mother; Jamie, Max, Ursula, Alfie and Diana take the next one; then Peter, Luke, Eleanor and Bradley the last. Once everyone's safely in their carriage, we begin to make our way slowly round the park in convoy.

We take a long, leisurely route through Central Park, waving to tourists and even New Yorkers, who, on seeing we're a full wedding party, unusually stop to raise a hand, and sometimes applaud. I smile, not only because I'm happy, but because I'm reminded of another occasion, when I'd just met Jamie and Oscar had ridden on one of these around the park searching for me, singing and calling out my name as he did so.

Sean has brought back so many happy memories for me today, of places we visited together and of the people who are now accompanying me round Central Park. Even this bridal Pied Piper I'm playing today has brought back memories of when Sean led me on a treasure hunt around the streets of New York, finally proposing to me on the Brooklyn Bridge at the end. In fact, the bridge is one of the few places we haven't visited today.

But even though I've thoroughly enjoyed this prolonged magical journey to my own wedding, I'm starting to get impatient now to see Sean and become Mrs Bond.

We've talked about the name change – Sean obviously wanting me to take his name – but I like being an O'Brien. I don't have much family and I don't want my side of the O'Brien family to end with Dad. So in the end we've agreed that in our business lives we will both keep our own names, but we'll actually become O'Brien-Bonds to every-one else, which I think has a lovely ring to it!

We continue in the carriages along Terrace Drive, past the Bethesda Fountain, with the Angel of the Waters as always calmly watching over proceedings below, and we're just making our way towards Strawberry Fields when suddenly our horses pull up.

My father alights from one side of our carriage to help me down.

I look back at everyone else. 'Aren't you all coming this time?' I ask as they remain in their carriages.

But they just wave as their horses pull round ours and continue up the West Drive.

'This way,' my father says, taking my hand and leading me along a little path to a sign that says, WAGNER COVE. We make our way down some hidden steps and I find myself at one of the larger lakes in the park.

There's a small rowing boat waiting at the edge of the water, and at last waiting inside the boat is Sean.

Forty-six

Sean stands up in the boat to greet me, and wobbles.

'Careful,' I call. 'I don't want you falling in now! It's taken me long enough to get here.'

Sean climbs out of the boat onto the grass. He's wearing a beautiful black suit, white shirt and, like my father, a black bow tie. 'You look absolutely gorgeous,' he says, kissing me gently on the cheek.

'You don't look too shabby yourself,' I reply, overjoyed to finally see him.

Sean still can't take his eyes off me. 'I can't believe you're actually going to be my wife in a few minutes. You really do look breathtaking.'

'Sean, please don't say anything else,' I mumble, taking a deep breath. 'I haven't cried so far and I really don't want to start now.'

'Well, this is it,' my father says, as he lifts my hand and turns me towards him. 'Scarlett, I've loved you since you were a baby,' he says sombrely. 'In fact, my love for you began before you were even born, when you were just a promise in your mother's tummy. I watched you grow into a delightful, if cheeky little girl –' he winks '– then mature into the amazing, wonderful young woman who stands before me now. And although you've often given me grief over the years,' he smiles, 'I can tell you I've never been prouder of you than I am at this very moment.'

'I need a tissue,' I gulp, as tears begin to spill onto my cheeks.

My father pulls out a white handkerchief, and I dab carefully at my eyes.

'Take good care of her,' he says, passing my hand to Sean. 'She's very precious to me.'

Sean takes my hand in his and then holds out his other one to my father.

They shake formally.

Then Sean lets go of me for a moment to hug Dad. 'You know I'll look after her, Tom,' he says, patting him on the shoulder. 'She's very precious to me too.'

My father nods, then turns and begins to make his way up the steps again.

'Where's he going?' I ask.

'To find the others,' Sean says, stepping into the boat again. 'And so will we in a moment. Come on.' He holds his hand out to me and helps me into the rowing boat. Then he takes the oars, pushes us away from the side and begins to row us across the lake.

This is very romantic; after all the excitement, hustle and bustle of the last couple of hours, now it's just Sean and me as we make our way over the calm water.

'You're quite good at this,' I tell him as he pulls powerfully on the oars. 'I could get used to it.'

Sean raises his eyebrows. 'This,' he says, 'is a one-off.' Then he winks. 'But a very special one-off, for a very special lady.' He looks behind him, and then for the first time I see where we're heading.

Ladies Pavilion sits on a tiny rocky outcrop that juts out into the lake. It's a small, ornate pavilion with a slate roof and pretty cast-iron detailing, and allows wonderful views across the lake to the city beyond. I've rested here a couple of times when I've been wandering around the park, and I've enjoyed the pavilion's peaceful ambiance while I sheltered from the sun or the rain, depending on the season.

'We're getting married there!' I exclaim, as our other guests now come into view as we get ever closer to the shore.

'Are you pleased?' Sean asks, expertly steering the boat in the direction of the pavilion.

'I can't believe it! Yes ... yes, of course I'm pleased. It's beautiful, Sean. I just hadn't expected an outdoor wedding in December!'

'Full of surprises, me,' Sean says, obviously overjoyed

I'm so happy. 'I've even arranged the weather,' he says, glancing up at the blue skies above us.

'Well, you've certainly kept me guessing all morning, that's for sure!'

'Plenty more of that to come,' Sean says as we float closer to the shore. He throws a rope out to a waiting Peter, who pulls the boat in so we can disembark safely.

'Much better than The Plaza,' Peter says, whispering in my ear as he helps me out of the boat. 'You know what we always say, Scarlett – everything happens for a reason!'

I give Peter a little hug. 'A hundred per cent better,' I agree, smiling.

Oscar fusses around me, straightening my dress and cloak, and adjusting my hair.

'How I ever agreed to you being dragged across the city on every mode of transport possible I don't know,' he says, tutting at Sean as he climbs out of the boat behind us. 'However, darling,' he smiles at me, 'you have managed to do it all with much grace and remain beautiful throughout. I made a good choice.'

Peter returns to the other guests, while Oscar, Maddie and Gabi form a line in front of us to make the bridal procession. Then we begin to walk up a small path to the pavilion.

Inside the pavilion, along with the guests I have collected at various points around New York, an officiant waits to perform our service, and as she welcomes everyone and begins the wedding ceremony, I allow my eyes to roam across our family and friends. With each new mode of transport this morning I collected people who are important in Sean's and my life. Along with our close family and friends, a few more guests have arrived to join us now too, so there's quite a crowd spilling out of the pavilion onto the grass of Central Park, and all I can think about as the officiant continues to talk and our ceremony progresses is how perfect this is, and how I wouldn't want to be anywhere else in the world right now than standing here, in one of my favourite places in the world, marrying my gorgeous and wonderful Sean.

When the ceremony is over, our rings have been exchanged and everyone's tears have been dried – the vast majority of them shed by Oscar, who bawled his eyes out through the whole ceremony – there are of course photos to be taken.

When all the shots of family and friends are complete, I begin to notice that one by one our guests seem to be disappearing.

'Where's everyone going?' I ask Sean as we stand face to face preparing for another close-up.

'Just somewhere,' Sean says mysteriously. 'You'll see soon enough.'

Finally the photographer is satisfied he's got every possible shot of us he can and we're allowed to depart.

Sean walks us past where my carriage dropped me off before the ceremony, and then we walk a little further out of the gates of Central Park to discover the original white Jaguar waiting for us, this time without my film-star chauffeur.

Sean opens the door for me and I give him a puzzled look as I climb inside. He just hops into the driver's seat and we head off downtown again in the Jaguar. This time as we drive, we stay close to the Hudson River until we reach West 30th Street, where Sean turns a swift right and pulls up at the Port Authority Heliport.

'You've got to be kidding me!' I say, looking up. 'We're not.'

But we are.

Within a few minutes Sean and I are swooping across the skies of Manhattan in a little blue helicopter!

'This is amazing!' I call out to him, over the noise of the blades above us. 'You're amazing! The whole day is amazing! I love you!'

Sean can only make out the 'I love you' part and he mouths 'I love you too' back at me.

The helicopter ride is over all too soon. We fly across every major landmark in the city, including the Brooklyn Bridge, and Sean holds his hand out to me across the inside of the helicopter when we do.

We finally land at a different heliport than we started at in downtown Manhattan. The blades cease spinning, and we both climb down and thank the pilot. Then Sean leads me across the tarmac to what he promises me is the last stage of our journey, where a man waits on a black and white two-person rickshaw.

'OK, this bike really has to be it now!' I tell him as we set off. 'We've covered just about every mode of transport there is. I've gone by boat, car, bus, carriage and train; I've even flown today!'

'Yes, this is very definitely it,' Sean says, taking my hand. 'But the question is, have you enjoyed it?'

'Of course I have. I was trying to tell you in the helicopter – it's been amazing. You're amazing, Sean.' I lean over and kiss him. 'But even after all that wonderful, exciting stuff, by far my favourite part was taking our vows in Central Park. The venue was so simple yet so perfect.'

'It was,' Sean agrees. 'I knew you'd like it. Which is exactly why I know you'll love what's going to happen next.'

We're now crossing the Brooklyn Bridge. I feel a bit sorry for Dan, our little rickshaw man, pedalling away on his bike at the front while Sean and I are tucked up cosy and warm beneath a blanket behind him. But he seems happy enough as we reach the exact point where Sean proposed to me.

'You didn't think I'd leave this part out of our special day, did you?' he asks, squeezing my hand under the blanket as the rickshaw slows down.

'Of course not. I remember it as if it was yesterday.'

But we don't pause and turn round as I expect is going to happen now we've reached the section of the bridge that's so special to us; instead we continue along the bridge across into Brooklyn.

'Why are we going to Brooklyn?' I ask. My mind is racing with all the possibilities. Has Sean perhaps booked the River Café for our reception?

But as we turn into a couple of familiar streets, I know exactly why!

'Sunnyside?' I ask hopefully.

Sean nods. 'Sunnyside.'

Forty-seven

We're going to see the children at Sunnyside on my wedding day! I can't believe Sean has included them too.

The rickshaw pulls up outside the front of the house and Sean helps me out. Then we walk down the path through a very tidy-looking garden to the front door, which today has a huge red bow on it.

'Go on, then,' Sean encourages me. 'Knock.'

I rap hard on the brass doorknocker and wait.

After a few seconds Bethany opens the door; she's beaming with excitement and obviously desperately trying to stay calm. She comes out onto the front step with us and pulls the door to behind her.

'Congratulations, Scarlett and Sean,' she says in a tiny voice. 'Here.' She hands me a large homemade card. On the front is a child's drawing of a bride and groom; the bride is wearing a very traditional dress of white lace with lots of flowers in her long, black hair, and the groom a very tall black top hat and tails. I open it up; inside, all the children have signed it and written lots of different congratulatory messages.

'Thank you, Bethany,' I say, giving her a little kiss on the cheek. 'It's beautiful. Can we possibly come in for a bit, do you think, and thank everyone?'

Bethany pushes open the door a little and pokes her head through the gap. Then she retrieves it and pulls the door to again.

'Yes, you can now!' she declares, as she throws the door open wide.

We step inside the hallway, which is usually covered in coats, shoes and toys, but today is pristinely tidy, just like the pathway was. There's a large, cheerful-looking Christmas tree standing in a bright red pot in the corner with its lights twinkling, and colourful homemade bunting hanging from the walls, stairs and light fittings. In the centre of the hall, at the top of the staircase, a huge banner declares, CONGRATULATIONS, SCARLETT & SEAN! Except whoever made it obviously ran out of space as the letters on the 'Sean' part curve round the edge of the paper.

Before I have time to declare my delight at the banner, two children wearing their smartest clothes come down the stairs, stop on the bottom step and begin to sing the first line to a song I recognise immediately Then a further group of four children emerges and joins in with the next line.

Children appear line by line throughout the song from all over Sunnyside, until every one of its residents is lined up on the stairs singing the infamous Wet Wet Wet song 'Love Is All Around' from the movie *Four Weddings and a Funeral*.

'Was this your idea too?' I whisper to Sean as the children sing before us.

Sean shakes his head. 'Nope, this was all them.' And I notice his eyes are misty.

When the children finish, I'm about to applaud, but Jack stops me by putting up his hand.

'We love you, Scarlett!' the children call in unison. 'And now we love Sean too! Congratulations!'

I wait just a moment to check they've finished this time, then I hold my arms out to them and they all come bounding down the stairs to surround Sean and me, jumping up and down on the spot with excitement. Then, as if everyone's appearing magically from special hiding places all around Sunnyside, our other wedding guests now join us, along with Kim and the rest of the Sunnyside staff.

'I hope you don't mind holding your wedding reception here?' Kim asks apologetically. 'It's going to be a bit rough and ready!'

'Are you kidding me!' I reply as yet another child wants to hug me. 'It's my wedding day – where else am I going to find all this love under one roof!'

*

The party at Sunnyside is, as I'd hoped, full of love and laughter. Sean has had food catered in, even though he tells me he had a real battle with Kim, who wanted to cook it all herself. But the food I find myself ravenously digging into, when I realise just how long it is since I last ate anything, is not your usual staid and boring wedding food, but fun and scrumptious things such as cupcakes, iced doughnuts, tiny chocolate mousses and trifles filled with delicious custard. There are finger sandwiches with every filling you can imagine, from plain cheese through to smoked salmon. And there are also lots and lots of pretzels and crisps – or chips, as the children correct me on more than one occasion.

The children and guests all tuck in and mingle together, and it makes for one big, happy party in the large playroom, which has been transformed into the perfect reception venue, with twinkly lights, large helium balloons, more homemade bunting and pretty posies of winter flowers dotted about everywhere.

I sigh when I finally have a moment to myself to look around at everyone enjoying themselves. It's just perfect.

How many times have I said that word already today?

Sean has made our wedding day absolutely perfect. He has thought about everything and everyone that is special to me and made sure he included it in our big day, just like he said he would. I feel quite guilty; it feels like this wedding day is more about me than about him. I'll definitely have to make it up to him on our honeymoon.

If we have a honeymoon booked . . .

I'm just about to ask Sean about it when Peter attempts to gain everyone's attention on a microphone and some serious-looking sound equipment that's suddenly appeared in the room.

'Ladies and gentlemen, boys and girls,' he says, if you could now all please arrange yourselves in two parallel lines down the middle of the room, and if you have a partner here tonight, or maybe someone you admire from afar, please face them!'

I look at everyone busily arranging themselves along both sides of the party room as tables are pulled back and drinks, both soft and alcoholic, are placed well out of harm's way.

'What's going on now?' I ask Sean as he pulls me to the top of one of the lines and stands facing me.

'Haven't you learned yet today not to ask questions and just to let it all happen?' Sean calls, grinning.

I sigh and accept my place at the top of the line.

'What you'll notice,' Peter says as we stand looking at each other now, 'is just how many of you are now partnered up with the man or woman of your dreams simply because your lives have been touched by our beautiful bride, Scarlett!'

I look along the line. Peter is right. There's my father and Eleanor, Gabi and Max, Oscar and Luke, a couple of Sean's friends who have met through me too; even my mother is eyeing up a worried-looking Bradley right now. Maddie is hanging back a little by the far wall; sadly she didn't ever work things out with Felix, but Jamie, seeing her embarrassment, gallantly takes her hand and leads her to the end of the line.

'She's quite the little matchmaker, is our Scarlett,' Peter says. 'Very much like the Hitch character from one of her favourite movies! But who am I to decide if that's a fair comparison? Let's let the star of that movie decide himself ...'

I stare up at Peter. It couldn't be ...

But it is. Seemingly out of nowhere Will Smith bounds into the room and the children scream with delight! Actually, I think I may have joined in with them. They rush over to Will, who good-naturedly ruffles their hair and high-fives them.

'Back to your places, kids!' he calls, taking the microphone from Peter. 'We've got some work to do!'

Amazingly, the children listen to him and return to their spots in the line, while I just stand there open-mouthed.

'You'd better close those pretty lips of yours, Scarlett,' he says, winking at me. 'You's a mighty fine-lookin' woman, but you don't wanna be catching no flies in there!'

Everyone laughs, while I hastily close my mouth. I just can't believe it; Will Smith is here. Right now. At our wedding!

'Now, I didn't actually record this first song I'm going to perform for you,' Will says into the microphone, 'even though it's from one of my movies. But because it's one of

Scarlett's favourite movies, I'm gonna sing it for you now. Hit it, Peter!'

Peter gives him a thumbs-up from behind a sort of mixing desk and the intro to the end song from the movie *Hitch* starts playing, 'Now That We Found Love'. Then Will joins in with the vocal, and everyone immediately starts clapping.

'Come on, Scarlett,' Will calls. 'You know what you gotta do!'

In complete shock I take Sean's hand and we begin dancing down the centre of the two lines of people, just like Will and Eva Mendes did at the end of *Hitch*, followed by all their guests. Then all *our* guests follow our lead and in pairs take it in turns to dance crazily down the centre aisle. By the end of the song, even Will is joining in and dances with me down the aisle while everyone applauds.

'Oh my,' I laugh when he finishes. 'Thank you so much for coming along today and doing that for us. I love that movie so much!' I almost add, 'And I love you too,' but I manage to remain relatively cool and calm.

'You have friends in high places,' Will says, waving a hand at Gabi. 'However, what really persuaded me to come along today was finding out where you were holding your wedding reception. The kids here are having a fantastic time, and they obviously adore you.' He leans in to me and whispers, 'I was here earlier when they sang to you.' He beats his fist on his chest. 'Got me right here, it did. You, Mrs Scarlett O'Brien-Bond, are one very loved lady!'

He kisses me on the cheek and it's amazing I'm still conscious to hear him call into his microphone, 'Right, you guys, I can't leave tonight without a little rap, now, can I?'

The children, and some of the adults, whoop and cheer with delight as the opening bars of Will's iconic *The Fresh Prince of Bel-Air* theme song are heard pounding from the speakers, and we all gather round to listen.

'But you might notice that this version has a few changes. Scarlett –' he salutes me '– this is for you!'

> *'Now in this song I'm gonna tell you how*
> *Scarlett's life got spun, turned round and round.*
> *Could you all take a moment just to sit right down?*
> *Gonna tell how she became the Queen of Manhattan*
> *   town.'*

I can't believe it – Will Smith is singing *The Fresh Prince of Bel-Air* rap, but instead of the usual lyrics, it has words written especially for me.

> *'In Stratford-upon-Avon, where she was raised,*
> *In the cinema Scarlett spent all of her days,*
> *Watchin' all the great movies she could see,*
> *From* Notting Hill *to* Love Actually.'

I have to laugh; it's perfect. Again.

'Then she went house-sitting in Notting Hill,
Met Sean and Oscar. Smooth going till,
A few weeks later, Sean said to her,
"You complete me; I hope I complete you too."'

'Aw's from around the room, and Sean reaches for my
hand.

'But it didn't stop there – you came to NYC,
Met your brother, Jamie, in front of Tiffany's.
If anything, I could think there couldn't be more,
But next thing you know you knocked on this door.'

The kids whoop as Sunnyside gets a mention.

'Then on Brooklyn Bridge Sean asks to marry you,
And now, a year later, just look at you two:
In the New York kingdom, the king and queen
Are finally living their movie dream.'

The cheer is so massive at the end of the song that I
actually wonder if Sunnyside's roof might be raised up into
the Brooklyn night sky.

'That was simply amazing,' I tell Sean, as Will is now
swarmed by children once again. 'This day seriously can't
get any better, Sean. You really have made it the best day
of my entire life!'

Sean kisses me, and for that one moment we forget all

about Will Smith, Sunnyside, our friends and our families; it's just us. Just like it's always been for the last few years, and just like it's always going to be forever.

We link our arms around each other and stand back to look at everyone in the room enjoying themselves.

'The kids adore Will, don't they?' I say, looking at the Sunnyside children still clambering all over him.

'He has that natural chemistry with children, a bit like you. In fact, you seem to have it with most people, Scarlett.'

'Aw, thank you. What a lovely thing to say.' I kiss him again.

'Would you like one of those one day?' Sean asks, looking at Will again.

'A Will Smith?' I tease. 'No, I'm a one-man woman, me!'

Sean pulls a face. 'No, I mean a child – would you like us to have a baby together?'

I turn and look at Sean properly now. He's serious.

'*From Notting Hill with Nappies ... Actually*?' I ask, grinning.

'From Notting Hill, from New York ... Who knows where we'll be when the time comes?'

I think about it.

'Yes, I think I might, one day in the future. But for now let's just be happy being us. A mini Scarlett or Sean might well be our next chapter ... '

Did you miss Scarlett's debut? Meet her in

She was just a girl, standing in front of a boy ...
wishing he looked more like Hugh Grant.

Scarlett loves the movies. But does she love sensible fiancé David
just as much? With a big white wedding on the horizon,
Scarlett really should have decided by now ...

When she has the chance to house-sit in Notting Hill – the setting of
one of her favourite movies – Scarlett jumps at the chance. But living
life like a movie is trickier than it seems, especially when her new
neighbour Sean is so irritating. And so irritatingly handsome, too.

Scarlett soon finds herself starring in a romantic comedy of
her very own: but who will end up as the leading man?

'Sparky, fun and endearing' Katie Fforde

'An endearing, romantic and fun read for
chick-lit (and rom com!) fans' *Closer*

'Joyous and carefree, a souffle of a book that will lift the spirits of
anybody who ever daydreamed about a different, more glam life'
Bernadette Strachan

Scarlett O'Brien, utterly addicted to romantic films, has found her leading man. She's convinced Sean is Mr Right, but the day-to-day reality of a relationship isn't quite like the movies. With Sean constantly away on business, Scarlett and her new best friend Oscar decide to head to New York for the holiday of a lifetime.

From one famous landmark to the next, Scarlett and Oscar make many new friends during their adventure – including sailors in town for Fleet Week, a famous film star, and Jamie and Max, a TV reporter and cameraman. Scarlett finds herself strangely drawn to Jamie, they appear to have much in common: a love of films and Jamie's search for a parent he never knew. But Scarlett has to ask herself why she is reacting like this to another man when she's so in love with Sean ...

*

'An irresistible, feel-good story infused with infectious humour and sprinkled with Manhattan magic' Miranda Dickinson

'If you like your books full of good-looking boys and celeb spotting, it's all here. A funny and light-hearted read' *Heat*

'A charming page-turner' *Star Magazine*

From the bestselling author of
From Notting Hill with Love . . . Actually

Breakfast at Darcy's

Ali McNamara

When Darcy McCall loses her beloved Aunt Molly, she doesn't expect any sort of inheritance – let alone a small island! Located off the west coast of Ireland, Tara hasn't been lived on for years, but according to Molly's will, Darcy must stay there for twelve months in order to fully inherit. It's a big shock. And she's even more shocked to hear that she needs to persuade a village full of people to settle there, too.

Darcy has to leave behind her independent city life and swap stylish heels for muddy wellies. Between sorting everything from the plumbing to the pub, Darcy meets confident, charming Conor and sensible, stubborn Dermot – but who will make her feel really at home?

'A warm second novel - ****'
Daily Mirror, Book of the Week

'Perfect easy reading' *Sun*

'Charming story of adventure,
discovery and affairs of the heart' *Candis*

How many lifetimes would you travel to find a love that lasts for ever?

When single career girl Jo-Jo steps onto a zebra crossing and gets hit
by a car, she awakes to find herself in 1964. The fashion, the music,
her job, even her romantic life: everything is different. And then it
happens three more times, and Jo-Jo finds herself living a completely
new life in the 1970s, 80s and 90s. The only people she can rely
on are Harry and Ellie, two companions from 2013, and
George, the owner of a second-hand record store.

If she's ever to return from her travels, Jo-Jo must work out
why she's jumping through time like this. And if she does
make it back, will her old life ever be the same again?

*

'Time-travelling, groovy fashion and music, a central mystery
and lots of wit. Most of all, like all of Ali's books, there's
a big, yummy dollop of romance' *Star*

'Feel-good fun at its best' *Sun on Sunday*

Love for Scarlett

'Sparky, fun and endearing' Katie Fforde

'An endearing, romantic and fun read for chick-lit
(and rom com!) fans' *Closer*

'Joyous and carefree, a souffle of a book that will lift
the spirits of anybody who ever daydreamed about
a different, more glam life' Bernadette Strachan

'Utterly enjoyable' *Stylist*

'If you love your rom coms and know your
Mark Darcy from your Daniel Cleaver then
you're going to adore this' Carole Matthews

'As adorable as a Richard Curtis movie, as funny as
that Welsh bloke in the baggy grey pants, this romantic
comedy is the perfect way to pass a winter afternoon
should Johnny Depp be unavailable' *Daily Record*

'An irresistible, feel-good story infused with infectious humour and
sprinkled with Manhattan magic' Miranda Dickinson

Don't miss the next treat from Ali – coming in May 2015!

THE LITTLE FLOWER SHOP IN CORNWALL

Poppy Carmichael, 30, certainly never intended to own a florist.
But when she inherits her grandmother's beloved flower shop
on the beautiful Cornish coast, Poppy has no choice but to
return to the pretty harbour town of St Felix where
she spent much of her childhood.

Returning to St Felix brings back sad memories for Poppy.
But when she makes new friends such as local flower grower
Jake, a young widowed father of two teenagers, Poppy begins
to overcome her fears, and discover for herself what's
so special about this little flower shop by the sea.

A sparkling summer novel by Ali McNamara, author of the
much-loved novel *From Notting Hill with Love ... Actually*